The Lotus Tree

Jenny Allen

For

River & Kaidan, the two brightest lights in my life. I love you both.

Eric Deardorff, my husband and the love of my life. I can't imagine my life without you. You are the best decision I have ever made and the one I want to continue making for as long as I have the choice.

Special Thanks to:

Emily Kirk, **Kayla Bowers,** and **Danny Nagel**, my brainstorming partners and test bunnies.

Chris Howard, who creates all my beautiful covers.

And to all the people who have influenced and supported me.
Thank you.

Lilith Adams Series

Blood Lily
Rose of Jericho
The Lotus Tree
Ghost Orchid

Trigger Warnings:

Kidnapping. Torture, Brief Mentions & Instances of
Domestic Violence, Implied/Brief Sexual Assault,
Body Horror, PTSD, Survivor's Guilt, Stockholm's
Syndrome, Drug use, Execution.

For more information about permission to reproduce selections
from this book, write to Permissions, Jenny Allen Books &
Original Art, 872 Stoverstown Rd., York, PA, 17408

Manufacturing by Ingram Spark.
Book Design by Jenny Allen
Editing by Lyndsey Smith with Horrorsmith Editing

Cover Art by Blonde Design and © held by Jenny Allen.

ISBN: 979-8-9892492-1-3

Jenny Allen Books & Original Art, 872 Stoverstown Rd., York, PA 17408
JennyAllenBooks@gmail.com
www.JennyAllenBooks.com

The Lotus Tree

Jenny Allen

Jenny Allen Books & Original Art
York, PA 17408

Chapter 1 - *Cassie*

A heady exuberance infused the crowd leaving the Fred Astaire Dance Studio in Richmond, Virginia. They picked their way through the nearly vacant parking lot, pulling their coats tight against the bracing chill, while discussing promenades, underhand turns, and rumbas beneath the light of a full moon. One by one, people said their goodbyes and climbed into their vehicles until the group dwindled to three middle-aged women.

A tall man in his mid-thirties sporting a jacket with the studio's logo called out as he locked the door. "We'll go over those waltz steps next Friday, Cassie! Wonderful moves on the floor tonight."

"See you then!" Cassie shared a brilliant smile that made her appear far younger than thirty-four as the cold February air bit at her cheeks. "Have a great night, Steve!"

"You too." The man waved before jogging toward his SUV.

While Cassie's eyes scanned the lot, the other two women swayed and did pirouettes between vehicles. Ensuring the safety of others was an occupational habit, which explained why she had a hard time letting loose. The ballroom lessons were meant to help her relax, something that never came naturally.

Once Meg and Tamara were secure in their cars, engines rumbling and reverse lights on, Cassie headed for her modest Honda Civic sitting under the last streetlight.

"Good night, Cas!" A woman with long blond hair waved as she drove past.

Although Cassie couldn't recall the woman's name, she waved back with a smile before digging for her keys. By the time she found them in the bottom of her enormous bag, the parking lot was empty.

Beyond the miniscule strip mall's floodlights, the windows sat dark from the dance studio to the daycare which, according to its sign, offered "A Little Peace of Mind." It felt so odd. Seconds ago, excited voices and happy faces had filled the place, and now, it was silent as a tomb.

Cassie shrugged off the eerie sensation and started to swing open her car door, when a voice startled her. She turned, shielding her eyes from the bright floodlights as she tried to locate the source. A teal car sat beyond the daycare, peeking out of the darkness. She shifted her gaze, searching for the vehicle's owner, until she spotted a tall, slender man waving his arms at her from the sidewalk in front of Carlson Photography.

When the man began jogging toward her, Cassie immediately reached into her purse—another occupational habit.

The black wool peacoat and dark pants he wore explained why she hadn't seen him at first. As he came closer, she noticed the T-shirt beneath his coat sported the Fred Astaire logo, but when the light fell across his face, she didn't recognize him. Although, to be honest, it had been a full house with over fifty people packed onto the dance floor, not to mention the shy wallflowers.

"Hey there. Sorry if I startled you." The man flashed a smile filled with enigmatic warmth, sending a small tingle down Cassie's spine.

She'd obviously been single too long. Not that the guy wasn't attractive. He was…in an odd way. Although, he was a little too pale and thin for her tastes, and his hair seemed too black to be natural, but his eyes were a definite plus. Thick lashes surrounded a sea of brilliant blue with brown circling their irises.

Then Cassie realized that, while she was ranking his date-ability—he also didn't wear a wedding ring—the poor man was staring at her in confusion, waiting for a response.

"Uh, sorry. It's okay. I just don't remember you from class."

The man blushed slightly, fidgeting with the buttons on his coat. Somehow, the innocent expression appeared natural on him, though he didn't seem like the shy type.

"Well, I'm new. I've only taken a couple of lessons, but my instructor insisted that—"

"You have to go to your first party sometime," Cassie chimed in with the familiar mantra of the Fred Astaire instructors. They both chuckled in a moment of comradery, and their warm breath billowed like smoke into the chilly night air.

"Yeah. I tried to stay out of sight. I didn't want everyone witnessing my awkward mistakes, especially not a lovely lady like you."

The compliment made her blush, which widened the man's grin. She wasn't accustomed to flirting, not really. *What happened last year wasn't flirting. It was sheer stupidity, which is why I avoid these situations.*

In high school, a slew of extra-curricular sports had consumed most of her time—mainly track, soccer, and volleyball—with her rigorous study regimen taking up the rest. Cassie didn't have leisure time for boys, a fact that remained unchanged. The small bits of time her job didn't demand were consumed by workouts, running, and Netflix binges while doing extra research.

*Well, except for him...I never should have...*Cassie shook off the intrusive thoughts about her recent romantic tragedy and focused on the moment.

His sparkling blue eyes became too intense as they locked onto hers, so she smiled at the cracked asphalt instead. "Well, thank you for..."

Then she caught sight of his black sneakers and stopped in mid-sentence.

Huh.

The dance studio didn't allow black-soled shoes. Not only were they all wrong for the smooth, gliding motions, they also left scuff marks on the polished wood. The cleaning staff would be scraping them off for days, especially with a new student.

"You didn't dance in those, did you?"

The man's smile slowly spread, and he shook his head. "No." His relaxed chuckle eased her sudden suspicion. "I bought proper shoes during my last lesson. My instructor, Steve, said they'd make the moves easier, but the difference really surprised me. Anyway, that's my problem. When I changed shoes, I got distracted and locked my keys in the trunk. I'd call a locksmith, but my phone is in the glove box. You know what Steve says..."

"...No phones in the studio." They chimed in together again with a conspiratorial smile.

With her mind at ease, she moved toward her car. "One second." Cassie bent over the driver's seat to snatch her phone from the center console. "Here. Use mine."

When she turned back around, his eyes traveled along the lines of her body before reaching her face. Once upon a time, the lingering stare would have made her painfully nervous. Perhaps the dance lessons were paying off after all.

"Thanks so much." The man took her cell and dialed a number from memory.

Odd…

Before she finished the thought, he glanced at her. "I don't suppose you'd wait with me until the locksmith arrives. If they can't find the address, they might call back, and…I'd love the company."

All her natural skepticism withered in the brilliance of the man's intense eyes. Besides, she could handle a 160-pound man if things took a turn.

"Sure. I don't mind." After locking her car, she fell in step beside him, pulling her coat tight against the brisk wind. He stood slightly taller than her, and his movements appeared rather graceful despite the disparaging remarks he had made about his dancing.

"Hi. Yeah. I'm locked out of my car…Uh-huh…" The man's dashing smile became infectious. "Sure. I'm at 100 Arboretum Place, Suite 110…Yeah, in the Arch Village Shopping Center…It's a teal Toyota Camry. My name is Vélos Ambrose…Yes, it's a real name." He rolled his eyes with an expression of playful frustration, and Cassie almost giggled. "Thank you."

"That's quite an unusual name." She leaned against his car, studying him in a little more detail.

The man had a slight bump to his very straight nose and a subtle olive undertone she hadn't noticed earlier. *If he spent any time in the sun, he'd probably tan well. Greek, perhaps?*

The new tidbits of information caused her to re-evaluate her opinion. Sure, he appeared too thin for his five-foot-ten frame, but he was also quite charming, and something about his voice felt familiar and comforting. At first blush, he didn't seem like her type, but perhaps that was a good thing. *Especially considering my last relationship…if I can even call it that.*

Vélos nodded and slid her phone onto the hood of his car. "Yeah. My mom was very traditional. Old World Greek."

"Like the gods of Olympus and whatnot?" The unusual confession piqued her interest.

"Yeah, but you can call me Art, my middle name. And you are…Cassie, right?"

The blush blossomed over her cheeks again before traveling down her neck. "How did you know?"

A roguish grin stretched his thin lips as he leaned forward, his hypnotic eyes staring intently into hers. His words escaped in a plume of condensed breath. "I might have asked the instructor…"

Cassie's heart fluttered as he loomed closer, mere inches away. Tendrils of electricity crackled over her skin, leaving goosebumps in their wake. If she lifted her chin, her lips would touch his.

"…but I didn't."

Her puzzled frown barely formed before a sharp pain flared in her left thigh. The world slowed to a crawl, and she stumbled away from the car, staring at her leg like it was a foreign object. When her eyes flashed back to Art, she tripped over the curb and landed hard on the frigid sidewalk.

"What did you…"

The handsome man crouched in front of her, his once warm eyes now calculating, as he studied every move with calm detachment. The stark contrast from his shy, flirtatious persona sent chills down her spine.

"What did I give you?" His hand slid into her dark brown curls, caressing them. With the other, he held up an empty syringe. "A fun combination of Versed and fentanyl. You'll lose consciousness and fall into a deep sleep where pain won't touch you. You probably won't remember this moment…sadly."

Tears ran down her cheeks as she threw a punch, but her arm fell to the ground before hitting her target. Her body felt like a lead weight, dragging her to the ocean floor. *This can't be happening. To me of all people.* Training didn't matter if she was too naïve to see bad things coming. As the blinding panic swelled, her chest constricted, each breath burning like fire.

"Why? What do you want?" She screamed the words, hoping someone might still be around to hear her, but she knew better. She'd made sure everyone else left safely.

Art's fingers tightened around her hair and wrenched her forward, his enigmatic eyes sparkling with malice. "We'll have plenty of time to answer questions…and much more."

The man's gaze lifted to a silver sedan pulling up next to the curb. Before Cassie got a look at the driver, her right cheek exploded in pain, which made the world spin faster. Her left temple cracked against the icy concrete, and a blissful euphoria seeped through her bones, dragging her into an unnaturally peaceful surrender.

Chapter 2

Lilith stared at the drop ceiling, counting tiles to avoid acknowledging the intrusive person sitting across from her. Despite the woman's frustrated grimace and non-stop pen clicking, Lilith stayed resolute. After all, she'd survived scarier battles.

When the timer finally buzzed, Lilith breathed a sigh of relief and hopped off the couch. "Guess that's our time."

"No. Sit! You cannot keep avoiding me." The voice sounded annoyingly shrill, or perhaps that was a matter of context and perspective. "You've sat here once a week for the past eight months and memorized every detail of my office but haven't spoken a word about what happened."

A new water spot in the corner of the ceiling caught Lilith's attention as she sank back into the sofa. The brownish discoloration blossomed out like a dying flower, by far the most fascinating thing in the room.

"Ms. Adams, you either tell me what took place last year, or I will *not* reinstate you." Her words rang with finality, and she slapped the pen down on her notebook for emphasis.

Lilith closed her eyes, violent scenes flashing through her mind—blood pouring down Alvarez's shirt, Richard Coffee's screams, flames, Chance choking on blood, the scalpel carving through Cohen's skin as his shrieks echoed off the walls. If she couldn't stop the torrent of horrors, she'd put them to use. A rebellious fire burned in the pit of her stomach, and she remained silent.

"Fine. You can leave and consider a career change." Dr. Price stood abruptly and gestured behind her. "There's the door. Talk or get out."

Lilith couldn't finish her mandatory therapy if the woman refused to see her again. *Damn it. Why does this have to be so complicated?*

"I'm required to see a therapist for one year. That doesn't mean I have to talk. My uncle Aaron hired you, and I don't trust him, which means I certainly *don't* trust you. Four more months and I'll be off suspension."

After she cast a piercing stare at the woman wearing horn-rimmed glasses, Lilith surveyed the built-in shelves. Anything to keep her mind distracted from the ghosts haunting her.

The doctor owned an eclectic range of books—Joseph Campbell's *The Hero with a Thousand Faces*, *Dianetics* by L. Ron Hubbard, *The Complete Book of Herbs*...Lilith even spotted a first edition *Interview with the Vampire*, which she found funny, considering the woman's profession as a vampire therapist.

"Actually..." The smug tone meant Lilith wouldn't like what came next. "That would be true *if* you were a cop and I worked for the NYPD, neither of which *are* true."

Dr. Price eased into her seat and waited until she held her patient's undivided attention.

"Let me explain your situation. You are an independent contractor working with the police department as a crime scene investigator. You are not directly affiliated with them, and I am *not* Internal Affairs."

"I know..."

"Within a two-week period, you were kidnapped, tortured, and nearly killed multiple times. You lost your partner of six years, most of your family—including your father—and you shot an unarmed assailant. Solasta has concerns, valid ones, Ms. Adams. The company requires a *minimum* of one year. It is my job to say when and how you return to active duty, which is contingent on your cooperation."

The pretentious tone rubbed Lilith the wrong way, but if the doctor was right, it meant she had wasted the last eight months.

After a tense moment of silence, the woman's satisfied smile melted into an expression of professional concern. "How many therapists do you think have the clearance to know what I do?" When Lilith still refused to speak, she sighed heavily and adjusted her glasses.

"Everything here is confidential in the strictest sense. It doesn't leave this room. I do not discuss my patients, I am not an investigator, and I don't provide reports. I simply tell them if you are well enough to work or not. Now, why don't we start with why you left for Tennessee."

The mental image of that fateful night brought tears to Lilith's eyes. She recalled the warm smile stretching Gregor's lips when she had arrived at the

Italian restaurant. Although she glimpsed the guilt already heavy on his shoulders, she hadn't understood its significance until it was far too late.

She'd wanted to believe her father when he stated his only concern was about the Elders' plan to go public and how Duncan's disappearance might complicate that. She'd seen the tells, she'd known he was holding back, but she didn't question him. As a result, people died…good, innocent people. Everything still felt so fresh, but she couldn't form the words to relay any of it, even if she wanted to.

"So, I'm just supposed to take your word? And don't quote your legal oath. What am I gonna do if you lie and start blabbing? Take you to court? Vampires work outside the law out of necessity. I can *assure* you that my uncle doesn't give a damn about helping me. So, what's your angle?" Lilith sank into the couch cushions with a skeptical stare and folded her arms across her chest in a clearly defensive posture.

Dr. Brittany Price pushed a stray blond hair toward her tight bun before shuffling through her papers. "Should we discuss why you distrust your uncle?"

"Should we discuss why you have three cats?" Lilith tilted her head with a malicious grin as the good doctor's mouth opened in shock.

"How did you—"

"Here's a tip. With three long-hair cats at home, avoid wearing black. It's stark against your pale complexion anyway. I'm guessing the British Isles. England or Scotland?"

The woman stiffened. "Welsh, actually. Why don't we begin with something innocuous this week and build from there?"

"Did you get that from your word-of-the-day calendar?"

"Ms. Adams. Hostility won't make this go any faster. If you want your badge back, start talking. You may not trust me now, but if you wish to continue working for Solasta, you better learn quick." After a brief pause, she managed to pull on a mask of professional indifference again. "Are you still having nightmares?"

Lilith's focus fell to the floor, dark memories rearing to the surface. Trust wasn't her only problem. Talking acted like an ancient summoning spell—each time she dredged up the horrific events and said them out loud, she relived everything in vivid, mind-flaying color. In a way, it felt like she had never defeated Ashcroft, Farren, Luminita, or Peisinoe. They merely left the physical plane, to live in her mind where they could torment her forever.

She sighed softly, still refusing to look the woman in the eye. "Who says I'm having nightmares?"

"You're joking, right? I read the preliminary report. The company's version, not the scrubbed mass of inconsistencies you turned over to the FBI. No one goes through all that and comes out clean. Look, I am not here to dig for information. I am here to help, Lilith."

Dr. Price placed her pen and paper on the side table and leaned forward.

"You lost a lot in a very short time. You suffered profound shifts in your life, and the mind rarely deals well with change, especially as violent as yours. Talk to me."

The woman wasn't wrong. Lilith hadn't escaped unscathed, either emotionally or physically. She still bore the scar on her chest from Phipps Bend, her left arm ached in the cold weather from the nasty break, and horrific dreams kept her from a decent night's sleep. Hell, life without her father and Alvarez seemed like too much of a struggle most days.

Beyond all that, she had lost Gregor's companies to her morally bankrupt uncle. Apparently, the board members decided he was a more appropriate and experienced replacement. Now, he controlled Solasta, which wasn't only the largest research lab in the U.S., but also her employer, and he seemed determined to hold her job hostage until he got what he wanted.

"Fine. Say you're right…" Lilith pushed away the dark thoughts and faced Dr. Price. "I don't see how that prevents me from working."

"I am not here to determine if you can perform your job. I am here to judge whether returning to work will be harmful to your mental health. I am *not* the enemy here, as much as you hate to hear that. I have no ulterior motives. Despite what you think about Mr. Bogdan…."

"You know his last name means *Gift of God* in Romanian, right? How conceited do you have to be to choose *that* as a surname? It's hard to believe he's even related to me."

"Lilith, your uncle needed a safe intervention to prevent further police investigations. I may be the answer to his dilemma, but that doesn't mean I can't help you. Can you tell me about your nightmares?"

An uncomfortable silence settled over the room again while Lilith waged an internal battle. They were only dreams. Even if this therapist reported them to Aaron, they wouldn't mean anything to him. What would be the harm?

Dr. Price kept her blue eyes fixed on Lilith, as if looking away would break the tenuous bond of cooperation, and slowly retrieved her pad and pen.

When Lilith opened her mouth, she had every intention of being honest. "They are about Peisinoe...mostly."

Well, partial truth is better than nothing.

Lilith focused her attention on the bright window, wishing she could absorb the sunlight into her bones and chase away the darkness lingering there.

"And what happens in these dreams?"

When the woman scribbled furiously, Lilith felt slightly guilty for lying. Sure, she still dreamed about Peisinoe, but a different monster tormented her most nights.

With a reluctant sigh, she forced out the words. The cat was out of the bag, and she couldn't turn back now.

"The effect she had on Chance."

Flashes burned through her mind—his emotionless face and vacant eyes, his hands tight around her throat, Peisinoe's high-pitched shriek echoing through the stale air, Lilith's toes scraping the floor as she fought to draw breath, the burning in her lungs from oxygen deprivation. Even after eight months, the memories remained raw, which lent credibility to her story.

"One dream repeats more than the others." *Technically the truth, although not the one I'm about to describe.* "The first time I had it, we were still on the case."

Lilith pulled her knees up to her chest, hugged them close, a chill trickling down her spine, and dredged up real memories she'd tried hard to bury.

"She used her mind control tricks on Chance. He started choking me, and she laughed while I died. I still remember the blind adoration in his eyes and the grip on my throat sometimes." When a tear welled in her eye, she wiped it away, angry at her body for giving into the process and expressing emotion to a shrink. *Damn it. Why did I bring up the siren of all things? Stupid.*

"And how has that affected things between you, your relationship?"

The unexpected question cut through the flashbacks, bringing her to the present, and she swung around to glare at Dr. Price. "It hasn't. It's a stupid dream. I put a bullet in her face. She can't hurt anyone anymore."

"It hasn't made you distrustful or skittish around him? You don't pull away when you wake up from one of these dreams?" The woman's disbelief shone so crystal clear, it could have auditioned for a sparkly vampire movie.

Lilith dropped her feet to the floor and leaned forward, resting her elbows on her knees. "The first time I had it, when she was still alive, yeah. It was so real. I smelled her cheap perfume, felt his bruising strength, tasted the tears in my throat. But now…No. Chance would *never* hurt me unless forced by a super-powered banshee, and like I said, she's dead."

The shrink held her hands up in surrender. "Got it. That is sound logic." Something in her voice suggested that logic and the truth existed as two separate things. "Tell me. Do you ever dream about her death?" The shrink's eyes fixated on her with such intensity, heat crept up Lilith's cheeks.

As if summoned by the doctor's question, the entire scene played through her mind. The siren's round face grinned up at her, blood trickling from her pouty lips and her signature platinum curls disheveled from the scuffle. The gun, pressed against Peisinoe's temple, weighed heavily in Lilith's hand. She warred between self-defense and murder, her finger hesitating on the trigger. The gunshot cracked like thunder, bits of bone and brain matter splattering against the white tile. Then Lilith stared at the 9mm in her blood-drenched hand and simply tried to breathe.

"No." The clipped word didn't sound remotely convincing to Lilith, and she *wanted* to believe it was true.

The doc merely raised a cynical eyebrow and waited.

"Fine. Yes."

"Do you feel remorse?"

The question seemed obvious and innocent but hit Lilith like a tidal wave. She never allowed herself to dwell on that subject.

"Peisinoe set fire to anything and everything for the sheer joy of watching it burn. When she took control and made Chance strangle me, he remembered everything—my tears, pleas, fear, heartbreak, all of it. She would have forced him to relive those memories for decades. Escaping didn't matter if she was still alive. The monster would have never stopped hunting us. She *had* to die."

There had been no other way. Lilith knew that. Still, the words seemed hollow. She had crossed a line she could never uncross and spent all her time trying to ignore the consequences.

"That doesn't really answer my question. Do you *feel* remorse?"

Every muscle tensed, and she frowned up at Dr. Price. "I've never killed anyone in cold blood before, justifiable reasons or not. So, on some level, I suppose, but I made the right choice, the *only* choice. She couldn't be allowed to live."

"And it was your responsibility to ensure that?"

A surge of righteous indignation burned through Lilith's veins, and she sat up tall. "Who else was there? You have no idea how dangerous she was! I couldn't drag her into a courtroom. There was no one else. I had an opportunity, and I took it. I did the world a damn favor."

Judging by the woman's lifted eyebrow and lopsided frown, she remained unconvinced, which aggravated Lilith to no end. Thankfully, she let it go.

"Tell me about the medical facility. What really happened that night?"

Before the flashbacks took over again, Lilith leaned over and grabbed her purse. "I think our time's up, Doc."

"We have to talk about it sooner or later. Mr. Bogdan won't let you return to duty without my endorsement."

"I choose later. Much later. I have somewhere I need to be."

When Lilith rose to her feet, Dr. Price did the same and held out her hand. "Ms. Adams. I want to work with you, and I have a feeling you need my help. Think on it, and perhaps next week we can make a fresh start. If you change your mind before then, I'll squeeze you in."

After a moment of hesitation, Lilith shook the woman's slender hand. Surprisingly, the doctor's palms were sweaty and warm—not an encouraging sign.

"Maybe."

Trust was something she had in short supply, especially these days.

Forty-five minutes later, Lilith's cab pulled up to a monstrous brick building on the corner of Lexington in Midtown Manhattan. Once she pushed past the crowd rushing out of Barnes & Noble, she slid in the side entrance and took the stairs to level B1. At the end of the hall, a black and white sign featuring a tiger read: "NYC Shotokan Karate Dojo."

As she hurried through the door, shouts and grunts of students greeted her, echoing a strength and determination she desperately needed after the brief delve into her psyche.

Kids, teens, and young adults in varying shades of white uniforms filled the blue mats, all moving in unison. For a moment, she merely observed the rhythmic motions, allowing them to soothe her jangled nerves.

Then her eyes drifted further up the room, where the instructor stood before the class—a six-foot-three wall of lean muscle with ruffled chestnut hair and hazel eyes. Although his black *gi* was quite flattering, the grace and strength of his movements made the man a true sight to behold. She watched his hands gliding through the air in smooth motions. Like the musical tones of a snake charmer, they lulled her into a tranquil state, quelling the panic and chaos in her head.

As she smiled, the man in black glanced up at her in mid-motion, breaking the hypnotic spell.

Lilith shrugged, mouthed *I'm sorry*, and ducked into the dressing room, her cheeks turning pink. She hated being late. Not only did she find it rude and disruptive, but it also made her the center of attention—something she always found painfully uncomfortable.

After opening her locker, she unzipped her duffle and pulled off her shirt. The shrink's question still buzzed around her head. "This is why I hate therapy," she mumbled, tossing her top into the bag.

When she reached for the clasp on her jeans, the door swung open and she whirled around, covering her bra with a dart of startled embarrassment.

"Don't let me stop you." The handsome instructor leaned against the doorframe with a mischievous grin.

"Hey, what are you doing? You have a class out there." Lilith frowned and shimmied out of her jeans.

"It's fine. Jeremy took lead for a minute. He needs the practice if he wants to take over the eight to eleven class. *You* are late."

The amused tilt of his lips usually made her melt, but today was not a typical day.

"I'm sorry. This damn therapist..." She shoved her clothes into the duffle with a little too much enthusiasm.

"Still refusing to reinstate you?" He crossed his arms over his chest, his grin giving way to concern. "Talk to me, *mon petite cherie.*" The Cajun undercurrent in his voice only became more irresistible when he spoke in French.

"The woman threatened me. Talk or no job. I don't know how much more I can take, Chance."

Chance Deveraux, head of security for her father's companies, was one of the few things holding her life together. If she ignored the trauma, loss, grief, and guilt, the past eight months with him were the happiest of her life.

While she stared into her duffle, conflicted and overwhelmed, he padded barefoot across the tile floor and slipped his hands around her hips. Then he tugged her back against him, enveloping her in warmth, his breath whispering against her neck.

"This might be a radical idea, but what if you just talk to her, and…"

Lilith frowned over her shoulder. "You know who hired her, right?"

"…and tell her what she wants to hear." Chance spun her around, kissed the tip of her nose, and playfully swatted her ass. "Now finish getting dressed and get out there. We can talk more after class. I'm making dinner."

Lilith bit down on the smart-ass comment that almost escaped her lips as he strolled out of the locker room. Making a glib remark about his lengthy *dating* history didn't feel right anymore.

While they were in Tennessee, she discovered Chance's carefully guarded secret—for the past thirteen years, he'd held a torch for her and filled the void with a laundry list of one-night stands. He never deceived the women he dated. Chance was always honest, but that never stopped them from trying to change his mind. Apparently, no one had succeeded.

However, she had grown up with the image of Chance, the playboy, and thinking in those terms was a hard habit to break. She still expected him to snap out of the trance, realize he'd spent more than a decade pining over a flawed, broken woman, and run.

Of course, any time she voiced that fear, he dismissed the very possibility as ludicrous, and she wanted to believe him more than anything. Since his confession, he'd been nothing but sincere with her, even about things she didn't want to know.

Once she drew in a cleansing breath, Lilith shimmied into her *gi*, tied her orange belt, and hurried into the dojo. After the traumatic events of last fall, she'd attended every one of Chance's karate lessons. Not only did the suspension bore her to tears, but after everything that happened, she needed the training, and it didn't end with martial arts.

Lilith also spent Monday, Wednesday, and Friday mornings running with her new partner, Nicci DeLuca, for the same reason. Nearly becoming lunch meat to a zombie horde had been too traumatizing to ignore the first rule of *Zombieland*—cardio.

Meanwhile, Timothy Bardow, Chance's best friend and co-worker, was coaching her on the second rule—the double-tap—as well as teaching weapon endurance and accuracy. Lilith wasn't a bad shot, but aiming a gun for longer than forty-five seconds was a lot harder than TV led people to believe.

A traumatized girl becoming tougher, stronger, better, sounded like a standard movie montage. However, snatching some modicum of control in her chaos-strewn life wasn't her only motivation. Things didn't feel *over*. Cohen and the Durand Council still had leverage on them, they didn't have any leads on Malachi's virus, and everything else felt…unfinished. The theoretical sky darkened, and the whisper of a storm tingled over her skin. She wanted…No, she *needed* to prepare herself.

If she told her therapist the truth, Dr. Price would probably say Lilith craved drama and sought it out to avoid the happy things she didn't feel she deserved. But that sentiment only applied to normal people, not her, not someone who attracted death like a damn bug zapper.

Too many monsters targeted her for one reason or another. She didn't expect the pattern to end with Ashcroft, Farren, and Peisinoe. Besides, Luminita was still out there somewhere with the Voynich Manuscript.

Serenity suppressed her wandering thoughts as she stepped barefoot onto the mat. Somehow, standing on the vinyl acted like a splash of cool water on her face.

Chance resumed control of the class, restarting forms from the Tekki kata—a personal favorite of hers, with an emphasis on close combat. Lilith shook her shoulders and bounced on the balls of her feet, attempting to shake off the stress weighing her down, before joining in.

T wo hours and a hot shower later, Lilith sat across the table from Chance, poking the meatloaf with her fork. Although dimly aware of him studying her, she allowed one thought to consume all her attention. To her dismay, the peaceful focus she'd gained from the karate lesson faded before she stepped foot in the cab. The doctor's question kept repeating in her mind.

She'd lied about her nightmares to protect herself and had ended up more conflicted than if she'd told the truth. *Do I feel remorse? The morally correct response is yes, but do I really feel that way? And if not, what does that say about me?*

"Lily?"

She glanced up, confused by the expectant look on his face. *Did I miss an entire conversation?* "I'm sorry." After pulling on a polite smile, she slid her fork onto the table. "What were we talking about?"

"Tim borrowing my truck until Saturday to clear out his old apartment. What has your mind playing Scattegories?"

She rubbed her face and took a deep breath, trying to put her thoughts into coherent sentences. "Nothing. It's just something Dr. Price asked. So, what time is your flight?" When in doubt, change the subject as fast as possible.

Chance stared at her for a few moments before he answered. "Plane leaves at ten tonight. I should be back around the same time Thursday…"

He hesitated again.

"Are you sure you're all right, *cherie*? I can always postpone the trip. It's just security updates for Aaron's L.A. office. Nothing that can't wait a week or two." The hint of Cajun in his voice felt like a caress of warm velvet.

"I'm okay. I can survive two days without you holding me together." The words emerged sharper than intended, and she quickly slid her hand over his to soften the blow. "Seriously. Go. Aaron doesn't need more reasons to hate me."

"Come with me."

"What?" Lilith frowned at him, as if he had started cursing in indecipherable French.

"Come with me." Chance leaned over the table to push a stray strand of hair behind her ear. "You don't have any obligations, and you could use a change of scenery. A little sunshine, some sightseeing…So, why don't you just come with me?"

"You'll be working, and I have zero desire to see Aaron. Not to mention, the hometown of my alma mater is *not* my favorite place in the world."

A shiver ran down her spine, and a flood of bad memories roared to the surface.

"I mean, what would I do, hole up in a hotel room and watch HBO?" Lilith leaned in and kissed his lips before sinking back into her seat. "Don't worry. I'm running with Nicci in the morning, then having dinner with

Gloria. At least she's not setting me up on another horrific blind date." She flashed a cheeky grin, and the mood suddenly lifted.

"She damn well better not." Chance squeezed her hand with a wink. "I plan on keeping you."

Lilith quirked an eyebrow, unable to resist an opportunity for sarcasm. "Well, that sounds vaguely stalker-ish. You don't have a cage in the basement, do you?"

Chance chuckled, and the warm, bright sound filled the room. "No cages, I promise. I'll just give you plenty of reasons to stay."

"Hmm, well, I don't think the meatloaf is doing you any favors." She poked at the dry slab of meat covered with ketchup. "Next time, I cook."

Although he appeared offended, she knew it was all for show. He freely admitted he couldn't make anything except Cajun food but never stopped trying to expand his menu.

"It's a date. See? Still got reasons to stay."

After rolling her eyes, Lilith took a bite of the surprisingly delicious potatoes.

"Speaking of which…I thought you could stay at my place while I'm gone," Chance added.

"Why? You know, you don't have a cat or live plants, right?" She chuckled and took another bite.

"I know, but…I'd feel better knowing you're here." Something still lingered in his face, some unasked question on the tip of his tongue.

As he bit the corner of his lip and glanced down at the hardwood, she wondered why he seemed so nervous. *What is he not saying?*

"Okay…" She narrowed her eyes in suspicion, studying each line of his face. When he didn't continue, she prompted him. "…And…"

"Well, I was thinking…" His eyes found hers with sudden confidence. "I own the building, and you pay a fortune in rent…" The hopeful expression he wore almost quelled the rising panic in her gut. *Almost.* "I thought you could move in here."

As soon as he rushed through the words, his nervousness set back in, but he managed to maintain eye contact. Both her eyebrows flew up in complete surprise.

"I, uh…" Her brain seized like a motor with no oil, and his confident swagger faded with each passing second. Once again, Lilith rubbed her face and forced her thoughts into some semblance of order. "I haven't lived with anyone in a very long time, Chance. I mean, that is a *huge* deal."

"Trust me, I know how big it is…and also, phrasing." His impish grin quickly dissolved into a serious poker face when she didn't rise to the bait. "Look. You spend most of your time here anyway, and it's not practical to pay so much for an apartment you barely use. Plus…I love having you here, *amour de ma vie.*"

When she stared into his deep hazel eyes brimming with hope, she couldn't dash his dreams, especially not over old wounds that had nothing to do with him.

"I love you too, handsome. Okay, I'll stay here while you're gone and think about it. We can talk more when you get back. Deal?"

Chance nodded, rose from his seat, and strolled over to her with a brilliant grin plastered on his face. When he held out his hand, she couldn't help but smile as she took it.

In a sudden motion that made her yelp in surprise, he tugged her close and pressed his lips against hers in a feverish kiss. Deliciously familiar thrills raced down her spine until he pulled back enough to rest his forehead against hers, breathless.

"Are you trying to—"

Before she finished the sentence, he tossed her onto his shoulder as if she weighed nothing.

"Chance!" Lilith panted with each laugh, swatting his back as he carried her up the stairs toward his loft. "What the hell are you doing?"

"What I damn well want." The happiness in his voice chased away all lingering doubts about her sanity. "Unless you want me to put you down…"

"You better not!"

Chance laughed wholeheartedly and jogged up the remaining steps in triumph.

Chapter 3

"**N**o way! He asked you to move in?" After two miles, Nicci didn't sound the least bit winded. In fact, her New York-Italian accent became more prominent when excited, and Lilith found her partner's perfectly even respirations insulting on a deeply personal level.

When Lilith merely nodded with a grimace, Nicci slowed to a casual walk, and her long brown ponytail swung like a metronome with each purposeful stride.

"So, what did you say?"

Lilith shrugged and inhaled several jagged breaths, her hands on her hips. "I said we could talk more when he gets back from L.A."

A sudden muscle cramp made her clutch her side with a groan. After bending over and breathing through the pain, Lilith glanced over at her partner, who was clearly questioning her sanity.

"Come on. Living together is a huge decision, and it's only been eight months. What if I can't stand where he clips his toenails, or he hates my laundry piling up? What if our entire relationship is built on shared trauma, and we can't deal with everyday life together? What if he gets bored?"

Nicci's heart-shaped face pulled into a scolding frown. "You haven't figured that out by now?"

After swallowing the nervous lump in her throat, Lilith stared at the cracked pavement, unable to come up with an answer.

Nicci snorted in disbelief. "I only met Chance eight months ago, and even *I* know you're mental if you think he's going anywhere. The boy has it bad."

"What, because he's had a crush on me since we were teens? The fantasy he created over the past thirteen years and reality are two very different things. I'm only human…" After a pointed frown from the petite detective,

Lilith amended her words. "You know what I mean. I have flaws like everyone else, whether I'm human or not. What he built in his head is impossible to live up to."

Nicci stared up from her five-foot-nothing height. "You think you have to be perfect around him?"

"Well, yeah…" She rubbed her arms with a surge of self-consciousness. "Sometimes, things are so easy, so natural, but other times…"

"You gotta deal with that before you move in with him, Lil. No one is one hundred percent all the time."

"Exactly my point! Can we talk about something else? I have enough people probing my brain." She started walking, leaving Nicci to catch up.

"Oh yeah, the therapist. Still giving her the silent treatment?"

"More or less."

"Any idea when she's gonna reinstate you?"

"Current signs point to never. If I don't start talking, she won't give my badge back…but she's on Aaron's payroll."

"Damn. That's too bad. We had a juicy case last night, and I could use your help." The tauntingly melodic voice was clearly meant to pique her interest—it worked.

"What kind of case?"

"Well, I'm not sure I should tell you since you're still suspended…" The detective winked and picked up the pace to an easy jog.

Apparently, Nicci wanted her to work for the details, but patience wasn't a virtue Lilith possessed. "Come the hell on. Just spit it out."

"A vamp victim." She grinned at the wide-eyed expression on her partner's face. "I know. It's been a while. Close to six years, if you don't count last fall."

Lilith flinched but suppressed the litany of horrible memories beginning with Duncan's kidnapping. "So, what was the cause of death?"

"No idea."

"What? Who worked the scene?"

"Boyd, but the autopsy and toxicology reports aren't back yet. Peters is on vacation, so the detective oversaw the fill-in techs from homicide."

Detective Boyd was young, sweet, human, and very naïve about the dark depravities the world contained. Although Lilith liked him, she also liked beagle puppies. It didn't mean they could lead a homicide investigation.

"Wait. If he controlled the scene, how did you find out the victim was a vamp?"

"Frank caught it at the morgue and messaged me this morning."

"Right…" Of course. It was standard protocol for the medical examiner to test every corpse as a security net, but it hadn't yielded results since Solasta placed Lilith in Major Crimes.

"Can you sweet-talk that therapist into reinstating you? If you don't want anything getting back to your uncle, just make up stuff or something."

"Funny. Chance said something similar." They both came to a stop, allowing two moms with fancy cross-country strollers to pass.

"See? He's a smart cookie. A definite keeper."

"Because he suggested I lie to get what I want? You have weird criteria."

Nicci ignored the smart-ass comment and turned to face Lilith. "Hey, maybe you could peek at the file anyway…off the record."

"If Dr. Price gets one whiff of me working a case, I can kiss my badge goodbye, permanently."

After lightly jabbing her shoulder, the pint-sized detective circled in front and jogged backward. "Come on, I won't tell your therapist if you don't. You know you want to…I'll be home by seven…" The woman's Cupid's-bow mouth stretched into an impish grin that became contagious.

"Fine. One look. I'm having dinner with Gloria and the girls, but maybe I can swing by after, if it's not too late."

Nicci nudged her partner forward. "All right, then. Show me what you got."

The petite woman took off, and Lilith tore after her at full speed, despite the fatigue burning through her body. Of course, Lilith still didn't come close to catching her.

"Mom! Erica's not helping!" Sofia, a feisty nine-year-old, huffed and stormed over to grab the last plate. As she stomped back to the sink, her dark brown braid swung angrily from side to side.

Erica, still perched on the counter, typed fiercely on her cell with the same engrossed grin Lilith had witnessed on countless teenagers. It was the default expression of a generation. Meanwhile, Sofia and her younger sister, Rose, were stuck cleaning the dishes.

Poor Rose. The six-year-old was never talkative, but after losing her father, she barely spoke at all. Rose stepped onto a blue stool and began rinsing off plates without a peep, and a familiar guilt settled over Lilith's shoulders.

After flashing a pleasant smile, Gloria slowly scooted away from the table and stood. Of course, Lilith didn't believe the middle-aged woman's calm facade. This was merely the quiet before the storm.

Suddenly, the woman's Spanish-flecked voice boomed across the kitchen with commanding authority. "Erica Maria Alvarez! *Entonces ayúdame dios.* Put that phone down, or it goes in the garbage disposal. Help your sisters, now!"

To Lilith's surprise, the teenager rolled her eyes at her enraged mother, shrugged her shoulders, and hopped off the counter.

"Fine. Don't be so dramatic, Mom."

Gloria smoothed her button-up shirt and slid into the seat once she regained her composure. "That girl will be the death of me yet."

"I thought you were adamant about her only using the landline? When did you give her a smartphone?"

Gloria sighed and sunk into the chair. "I pick my battles, *bonita*. With Felipe gone, I need to keep a closer eye on Erica, and the phone's parental controls let me do that."

"GPS can be a wonderful thing." Lilith took another sip of coffee and soaked in the chaotic family atmosphere that would have felt like home a year ago.

It still seemed weird, sitting in the Alvarezes' kitchen. She kept expecting her old partner to waltz through the door, kiss his wife, hug the girls, and settle in to bitch about pop culture or their incompetent police lieutenant. But Felipe would never walk through those doors again.

The image flashed through her mind for the millionth time—her partner kneeling on the dark concrete, his head tilted to one side, blood flowing down the front of his shirt. Then she blinked, and it was gone.

Come on. Get a grip. As she repeated her usual pep talk, her eyes drifted to the kitchen floor where she had fought her father—*No, the reanimated corpse of my father.* Her gaze lifted to the backdoor where the siren had nearly killed her…again. Outside, in the backyard…*Stop, now, before you disappear down the rabbit hole.*

"*Bonita*, I worry about you."

Lilith glanced up at an all-too-familiar expression of sympathy. It always left her conflicted—grateful and resentful at the same time.

"I'm doing okay, Gloria. Really. I'm staying busy. Things are great with Chance. I'm all right."

The woman snorted and tilted her head. "Not even you believe those words."

"Come on. Back off." Lilith frowned into her coffee cup, unable to handle another person telling her what to do, how to feel, or what to think. Whatever happened to the *fake it till you make it* style of coping?

"Lily. You can talk to me." The combination of the woman's empathetic tone and gentle touch on her arm made Lilith snap.

"What am I supposed to say, Gloria? That I see violence and dead bodies wherever I go? That I still have nightmares of my family and friends being killed, tortured, slaughtered? That I feel guilty *each and every* day for surviving when they didn't? That I am the reason Felipe is not here and that it haunts me to my very core?" Tears burned in her eyes, and she tightened her grip on the coffee mug. "Everyone wants me to talk about it, but that's the last thing I want to do!"

Silence settled over the entire room, and Lilith glanced up. Erica, Sophia, and Rose stared at her wide-eyed, their faces frozen in a soundless gasp. *Shit.* When she opened her mouth to apologize, her brain seized at the horror and disbelief filling their eyes.

"Girls! Upstairs…" When they didn't move a muscle, Gloria shoved away from the table and surged to her feet. "*Pon tu tresero arriba ahora mismo!*"

The commanding voice broke the spell, and they darted out of the room.

"Erica! Draw a bath for Sofia and Rose!" she called after them as they raced up the stairs.

"I am so sorry…" Lilith stared into the unfathomable depths of her coffee cup, feeling about an inch tall.

"No, no. I prodded." Gloria settled back into her chair with a strained smile. "They are tough…More than me at times, I admit."

The Spanish woman took a slow sip from her cup, gathering her thoughts before continuing.

"I've said this before, but Chance spoke the truth at Felipe's funeral. You aren't to blame, and you are *not* a pariah for surviving, Lily. The voids in your life can't be filled, not even by a handsome Cajun."

"I understand what you're saying, but—"

"Let me finish. The jogging, karate classes, shooting range, a new romance…You're running full speed to avoid the ghosts behind you, but you cannot run forever, *bonita*." The woman's deep brown eyes stayed locked on her, waiting patiently.

"You're right." She glared at her mug, wishing she could hide from all the people who wanted to pick her brain. "Nothing feels right. Felipe and Dad are gone…My father lied to me about my mother's death and basically everything else…and the only blood relatives I have left are a pack of vultures, circling the carnage."

Lilith eased her grip on the mug's handle to keep from shattering the thing.

"The worst part is, I can't even lose myself in work because Dr. Price thinks it's bad for my mental health. I'm teetering on the edge of a damn blade, and I'm scared to death of falling. I'm completely off-balance, and now is the time Chance asks me to move in." She rubbed her face as tears threatened to spill.

A warm hand smoothed over her back before her best friend tugged her into a sideways hug. "Do not worry about other people. If you need work, tell Dr. Price. Fight for the things that will help you. And as for Chance, he will understand, and if he doesn't, he is not the one for you."

"Thank you." Lilith hugged Gloria tight, surprised that the woman's insights helped. "I just feel awful for hesitating when he asked. I love Chance, but even if it was the right time, moving in is still a huge decision. I haven't lived with anyone since…" Memories flashed through her head. Dark, violent ones she had buried long before the tragedies eight months ago. "Well, since college. Shaking off the past is not an easy thing to do."

Gloria tilted her head and took a long, slow sip of her coffee, waiting to hear the story playing in Lilith's mind.

"It was a long time ago, and I'd rather not dredge up more painful—"

Before she finished the sentence, "Eye of the Tiger" tore through the quiet kitchen—Nicci's ring tone. Lilith released a sigh of relief, grateful for the intrusive *Rocky III* power ballad.

"Sorry. Could be important." After flashing an apologetic smile, she slid out of her seat and crossed the kitchen. "Hey, Nicci. What can I do for you?"

"Are you still coming over tonight?" The strained undercurrent in her partner's voice raised the hairs on the back of Lilith's neck.

"Yeah. I was about to leave Gloria's in a few. Is something wrong?" She already knew the answer, but, for some reason, Nicci insisted on playing her hand close to the vest.

"I got the tox report and autopsy back on my John Doe. You'll want to see this."

"Sure. I'll be there as soon as I can."

After hanging up, Lilith stared at the screen, her skin prickling with a mixture of fear and…excitement. Apparently, she hadn't learned her lesson about wishing for mysteries to solve.

When Lilith glanced up from her phone, Gloria pulled her into a hug that bordered on uncomfortable. Except for her parents and Chance, she wasn't much of a hugger, but some part of her needed it. For a moment, Lilith relaxed and tried to breathe in her friend's affection and support, like oxygen for her fractured psyche.

"We can talk more next time. Promise. Tell the girls I'm sorry and I love them."

"Of course, *bonita*. Be careful."

An hour later, Lilith sat in Nicci's home office, which contained a blend of high-tech computers, sports trophies, and memorabilia. The wall of photos Lilith had admired the first time she visited the apartment displayed various hobbies including rock-climbing, volleyball, triathlons …the list went on. However, her partner wasn't all brawn. The woman was also proficient in hacking and research.

"Okay. Show me what you got."

Nicci slapped a thin file into Lilith's hands before turning back to her computer and typing away at top speed. "Take a peek at that while I pull up the other reports. I want your thoughts."

Lilith flipped through the crime scene photos of a seedy motel room, complete with bloodstained carpet—none of it fresh—and peeling wallpaper. A man in his mid to late thirties lay slumped against the wall with his chin resting on his chest.

She saw no obvious signs of trauma. In fact, the only things differentiating him from a drunk sleeping off a bender were the pale skin and yellowish tint that didn't fit his ethnicity. The dingy tank top revealed a farmer's tan on his arms and chest, which indicated a lot of time in the sun. If he worked outside for a living, it meant he was a relatively young vampire or a half-blood, perhaps both.

A cellphone—an older flip-style model, most likely prepaid—lay on the floor by his outstretched hand. A battered suitcase containing about a week's worth of clothes remained open on the bed. He wasn't local…A tattered wallet sat on the dresser next to a well-worn map. He was traveling, but where to and why?

The rebel flag belt buckle indicated a possible origin in the South, but that wasn't a guarantee. These days, Confederate supporters lived all over the U.S. The stronger indicators were the dust on his dark jeans and the strong wear patterns on his soles. The victim spent a considerable amount of time walking, and not for work. The cowboy boots the man wore might be for hard labor. A blue-collar hitchhiker, perhaps?

"He's not from around here. Do you have an ID?"

"Yep. Clayton Barker, age thirty-five, half-blood." Nicci kept typing away as she answered. "Here we go." When she swiveled around, her expression mirrored Lilith's—afraid but thrilled. "Look at the cause of death."

Lilith leaned in and skimmed over the screen until her eyes widened in shock. "Complications of a viral infection?"

The detective flashed an eager grin and pulled up two seemingly identical pictures. "These are transmission electron microscope images of viruses. On the left, we have the one from our victim. On the right…"

"Malachi…" Lilith stared at the screen, her heart racing. Then a horrible thought occurred to her. "Where is Barker from?"

"Atlanta, originally, but he's traveled all over the state, working as a farmhand…and guess which lab he uses…"

"Goditha. Shit! Malachi isn't an isolated case." Lilith shot up to pace the floor, her mind racing through all the implications. "We need to test the blood supplies immediately."

Although the sentence seemed logical, when Lilith realized it meant speaking to her uncle, her jaw clenched. This was not a conversation she wanted to have for multiple reasons.

"It could be a coincidence." Her partner seemed to pick up on her train of thought and appeared apologetic. "Maybe we should gather more…"

"No. We can't take that chance. All the facilities need to be tested." With a resolute grimace, she glanced at the clock. "He should be awake."

Which meant she couldn't delay the call.

"Damn it, okay." After releasing a huff of air, Lilith dug out her phone and tapped the first contact on her list. "Good evening, Aaron."

"Lilith. If you are looking for Chance—"

"No. If I wanted to talk to him, I would have dialed his number and avoided—" She stopped short and swallowed the insult. Pissing off her uncle wouldn't help. "Anyway, I need to speak with you."

"In that case, how can I help you?" The trace of contempt in Aaron's cold voice made the question sound more inconvenient than sincere.

Oh yeah, this is gonna be loads of fun.

"We have a serious problem. I need Elder authority to check all blood supplies in the North American facilities for contamination."

"I'm sorry. I don't think I heard you correctly."

The patronizing tone intent on reducing her to a petulant child shook her confidence. *What if I'm wrong? What if the virus didn't originate in the lab? No. In my gut, I know I'm right.*

"I understand this is a huge request, but I have two confirmed cases of viral infections, both of whom received supplies from Goditha."

"The names?"

"Malachi Sanders and Clayton Barker."

"And you have proof that these so-called *infections* came from the blood supply?"

Lilith expected disbelief, or perhaps anger, but Aaron seemed more irritated than anything else, as if the call interrupted something he considered more important.

"Malachi was a pureblood who had very little contact with the community down South. Clayton Barker was a half-blood drifter from Atlanta. Goditha is their *only* connection, and I shouldn't have to tell you how rare this is."

The line buzzed with tense silence, and Lilith glanced over to Nicci, who anxiously watched. Each passing second deflated their hope a little more until Aaron finally spoke, confirming her fears.

"Two cases of a supposed *infection* are not enough to warrant testing Goditha's supply, let alone the entire country's. Do you understand how much money would be involved? Not only the cost of testing, but the productivity and inventory that would be lost. Not to mention, blowing a panic whistle that cannot be undone. You simply do not have enough evidence."

"Clayton Barker died from this, and the virus took hold in a pureblood vampire. It's confirmed. That should be enough proof."

"No." That one word rang with frustrating finality, and she fought the urge to scream. "You have no idea where this *virus* came from. Bring me evidence that it came from the blood, and maybe…I'll consider your request."

"Can I at least get a sample from Goditha to check?"

"No. That would raise too much suspicion. Find another way."

"How the hell am I supposed to prove it came from the supply when you won't let me test it?"

"Not my problem." Aaron hung up before she could formulate a response.

"Short-sighted prick!" Lilith released a disgruntled growl before shoving the phone into her pocket. "Our entire race is in danger, and all he cares about is his bottom fucking line."

"I take it that's a no." Nicci winced when Lilith answered with a hostile glare. "Too bad we can't test Miriah's blood. That would make three cases. Unfortunately, the FBI and Knoxville PD kept everything on lockdown, and Chance lost the samples he grabbed from Goditha when Luminita's men jumped him."

The petite detective leaned back in her chair brainstorming the problem. Then she lunged forward with an uneasy smile.

"But I think you know someone who can get us a sample."

Lilith stopped in her tracks. "That is a bad idea."

"Why? Because Chance gets his feathers ruffled by his very presence? Or because of his winning personality?"

"Both." Lilith sighed heavily continuing to think through the suggestion. "Besides, it wouldn't be enough. Malachi and Miriah were married. She could have contracted it from him directly. It still wouldn't prove anything, not to Aaron."

Nicci nodded, deep in thought, before she glanced up sharply. "What about you and Chance?"

"No. Gregor sent us with blood and capsules. He didn't trust the lab."

As she spoke the last sentence, Lilith wondered why? At the time, her father had said the supplies might be compromised or inaccessible. Was there a possibility he knew about the virus? If so, why wouldn't he have said something? *No. It doesn't matter.* Even if her father had knowledge of the threat, he was dead now.

"Damn." Nicci frowned and turned back to the monitors.

"Sorry, I didn't contract a deadly virus." Lilith chuckled and collapsed into the chair. "What about Solasta? I mean, they've been researching it for eight months. They must know something by now."

"Why don't I pick you up in the morning? We can go by the research lab and then the coroner's office."

"Perfect. I'd really—Shit…" Lilith sighed and rubbed her face again in pure frustration. "One foot in the coroner's office and Dr. Price will take my badge. I'm not exactly friends with Frank. You can bet your ass he'll report me out of sheer spite."

"Then wait in the car. I'll bring you the detailed report, and we can go through it over lunch."

"No. I want to inspect the body and ask questions."

That only left one option, and she really didn't like it, but Gloria was right. If Lilith wanted to find answers, she had to tell her shrink and fight to work the case.

"I need to see Dr. Price and make another deal with a devil. I'll go first thing in the morning. Hopefully, you can pick me up on your way to the morgue, and we can stop by Solasta after."

"She's gonna make you talk." Nicci grimaced again.

"Yep."

Lilith stared at the ominous virus emblazoned on the screen. The thing didn't appear threatening. In fact, it resembled a work of art, perhaps a Van Gogh painting of a sun with a purple teardrop in the center.

Somehow, this unassuming speck had managed to kill a vampire. It bested the insanely healthy immune system and physiology of a unique species never before susceptible to disease.

"Where did you come from?" Lilith whispered to the virus, enthralled by the beautiful and deadly puzzle piece.

Chapter 4 - *Cassie*

Somewhere in the dark void, Cassie struggled to reach consciousness, like a disoriented swimmer clawing for the surface. Her head spun in groggy circles, her stomach lurched and flip-flopped, and each time she opened her eyes, a suffocating blackness engulfed her.

For a moment, full-blown panic dragged her back into fitful dreams of dark-haired strangers—the man's misleading smile, a pain in her thigh, her face crashing into the ground, the click of heels on pavement, a trunk slamming shut, the rough scratch of cheap car upholstery.

The stranger...She should have known better. They *trained* her to know better. A few blushing compliments and she became as helpless as a doe-eyed cheerleader in a slasher film.

Cassie forced the memories aside and focused. Dwelling on the past wouldn't help her present situation.

"Come on. Remember, step one in the field—control your breathing." After squeezing her eyes shut, she took deep breaths and concentrated on the air moving in and out of her lungs. *One, two, three. One, two, three.*

Eventually, the terror receded enough to take in her surroundings. Although the inky blackness seemed impenetrable, it still provided critical clues. Her eyes didn't hurt, and she didn't feel the pressure of a blindfold, but absolute darkness was rare above ground.

"Okay. What else?"

Cassie inhaled deeply. Within the stale air lay a medley of other scents, predominately rotting wood, dust, dank humidity, and dead leaves—the unmistakable odors of abandonment and decay. The sort of stench that seeped into the marrow and spread hopelessness like a rabid infection, devouring every shred of light in a person's soul.

"Stop spinning out. What are you missing?"

After drawing in another deep breath, she discovered a delicate sweetness lingering in the air. Despite the overpowering scents, the subtle fragrance conjured a warmth she almost found familiar. *A flower? Perfume? Fruit?*

Her head tilted toward the sweet smell, attempting to single it out, but something halted her movement. A crisp awareness spread when she sensed the rough scratch of rope around her throat. As the dread bloomed, she detected similar restraints on her arms, wrists, waist, thighs, and ankles.

Terror bubbled in her tightening chest. "Think, Cas. Calm down, breathe, and think. One, two, three. One, two, three...Where are you?"

Unfortunately, she couldn't even discern her body's position in the disorienting darkness.

"Okay. Start with that." She closed her eyes, both to quell the roaring panic and because they were useless. Even if she couldn't see, she still had other senses.

After focusing, she felt her long brown hair on her shoulder, which meant she was upright, but her feet didn't touch the floor. When she stretched her toes, they met only empty air. They had her suspended on something. *Progress...*

Next, she systematically moved each body part, testing the ropes, but found no give. Something warm and coarse like wood sat against her back, but it wasn't solid. She only detected its weight at specific points—the small of her back, her neck, and above her wrists and ankles. Something circular? A giant wagon wheel popped into her head, but it made no sense.

"Breathe, Cas. Remember the training. Keep gathering info."

No one silenced her or asked questions when she spoke out loud, which suggested she was alone. In fact, now that she thought about it, she couldn't hear anything—no movement of air, whir of machinery, city sounds, birds... Only a deafening silence making her ears ring.

"I must be underground, someplace well insulated, isolated." Six deep breaths as the panic threatened to retake control. "I'm not dead, so they want something. A hostage, information. Wait."

Cassie stopped, her brain clicking into business mode. "The guy who drugged me...He knew things about the studio and wore their branded attire. He either attended classes or did a ton of recon. Putting that much time and effort into acquiring a target meant they wanted me specifically. But why?"

Her mind flicked through possibilities but came up empty. What made her so important, so unique? What did she know that no one else did? Could it be work-related, or was she the unlucky victim of a stalker who craved strong, athletic brunettes?

The stark thud of footsteps echoed from above, breaking the silence. She strained to peer upward, but a fine mist of dirt rained down on her face. When she coughed and shook her head, the rope rubbed against her neck, leaving it raw and sensitive.

The steps continued moving overhead from right to left. They sounded rich, like dress shoes on old wooden boards with a lingering echo, which answered a few questions. This wasn't a bunker, and the room itself wasn't soundproofed. Most likely, they were holding her in a light-tight basement with a structure above. The depth of the echoes indicated someplace large and vacant. Perhaps an old church with a catacomb? Plenty of them littered the East Coast.

For a moment, Cassie considered calling out for help, but logic stopped her. Anyone who had invested that much time and effort in kidnapping her wouldn't cheap out on a location. She had already determined the place was abandoned and isolated, so the odds of random people walking overhead were abysmal. *No.* Yelling would only advertise her conscious state, and as much as she wanted answers, she didn't think she'd like them.

The longer she played dead, the more time she bought. People would look for her, and there was evidence of her disappearance, like her car. Of course, the perpetrators probably moved the vehicle or torched it. There were still her friends, her dance instructor…but the only person who would miss her before next Tuesday was her partner, if she could still call him that.

A tumultuous wave of emotions threaded through her nerves. Her hopes of a rescue hinged on either surviving a week until someone missed her or relying on the burnt-out partner who had gotten her suspended. *I need more friends.*

The footfalls faded off on the left-hand side, and she breathed a little easier until the unmistakable thump of shoes on wooden stairs reverberated in the distance. A male, judging by the deep thud of heavy feet, was coming downstairs.

Before she dissolved into terror, she closed her eyes, took slow even breaths, and counted. Maybe if she still appeared unconscious, he'd leave and come back later. The man transitioned to stone or concrete, producing a sharper tone as he moved closer, and her calm began to deteriorate.

The footsteps came to an abrupt halt, but she had no idea where the man had stopped. The echoes made them impossible to pinpoint. The silence stretched out mercilessly, and she tried to keep every muscle from tensing.

Metal rattled and clanked nearby, and then a door swung open with a high-pitched squeal, sending her pulse racing.

Light fell across her face from what must have been the doorway, and the footsteps resumed at a leisurely pace. Each one sent her closer to full-blown panic, and her lungs nearly seized by the time the man stopped moving.

An ominous silence surrounded her as he stood there, inches away. Heat radiated from his body, warm breath rushed over her face, and cheap cologne accented the acrid stench of sweat.

The terrifying quiet stretched on forever until every wisp of air made her tremble and urine trickled down her legs. The resulting shame and embarrassment deepened her feeling of helplessness. She couldn't even control her bladder.

The light still illuminated her lids, and if she'd open her eyes, Cassie might catch a glimpse of her captor, but terror kept them glued shut. An internal war raged between the need for information and her crippling fear, her nerves prickling with dreadful anticipation. Then an abrasive fabric pressed against her face, and she whipped her head back, cracking it sharply on the wood. Pain blossomed along her skull as she writhed in a vain attempt to avoid the blindfold.

Strong hands stretched the material so tight across her eyelids, spots danced behind them. After a few failed attempts, she opened her eyes to filtered, unfocused light.

Cassie turned toward the man, hoping to glimpse him through the loose weave, but only saw a shadow silhouetted in the door's light. *I should have looked when I had the chance.* Even a quick glance could have provided important clues, especially since he decided to blindfold her.

Minutes passed, and the man didn't move. The silhouette stood still as stone, breathing heavily. The slight wheeze indicated he was overweight, but the breaths also held a skin-crawling undertone of desire.

"You don't have to do this." As the trembling words emerged from her mouth, she prayed his hesitation stemmed from cold feet.

Deep in her gut, she didn't believe that was the case, but what else could she do?

"You can still walk away." Her heart thumped violently, but the shadow remained perfectly still.

The snip of scissors broke the eerie silence, and fear seared down her nerves.

"No!" She struggled against the ropes until they burned into her skin, but the cold metal still touched her stomach.

A scream escaped, and her entire abdomen tried to retract. The scissors trailed up her body, gliding over her skin. The shearing sound of cut fabric filled her ears, and when her top gave way, cool air chilled her exposed torso. The scissors vanished for a moment and reappeared at each arm, cutting her sleeves.

The black silhouette reached out and tore away the remnants of her blouse. A calloused hand glided across her trembling skin, lingering over her lace bra, and tears welled in Cassie's eyes.

"Please…" The whimpered plea was an act of desperation. Logic dictated her simpering cries were more likely to fuel his twisted fantasies than deter them. However, in this situation, she was just another powerless victim begging for mercy as a last resort, not a federal agent.

The cool metal touched her again, tracing between her breasts, down her ribs, her stomach. The sudden snip of the scissors cutting the waistband of her skirt made Cassie jump with a startled cry, but the man continued until the chiffon fell away, leaving her unprotected.

Her eyes squeezed closed, and she fought for each breath through the tears streaming down her cheeks. When the rough hand glided along her hip in a lecherous touch, bile burned up her raw throat.

"What do you want from me?" She knew the answer but refused to admit it. *This isn't real. This is not my life. This is not how I end.* The thoughts kept repeating until they became her mantra, her escape.

The hand disappeared for a moment before sliding under her bra strap. *No. No. No.* The scissors clicked, and his fingertips brushed over her chest to the remaining strap. A quick cut and then the cold blades glided under the flimsy material between her breasts.

The mad man took his time. She heard each fiber break between the blades, her body shaking with inescapable panic. After the abrupt snip, he ripped away the tattered remains of her bra, and the frigid air slithered over her skin, coiling around her like a venomous snake.

"Please…Please don't do this." The words escaped in a hoarse whisper.

In silent reply, the man slid his hand between her thighs, and the air froze in her lungs. He hesitated, his sour breath rushing over her cheek as his grip tightened. Each second made her stomach lurch until she broke into a sickening sweat, filled with the urge to squirm away or fight back. The restraints made both impossible. She was powerless, helpless, vulnerable, humiliated.

He snatched her panties and tore them away in a swift and violent motion. Every inch of exposed skin shuddered, and sobs of defeat wracked her body. How could this be the end of her life? Cassie always strove to do the right thing and help others. She went to church, gave to charities, and participated in fundraising 5Ks. *I am a good person.*

Cassie thought of all the corpses who shared that same thought before they died, and her throat tightened. *Bad things happen to good people.* In theory, she should know that better than anyone, given her profession, but somehow, the realization still came as a shock.

Metal clanged sharply against concrete, bringing her back to the present. The black silhouette still loomed in front of her. *Did he throw the scissors away?* While her brain puzzled over the sound, the shadow vanished, and the light from the open doorway flooded her vision.

Every hair stood on end as she strained to detect some clue of what was happening—nothing.

No movement, footsteps, heavy breathing...

Only the deafening roar of her blood pounding.

What is he doing? Her chest burned with each labored breath, and a cold sweat broke over her chilled skin again.

Cassie focused so intently, the gravelly voice behind her nearly stopped her heart.

"You must be prepared."

"Prepared for what?" She latched onto the words like a lifeline, ignoring the ominous tone, but he didn't answer. "How? How can I prepare?" *Is he trying to help me? If so, why isn't he answering?*

A sweet smell flooded her nostrils—the same delicate fragrance she had detected earlier. Although she didn't recognize the exotic scent, it nagged at the back of her mind. While she thought through the possibilities, something smooth traced over her lips, and she pulled away.

"Take a bite." The sinister voice made the invitation far less appealing. "Now!" His tone sharpened, and he jammed the thing against her mouth with bruising force.

Reluctantly, Cassie took a small bite, and the flavor exploded across her dry palate in liquid fireworks. It tasted like…a slightly citrus plum but sweeter…like sunshine, warmth, and everything she desperately craved.

"Again!"

This time, when he shoved the fruit forward, Cassie eagerly complied. She hadn't realized how hungry she was…*How long have I been down here?*

Without waiting to be asked, she took a third bite, then a fourth. A euphoric sensation settled into her bones and warmed her naked skin. All the panic and stress tensing her muscles melted into a welcome exhaustion.

Calloused hands, wet with the sweet juice, caressed the crown of her head, and the raspy voice chanted in a foreign language. At times, she almost thought she recognized the words, but they didn't matter. Nothing mattered anymore.

When the liquid trickled down her hair and over her warmed skin, she stopped pulling away. It felt too good, like being bathed in sunlight and divinity. The juice was soothing and insulating, protecting her from the cold. Even the odd foreign chant transformed into a gentle lullaby, easing her toward peaceful slumber.

The slick hands smoothed over her neck, her shoulders, her breasts, and her eyes fluttered, fatigue wrapping around her like a soft blanket. If she slept, it wouldn't matter what he did to her or how long his hands remained on her skin.

It was her one escape, her choice, a way she could be free.

Chapter 5

"Let me see if I have this correct." Dr. Price pushed her horn-rimmed glasses up the bridge of her nose with a poorly concealed grin. "You want me to reinstate you so you can investigate a case. One you've already studied the file on…"

"Study is a bit of an overstatement. I barely glanced…" The muttered words died off when Lilith's psychiatrist shot a warning glare and continued.

"…despite being suspended and massively uncooperative in therapy sessions. Why would I do this?" One elegant eyebrow arched, and she tapped her pen against the paper. This time, it seemed more like the thump of a patronizing drum than a nervous tick.

"This is a crucial case, and I need to be involved." Lilith paused for a moment, considering the risks.

Revealing the sensitive details could prove dangerous, but if the woman was spying for Aaron, Lilith wouldn't be saying anything he didn't already know. If the therapist didn't incite community-wide panic, no harm, no foul.

"You need to understand. The virus involved in this case—"

"Virus?" The tapping pen stopped, and a confounded expression clouded the doctor's face. The reaction didn't prove Dr. Price's innocence, but if she *was* in cahoots with Aaron, it wasn't a two-way street.

"Yes. One with exponential ramifications. It's the first one to infect a vampire, and now we have two confirmed cases…Who knows how many more are out there."

Dr. Price recovered quickly and resumed her mask of indifference. Not a single micro-impression of surprise appeared after that initial response. She was either very good or…

"And you are an expert in virology?"

Lilith scowled and slouched in the chair. "No, but I know things about the case that Detective Boyd doesn't because he's human. I *need* to be involved. There isn't anyone else."

When the woman merely sat still, staring her down, Lilith gritted her teeth.

"Look…I'll tell you whatever you want. I'll come in once or even twice a week and tell you about the nightmares, Phipps Bend, the medical center, all of it."

The impervious stone face of Dr. Brittany Price finally broke into an expression of genuine interest. After laying her pen on the pad with quiet deliberation, she stared at the paper as if reading through her options. Once she decided on her terms, she returned her stoic gaze to Lilith.

"Start by telling me what happened at Phipps Bend. If you hold back, the answer will be no. If you are straight with me and answer my questions, I'll consider it."

Lilith drew in a calming breath, her mind racing. Telling the truth about Ashcroft's powers, Coffee's mysterious heritage, the Durand, and the abilities of Cohen's blood…It was all incredibly dangerous information she couldn't risk getting to Aaron. She could try altering the details, but Dr. Price was better at her job than Lilith was at lying.

Is working this case worth the risk? The full truth put a lot of lives in danger, especially if Aaron discovered it.

"If you aren't willing to talk…" The woman closed her notepad and started to stand, when Lilith held out a hand to stop her.

Two vampires, unconnected except for their blood supply, were infected by the same virus. *What if it isn't just Goditha? What if we are all walking time bombs?*

"Wait. Sit down."

The good doctor settled back into her chair with an expectant expression.

"I'll give you the highlights, and you can ask questions. Good enough?" Perhaps omission would work if she condensed things.

"For now." The tone clearly stated Lilith was treading on thin ice.

After a nervous sigh, Lilith settled in and began. "We split up when we got there. Cohen and his partner, Whitmore, took the back of the building. Chance, Humphries, and I took the front. Ashcroft must have got to Humphries somehow. He shot at us, but I took him down…"

"Before you continue, the report mentions Cohen is part of an underground organization. Care to elaborate?"

"I agreed to tell you about the basement. I'm not ready to give you specifics on him yet." Her jaw clenched on instinct, and she tried to moderate the anger in her voice.

Asking point-blank about the Durand seemed like an odd choice with a patient who harbored extreme trust issues. Perhaps Dr. Price thought the bold approach would shock her into a truthful answer, or maybe Lilith had over-estimated the shrink's skills. Whatever the reason, the tactic wasn't successful, and they stared at each other in awkward silence until the shrink gave in.

"Fair enough. So, you took down Humphries...how?"

The heat that blossomed across Lilith's face made the guilt impossible to deny. "I fought, got him on the ground, and beat his face to a pulp."

The quick summary held a clipped tone. She shifted in the seat and tensed, waiting for the litany of questions, but the doctor merely signaled for her to keep talking and scribbled a few notes.

"Chance was hurt, so I set him up someplace safe with a gun. That only left me. I had to go down in that basement alone."

Lilith gazed at the off-white carpet, the mental horrors creeping up her spine until they replayed in vivid detail.

"Ashcroft kept my father tied to a column and Duncan chained to the floor. The man wasn't my uncle anymore, more like a rabid dog gnawing at his own limbs. Alvarez sat on the concrete, restrained, while Ashcroft paced back and forth, waiting...for me."

A shiver made her arms shake until she clasped her hands together, determined to finish the story. Too much was at stake.

"Then Whitmore and Coffee dragged Cohen into the room. I assumed Ashcroft influenced them, like he did Humphries. Cohen's partner started making demands, but the monster never intended to keep his promises. Humans were nothing more than tools to him, and Whitmore served his purpose, so the madman slit his throat.

"During the commotion, I snuck into the room undetected and began untying my father. Only a few ropes remained when Ashcroft lost interest in the others and turned toward Gregor. That's when Alvarez started arguing with him."

Tears fell as the scene flashed behind Lilith's eyes—the blade slicing into skin, blood running down his shirt in thick streams and soaking into the concrete.

After swallowing the lump in her throat and drawing in a shaky breath, she continued. "I freed Gregor, but at a high cost. When I looked up, Felipe was dead."

"Did Alvarez see you?"

Lilith blinked and thought back, the scene replaying for the millionth time. Felipe's warm brown eyes met hers a split-second before he spoke up.

"Yes, he did."

"Then he made a noble and conscious choice."

"Don't you think I know that? I would have done the same thing in his situation and sacrificed myself. I get it, but understanding doesn't make things any easier! Felipe is still dead because of me, my father, and the monster he created."

"Did you trust your partner?"

Lilith frowned at Dr. Price, thrown off by the odd question. "Of course, I did. We were partners for six years and, more than that…best friends. I trusted him with my life."

"Then pay homage to that bond by honoring his choice. When you hold yourself responsible, you take away his decision's power. He knew exactly what he was doing, Lilith. Let go of the guilt and respect his memory by moving forward."

For a moment, Lilith stared at the carpet and let the words sink in. She'd heard all the speeches before, but this time seemed different. Perhaps she shouldered the blame because it was easier than admitting why Alvarez had chosen to die. He felt her survival was more important than his, and accepting the truth meant living up to an impossible standard of greatness. The responsibility of proving he didn't waste his life terrified her more than wallowing in guilt.

"Do you want to continue?"

Dr. Price spoke so softly Lilith almost didn't hear the question, but after wiping her cheeks, she nodded.

"I…Uh, my father and I made it to the stairwell, but Ashcroft caught up with us. Then he dragged me back into that room and tied me up in Gregor's place." The thought of that column, the one where he had tortured her cousin for hours, sent her heart racing at full speed, and the words froze in her mouth.

"And what did you do?" The doctor's gentle prod broke through the memory of Miriah's mutilated corpse, allowing Lilith to speak.

"I goaded him. I wanted him to kill me. Death seemed better than enduring a tenth of what Miriah experienced, but Cohen had other plans. He took the monster's side and struck a bargain to keep me alive so he could study my *unique* properties."

The therapist's brow furrowed as she peered over her glasses. "What unique properties?"

Damn it. Watch yourself. "You'd have to ask Detective Cohen." Not a lie. She had no desire to explain that particular detail.

"And what did Ashcroft want in return?"

"He wanted him to join his crusade against vampires and anyone else who stood in their way. Andrew agreed to torture me under his guidance until the madman regained his calm."

"You believe he betrayed you?"

Lilith locked eyes with the doctor and truly considered her answer.

"I did at the time. Hell, even after. Every action seemed based on selfish motivations and self-preservation. My opinion didn't change until he tried to take a bullet to save my life. He begged his grandfather to kill him instead of me. Then, after the medical center…No…Cohen doesn't want to cause me harm."

"Doesn't? As in the present tense? But do you think he was swayed in Phipps Bend? Do you believe he merely acted a part and never intended to follow through on his promise to join Ashcroft Orrick?"

Lilith frowned at the question and thought through every possibility. "Honestly, I don't know."

The therapist nodded, satisfied, at least for now. "Okay. A fair answer. Then what?"

"Coffee found Chance and brought him down to the basement. Ashcroft's excitement permeated the room, and I lost all hope. Cohen followed orders and stuck needles in my arms—one to drain blood and the other to replace it…"

"Why?"

"Ashcroft preferred to feed on blood steeped in fear and agony. He believed it gave him more power." A small measure of defensiveness edged into her voice.

"Continue."

When Dr. Price didn't push for more information, Lilith relaxed into her chair and breathed a little easier.

"I don't recall much past that point. Dad came in, firing a shotgun, and some pellets ripped open the donor bag. I lost a lot of blood that was no longer being replaced and fell in and out of consciousness. I remember Coffee and Gregor pinning Ashcroft to the furnace while Chance freed me."

Lilith chuckled when a ridiculous memory popped into her head.

"For a moment, when Cohen tried to help unlock the manacles, I actually thought Chance betrayed us and was working *with* Cohen."

"And why did you think that?"

"I was half-conscious from extreme blood loss. My brain jumped to stupid conclusions because Chance let Cohen help him."

"Hmm. Are you sure some part of you didn't want him to be the enemy?"

Lilith's jaw dropped in utter shock, and she was unable to follow Dr. Price's train of thought. "I'm sorry. What?"

"Well, relationships come with an array of complex emotions. Sometimes, villainizing your partner is easier than dealing with those emotions."

"Can we skip the Nicholas Sparks shit and keep going?"

"So, you don't think I have a valid point? Or do you merely want to avoid discussing Chance?"

Lilith's jaw tightened, her anger bubbling to the surface. "I *know* what a bad guy is and have no desire to repeat the experience. No. I didn't *want* Chance to be an enemy, subconsciously or not."

"My apologies." After holding up her hands in surrender, Dr. Price scribbled a few more notes. "Do you remember anything else?"

"Um, yeah. We couldn't let that monster leave the basement, so Richard Coffee and my father intended to keep him pinned while we escaped. Ashcroft had filled the basement with flammable chemicals, probably his plan to hide his crimes, but during the scuffle, the lanterns broke, and the flames were closing in. Coffee was adamant about staying behind, but Chance forced Gregor to run. We barely made it outside before the entire place went up."

"So, they both died?"

"Well, Richard was mostly dead before we left. Ashcroft was clawing through his body to escape." The image flashed through her mind—entrails glistening against the concrete, talons shredding fresh, agonized screams echoing off the walls. Lilith rubbed the goosebumps from her arms, trying to banish the disturbing scene.

"I've read the reports, but I still don't understand. What made Orrick such a dominant threat?"

"What did the Goditha report say?"

"The entire thing seemed purposefully vague. It mentioned a faster healing ability, but nothing screamed *monster* except his psych profile."

Lilith straightened in the chair and decided on the truth. Even if the woman reported to Aaron, it wouldn't compromise Cohen if Lilith didn't reveal their common ancestry. Besides, some measure of truth appeared to be a necessary evil if she wanted her badge back.

"Chance shot him point-blank in the head, and half his brain splattered on the floor. Despite that, we both witnessed him claw at Dr. Nichols. Then he began to regenerate brand-new tissue. The thing healed missing brain matter and bone in mere seconds."

Dr. Price's eyes widened, and the pen slid from her frozen fingers. "How is that possible?"

"It isn't. That's the point. Nothing about Ashcroft was possible, but it all happened. Even his blood sample we tested defied the laws of nature. I don't know what he was before Gregor turned him, but he wasn't human." Lilith silently prayed the doctor's shock would distract her from detecting the lie. Revealing the Durand still seemed like a bad idea.

Of course, once they reached the insanity that had followed their return to New York City…How could she properly explain Peisinoe, Isadora, and Luminita without talking about Cohen's species? Nothing in the medical center would make sense without discussing the Durand to provide context. *A bridge I'll cross when I get to it.*

The shrink still appeared shaken, and Lilith didn't blame her. It was a hell of a lot to take in.

"So…" Dr. Price frowned at her paper as if it contained nothing but Greek scribbles.

Before she completed her thought, the door swung open, shattering the tense silence. "You ready for lunch, hon?" A woman breezed into the room, and her short silver-blond hair bobbed as she strolled straight toward Dr. Price.

"Um, Renee…" The doctor gestured to the couch by the door. "I'm with a client."

The woman stiffened before turning, an appalled expression on her heart-shaped face. The fine lines around her eyes and mouth indicated mid-thirties or early forties, and their patterns pegged her as a smoker. Lilith glanced at Renee's hands, spotting a faint discoloration on her left middle finger, which meant she either spent considerable time smoking in the car or was left-handed.

"Oh, God. I am so sorry! Hank wasn't at his desk, so I assumed..."

When Renee flashed an apologetic smile, Lilith noticed the woman's green eyes were slightly bloodshot. Perhaps she suffered from insomnia or indulged in alternative forms of relaxation.

"It's all right." Lilith stood and cast her shrink a significant stare that spoke volumes. "We were just wrapping up, right, Doc?"

A tight smile pulled at the therapist's lips, and she slid her pad and pen onto the table. "Yes. I think we made real progress today." Dr. Price rose and followed her patient toward the door.

Renee awkwardly backed up to the desk, putting distance between them. The uncertainty indicated a new relationship, an unfamiliarity with reactions and repercussions.

Dr. Price placed a hand on Lilith's shoulder and kept her voice low. "I'll notify the company. I am clearing you for this one case. I believe your assessment is correct. The matter is urgent, and you displayed an honest willingness to work with me today. Besides, I get the sense you really need this."

Lilith nodded as a weight lifted from her shoulders. "Thank you. I appreciate it." She turned to leave, but the doctor's hand on her shoulder didn't move.

"Oh, one more thing. I am well versed in profiling, so if I can help, please don't hesitate to ask. Any insights I provide will be shared only with you, confidentially and strictly off the books."

Lilith struggled to keep the disbelief and suspicion off her face but apparently didn't succeed.

"I am not Aaron's lackey. He does not own me, and I hold no allegiance to him. I'm a professional, and I'm sure you've done enough research on me to know that."

A faint blush crept across Lilith's cheeks. The moment she had seen Dr. Brittany Price's name, she ran every possible check on her, including credit. Aside from a few parking tickets, one bad review from a schizophrenic in Albuquerque, and a penchant for shopping on Amazon, Lilith had found nothing suspicious. As far as she could tell, the woman had never worked for Aaron before or for any of his family. Still, Lilith had trust issues for a reason, several of them, in fact.

"I'll consider your offer."

"Please do, and I apologize for my girlfriend, Renee. We were supposed to have lunch, and this session was a little impromptu. I left her a voicemail, but who actually listens to those?"

"It's okay. So, the usual time next week?"

"That will be fine. Thank you for finally opening up and talking to me. If you continue being honest, I think I can really help you."

Lilith nodded with a conflicted smile. After what she just experienced, she didn't doubt the woman could help her, but being honest represented a significant hurdle.

The doc held the door open for her, and Lilith crossed the vacant waiting room. The second she stepped into the hall, she dug her phone out and called Nicci.

"Hey, do you still have time to pick me up?"

Chapter 6

"Y ou're late." Dr. Frank Morgan remained focused on the corpse while his gruff voice boomed through the morgue like that of an angry troll guarding his bridge. The comparison wasn't much of a stretch. They both shared a cranky disposition and a territorial nature.

"Sorry, I had to pick up someone." Nicci strolled around the autopsy table, and Lilith followed close behind.

When Frank glanced over the rim of his glasses, an immediate frown crossed his face, his nostrils flaring. "No. *You* are not supposed to be here."

Lilith lifted her hands in surrender. "Relax, Dr. Morgan. My therapist cleared me for this case. You can call her, if you like."

Frank's left eye twitched, and he stared her down, a rather common occurrence. "No! This is my damn autopsy, *Ms.* Adams. You can wait for my report. Now get out!"

Most medical examiners—especially the older males—didn't appreciate a young upstart second-guessing their work. However, Dr. Frank Morgan took that dislike to a new level. Since he began studying corpses over two hundred years ago, Lilith understood why he considered himself an infallible authority.

"I'm not here to cause trouble. I need information. If this vampire died from a viral infection, the implications are dire."

As soon as the words left her mouth, she recognized her mistake.

"*If…?*" His wrinkled face scrunched into a scowl, exposing a vast network of wrinkles, and Lilith wondered about his true age. Physical appearance was often misleading, especially with vampires of varying lineage.

Dr. Morgan slammed his probe down on the tray, and the sudden racket cut off her distracted thoughts. "I assume you read my preliminary report?"

When her eyes fell as she nodded, his lips split in a malicious grin.

"Of course, you did, or you wouldn't be here. The cause of death said *complications due to viral infection.* You can read English, correct?"

"Whoa, okay." Nicci exuded more authority than a five-foot-nothing Italian should possess. "You guys can measure brain size later. Frank, walk us through this, please."

After one final scowl at Lilith, he limped toward the opposite table. Scar tissue from an old accident prevented his left knee from bending properly. Dr. Morgan didn't trust the Solasta surgical staff, but shopping around for an orthopedic surgeon was problematic at best for a vampire.

"Well, come on. I don't have all day." With a little too much zeal, he unzipped the bag and peeled the white plastic away from the body.

The corpse's skin displayed the same pallor Lilith had noticed in the photo, but without the clothes, she also spotted odd bruising in random places. None of them seemed like ligature marks or contusions, merely blossoming areas with various shades of black, blue, purple, green, and yellow.

"All right, kids. Clayton Barker, age thirty-five. No signs of external trauma. Suffered multiple organ failure due to transient aplastic crisis secondary to a viral infection. As you can tell by the jaundiced skin"—he shoved open the eyelids, revealing milky yellow orbs with a hint of color in the irises—"and eyes, hepatic function failure occurred first, which suggests the virus attacked the cells directly. Most of the other major organ systems, including the kidneys and heart, only show evidence of ischemic damage."

He paused, peering at them with squinted eyes.

"We good so far?"

"Not enough blood and oxygen to the organs." Lilith tried for a genuine smile, but he still grumbled as he turned back to the body.

"The bone marrow examination revealed large, multinucleated normoblasts and pronormoblasts, and the late normoblasts were completely absent. I also discovered alterations in the mature erythroid progenitors."

This time when he stared over his glasses, Lilith and Nicci wore blank expressions.

After a heavy sigh, he shook his head. "The man no longer created or matured red blood cells. That, coupled with his species-specific problem of low hemoglobin levels, became lethal." Once the recognition finally sparked, he appeared satisfied and returned his attention to the corpse.

"Frank." At the sound of Lilith's voice, his spine visibly tensed before he glared up at her. "Can I ask a few questions? Please." She kept her tone respectful, a near-impossible feat when he lashed out like a cranky troll, but the threat to her species outweighed her pride.

"Well, go on. Spit it out. You can't go ten minutes without opening your mouth."

Instead of rising to the bait, she ignored his outburst and asked her first question. "What's with the bruising? They seem random, not typical fight patterns, and..."

"Because they aren't contusions." Frank huffed impatiently. "The bone marrow was compromised, which not only affected the red and white blood cells but..."

"Platelets. They're areas of ecchymosis due to thrombocytopenia."

When she finished the sentence for him, he didn't appear entirely displeased. Lilith realized her partner might require an explanation with less scientific jargon.

"So, the bruises stem from an inability to clot. Random vessels ruptured and caused minuscule spots of internal bleeding. I'm sure that didn't help with the acute anemia."

Frank nodded and waited.

"Do you know the strength of his lineage?"

"Actually, not a stupid question."

Once again, she let the slight slide. Besides, coming from Frank, it was almost a compliment.

"Judging by the rate of decay, he was maybe one-eighth vampire—a diluted ancestry. He probably used replacements every six to eight weeks when healthy."

"One last question. Can you tell how long he's been infected?"

"I found a few human blood cells carrying the virus in the sample I took. Exposure occurred no more than sixty days ago. The infection altered how fast he broke down donor cells, so I can't be more specific than that. Before you ask, there is no way to tell if he's had repeated exposures."

"Wait. You said the human cells carried the virus. Does that mean it came from the donor blood?" Lilith couldn't help but get her hopes up. If Frank confirmed the source...

"Can't read *and* can't count. One question, my ass..."

"Please, it's important."

After another huff, he gave in. "No."

Well, shit.

"It means they were infected. Could have been before he ingested them but might have been after. There is no way to tell."

"Does that mean humans can be infected?" Nicci paled as she posed the question.

"Difficult to tell. They are capable of being carriers, but I have no way of knowing if the virus would become symptomatic with human physiology. Now, may I finish?"

They both nodded with a mixture of disappointment and relief. There had to be some way to figure out how he contracted this thing.

"Lastly, I discovered mild encephalitis—inflammation of the brain. Compared to the other systems, the damage was minor, and I doubt he experienced symptoms."

"So, Doc. Any thoughts on what it is?"

When he turned to Nicci, the smile held none of his usual malevolence. At least he liked one of them. "If this was a human corpse, I'd say he died from parvovirus B19. The damage caused is similar."

"And in a vampire?"

"I've never seen evidence that a virus could infect a vamp one thirty-second or higher, so I'm at a loss to how it infected him. Of course, I'm not a virologist."

"But if it suppressed the bone marrow, wouldn't that include white blood cells too?"

Both Lilith and Frank gawked at Nicci like she'd grown a second head.

"What? I took anatomy and physiology in college."

"A fair point, but the virus took hold and inflicted a lot of damage *before* reaching the marrow. In theory, a virus could only infiltrate a vamp's system if it killed the defenses first, not as an aftereffect."

"Okay. Anything else you can tell us?" The petite detective peered up from her notepad, pen at the ready.

"Close as I can tell, the thing is blood-borne, unlike parvovirus B19, which is carried in the sputum. That's all I got." Then he rounded on Lilith with a scathing glare. "Do you want to inspect the organs and make sure I didn't miss anything?" The clenched jaw dared her to say *yes*, but the guts wouldn't tell her anything new.

"I trust your work." As she moved to leave, something dark caught her eye. "You didn't mention these." She leaned closer, her fingertips tracing over two puncture wounds nestled in the antecubital space of his right arm.

"Track marks. Not an unexpected find with a drifter, and he has a matching set on the left."

"Anything on the toxicology report?"

"It's most likely heroin, which only remains in the urine for two days. Hair follicle tests can show a longer timeline, but a ton of factors interfere with the results, making them unreliable."

"Hmm." Lilith nodded and stepped away. "You're probably right."

When Frank narrowed his eyes with a suspicious frown, she couldn't help poking the bear.

"Besides, if I think of anything else, I'll call."

"See yourselves out!" Without another word, Dr. Morgan limped around the table, stormed into his office, and slammed the door.

"Man, he *seriously* hates you." Nicci chuckled and tucked her notebook into her jacket pocket.

"The struggle is real." Lilith's eyes lingered on the body. If the virus was blood-borne, the intravenous injections were a possible vector. What if Barker didn't contract the virus from Goditha, but a dirty needle? So far, the morgue trip complicated her investigation instead of strengthening it. Malachi wasn't a drug user, and Aaron demanded definitive proof to consider testing one lab. "Think I'm done here."

"What the hell did you do to him?" They headed for the door, her partner grinning, eager to hear the full story.

"Who?" With her mind distracted by the puzzling case, Lilith lost track of the conversation.

"Um...Frank."

"Oh, of course. Sorry. A few years back, I assisted on a case, a human one, because the department was short-handed. The cause of death was penetrating trauma to the guy's skull. In court, Frank testified that a cylindrical object like an ice pick caused the fatal blow."

"And you disagreed?"

"After studying the X-rays and the wound track, I concluded the object was tapered and flat on one side. Then the girlfriend confessed. She walked in on him banging her sister, blacked out with rage, and slammed her stiletto into his head. Frank has never forgiven me for being right."

"Damn." Nicci bit back a chuckle. "You don't make many friends, do ya?"

Although her partner meant it as a joke, the comment hit a little close to home.

"Speaking of which, why does he like you so much? He may hate me, but he doesn't *like* anyone."

"Well, I take measures to ensure my professional relationships work smoothly. Once a month, I bring him some Castellare Chiante Classico and a pan of homemade lasagna."

Lilith burst out laughing as they exited the building into the warm July sunshine. "See, this is why I don't have friends. I never excelled at bribery."

"Hey. Being at the top of Frank's list is worth a twenty-dollar bottle of wine and some food. Plus, he lets *me* ask questions without exploding in anger." Nicci winked and opened the driver's side door of her red Fiat. "To the lab? See if they found anything useful?"

Lilith nodded over the hood of the tiny clown car. Although it was a practical vehicle, especially for the city, she missed the spacious NYC cabs with plenty of legroom. Folding her five-foot-nine frame into a micro-economy car didn't top her list of fun things to do.

"And food on the way? Talking about lasagna made me hungry."

Forty-five minutes later, Nicci and Lilith pulled up to a concrete and glass building in New Rochelle, which resembled a 1960s hospital complete with an emergency entrance and enormous backup generator. "SOLASTA" graced the side in bold red letters with no other signage.

Unlike Goditha, Solasta kept everything in top shape, including the meticulously groomed landscaping. In the outskirts of Knoxville, an unkempt office park didn't stand out, but here, the surrounding middle-class community consisted of exclusive business parks and shopping centers. The area conveyed a particular level of success, and Solasta blended into the crowd.

When they reached the entrance, Lilith swiped her badge, and the door popped open. No one stood guard inside. Solasta believed posting anyone within sight would invite unwanted questions. Instead, they filled the empty foyer with a few plastic trees and a dozen cameras, which covered every square inch.

Although the lack of an information desk or directory might appear inconvenient, everyone with access knew where to go. Most vampires only used the medical services and blood banks, which they accessed from the

Emergency Department entrance. Besides, if someone made it past the front door, they'd be flagged by facial recognition software and greeted by armed guards in seconds.

"Is it always this quiet?" Nicci asked. They crossed the granite floor toward the elevators, their footsteps echoing through the cavernous space.

"Never been in this section before?"

"Once…" Nicci glanced around at the unused armchairs as her partner pressed the down arrow.

"Alvarez never came with me to the lab." A distant smile brightened Lilith's face. "He said it was squint-work, not police work."

"What?"

"I think he got it from a TV show Gloria used to watch. He said all the techs do is squint into microscopes—squint-work."

A ding signaled the elevator's arrival.

Nicci chuckled as they stepped inside. "Makes sense. So, there are guards here, right?"

"Solasta keeps about twenty on payroll, but honestly, I've never seen one."

Once the elevator opened on the first basement level, they strolled down the lengthy corridor to a door marked "Research."

"So, the director is a bit of an acquired taste…"

"Like Frank?" Nicci flashed a grin. "I can handle grumpy bears."

"Uh, no. Different kind of weird." Lilith rapped her knuckles against the frosted glass, hoping today wasn't one of his endless-conspiracy-theory days.

The door swung open to a state-of-the-art lab and a dozen people working at various stations. The woman who answered peeked at them from beneath thick bangs and appeared to be mid-twenties, probably a grad student or intern. The messy bun and bags under her eyes were telltale signs of a newbie. Plus, Lilith didn't recognize her, and she knew everyone on Dr. Scott's team.

"Can I help you?"

"We came to speak with Director Gerald Scott."

They flipped open their badges in unison, and the woman went pale, her left arm trembling—definitely new if law enforcement rattled her. Her eyes halted on Lilith's badge, and she glanced up with a deep frown.

"I was sorry to hear about your dad…and everyone else."

Apparently, the complete list was too much of a mouthful, not that Lilith blamed her. The tally included a lot of names.

After stowing her badge, she forced a polite smile. "Thanks. I appreciate it. Can you escort us to the director?"

The girl nodded with enthusiasm, her heavy bangs bouncing with each movement. "Yeah. Follow me." She spun around and rushed over to a hefty guy with red hair. "Um…Dr. Scott?"

The tentative tone earmarked her as the director's intern. He believed trial by fire and an overbearing work ethic created better scientists. Most of them ended up traumatized.

"There are some people here to see you."

"Come on, Claudia. How many times do I need to repeat the protocol? Names!" The man jotted down a few more notes while the woman struggled. "Uh…"

The man swiveled on the stool, his boyish face furrowed in a disappointed frown. "Idiotic! Did you even ask? My cat could do better—" The sharp retort died in his mouth when his eyes fell on Lilith.

"Ease up, you old bastard. Let the poor girl get back to work."

"Since when does texting at her desk for eight hours a day constitute work?" Gerald grimaced and waved a pasty-white hand at the rattled girl. "Go do something constructive that doesn't involve that infernal phone riddled with spyware."

Without another word, the intern shoved her cellphone in her pocket and scurried away.

"You work in a lab that handles highly sensitive information and still invite Google into every aspect of your life. Fucking useless generation." He glared daggers at his assistant before turning his attention to Lilith and Nicci. "As for you. The bastard part, I happily claim for a multitude of reasons, but who are you calling old, lass?" Gerald raised one scorching-red eyebrow, eased back in his seat, and crossed his arms over his chest.

The faint undercurrent in his voice came from the British Isles, but decades, or perhaps centuries, in America had diluted the accent to occasional hints overlooked by most people—until he used an odd word like *lass*.

"Your skin reacts when you sit near the blinds too long. Only an idiot would think you're as young as you look."

Her uncle Duncan, who had pioneered the biological exploration of their species, never explained why they aged at different rates. A one-hundred-and-fifty-year-old vampire could look twenty-three and another sixty. Perhaps a fancy explanation didn't exist. After all, humans didn't age the same either. It was all in the genes.

"Hi, there. I'm Nicci DeLuca, NYPD."

"I assume you're the new partner?" He shook his head with an apologetic sigh. "I'd consider a transfer." Gerald held up his chubby hand, shielding the words from Lilith as he whispered, "She can be a downright temperamental bit—"

"All right! That's enough." Lilith huffed and leaned against the counter. "The poor woman has enough reasons to run for the hills without your nonsense." The humorous expression didn't quite reach her eyes.

"And she's still here?" The laugh sounded richer than his nasally voice. "Come on, Lil. You don't call. You don't write. Been avoiding me?"

"Paid suspension." She crossed her arms over her chest and flashed a weary smile. Telling the same story for the past eight months made it a touchy subject.

"What for? Did you run your smart mouth to the wrong person again? I said before, you catch more flies with honey."

Although the man's grin consisted of crooked teeth, she still found it endearing. When Gerald avoided the downward spiral of paranoia, he was a funny and likable guy.

"Nothing so dramatic. Chalk it up to a rough year." Before he could offer his condolences or ask awkward questions, she cut him off. "And since when do you *ever* use honey? You make grown people cry and suffer nervous breakdowns on a regular basis."

"I said *you* can catch more flies with honey, not me. So, is this a social call? Ya missed my handsome face?"

"Nope. Pure business. Can you tell me anything about the Malachi Sanders case? Have you made any headway?"

His beady gray eyes bounced between Nicci and Lilith, the playful grin sliding off his face. When his brow furrowed, she got the impression it had less to do with the abrupt subject change and more to do with the virus.

"If you're suspended, I don't think I—"

"Gerald, my shrink cleared me for this one. I think she's testing me to see if I unravel, but it doesn't matter. This case is crucial."

"Lil...This thing is scary, and the vic was butchered by—"

"Stop. I don't need a refresher. We discovered a second victim."

Before she finished, the hefty man jumped up from his stool faster than expected. "Another case? Why am I just now hearing about this?" Gerald's faint accent grew thicker, perhaps induced by stress or straight-up fear.

"Whoa, calm down. Frank only completed the autopsy this morning. He will send you samples, and…The guy died from a lethal infection."

"How?" His red eyebrows knitted together in furious concentration. "I need details."

"I made you a copy of Frank's report."

As soon as Lilith held out the folder, Gerald snatched it up, flipped it open, and scanned the contents.

"So, have you learned anything about where it came from?" she asked.

When he glanced up, the defensive hostility caught her off guard.

"You do realize that studying a new virus can take years, even decades? Eight months is not a lot of time."

"Come on. I'm not attacking your work ethic. I know you barely see your cat." The long-running joke about his non-existent cat tempered his anger enough for her to continue. "I understand, but I'm desperate for anything that can point us in the right direction. I called Aaron and requested to test the blood for contamination but—"

"Let me guess. He vetoed the idea." The stocky man huffed and tossed the autopsy report on his desk. "Scrooge lives for the numbers. The tyrant tried to downsize my budget by twenty-five percent. Of course, he changed his tune when I mentioned Goditha's research department won't be operational for another year, at least."

"I'm not surprised. Scrooge is an accurate nickname. There's not a frivolous bone in the man's body, and he has the emotional warmth of liquid nitrogen. Is there anything at all you can tell us?"

"A few things, but not enough to convince your uncle to spend a fortune testing the labs. The thing is a retrovirus, like AIDS, but with a unique RNA genome that places it closer to the human parvovirus B19."

"That's the one Dr. Morgan mentioned. He said the damage mimicked an extreme case."

Gerald nodded while lost in thought. "That makes sense. Malachi started showing signs of bone marrow suppression." He shook off the theories and refocused. "Our immune system poses a serious challenge, but with repeated exposure, the virus begins to take hold. Not to state the obvious, but the weaker the lineage, the weaker the immune response. Therefore, fewer exposures are required."

"Could it be new or engineered?"

"I ran the RNA genome through every database. Malachi is the first documented case. However, sections appear in several modern viruses. It appears more primitive than engineered or spliced, like the predecessor to parvovirus. I don't have direct evidence yet, but I think it went extinct before the scientific viral record."

"Okay. So, something we eradicated a few centuries ago?"

"No. Edward Jenner developed the first vaccine for smallpox in 1796. This is much older, perhaps ancient."

"Like the Middle Ages, the Black Plague…"

"Although I can't rule that out, I'm thinking more Bronze Age. The thing barely resembles modern-day samples, and evolution takes time."

"What? A prehistoric virus?" Lilith couldn't hide her skeptical frown. The whole thing sounded ludicrous.

"The concept is not as far-fetched as it sounds." A happy glint lit Gerald's eyes as he spoke. "Plenty of archaic bacteria and viruses still exist in glaciers and burial chambers, cut off from the world. What we see today are their evolved counterparts. If one of them entered our ecosystem, they would wreck a modern human's immune system, which is no longer equipped to handle these ancient microbes. That makes them quite lethal. There *is* someone I can refer you to…"

"And they can supply us with more answers?" Nicci asked, pulling out her pad and pen.

"If I'm correct in my assumption, yes. She's a research professor at Penn State University in York, Pennsylvania. Doctor Rachel Thomas is a prominent paleovirologist. I have her card here somewhere." After swiveling on his stool, he rummaged through his workstation. "She's human, so I'll isolate the infected donor blood cells. Wouldn't want awkward questions about the vampire-blood medium. Ah, here it is!"

"How did you meet a human paleo…whatever?" Lilith took the business card and stuffed it in her jacket pocket.

"Paleovirologist. The American Society for Virology seminars. I like to stay current, and we are handling more and more human cases lately. She gave an excellent lecture on a thirty-thousand-year-old virus extracted from a deep layer of the Siberian permafrost."

"Wait. You attended a seminar…outside the lab?"

The man released an indignant snort. "I mention an exciting discovery, and that's your takeaway? Some conferences are held virtually, but sunblock works for short stints. Besides, scientists don't hold presentations poolside."

"Hmm. Point to you. One question before we go. The coroner said the infection caused transient aplastic crisis. Doesn't that mean the virus should become lethal faster in a pureblood?"

"Yes and no. A vampire with a strong lineage will have frequent exposure, but their immune response is also *much* stronger. However, once the infection eradicates the defenses, they would decline rapidly without constant transfusions. A half-blood won't be exposed daily, but their immune systems are inferior. They would be infected quicker, but the symptoms would progress slower. If you consider the different feeding schedules, the timelines would be similar...in theory, assuming it could conquer a full-powered immune system."

"If? But Malachi *was* infected. Wouldn't it have killed him eventually?"

"I don't know. The coroner's report showed only minor suppression in the bone marrow. The virus put up a hell of a fight, but his defenses kept things in check. The thing may never have turned lethal, but viruses evolve. Hell, if someone introduced it on purpose, this is a strong starting point to engineer a stronger variant. No matter your lineage, this thing poses a serious threat."

"And you think a human in middle-of-nowhere, Pennsylvania, can help? I mean, how could she possibly assist with our investigation?"

"Assuming I'm correct, understanding this microbe—where it came from, how and why it disappeared—would be a tremendous help. Not only could the origin narrow the list of suspects, but it could help us identify racial susceptibility or resistance, possible sources of antiviral treatments, and even immunizations."

"Can't you send her the information electronically? Do we really need to drive to York?" Nicci asked, jotting down notes.

"No, I can't just *send her the info.* What is the younger generation's issue with handling business face-to-face?"

Although his words emerged in a harsh tone as he stood to tower over her, Nicci was no intern and not easily intimidated. When she merely stared Gerald down with her pen poised over the paper, he huffed and settled back into his seat.

"She'll need a *live* sample, and something this important shouldn't depend on UPS. I can't leave the lab with the overflow from Goditha pouring in and the summer surge of trace evidence from the NYPD. Something about cramped conditions and heat makes humans nuts. June, July, and August are our busiest months."

Then he swiveled back to his desk, pawed through the second drawer, and dropped a thick manila folder on the table.

"My notes will speed things up for her, though. I'll prep the specimen. It'll be ready by morning."

"Thank you, Gerald. We appreciate your help."

"Just find out where the hell this came from and how it was transmitted. That will be thanks enough, and don't be such a stranger!"

After rubbing his sweaty neck, he turned back to the workstation, giving them the cue to leave.

"I didn't realize you did a lot of work for research." Nicci let the unspoken questions hang in the air as they strolled back to the elevator.

"I interned at the lab after college, and I still run packages for him on slow days. Gerald collaborates with the other facilities on various projects. Plus, I have an office here, and Gerald oversees trace evidence, especially on suspected vamp activity."

"Wait. You have an office?"

"Technically, but I rarely use it. Most of my cases happen on the other side of town, and home is more convenient."

"I bet it's bigger than my broom closet at the station," Nicci grumbled with a smirk before glancing down at her scrambled notes. "So, what now?"

A sigh escaped, and Lilith tried to untangle the random bits of information in her head. "I'm going to study these files from Gerald and Frank at Chance's place. Maybe I can make some sense of all this."

"How can I help?"

"Well, if someone *did* infect Goditha's blood supply, it might be an inside job. Can you pull a list of employees with access and a breakdown of their security measures? We can meet up in the morning, compare notes, grab the specimen from here, and then head to York."

"Sounds like a plan, partner." Nicci bumped Lilith's shoulder, her long ponytail swishing back and forth. "Happy to have you back."

"Already missing the zombie chases and ear-splitting banshees?" Although she chuckled, guilt lingered in the words. Being her partner hadn't exactly been beneficial lately. In fact, the position should've provided hazard pay.

Hopefully, this case will be different. As the thought flashed through her mind, Lilith knew it was a delusional lie.

Chapter 7 - *Cassie*

The absolute darkness made time impossible to track. *Is it even real? Had it ever been real?* In extreme isolation, the concept of time became an obsolete idea imposed on nature by humanity. Who decided how many hours comprised a day or how many minutes constituted an hour?

The perpetual never-ending night abolished the notion from her mind. Cassie's entire world narrowed to three things: the wood at her back, the rough ropes, and the dank air slithering over her naked body.

If only she could disappear inside the euphoric delirium from the odd fruit, which conjured feelings of warmth and safety. Somehow, the exotic juice allowed her to detach from the miserable prison and rise above it.

However, the harder she tried to reclaim the blissful utopia, the more it eluded her. Instead, the opposite happened. She became hyperaware of each change in air movement, sound, smell, and sensation, making her imprisonment more vivid.

The vertical position of her body was torturous. Although the restraints supported her torso and thighs, her outstretched arms and legs burned like fire. When she relaxed into the ropes, allowing them to hold her weight, the rough fibers burrowed into her skin like hot glass.

Once the pain reached an intolerable level, she summoned her remaining strength and carried her weight until her body screamed for relief. The continual cycle hurt more each time, and eventually, her muscles would refuse to comply.

Cassie attempted to swallow the lump of fear in her throat, her impossibly dry tongue sticking to the roof of her mouth. Meanwhile, her stomach churned and roared. *How long has it been since I've eaten?*

Despite the heavy sensation in her eyelids, she couldn't tell if they remained open. The same inky black engulfed her whether she opened them or not. She only knew one thing for certain—she was alone. The silence still rang in her ears. A few times, the sound of tiny scurrying feet broke the monotony, but nothing that resembled human. *Do they plan to starve me to death?* A slow and painful way to go, but better than some alternatives.

The sudden click of high-heeled shoes echoed from above, each step making her jump. After days, weeks, or longer of absolute silence, a pin hitting the floor would sound like a pistol shot, and as much as she craved a reprieve, she dreaded the possible outcome.

Only one ray of hope persisted—the mystery guest might bring another taste of serenity. The odd and unexpected craving of that fruit made everything else inconsequential, scaring Cassie more than the theoretical horrors awaiting her.

As the heels clopped down the stairs, new footsteps resonated above her. *Two of them?* Cassie strained her overstimulated senses, trying to separate the painful sounds. *No, three of them. Wait…four, five, six…*

She lost count.

A parade trampled across the floor, everything merging into an overwhelming cacophony. *Why invite an audience?* The stilettos ruled out a rescue mission. No one outside of TV and movies wore heels on assignment.

Cassie trembled and pooled her remaining strength, letting the rough ropes carry her weight. Her respirations quickened until her chest burned. Then the heels stopped as the crowd hit the stairs. *Is she waiting for them?*

While the steps continued, the door swung open. With the sudden outpour of blinding light, Cassie squeezed her eyes shut and whipped her face away, but the brilliance had already scorched her retinas, as if she'd stared into the sun. Cassie blinked, trying to clear her vision, but it was reduced to an angry red rectangle.

"Hello?" Cassie didn't recognize the quiet croaking voice that escaped her lips.

In reply, the clicking heels moved closer. Cassie continued to blink, willing her eyes to work, to show her something, anything. There was a brief glint of something gold, then everything went dark as fabric slid over her eyes. Unlike the previous blindfold's loose weave, this one blocked the light but didn't scratch her hypersensitive skin.

Tears fell, her sobs filling the room. Never had she been surrounded by so much darkness. Bright sunny days lying in the sweet grass, running her fingertips through the sun-kissed surface of Fountain Lake, soaking up rays on Buckroe Beach—that's how she had spent her free time when given the chance.

This new existence, engulfed in the cold, dank black, crept inside her bones and leeched her strength. *If only I could feel the sun on my skin one more time…*

Something metallic pressed against her lips, and Cassie pulled away from the unexpected sensation.

"Drink." The female voice sounded so…normal, like a middle-aged soccer mom telling her bratty kid to behave.

Although Cassie's rebellious side wanted to refuse, her body complied without hesitation. She lapped at the crisp water rolling over her parched tongue. The cooling sensation gushed down her throat, pooled in her empty stomach, and seeped into each cell. She gulped down every drop and gasped when the cup disappeared.

Before she could ask for more water, the deliciously sweet scent of the strange fruit wafted past her nose.

"One bite," the woman instructed with a warning tone.

The peel touched her lips, and Cassie took a savage bite, then chewed slowly. She savored every burst of flavor, the euphoria hovering on the horizon, so close but still not quite in reach. *One more bite, and…*

"Clean her up before the others join us."

Heavy footsteps approached with familiar wheezing breaths—the man who had prepared her. He wiped her down with rough towels, the freshness of unscented soap surrounding her. Humiliation burned across Cassie's cheeks. Possessing no control over her body made her feel less than human. Not even an animal needed someone to wipe their ass.

When the man lingered too long, the woman spoke up with a boom of authority. "That's enough. Grab the bucket, empty it upstairs, and then you can rejoin us."

The rough towel disappeared, wood scraped softly against the concrete, and then the heavyset man walked away and opened the creaky door.

Cassie forgot about the crowd until they shuffled into the room. Most of the people moved deeper into the space, followed by metallic scrapes and screeches, probably from folding chairs. The stilettos followed suit, taking the fruit and its power of blissful escape with her. The final set of footsteps stopped in front of Cassie.

Questions flooded her brain. *What are they going to do to me? What do they want? Why are there so many? Why isn't anyone talking? What are they waiting for?*

The silence stretched on until she doubted her sanity. *Is anyone even there? Did I make it all up?*

Fingertips brushed her collarbone, and the sudden sensation stole her breath. Her muscles stiffened, which pulled at the unforgiving ropes, sending sticky blood trickling down her arms.

"Please." Cassie's voice broke with trembling tears as she shook. "Just tell me what you want."

The fingertips leisurely traced her shoulder, her arm, the delicate dip at her elbow, and her forearm, avoiding the blood. A light touch on her palm preceded the tight grip around her pinkie that sent her heart racing. She braced herself, but the hand remained still.

"I want to tell you a story."

That voice.

She recognized the voice emanating from deep in the room—the man from the parking lot. He had a strange name, not that it mattered. What kind of kidnapper used a real name? However, all lies contained a grain of truth. *What was his name?* Cassie focused on dredging up the information as a distraction, but it didn't help.

The tense silence ended with a crack, like thunder. Milliseconds later, the pain finally registered, and she cried out. The hand left her broken pinkie and gripped her ring finger.

"No, no. You don't have to—" The tears made her voice break as true panic set in.

"I must ensure your complete attention, Cassie. We must know pain to know reward."

A mumble followed his words, like a concert of whispered agreements, a mindless cult revering their prophet.

She panted and sobbed, trying to curl her remaining fingers and escape the man's grip, but it was a futile effort. He snapped her ring finger like a twig. Her scream echoed off the walls, and before she could catch her breath, the cruel hand grabbed her middle finger. This time, he did not pause. The bone cracked, and the torturous pain followed right after.

"Dammit, please. Stop! I'm listening. Tell me whatever you—"

The vicious hand snapped the final finger, and the raw scream burned as much as her mangled hand.

"Leave the thumb."

The Lotus Tree

Somewhere past the excruciating agony, she heard the man take a single step back. Cassie sucked in air past the sobbing moans, and the ringleader cleared his throat.

"I will begin now. There once lived a beautiful young woman named Leto. Her parents named her after the Titaness, mother to Apollo and Artemis. Praise be to Leto, bringer of the divine."

"Praise be to Leto." The chanted chorus followed his words instinctually, with all the faith and conviction of a Catholic mass but twisted into something demonic.

The sound made Cassie's skin crawl.

They continued to chant with increasing vigor until their voices became more stifling than the endless darkness.

Chapter 8

W hen Lilith arrived at Chance's place, she kicked off her shoes, paced through the empty apartment, climbed the stairs to the loft, and spread the files over the king-size bed. Then she sat on the toffee-colored comforter and started arranging the puzzle pieces.

According to statements gathered by police, no one knew Clayton Barker. The manager said he had arrived in rough shape a few days ago and paid with a handful of crumpled bills. The man never left his room, none of the neighbors spoke to him, and no one signed in to visit him.

Honest hotel owners in the seedier areas often kept guest books to assist with investigations. Of course, their motivation didn't stem from an altruistic sense of duty. They merely wanted to keep the frequent police involvement brief so it wouldn't scare away the clientele. Even a fake name gave the cops a place to start and often came with a physical description.

"Okay. Focus and stop internally rambling. Barker lived in Atlanta, so why travel to NYC? Vacation? Business? Personal? Or did someone stage his death here for attention? No. The witness statements of him checking in ruled out that possibility. The man came here for a reason."

If the man had been aware of the infection and suspected Goditha, Solasta was the closest facility with major medical support, but the reports indicated he never left his room.

"Why trek up here for help and then hole up in a crappy hotel room for days?"

The timeline and lineage issues further complicated things.

"If someone introduced the virus to the entire Goditha supply at one time and half-bloods like Barker were more susceptible, why did it take nearly a year to become lethal? Does the thing have an incubation period? Is that the normal course of the disease? Did the perp infect portions of the blood at different times to minimize suspicion, or am I flat-out wrong about how Barker and Malachi contracted the virus?"

Miriah and Malachi's neighbor Ida said they were trying to have a baby. The contamination could have stemmed from their infertility treatments, though Lilith doubted that was the case with Clayton. Drifter vamps were not known for their secret desire to pursue domestic bliss. Either way, Goditha was the key, and it had to be an inside job. She couldn't picture any way around it.

"So, assuming someone infected the victims on purpose, why? What was their motivation? Why target vampires? Was there an ominous objective, or were they just guinea pigs? They certainly weren't a choice of convenience."

To infiltrate Goditha and complete their mission, the person responsible would have to be a vamp, another supernatural race, or a human with far too much information. Humans did work on-site—vampire scientists didn't grow on trees—but only in a limited area. They focused on engineering blood substitutes and treatments for thalassemia. The lab guarded anything pertaining to their species with strict security protocols. The likelihood of anyone stumbling across sensitive info, or even actively searching for it, was virtually nil.

"Of course, if the perpetrator isn't targeting vamps, what is the motivation for decreasing the already depleted supply of national donation centers and sabotaging medications for a debilitating disease? What is their objective? Are they making a statement against the creation of cloned or synthetic blood? Raging about scientists meddling with nature, like an activist attacking GMOs?"

Perhaps they had a religious purpose. Some cultures and faiths believed the soul or spirit lived in the blood. Devout Jehovah's Witnesses, for example, refused transfusions because their Bible stated taking life from another is an affront to God.

"Replicated and artificial blood could be interpreted as abominations, but is it reason enough to kill?" Lilith wanted to say no, but terrorist attacks and abortion clinic shootings had proven the violent capabilities of fanatics in the name of faith.

Without a single break, she studied every scrap of paper, organizing and reorganizing for hours.

"Lily, *cherie*, you up there?" The sudden voice made her jump. The elevator's noisy rumble hadn't even registered past her laser-like focus.

"Yeah, up here." After combing through the property manager's account, she still couldn't piece anything together. *Dammit.* Her eyes scanned the piles, but the same thought continued to nag her. She needed the list of people with access to the secure labs.

Perhaps someone would stand out, or maybe it would help narrow the suspect pool, which was pretty much everyone who ever set foot in that building.

As if she'd summoned the information from the void, a high-pitched chime signaled a new email. Lilith snatched up her phone and opened the message from Nicci entitled "Goditha."

A shadow stepped into the doorway while she avidly scrolled through the names. "Uh, Lily. What the hell is going on?"

Without glancing away from the screen, she waved in the direction of the door. "Sorry. It's for a case. I'll clean up as soon as I finish this email."

A bag thudded on the floor, and in her peripheral vision, she spotted Chance leaning against the doorframe, his arms folded over his chest.

"You're on suspension. You aren't supposed to work cases."

Lilith sighed wearily. *How many times do I have to explain this?* "My therapist cleared me. Well, for this one case anyway." She skipped to the list of those with access in section two. "Dr. Price gave her endorsement in exchange for my willing cooperation in our sessions. I'm doing everything by the book. Scout's honor."

A name appeared on the screen, and Lilith froze. Dr. Nichols, the scientist Ashcroft clawed to death, had been head of the research department. Nothing she recalled indicated his involvement, but the connection nagged at her gut for some reason.

When Dr. Nichols had tested the blood vial she found at Duncan's, he exploded with excitement over the results, not that Lilith blamed him. Ashcroft's blood represented an unprecedented and groundbreaking discovery, but then, so did a virus capable of infecting a vampire.

As she gazed at his name, she wondered how far he would have gone in the name of science. Since he headed the research department, he had access to everything—the blood banks, fertility, medical treatments, patient files, and anything else in the building.

The man had run Goditha with Duncan as his only oversight, and her uncle had given up on the lab months before he disappeared. Nichols could have tracked the virus's progression through checkups and fertility visits, even if he didn't conduct them personally.

Jenny Allen

However, Clayton Barker was an odd choice. Sure, the doctor might have chosen him for his diluted lineage, but as a drifter, tracking the progress would be problematic at best. Perhaps Dr. Nichols *didn't* choose Clayton Barker. Maybe the blood supply was contaminated after all.

While lost in her thoughts, she missed Chance's response.

"Lilith." He grabbed her phone and took a seat in front of her. "Did you hear me?"

When her cheeks heated, he sighed.

"This is your first case since the medical center, and you're latching onto it like a damn lifeline in Arctic waters. Look at this!" He gestured at the papers covering every square inch of the bed. "This is not healthy."

She frowned up at his handsome face while organizing her scattered thoughts. "It's sweet that you're worried, but I'm fine. This is important. It's not just any case."

"And only you can solve it?" His fingers caressed her cheek and slid into her hair, concern flooding his hazel eyes. "You aren't the only champion. Not long ago, you told me I can't save everyone. The same applies to you."

Although some part of her wanted to smack his hand away and storm out, Lilith melted into his touch for three simple reasons—she missed him, he wasn't wrong, and she couldn't get mad at him for making sense.

"I understand what you're saying. I do. I get that this looks nuts, but it's a vamp case…"

"And Nicci can handle it." With his familiar grin, Chance leaned close, brushing his lips against hers to serve as a distraction. *Cheater.*

"The vamp died from the same virus that infected Malachi."

Chance went still and then sat back with a shocked expression.

"Yeah, the guy *died* of a virus. Also, he came from Atlanta, and his normal supplier…"

"Goditha." He whispered the word, his eyes drifting to the papers and photos littering the bed.

"Exactly! I asked Aaron to test the blood banks, but he wants conclusive evidence first. He won't even give me a sample from Goditha because he doesn't want to incite a panic." Her jaw clenched at the memory of her uncle's dismissive attitude.

For a moment, Chance remained silent. Then he met her eyes with resolve. "You aren't working this alone."

"Of course not. Nicci is—"

"Not what I meant. You need someone who has experience with Goditha's security protocols and systems, so fill me in." Without another word, he rolled up his sleeves and picked up a pile of police reports from the corner of the bed.

The firm set of his jaw and the tightness around his eyes made arguing a futile endeavor. Besides, she didn't *want* to refuse his help. Chance acted as an emotional anchor, keeping her rooted in the present, something she'd need even more if they had to go to Goditha. The thought of setting foot in that place made her skin crawl.

When she remained silent, he glanced in her direction. "What? I'm not kidding. You can't shut me out of this." The muscles in his arms tensed, bracing himself for her rebuttal.

"I know." While filled with more gratitude than she could ever express, she leaned forward and kissed his stubbly cheek. "One of the many reasons I love you." The bright smile reached her eyes and erased his frown. "How did your trip go, by the way?"

"Fine. Aaron's a conceited prick, but the system needed modifications. Now, stop changing the damn subject and talk."

Lilith held up her hands in surrender before pulling out Dr. Morgan's autopsy report.

"Lily, the cab is here," Chance's voice boomed from downstairs as a horn blared again, ricocheting through the building.

"One second." Lilith frantically scanned the room, patting her pockets to ensure she had everything. When her hand touched the empty holster at her hip, she stopped and grabbed her Beretta still sitting on the dresser.

Sure, the likelihood of a gunfight on the way to breakfast was remote, but she had endured too much to remain naïve. Bad things happened to her, especially when she didn't expect them, so she never left the house unarmed anymore, not even for groceries.

After clicking on the safety, she jammed the gun in its holster and snatched up the case files. A weird mania prickled her skin, making her feel like an anxious kid on the first day of class. Perhaps her nerves merely stemmed from having been out of the game for eight months, but she couldn't shake the thought that things were going to get worse.

The image of Clayton Barker's face kept flashing in her mind—the first fatality, but not the last. She needed to find answers before things reached a tipping point.

After a deep breath and a final sweep of the room, she raced down the stairs.

"Got everything?" Chance lifted the elevator gate, holding it up as she jogged by with a stack of files. "You did leave my kitchen sink, right?" He slid in, closed the gate, and punched the down arrow with a sly grin on his face.

The elevator roared to life with a lurch she still wasn't used to, and Lilith hugged the towering papers closer to keep them from toppling.

"Smart-ass."

Of course, the retort only made his impish grin widen. "In all seriousness, though. How is there so much for two bodies?"

"Ninety percent of the job is paperwork—reports from the crime scene, autopsies, toxicology, witness testimony, character statements, suspect lists. Plus, Dr. Scott gave me copies of all his research on the virus...I wish a tech could condense this crap into the Cliffs Notes, but such is life."

"I think I'll wait for the movie."

Although she chuckled at the joke, it sounded halfhearted, even to her. Chance continued to study her, the grin slipping from his lips, and he leaned against the wall.

"What's bothering you, *cherie?* It's not only this case. I can tell there's something else eating at you. Did I—"

"No."

When she immediately interrupted him, it seemed to ease some of his tension.

"You haven't done anything wrong. I just have this feeling..." Lilith frowned, trying to pin down her thoughts. "It feels like I should know what's coming, like I've seen this all in a dream but can't remember. Things feel...*wrong.*" Goosebumps crept up her arms as the elevator came to a halt.

After pushing off the wall, Chance lifted the gate again and grabbed the precarious stack of papers. "Let me take these." Then his green-flecked hazel eyes rested on her until she met his gaze. "We'll figure this thing out, Lily. We always do."

She still harbored doubts but didn't voice them. Instead, she stood on tiptoe and kissed his cheek, desperate to believe his words. "Let's just grab breakfast with Nicci so we can hit the road, okay?"

When he flashed a lopsided grin, it eased the gloom and doom in her head, making her feel a bit lighter.

"At least we're not flying this time."

Chance hated flying, even *before* armed men had handcuffed them to a plane. She'd probably have to drug him like Mr. T from *The A-Team* if they had to fly again.

"If I see another plane again, it'll be too soon," he groaned, echoing her thoughts.

Lilith passed through the dilapidated first floor of the rehabbed warehouse, an amused smile lingering on her lips. However, when she reached the front door, she abruptly stopped, and Chance almost ran over her. Her eyes widened at the slender man with tousled blond hair, leaning against an extended town car where their cab should have been.

"I would have knocked, but it seems you misplaced your door." His voice held a familiar mixture of accents—Southern with hints of Old World European.

"What are *you* doing here?" Although Chance didn't sound openly hostile, the words were *not* friendly.

The man pushed off the car with inhuman grace, a smile curving his lips. Lilith knew he enjoyed pushing buttons, but the amusement didn't reach his blue eyes this time. The confidence was a facade, hiding the damage from the worst betrayal she had ever witnessed. The hollow smile pulled at the faint scars crossing delicately over his face, permanent reminders to never trust another soul.

So why is he here?

"I came to talk business with Lilith, as long as her bodyguard doesn't mind me stealing her."

To Chance's credit, he tensed but didn't rise to the obvious bait.

"Oh, come on. Where's your sense of humor! I come in peace." The man spread his hands with sincerity tinged by exhaustion, as if too tired to play the villain anymore. "I'm not here to fight. I have better things to do with my time."

"Cohen…" After placing a steadying hand on Chance's chest, Lilith strode over to the town car, toward Detective Andrew Cohen. "This isn't the best time. We're kind of in the middle of something big right now. We're meeting Nicci and then heading out of town."

It took several seconds for his eyes to drift from Chance's imposing figure to Lilith. "This is important. You, of all people, know I wouldn't come *here*"—he nodded toward the angry half-blood behind her—"if it wasn't crucial. Let me give you a lift, and I can explain on the way. If you don't like what you hear, I'll walk away. No strings. I give my word."

"Your word?" Chance scoffed and strolled forward, still clutching the tower of papers. "Like that's worth anything. What happened to the cab?"

The detective crossed his arms over his chest with a nonchalant shrug, either defensive or bored with the conversation's turn—probably a mixture of both. "Well, I figured if you called a cab, you needed a ride, and here I am with a car. I thought I'd save you some money, so I paid the driver and sent him on his way."

"Leaving us no choice but to listen to your bullshit. *Kass twa.*" Slipping into Cajun-French was a warning flare. Chance frequently dissolved into the language from his trauma-ridden childhood during emotionally charged situations, which Cohen typically instigated.

After balancing the stack of files on the sill of a broken window, Chance dug out his phone.

"Thankfully, this is New York City. There's always a taxi or an Uber driver within five minutes."

"Wait." Although she couldn't explain why, Lilith needed to hear the demon out. "I'm sure he came to us for a reason. If it wasn't critical, he would have called and saved himself the trouble."

"*Vous vous moquez de moi.* You didn't get your fill of tragedy last time?" Chance raked a hand through his hair after shoving his phone back in his pocket. He had valid reasons for his mistrust, but he hadn't been there when Farren held her at gunpoint. Chance hadn't been held captive in the medical center, when Cohen's only friend and confidant tortured him, intent on turning him into a monster. As hard as he tried, he couldn't understand the bond Cohen and Lilith had formed over those fateful days.

"First of all, please stick to English."

Chance merely glared at her in response.

"Second, it won't hurt to hear what brought him all this way. No obligations."

"Yeah, that worked out so well last time." As soon as the words left his mouth, Chance visibly regretted the reminder of Gregor's murder. With a sigh, he flicked his eyes between them, and Lilith expected him to refuse. To her surprise, he grabbed the files and slipped into the vehicle without another word.

"Huh. You successfully domesticated him. I'm impressed." A wide grin stretched the detective's thin scars, and he opened the door, making a gallant sweeping gesture.

Before climbing in, Lilith stopped inches away and stared him down. "Don't antagonize the one person willing to work with you, Andrew."

The playfulness bled from his face until he nodded with a solemn expression.

Once inside, they scattered. Chance and Cohen claimed the corners, while she sat across from them—maximum distance. Then an awkward silence settled over the car, both men trying to ignore each other's presence.

"So…where are you heading?" The nervousness in Cohen's voice seemed so uncharacteristic, it took her several seconds to respond.

"We're meeting Nicci at Baz Bagel in Lower Manhattan."

After he relayed instructions to the chauffeur, the glass partition rose, and the uncomfortable quiet settled in again. Although playing referee between two grown men became exhausting, Lilith understood the complex motivations, or at least she thought she did. Perhaps there was something else, a deeper issue neither of them felt comfortable sharing.

"All right. Start talking. What brought you to New York?"

Before he answered, his blue eyes moved from her to Chance, who leaned against the door in rapt attention, arms folded over his chest. For some reason, the posture rattled the demon. *Weird. Chance never had that effect before…*When Cohen finally pulled his gaze back to her, the calm confidence had returned.

"Right. Over the past few months, I've received scattered reports of odd behavior among the Durand."

Chance's left eyebrow almost reached his hairline. "*Odd behavior?* That's a broad term, especially considering the source."

For a moment, the Southern detective's jaw tensed, but ultimately, he released a long breath and nodded. "Point taken. Let's call it uncharacteristic behavioral changes. Trouble with perception, hallucinations, unprovoked aggression—"

"How is that different—" Chance started the smart-ass comment but stopped short after a glare from Lilith.

"Not helping."

Once he held up his hands in surrender, she returned her attention to the demon.

"I'm sorry, Andrew, but I don't see how we can help." The problem sounded fascinating, but abnormal psychology wasn't her specialty. She was more adept at acquiring emotional trauma than resolving it—hence the mandated therapist.

"Patience. I'm getting to that part. All these cases popped up around the Southeast, with a strong accumulation in Atlanta. After some persuasion, a subject agreed to testing—"

"I bet they *agreed.*" Although Chance muttered under his breath, in the confined space, the retort wasn't quiet enough to escape notice. Lilith fixed him with another warning glare, and he straightened in his seat. "Sorry. It's habit. Continue."

"We put the subject through a series of tests, including a psychological evaluation, tox screen, full blood workup, CT scan, and MRI. After compiling the data, the team decided these symptoms were caused by acute encephalitis."

The last word caught her attention, like a flare in the night sky. "Viral encephalitis?"

Cohen's eyes widened at her unexpected question. "Precisely. How… did you know that?" He shifted slightly, his stare bouncing between them with growing suspicion.

"Was this demon…sorry, *Durand,* susceptible to a virus?"

Lilith was well aware that Andrew hated her referring to his kind as demonic, but Durand sounded more like a proper surname, not the name of a species. Of course, *vampire* probably sounded that way too at one time.

"No. Not a single documented case of a viral infection exists among our kind. Quite the opposite. Centuries ago, we quietly eradicated smallpox from a few villages by adding some of our blood to the central well. What aren't you telling me? The fear and excitement are rolling off you in waves."

"I'm not ready to share my toys yet," she whispered, leaning back and contemplating the possibilities. *The signs and symptoms differ, but can it really be a coincidence? What are the odds?*

A sudden thought occurred to her, and she glanced up at the detective.

"Why come to me with this? With research staff at your disposal, I fail to see how my help benefits you."

"A valid question. The *research team* consisted of two men who worked after hours, off the books."

"Wait. Didn't you inherit Farren's company? The one with a skyscraper in Huntsville? Surely, you have access to more than two guys donating their time."

"Not quite. While I am the public face of Farren's company, I'm nothing more than a glorified figurehead. All the real decisions happen behind the scenes, in a seedy world of underground politics that I am not privy to anymore."

"So why not take this to the Council? This seems like something they'd investigate."

After an elegant shrug, Cohen slouched into his seat. Once again, Lilith noticed the absence of his typical self-important demeanor. In fact, he appeared more exhausted than anything else.

"I took Farren's seat, but half of them don't take me seriously, and the other half doesn't trust me. Both Farren and Luminita broke their covenant by acting against the Council, and I have ties to them both."

A haunted shadow passed behind his sky-gray eyes, and she knew what flickered through his mind—Luminita carving his flesh, his grand-father's long history of abuse before Andrew put a bullet in his head. Those two people irrevocably changed him in horrifying ways.

"Anyway, they didn't deem the behavioral patterns worth investigating. Once I had proof, they said validating any claims would cause unnecessary panic. All the cases so far involve half-breeds or families low on the totem pole. The Council consists of the oldest families among the Durand, and many of them still put stock in a theoretical caste system. The bottom line is, they don't think it's important."

"Well, that sounds familiar." When Cohen merely frowned in confusion, Lilith elaborated. "My uncle Aaron said the same thing. He runs—"

"Okay. So, the inner circle is ignoring the problem." Chance cut her off with a warning glance of his own, not that she blamed him.

Explaining their current hierarchy wasn't the most prudent use of her time, and freely handing information to a vicious species like the Durand wasn't smart. Sometimes, she forgot Andrew wasn't simply a friend and confidant. He also represented a race of manipulative cutthroats who didn't care much for vampires.

"I still fail to see how we can help." Chance kept his voice neutral despite the tension in his shoulders. At least he tried to play nice.

A weary chuckle escaped Cohen's lips, and he dragged his fingers through his hair. "Who else do I have?"

They both stared at the man in disbelief, too shocked to respond.

After a heavy sigh, he leaned forward against his knees. "To be blunt, you two are the only ones I thought might listen, and you have resources. Besides, if this thing can affect us, perhaps it will eventually infect your..." The words trailed off as an epiphany blossomed in his eyes. "It already has, hasn't it? Shit. That's why you jumped at the virus angle? You already found it!"

Lilith swallowed the sudden lump in her throat, and Chance caught her eye with a slight shake of his head. Saying anything was a risky move, but if they once again shared a common enemy...

For a moment, she ignored Detective Cohen and focused solely on Chance. She needed him to understand. "The timing, affected area, symptomology...There are too many similarities for it to be a coincidence."

Once he gave a reluctant nod, Lilith swung her attention back to the demon.

"Before I explain, I need to make a call." Without another word, she dug out her phone and dialed Nicci. "Hey, are you at the restaurant yet?...Cool. Can we meet at your place instead? We have a guest and need more privacy than the diner can provide...Okay, be there in ten."

Before she hung up, Cohen rapped his knuckles against the glass partition and gave the driver Nicci's address from memory. *Odd. Perhaps he looked for me there first, hoping to avoid Chance.* It wasn't the worst idea, especially since he didn't know about her suspension—one more tidbit she could add to the pile of things he didn't need to know.

"Did your men learn anything about the virus?"

"Not much. It's bloodborne, although my people believe it could be sexually transmitted as well. My guys are capable, but they aren't experts or virologists." A faint blush crept across his scarred cheeks, and he stared down at his palms.

"Perhaps we can help each other find answers." The thrill of excitement she experienced over the new bit of info was short-lived. The optimism fizzled when she glanced at Chance.

He didn't object or refuse. Chance merely stared at her, his jaw clenched in an all-too-familiar expression.

Working with Cohen meant exposing themselves to the Council again. When they had accepted his help in Tennessee, the Durand ended up murdering her father, kidnapping them, and forcing them into servitude to find her uncle's missing book. The infighting was the only reason they survived the ordeal. Still, Andrew's data and information about his species could prove extremely valuable.

After ten silent, uncomfortable minutes, they finally arrived at Nicci's building. Cohen hopped out as soon as the vehicle came to a stop, but when Chance began to climb out, Lilith grabbed his shoulder, holding him back.

"Cohen, can you head inside and tell the guard we're here to see Nicci? We'll join you in a second."

His eyes flickered between them again. He hesitated, then nodded and breezed through the doors. Once he disappeared, she rounded on Chance.

"Talk."

His brow furrowed in confusion. "About what?"

"Cohen. You need to tell me what is going on."

With that, he leaned back into the seat and gazed out the window, pointedly avoiding her eyes. "I don't trust him, *cherie*. I've never kept that a secret." For a split second, he bit his lower lip—he was holding something back.

"I read faces. You aren't telling me everything, so spit it out. I can't do this without you on my side."

"*Mon petite cherie*, I am *always* on your side. I don't like the way the man operates. Even when he means well, he's underhanded. Today is a perfect example. Instead of calling you, he showed up on *my* doorstep and coerced us into accepting a ride by getting rid of our cab. What was his plan if we intended to stay in for the day? Was he gonna sit on the sidewalk until one of us left the building, or did he already know we had plans? The bastard doesn't understand the basic concepts of consideration and cooperation."

While he spoke, Lilith studied each microexpression and body movement—he bit his lip three times, the skin beneath his eyes quivered, his right shoulder raised twice, and his thumb rubbed his palm in a self-soothing motion. The tics didn't indicate a lie, but they did reveal stress, anxiety, a lack of confidence, and an attempt to keep something from her.

"You aren't wrong, but there's something more personal. Dammit. Please, just talk to me."

His eyes searched hers for so long, she thought he might not answer. "Can we let this go for now? This isn't the time. We have more important things—"

"And when *is* the right time? If things are as bad as I suspect, we'll need Cohen's help. Please. I can't solve a problem if I don't know what it is."

After a heavy sigh full of frustration, he raked a hand through his chestnut hair. "You are your father's daughter." A halfhearted smile stretched his lips, and his resolve melted. "You know those fun side effects from Cohen's blood? The ones that went away for you after a few days? Well, they didn't for me. They are still as potent as day one."

A billion thoughts whirling in her brain came to a standstill as his gaze drifted to the floor. She knew he still sensed things, but she had no idea the ability was still that strong. *How is that possible? What does it mean for him? Did Cohen's blood permanently scar him? Worst of all, why didn't he trust me?*

"Why didn't you tell me?"

When he glanced up at her, faint tears misted his eyes. "Honestly? I didn't want you to be afraid of me."

"Afraid…" Lilith shook her head and slid into the seat beside him, but he stared at the floor, refusing to meet her eyes. "I couldn't…"

"You could." After a tense moment of silence, he stole a sideways glance at her and exhaled. "We can talk about this later. In private."

The sudden lump in her throat blocked any words from escaping, so she settled for a simple nod. Without another word or even a backward glance, Chance slid out of the car and grabbed the stack of files.

Something still nagged at the back of her mind, but Chance keeping a secret this big because he thought it would scare her dominated her thoughts. When she climbed out of the vehicle, she studied his face again, but Chance merely stared stoically at Nicci's building, refusing to give up anything, which was still a tell. However, he was right about one thing—they had more important things to deal with, so his secrets would just have to wait.

"We need to talk later. This isn't finished."

Chance met her stare for a brief second, a lingering sadness in his eyes. "I know, *amour de ma vie.*"

Once she turned and spotted Cohen waiting by the elevator, a litany of questions unfurled in her mind. *What happens if I tell Cohen? Will there be another trial like her father's? Would they lock Chance in a lab and study him, or would they just put a bullet in his brain?* No. She couldn't let the Council know about him.

Still, Andrew didn't seem very fond of their leadership at the moment. Perhaps he'd help them…

With a sudden rush, she remembered first meeting Luminita in Farren's skyscraper. The woman had questioned Chance's heritage with unusual curiosity, and when she discovered the side effects, Luminita started to say something, but Cohen had stopped her. *True, the information tease might have been nothing more than a manipulation tactic, but what if Luminita knew something? If so, why did Cohen interrupt her? What does he know?*

"I'm sorry, *cherie*. I'm not trying to keep things from you. We *will* talk, and I *will* tell you everything. I promise." Chance bumped her shoulder, shaking her out of her thoughts. "Are we good?"

"Yeah. We're good." Taking a deep inhale, she shoved open the door and crossed the lobby with a purposeful stride. As much as she wanted to grill Cohen for information, the virus was their priority. Everything else had to wait.

"Are you all right?" Andrew studied her, concern pulling at every muscle. Of course, like Chance, Cohen sensed all the tumultuous emotions boiling beneath the surface.

"Yeah, everything's fine." The words emerged more clipped than she intended. *Guess I need to work harder on burying shit. That's why Chance didn't tell me.*

As if someone had flipped a switch, Lilith realized she'd spent the past eight months complaining about everyone trying to get in her head. Meanwhile, Chance had a first-row seat to every emotion she'd experienced, including the guilt and self-loathing she tried to hide. He hadn't wanted her to put on a show or run away, and if she'd known the truth, one or both would have happened.

Before Cohen responded, a loud ding announced the elevator's arrival. The trio hurried on board, and she jammed the button for the fifth floor harder than necessary.

Neither of the men next to her deserved hostility. *She* had decided to pass Cohen's blood on to Chance when Humphries shot him. *Wait. Maybe that's the difference—my pureblood mixed with the Durand's.*

While she theorized the possibilities, the elevator came to a stop, and they strolled down the hall to Apartment 507. If answers existed, they'd have to wait. Lilith shook off her spiraling thoughts, squared her shoulders, and knocked.

When Nicci swung her door open, her jaw dropped in surprise. "You called *him*? Is he going to get us Miriah's samples?" The giddy excitement in the detective's voice might have made some people question her sanity, especially Andrew, who appeared lost.

"I'm sorry, what?" Cohen frowned, glancing back at Lilith and waiting for her to fill in the gaps.

Of course, he wasn't the only one. Chance's eyes weighed heavy on her too.

"No, Nicci. I didn't call. Can we all sit down and start from the top? Please?"

"Uh...sure." Nicci's eyes bounced around the group as the tension thickened to intolerable levels.

After flashing a strained smile, Nicci spun on her heel and led them into the living room, where files, photos, and reports covered the coffee table. Chance added their weighty stack to the pile before claiming a seat.

"Did you read through the email I sent last night?"

"Yes, and I have a theory..." A sudden cough from Detective Cohen interrupted Lilith's thoughts. "Right. First, I should explain why Andrew is here. Some of his people are developing viral encephalitis, which is causing extreme behavioral changes."

The petite detective's eyebrows shot up. "You think it's related?"

"Perhaps." She turned to Andrew as he slid into a seat as far from Chance as possible. "Besides the encephalitis, did the body display any other signs of viral damage?"

Cohen shifted his vision around the room before he reluctantly answered. "Yes...minor liver damage and bone marrow suppression, but nothing as extreme as the psychotic behavior."

"Did your team isolate the virus? Any electron microscopy we can compare?"

"I have no idea what that means, but my guy sent me this." Cohen pulled up an image on his phone and passed it to Lilith.

With one glance at the Van-Gogh-like image of vibrant yellow and purple, certainty burned in her gut. "What do you think?" She slid the phone over to Nicci, eager for a second opinion.

"I'm no virologist, but...yeah. It looks the same. We could ask Dr. Scott."

"No." Lilith quickly interjected. "He would ask too many questions we can't answer at the moment, like where we got the sample." She leaned into the squishy chair and tried to focus on a different angle. "So, your victim showed severe encephalitis, where ours displayed significant liver damage and bone marrow suppression. It makes sense, in a way."

"How does that add up to the same virus? The effects sound completely different." Chance frowned and leaned forward against his knees.

"The path of least resistance…Both species suffered the same symptoms but in varying degrees due to different vulnerabilities. Frank spotted mild encephalitis in the vampire victim, but our liver and bone marrow have an innate weakness forming hemoglobin."

For a moment, she fell silent, following her train of thought.

"I haven't studied the Durand's anatomy, but their abilities and manner of feeding are more…cerebral. I imagine there are extremely complex brain chemistries at play."

"Hell. You make it sound like an evolving supervillain hell-bent on wiping us all out." Nicci shivered and curled deeper into the chair.

"I'm the first to admit I'm not an expert, but I don't think it's changing or evolving into different strains. Our physiology is vulnerable in different ways. We've simply never had the opportunity to study it before because no microbe has beaten our innate defenses."

An uncomfortable silence settled over the room, like a dark cloud.

"What if this thing infects humans?" A hollow tone had crept into Chance's voice.

"Frank said the virus was visible on human donor cells. However, he's not certain if that means humans can be infected or if they're merely carriers. Without testing, we can't know for sure."

Meanwhile, Cohen raised his hand and waited until the group acknowledged him. "Excuse me. I've been quite patient through this little brainstorm session, but can you start from the beginning and tell me what the hell is going on?"

Within forty-five minutes, they had caught him up to speed on the new crime scene, the autopsy report, the victim's connection to Malachi, and Dr. Scott's theory on the virus. Detective Cohen seemed enthralled by the wealth of information.

"So, you think this guy is right? This is some sort of ancient virus?" He kept scanning through the various virology reports with eager excitement, though Lilith remained certain he didn't understand most of it.

"No idea, but it's our only lead. I'm throwing darts in the dark here." She slumped into the once-cozy chair, lost in a sea of unanswerable questions. "I'm still trying to figure out how it infected your species. If I'm right about Goditha's blood supply as a point of origin, how would any of your people be affected?"

Cohen rubbed at his chin, mulling over the question. "If blood is the only mode of transmission, it would cause far fewer cases."

"Well, you mentioned the path of less resistance. Could that extend to the vector as well?" Nicci glanced between Lilith and Cohen, and their brows furrowed. "From what I know about the Durand, sexual transmission is an ideal way to spread among them."

"I'm sorry. What?" The demon's eyebrow raised, and his jaw clenched. *Someone hit a button.*

"I mean no offense. Okay, well *mostly* no offense." Nicci grinned despite herself. "You told us your people feed on sexual energy to keep from causing harm to the...donor..."

"Uh-huh." The skeptical tone overpowered his wry smile, warning the petite detective to tread carefully.

"All right. Dial it back. It's fun to speculate, but we are not experts. We can ask Dr. Scott when we get back." Lilith wrapped up the discussion with a pointed glance at her partner. They were having a hard enough time keeping Cohen in a productive mood with Chance around. They couldn't afford to keep pressing buttons without a definite payoff.

Thankfully, Cohen jumped at the cue for a subject change. "Do we know anything about this Doctor Thomas?"

"Well, she's a tenured professor and perhaps the best paleovirologist in the country."

"Probably the *only* paleovirologist in the country." The frustrated tone stated Cohen remained unconvinced of the information's validity and value, something Lilith related to. They had learned a lot but only scratched the surface on a subject they had amateur knowledge of at best. It felt like unearthing a pyramid with a plastic spork.

"This is the only lead I have. If you want in on this, have your men send their research and samples to Dr. Gerald Scott at Solasta Laboratories in New York City. I'll text you the address. Also, can you persuade the FBI to release Miriah's biological materials? With Aaron blocking my every move, there's no way we can exhume the body."

"That will help?"

"Well, yes and no. It won't positively confirm the infection originated at Goditha, but every bit of info helps. My uncle won't let me test the supply until I give him proof it's compromised."

"Can't you take a sample and know for sure?"

Lilith smirked. "Preaching to the choir. He thinks it'll incite a riot."

"So, instead, he wants you to run around, backtracking the virus until you prove the origin *before* he lets you test to confirm? That is idiotic."

Lilith found his expression of astonishment oddly satisfying.

"Like I said, *preaching to the choir*. So, what do you think? Can you retrieve samples from Miriah's autopsy?"

Cohen nodded. "I may be able to pull some strings. The agents in charge of the mess in Tennessee—John Gorman and Eileen Hersch— seemed agreeable as far as FBI agents go. I'll call and ask them to contact Nicci since she's a detective and not connected to the case. It'll lessen suspicion."

"Chance, can you call security at Goditha and request Dr. Nichols's computer?"

"The doctor Ashcroft attacked? I'm not following."

"It's just a hunch, but the man headed research and development for the entire lab. I think if he wasn't directly involved, he may have pertinent information. There's a chance I'm wrong, but I'm hoping not."

"I can have them overnight the laptop, and I can bypass the standard encryption with my security clearance and protocols. However, if he added any additional security measures, you'll need—"

"Me." Nicci flashed a grin that verged on impish. "I can handle any special encryptions. In fact, why don't I stay behind. We don't want to overwhelm this lady with a busload of people. Plus, I can dig into Goditha's records—shipments, personnel changes, internal memos, etc."

Lilith's smile was strained at best. "Sounds good." Although her partner had made valid points, the thought of sitting in a car for five hours with Chance and Cohen was on par with being caged between two starved wolves.

When she peeked over at Cohen, he frowned at her as if trying to figure out a puzzle. If she took the risk and told him about the side effects, he might be able to help somehow, but was it her risk to take? Chance sure as hell didn't want her sharing his secret, but did they honestly have a choice? He needed answers, and short of tracking down Luminita, Cohen was their only other option.

"Let's get moving. It's already noon. We'll need to break a few speed limits to reach the campus during her office hours." Although Chance meant to address the entire group, his eyes stayed locked on Lilith with severe apprehension.

Great. Locked in a car with two emotional litmus tests full of secrets. What can go wrong?

Chapter 9

Since Lilith had failed to renew her license and still experienced nightmares about the last time Cohen drove, Chance took the driver's seat. Although the odds of being T-boned by another assassination squad were remote, why tempt fate? The driver Detective Andrew Cohen arrived with had stayed in New York, but not by choice. Chance required as much control over the situation as possible, even if it only amounted to playing chauffeur.

With that decision settled, Lilith claimed the passenger seat—the all-around safest decision—which left Cohen stranded in the cavernous backseat. Abandoning Chance would only aggravate him, and she had little desire to be confined to the backseat with Andrew for five hours. She didn't possess the energy for social niceties. Especially when she'd only shared life-and-death situations with him.

However, the front didn't provide much protection from the awkward tension, which became so thick she could cut it with a knife.

The trio stopped by Solasta, picked up the sample Dr. Scott had prepared, and then headed out of the city, the awkwardness continuing.

After half an hour of road rage, traffic jams, and rigid body language, the detective broke the silence. "Do we need to talk?"

"Nope." Chance swerved into the fast lane to avoid hitting a white Celica that had slammed on its brakes for no damn reason.

"Really? Because things seem more complicated than usual. I'm trying to play nice. I'm not used to relying on others, and coming to you for help took a lot."

Silence settled over the car until her ears began to ring. *Tinnitus is a cruel mistress.*

Lilith watched in the rearview mirror while Cohen glanced between them with an expectant frown.

"The silent treatment? Honestly? Are we in grade school?"

She couldn't take any more of the male posturing. If they wanted to work together, she needed to come clean. After turning around, she stared at Cohen, who slumped into the far corner. "The side effects—"

"Lily…," Chance interrupted with a growl, which could be hot or intimidating, depending on the context. Either way, it didn't deter her.

"No. We need to clear the air. I'm tired of everyone keeping crap to themselves because they think it's noble, myself included. Besides, he might help."

"And what if you're wrong?"

She ignored the question, returned her attention to the demon, who already appeared worried, and hesitated. *What if I am wrong? What if he turns us over to the Council?* No. Lilith couldn't believe he would do that, and they needed answers. "He's still suffering from the side effects."

With a bone-weary sigh, Chance chimed in. "Still as potent and annoying as day one." Then he stared the man down in the rearview mirror. "I pick up *everyone's* emotions."

A faint blush crept over Andrew's lightly scarred cheeks—a reaction so uncharacteristic, Lilith thought she imagined it.

"Uh, yeah. I see." After clearing his throat, he began fidgeting with his navy tie. "What about healing?"

"No one's shot me in the chest lately, but bruises and scratches disappear quick."

"Huh. Well, either it takes longer to leave your system because you're a half-blood, or…"

"Or…" A clear warning echoed in Chance's voice.

"Or the effects may be permanent." Cohen appeared less than pleased at that prospect.

"Permanent how?" As soon as Lilith spoke up, Cohen flashed her an expression that clearly questioned her intelligence.

"Permanent. Perpetual. Forever. Everlasting. As long as he lives. Stop me when the definition sinks in. If he's still healing at an abnormal rate, he could live a very long time. Perhaps longer than you, assuming he doesn't get himself killed by occupational hazards. Keeping you in one piece isn't an easy job."

After a pointed glare, Lilith fell back in her seat and mulled over his words. If the constant onslaught of everyone else's emotions didn't drive him insane, Chance might outlive her. For the Durand, learning to control and use those gifts from childhood provided a hefty advantage, much like learning a second language. With Chance starting in his thirties, adapting would not be easy.

When she glanced toward the driver's side, his conflicting feelings were fluctuating across his face in a myriad of microexpressions. All this time, Lilith had never recognized his struggle because she buried herself in pity and remorse. *I failed him.*

Once again, Cohen broke the silence, and she wasn't entirely ungrateful. "So, besides the blood replacements and longevity, what makes a pureblood different from a human?"

"Not much. Our superior immune system is a huge plus. This is the first infection, and there are no documented cases of cancer. On average, we possess slightly better senses, stamina, strength, and agility, but not superhuman. Professional athletes test the limits of what's possible more than we do. The allergy to sunlight is a racial trait that theoretically emerges in old age, but some vampires never develop the reaction."

"Interesting. Continue."

"With the development of blood sources and the new hemoglobin-packed capsules, it isn't difficult to blend in. The only issue is covering the long lifespan of purebloods—which varies based on lineage—in this new digital age of Homeland Security, facial recognition software, and social media. People start to ask questions when you look thirty but were born in 1908."

"A hardship I am all too familiar with."

While Lilith wondered how old Detective Cohen really was, he continued to ask questions.

"Do you know how your immune system works?"

Lilith frowned, surprised by the seemingly random inquiry. "UCLA didn't offer a course on Vampire Microbiology."

"I'm only curious. I'm no expert, but perhaps Chance's body integrated the unique properties of my blood to overcome his...inadequacies."

A piercing glare from the front seat caused him to pause before he addressed Lilith.

"What I mean is...perhaps the effects disappeared for you because you didn't need the benefits due to your bloodline."

The concept made sense, especially when she recalled Ashcroft's blood sample. The two complete strands of DNA had fused, pulling strengths from each species to form something more powerful. If Ashcroft hadn't been a masochistic, egocentric psychopath, the Durand might have heralded him as the next leap in evolution—Luminita did, regardless of the body count.

"Dr. Scott knows much more about our cellular physiology. We can pick his brain once things calm down." She didn't miss the pointed scowl from Cohen. "With your permission, of course. Confidential and off the books."

"That is dangerous territory. You know first-hand how serious the Council is about potential exposure. Handing information this volatile to a stranger isn't worth it, no matter how noble your intentions." Cohen crossed his arms over his chest with an air of finality.

"I wouldn't broach the subject if I didn't trust the man. I've worked with him for years."

"Yeah. I knew Luminita most of my life and trusted her implicitly. One thing I've learned in the past year is that you can't trust anyone that much."

"Let me finish, please. Dr. Scott and I have a history of working on confidential projects, including this virus. Not a shred of info has leaked from his lab. We need to know everything we can about how your blood affected Chance."

"Can you stop talking about me like I'm not here?" Chance's jaw clenched, and his lips tightened.

Lilith didn't need Durand blood to feel the anger and discomfort rolling off him.

"Sorry. I didn't mean—"

"I know." The words emerged in clipped tones, and his hands flexed around the steering wheel.

"May I ask one question before we change the subject?" For some reason, Cohen interpreted Chance's death glare as *yes, please do.* "How often have you needed blood in the past eight months?"

Chance's stare turned icy, and Lilith scooted farther into her seat with a blooming sense of apprehension.

"Once."

At first, she thought she'd misheard. It wasn't possible. Even the weakest half-blood required nourishment at least every two months, and that was severely pushing the boundaries. Chance lived on a three- to four-week schedule, and she had witnessed him taking the capsules multiple times since the events last fall.

His eyes darted over to her shocked face, displaying all the markers of guilt and anxiety. "MegaRed Omega 3 supplements…"

"Why the hell didn't you tell me?" *Light omission is one thing…but this? Actively deceiving me?* The anger of betrayal warred with her sadness at utterly failing him. *He felt he couldn't talk to me about this, so he hid it.*

"Can we discuss this later…in private? This one time, Lily, please let it go. This doesn't involve him. *He*'s not the one I'm dating."

When Lilith peered into the back seat, Cohen appeared like his old self for the first time since the medical center—lounging with a satisfied smirk of confidence and victory. Then he caught Lilith's eye, shrugged, and held up his hands.

"I was just curious about the extent of his side effects."

"*Putain de menteur!* Can I lock him in the fucking trunk?"

The feral growl in Chance's voice made the demon's smug smile falter, and when she didn't immediately answer, it disappeared entirely.

"You two need a break. Lucky for me, there's a solution." Lilith flicked the divider's control with a flourish and watched Cohen slowly disappear.

"Lily—" Chance started, but she cut him off.

"Nope. You wanted to talk later, so that's what we'll do." Without another word, she flipped on an oldies rock station and melted into the passenger seat.

Part of her felt childish for shutting Chance down, but she needed time to decompress. Everything raced around her mind at a million miles an hour, but each time she isolated a thought, it jumbled into an unrecognizable mess.

Besides, the tinted glass wouldn't stop Cohen from sensing everything. He couldn't read minds, but his finely honed ability to interpret emotions came too close for comfort. So, she allowed the hum of the moving car and the sweet tones of Boston's "Foreplay" to lull her into a peaceful nap.

Lilith blinked back the bright sunshine as the car rocked to a stop. When her eyes fully opened, she didn't see the university campus she'd expected. Instead, she stared at the anonymous face of a Country Inn & Suites Hotel.

"Where are we?"

"York, but between the traffic, construction, and back-road detours, I couldn't make it in time. I gave it my best shot, but Dr. Thomas's office closed over an hour ago."

"Dammit." She rubbed the sleep from her eyes and attempted to get her groggy brain functioning. "I should call—"

"I already did, in case she was working late. No luck, but I left a message about stopping by in the morning."

"Nice thinking. Thanks." Lilith stretched her aching neck, and her stomach growled ferociously. "Perhaps we should grab some dinner after we check-in."

"Well, I'm not sending you with Cohen after last time." Beneath the resentment lurked a lightness she desperately needed.

"What? You didn't like the Chinese food? I thought their pepper chicken was on point." She flashed a playful grin, and Chance quirked an eyebrow.

"I was a little more concerned with the blood and broken bones."

"Hey, he picked up fresh takeout after he dealt with the police, remember? I tossed the ones with blood on 'em."

Chance shook his head, and a lopsided smirk stretched his lips. "I'm still not letting him drive."

"No arguments there. Although, to be fair, a death squad T-boned the car, so they're the responsible party. Still…"

Knuckles rapped against the divider window, making them both jump.

"I almost forgot he was back there." When she flicked the control, the smoky glass revealed angry steel-gray eyes followed by a deep frown.

"Very humorous. Was that my time-out?"

"Well, that is not a very productive attitude." Lilith flashed a grin, and the divider started to rise again.

"Dammit. Stop. Okay, okay." Andrew held up his hands in surrender, and she lowered the glass. "I will play nice. I'm assuming we missed the doctor and will pick things back up in the morning?"

"Correct." She nodded and opened the glove box to retrieve her gun. "We were discussing dinner." The Beretta slid right into her holster, bringing an instant sensation of safety.

"I'll find my own, if you don't mind."

"Suit yourself."

Chance didn't appear broken up about the prospect of dining without Cohen's company, and Lilith needed a break from the overwhelming flood of testosterone.

Cohen narrowed his eyes at the back of Chance's head for an instant, long enough to make her suspicious. For the hundredth time, she wondered why their mutual animosity seemed disproportionate.

It was only natural for Chance to place some blame on Cohen for recent complications and vice versa. Still, Lilith couldn't explain the depth of their apparent hatred.

Perhaps Chance hated being around someone else who could read emotions. After all, he was a very private person, and having first-hand knowledge of the Durand's abilities could explain some of the defensive anger. Lilith had met him thirteen years ago, spent the past eight months as his girlfriend, and *still* knew next to nothing about his early life.

The man never talked about his family beyond brief hints at abusive behavior and drug use. Most of what she knew had come from her late father, Gregor, and didn't amount to much. Both Chance's parents had died in a car accident when he was ten. Then he floated around a few foster homes before he became a ward of the state of Louisiana and spent several years in an underfunded children's hospital. He buried a lot of pain and probably hated the Durand's intrusive abilities.

As for Cohen, he had seemed to enjoy needling Chance for a reaction at first and sometimes took things beyond teasing into dangerous territory. Now, some deeper animosity lurked behind his seemingly innocent goading, but why? Was it simply conflicting personalities?

"If you hear anything, please let me know." Cohen slid out of the town car and strolled toward the hotel office.

"It is a massive display of self-control that I don't knock every one of his smug little teeth out." Chance slammed his hands against the steering wheel with a frustrated growl.

"Dial back the testosterone. I know he gets under your skin, but—"

With a sudden movement, he swung around to face her, his hazel eyes burning with fury. "You have *no* idea."

Lilith blinked in surprise, but as his words sunk in, her defensive anger reared its ugly head. "No, I don't suppose I do since you elected *not* to tell me *any* of this or truthfully explain what is going on between you two." Before he responded, she stepped out of the car. "I'll get us a room." Then she slammed the door on a startled Chance and stormed toward the hotel. In her blind rage, she nearly bumped into Cohen.

"Whoa. Before you march up to the office, here." He tossed her a set of keycards, his eyes darting to the car. "With my apologies."

She stared at the cards for a long moment before meeting the demon's suddenly green eyes. The color-changing trick still creeped her out, even if he didn't consciously control it. "Let me guess. This room is right next to yours, isn't it?"

The slow grin pulling at his scarred face answered her question. "In my defense, the hotel only had a few vacancies, and these were the only two on the ground floor. I know your boyfriend likes an easy exit plan."

The stress he placed on the last sentence made it an obvious dig, but Lilith was far too tired to argue. "Thanks. Enjoy your dinner."

"If you hear from Nicci or the virologist, I'll be right next door. Room 105."

"Then all I have to do is speak up. and you'll hear me, plain as day."

With a warm chuckle, he patted her shoulder. "This isn't the Motel 6, sweetheart. You may have to knock on my door and deliver the news in person."

After a weary sigh, she turned her back on Andrew and spotted Chance leaning against the car, staring at his phone. When she approached, he glanced up, and she saw the apology in his eyes without him saying a word.

"I...uh...found a place for dinner. If you don't mind the walk."

Okay. Straight to chit-chat. Ignore the problem for now. "Are we talking 5K or early summer stroll?"

"Bit of both. It's about fifty minutes on foot through downtown, but I think it'll be worth it."

The lopsided smile dissolved her anger. *Dammit.*

"I want to say something first."

The man immediately tensed, bracing himself. "Okay..."

"Neither of us excelled at handling recent circumstances or communicating with each other the past few months."

He shifted forward, his mouth opening to say something, but she stopped him with a hand on his chest.

"Let me finish, please. I understand. You wanted to deal with this on your own and didn't want me to worry. Believe me. I know because I've been doing the same damn thing. I'm still having nightmares."

Confusion etched every line on his face. "How is that a secret?"

Lilith lifted her eyes to meet his with a heavy expression. "They are getting worse. Each one is more horrifying than the next, and Ashcroft always makes an appearance."

"Ashcroft? He's dead..."

"Yeah. So is everyone else in my dream, for the most part."

"But why him?"

"I don't know. Maybe because he was the first fucked-up thing that happened, and my dream brain is stuck on him as the source of all my trauma. God...I sound like my therapist."

"Why didn't you just tell me?"

"I didn't want you to worry. Sounds familiar, right?" She shrugged and exhaled slowly. "We both need to do better, act like partners, trust each other, allow the other to help—"

"I've never had that, *cherie*. I'm not used to relying on others or asking for help. I'm trying...I think once you officially move in—"

Her entire body clenched with irrational fear, and he stopped mid-sentence.

"I'm sorry. I know you sense how freaked out I am, but this is not about you. I promise." After taking a step closer, she nestled against his chest. "You are the one thing I *am* sure of, but for tonight, can we leave all the emotional crap here with the literal baggage?"

With a one-sided smile, he wrapped his arms around her, leaned down, and brushed his lips against hers in an intoxicatingly light kiss. "If that's what you want, then yes."

A soft smile lit her face, and she interlaced her fingers with his. "Lead the way to this amazing restaurant, but you may have to carry me at some point. I'm already tired."

An hour into their adventurous stroll, Chance stopped at a white brick church with a wine-red "V" painted on the side. "Now, that is an unusual venue choice for an Italian restaurant."

Victor's, as the sign pronounced, hosted several tables of chattering people on the red brick patio surrounded by a wrought-iron fence lit by strings of warm lights. The food looked amazing and smelled even better.

With a conspiratorial grin, they headed through the beautiful wood and glass doors. Every single time Lilith set foot in a church, whether it was still used as one or not, she thought of Hollywood. Countless movies and TV shows stressed the importance of holy ground. According to them, evil things—aka non-humans—could not stand in the presence of God in his own house. She didn't believe any of it, of course, but she still suffered from an unreasonable hesitation that gnawed at her stomach, telling her she didn't belong.

As soon as they passed over the threshold, however, the anxious energy dissipated. Although the church still boasted its original Tuscan plaster walls and stained glass windows, there was nothing stoic or sacred about the people. Raucous laughter, clanging glasses, and rowdy conversation filled the room with a bright liveliness they both needed.

The hostess led them to a table in the corner, and once seated, Chance kept true to his word and never broached taboo subjects. Instead, they smiled, held hands, cracked jokes, shared amazing food from their plates, and talked about everything except Cohen, moving in together, nightmares, side effects, and the bizarre virus.

After dinner, they shared a delicious tiramisu and sampled some waiter-recommended cocktails that packed quite a punch. Lilith barely finished her Winter Sangria, but Chance powered through three Habanero Heavens before they paid their rather hefty bill and began the trek back to the hotel.

"Are you sure you're okay to walk?" Her grin widened when Chance stumbled over the first curb in front of the Spring Garden Township Admin building.

He stared her down with a playful glare. "I lost my footing. Lay off. What are you, my designated walker?"

"I yield." Lilith chuckled, holding up her hands, and turned to face him. "But…" He growled a warning, but that no longer intimidated her. "I mean, you *did* try to order a stuffed martini before the waitress cut you off."

"They did *not* cut me off. They couldn't make it, so she brought the check. What's your point?"

"Well, if they made you a literal stuffed martini, they'd have brought you a frosty glass full of floating pimentos, blue cheese crumbles, garlic, and jalapenos. I think you wanted a stuffed *olive* martini."

"Semantics. They knew what I meant."

"Uh-huh."

"Laugh it up while you can, *cherie*." Chance darted forward so quickly, she had no time to react. In one smooth move, he pulled her into his arms and pinned her against the bridge's concrete railing. "I'm not too intoxicated to catch you." An impish grin curled his lips, and his fingertips traced up her neck.

While shaking off the delicious shiver, she positioned herself to one side. Then, when he was distracted, she shoved him sideways and danced free with a proud grin. "But too tipsy to keep me where you want me." With a wink, she jogged up the sidewalk.

When Chance caught up, he laced his fingers with hers.

The jubilant bubble they had created nearly lasted until they reached the hotel. "Eye of the Tiger" rang through the night when they passed over I-83, less than half a mile from their destination.

"Hey, did you find something?" Lilith asked.

"How involved was Cohen in the Tennessee FBI investigation?" Nicci's voice was firm, to the point, and more than a little irritated.

The tiny hairs on Lilith's arms prickled, and Chance picked up on her reaction right away.

The happy, intoxicated guy disappeared, replaced by a sober man wearing an expression reminiscent of a loaded gun searching for its target.

"Well, from what I understood, he worked closely with the agents, tying up loose ends until they closed the case. Why?"

"We have a big fucking problem."

Chapter 10 - *Cassie*

"Leto's family raised her in the old ways, by teaching her to honor the gods of Mt. Olympus who still walked among them. She devoutly considered herself a handmaiden to the goddess her parents named her after."

Cassie tried to make sense of the bizarre crap he spouted, but none of it rang a bell. *Ancient gods and handmaidens? What the actual fuck?*

"What does this have to do with me?" The frustrated cry emerged before she thought it through. Seconds later, a strong grip closed around her right pinkie and snapped the digit without hesitation.

"Not everything is about you." The sadistic man speaking over her agonized cry sounded bored, as if he had expected the question but hoped she'd be smart enough not to ask. "Again."

The ruthless hand moved to her right ring finger and cracked it backward. Bile rose, strangling her wild screams, when the flesh flapped limply against the back of her hand.

She tried to avoid flexing her broken digits, but the muscles tensed regardless. It was like a sore in her mouth that she couldn't stop rubbing with her tongue. The harder she resisted, the more the swollen, limp flesh quivered, sending jolts of pain up her arms. Only the middle and pointer on her right hand remained mobile.

She bit her tongue hard enough to draw blood, and her captor continued his monologue.

"Leto was born into an ancient, prominent family in Greece, but over time, their power and money dwindled. Too many of those who prospered from the gods' generosity forgot them. People no longer paid proper tribute, not even to Zeus. So, when the gods retreated from Greece, they took their blessings with them, to teach their children respect. The economic crisis worsened in the 1980s until even devout families began to suffer. Things grew so dire that in early 1990, Leto ventured to new lands, hoping to save her family."

The man paused as Cassie lost control of the mindless moans escaping with every ragged breath.

"Perhaps we pushed too far too soon. I assumed you would possess a higher tolerance, Cassie. *Tut, tut, tut.*"

The patronizing disappointment made her snarl, and hatred seared through her veins.

"Allow her another bite."

Heels clicked against the floor, and her mouth watered with desire the closer they came. As soon as the fruit touched her lips, she sank her teeth in, took a huge bite, and let the juice trickle over her tongue.

By the time the woman—a reasonable assumption, judging by the stilettos—returned to her seat, the pain had dulled to a tolerable level, and her chest loosened enough to breathe deeply. *What kind of fruit relieves pain like morphine?* None to her knowledge. *Do they spike it with drugs? Does it matter at this point?*

"Better. I hate to be interrupted." Each time the man spoke, he sounded more aristocratic and pompous. He pulled on the persona for the crowd, like a cheap suit, and gradually became more comfortable in his role.

Although real masterminds loved to lord their accomplishments, they rarely went on huge monologues this complex. Who cared about some woman from Greece or the economic turmoil? This madman and his followers did.

A sermon. The man wasn't revealing a crazy plot to dominate the world or take down modernist society. He was delivering a sermon to his disciples. The audience existed to build his ego and provide validation, so he attuned the fabricated lore to sway *them*, not her.

Still, the story could reveal something about his psyche and objectives, even if it wasn't aimed at her. *What does he want from his flock of sheep?* Every madman with a cult wanted something. Power, money, control—those were the usual motivations.

"Leto found employment as a housekeeper for a wealthy family outside Atlanta. The lady of the house was very detached and self-serving. The children were left in the nanny's care, while she spent her nights at fancy clubs and slept until dusk. In the brief moments of consciousness at home, the woman never had a kind word for anyone, especially not her husband.

The man brokered deals for international clients and conducted his business at night, so the two rarely shared five minutes in the same room, which didn't appear to bother them."

The ringleader's droning voice combined with the hypnotic lull of the fruit, making Cassie drowsy. When her muscles went slack, the ropes bit into her skin, but the pain quickly faded into the background. Her eyes fluttered closed.

Then she realized the man had stopped talking.

A thunderous slap to her cheek lit every nerve like the Fourth of July.

"That is your one and only warning. Next time, he will break the two fingers you have left."

She nodded sightlessly, agony and euphoria fighting each other for dominance. The audience hadn't made a sound when he struck her.

Aside from their original whispers of agreement and their odd chant about Leto, they hadn't made a peep, not even a gasp or groan when the bastard broke her fingers. A complete lack of dissension in the ranks rarely occurred, especially when it involved torture. Before she could consider the implications of that revelation, the narrator began speaking again.

"Unsurprisingly, the husband took quite a liking to Leto, who was young and curvaceous, with raven black hair and chocolatey-brown eyes— a true Grecian beauty. However, the man was not only drawn to her physical appearance. She treated him with kindness and thoughtfulness, something he was not accustomed to from his frigid wife."

The lengthy, nonsensical story began to burn through the bliss Cassie had garnered from the mystery fruit. *Why the hell does anyone need to know this? What is he trying to tell them, and what does this sicko want from...*

Amid her internal questions, sudden pain shot up her arm, the middle finger snapping back against the knuckle. Raw anger leaked into her scream, and she snarled at her cowardly host.

"I was listening! Fuck! What is your end game? Bore me to death with a damn soap opera while your minion breaks all my bones? You fucking coward!" Cassie's eyes roamed the darkness behind her blindfold, wishing she could use his stupid face as a beacon for all her hatred.

For a moment, the entire room became deathly silent, except for Cassie's panting breaths. Then footsteps approached and stopped in front of her. A soft hand—different from the rough, calloused touch of her torturer—slithered up her stomach, between her bare breasts, up her chest and neck, until he gripped her jaw. The fingers squeezed painfully tight while he lifted her face toward his.

"Dear, sweet Cassie. I do not need anyone to do my work for me. I simply like to share with the group. We are a collective, and each one holds equal responsibility." He released her with a shove that sent her head whipping into the wood, and spots danced before her eyes.

While she tried to maintain her tenuous grip on consciousness, the same footsteps echoed around her, then halted behind her left side.

"You must learn the history, as all my subjects do. They are here to participate and bear witness to your sacrifice."

Her brow furrowed in confusion. *My sacrifice? The histories?* "What the hell are you talking about?"

A heavy sigh rolled over her shoulder, the hot breath raising each tiny hair.

"Followers, I believe Cassie would like a proper explanation of her role."

A hushed murmur of voices echoed deeper in the room, making her skin crawl.

"Very well. Have you heard of *Basanos*?"

"No." Her voice quivered with trepidation, and her pulse began to race.

"The *Basanos* was a touchstone in ancient Greece used to test the purity of gold. Later, the word evolved and eventually encompassed torture used in the name of truth-seeking. See, just as pressing metal to the stone revealed its value, applying pain uncovers the value of one's testimony."

Cassie swallowed hard, his ominous words hanging in the air. "You don't have to—"

"Stop!" His voice snapped with a horrifying finality. "Do not placate me with promises of honesty to save yourself. Absolute truth hides deep in the body and must be coerced into the open through force. It is only through *Basanos* on the Breaking Wheel we prove innocence and extract the information we seek."

"You are…insane." Her whispered voice cracked with tears when her bleak future flashed through her mind.

"Pain is nature's truth serum, Cassie. That is why the testimony of a tortured slave surpassed even the words of a free citizen in the eyes of Ancient Greece."

"Please…I will tell you everything you want to know." Even as the words passed her lips, she knew they wouldn't make a difference, but the compulsion to plead and beg wouldn't be denied. She wanted to survive.

A hand slid across her shoulder, and she tensed as it made its way down her arm.

The self-important voice whispered in her ear with a sinister tone, "I know you will, Cassie, but first, I want you to scream for me."

"Why? Why are you doing this?" She sobbed uselessly, and his hand paused on the outer curve of her elbow.

"I've already told you. Pay attention! When the time comes, you will know your final purpose and gratefully welcome your fate." The madman snatched her hair, pulling her head back against the wood with a vicious grip. "Until then, you will listen without further interruptions."

The hand left her elbow just before a rush of air. Her nerves exploded with blinding pain when his fist struck the back of her elbow, sending the bones shooting forward, rupturing the skin.

Warm, sticky blood oozed from the break while her tormented screams filled the room. The agony was so unbelievable, her mind couldn't fully comprehend it. When the shrieks finally ended, she choked on tears until her throat closed and breathing became a struggle.

A leather strap tightened around her bicep and pinched, but it was a mere gnat in the electrical storm of agony enveloping her brain. The scent of seared flesh reached her nostrils seconds before the burning flared up her arm, and distantly, she realized they had cauterized the wound to keep her from bleeding out.

"Eat!"

Cassie wasn't conscious of the bites she took. Her body acted on instinct, trying to survive.

The delirious warmth worked quickly. The throbbing still existed, slicing at her mind like searing knives, but she felt disconnected from the sensation. Another bite and she pulled farther away from the pain until she floated above herself, watching three formless shadows stand around her broken body.

"Cassie, are you with me?"

The voice sounded familiar and warm, with the hint of a Philadelphia accent, one she knew better than any other. Tears streamed down her face in sheer joy. *He came to save me! I knew he'd come…*

"Cassie!"

The world shifted, and the voice morphed in mid-word, stealing all her fleeting dreams of rescue.

"I hope for your sake you are still awake."

When fingers drifted along her right arm, everything came into focus so quickly, it sent her stomach spinning.

"No, no! Please! I'm awake," she pleaded desperately.

"Good." The cruel hand patted her shoulder, and the footsteps receded deeper into the room.

Since collapsing in relief wasn't an option, she shifted her weight to support her broken arm so the ropes wouldn't pull at the shattered joint.

"Now then, where was I? Ah, yes. Leto and the man of the house. The two enjoyed a steamy tryst, carefully hidden from his wife's eyes. The man was powerful and charismatic, like Zeus himself, and Leto could not resist. Now, his wife may have been frivolous with *her* affections, but she lorded over each possession, including her husband. After three months, he grew too scared of being caught to continue. The man promptly made Leto pack her bags, handed her a few hundred dollars, like she was nothing more than a common whore, and kicked her to the curb.

"However, this is only the beginning of her story. See, the man she'd worked for left an unexpected severance package—she was pregnant with twins. Leto took the news as proof of the old gods' existence. They showed their approval by bestowing the same divine gift as her namesake from Grecian myth.

"For the next several months, she lived a humble life, pouring all her energy into keeping the twins healthy, no matter the cost. She no longer had the money to send back home, but they would understand. She had a higher purpose from Zeus, chosen to carry his new children into the modern world. The boy and girl growing inside her, like Artemis and Apollo, would rise to power and reclaim the glory of Mount Olympus."

Chapter 11

Lilith pounded on the door to Room 105 with the same force her heart exerted against her ribs. *I should have known better. Things are never that damn simple. How could I be so stupid?*

A second later, the door swung open with a sudden swish, and all her racing thoughts crashed and burned like a five-car pile-up. Her eyes automatically moved from Cohen's almost handsome face to the faint scars littering his torso to…everything else while he stood there stark naked.

When she still couldn't find her words, he cleared his throat, which jolted her from the weird trance.

"Dammit, Cohen!" Lilith turned and covered her eyes with a fierce heat burning her cheeks.

"Did you need something?" An amused lilt hid beneath his calm indifference.

"Can you put some damn clothes on first?"

"If you insist."

She listened to him padding barefoot into the room, followed by a swish of fabric, but a soft moan surprised her into glancing back, despite every instinct. On the bed lay a woman with vibrant red hair, and when he stole the sheet to wrap around his waist, Lilith got more than an eyeful of her nude figure.

"Sufficient?" When she didn't respond, he followed her line of sight to the bed. "Told you I'd find my own dinner."

Once Lilith tore her gaze away from the sleeping woman, she rubbed at the blush still warming her cheeks. "Apparently, we went to *very* different restaurants…" Then she stopped short and shook her head. "No. Not my business." *Focus. Focus.* "However, the FBI investigation in Tennessee *is* my business." *There we go. Back on track.*

A seemingly genuine frown pulled at his brow, but she found it very hard to believe, given the circumstances. After everything they had endured together, she wanted to trust him, but this?

"I'm not following."

"You told us...You told *me* the FBI closed the case. *No loose strings.* That's precisely what you said." The anger leeched back into her voice, her righteous fury resurfacing.

His blond eyebrows shot up in surprise, and he leaned against the doorframe in Chance-like fashion. "Yes, because it's the truth. You are awfully worked up." After studying her face for a moment, he stuck his head out enough to peer down the hall both ways. "Where is your stronger, angrier counterpart?"

"I asked him to stay in the lobby because I need him not to kill you." Asking Chance to wait next door would have been an absolute waste of time. He'd sense everything he didn't overhear, and considering how Cohen had opened the door, the result would have been apocalyptic, probably involving an endless stream of French Lilith wouldn't understand.

"Well, I suppose I should thank you, but somehow, I don't feel that's appropriate yet."

"When did you plan to tell me about the third party who took custody of the biological materials from Miriah, Goditha, and Phipps Bend?"

The amusement abandoned his face, and he stood bolt upright. "What?"

"You heard me. Who has all that *extremely* damaging information, Andrew?"

"I honestly don't know what you are talking about."

Her eyes narrowed while she stared him down. "How could you *not* know? After all, you were *central* to the investigation, or so you claimed."

"It must have occurred after they closed the case." His sky-blue eyes drifted to the floor, his voice trailing off as he thought through every scenario. "That's the only thing that makes sense."

"Nothing *makes sense*, Cohen. Not one damn thing. Why the hell would the FBI hand over evidence? Not to mention, why would anyone know enough to want it?"

"Andy? Who's at the door? Is something wrong?"

The drowsy female voice seemed intrusive, and apparently, Lilith wasn't the only one who thought so.

Cohen turned to face the room, a deep frown developing across his features. "You need to leave." Flat practicality infused his voice, and he held the door open wider.

"What?" The woman sat up, covering her chest with a sudden sense of modesty. "But—"

"*Now.*" That one word rang with a chilling finality even Lilith found abrasive.

The redhead froze as if his words hadn't sunk in.

"I said now!"

The sharp order set the woman into motion. In a frenzy of embarrassed anger, the woman stormed around the room and shimmied into various articles of clothing. "You are such an asshole!" Finally, the woman threw her shirt on and shoved past him without buttoning it.

When she nearly ran over Lilith, she came to a screeching halt. Stormy eyes looked the vampire up and down with open contempt, and before Lilith could say anything, the furious redhead spun on her heel and slapped Cohen in the face with commanding force.

"Prick."

He stood perfectly still, maintaining his bored expression without bothering to meet her eyes. "If you're done, you can leave."

The woman's face hardened into an icy stare, and after straightening her haphazard clothes, she marched toward the lobby.

"Wow, *Andy*. You sure know how to make friends, don't you?"

Cohen glared up from beneath his furrowed brow with a clear warning. "Do *not* call me that."

Lilith held up her hands and shook her head. "You could have just told the poor woman you had business."

While she spoke, he pushed off the doorframe to stand mere inches from her, and for the first time since Tennessee, she felt intimidated by him.

"I don't know anything about this, and if you think I did, it means you *still* don't trust me."

Any response died in her throat when he leaned closer, an odd mixture of anger, betrayal, and sadness in his hazel eyes.

"After Phipps Bend, Farren, the medical center, what Luminita—" Tears welled along his lashes, and he dropped his gaze to the ground, suddenly lost in dark memories of excruciating betrayal.

Although Lilith wanted to reclaim her personal space, this volatile, emotional version of Detective Andrew Cohen felt alien and unnerving, which left her frozen in place. When she mustered the bravery to step back, his eyes snapped up to hers and bored through them.

"They didn't mean anything, did they? Something fucked-up happens and you assume I'm behind it." His jaw tightened, anger burning away all the other emotions. "I fucking *begged* my grandfather to put a bullet in my skull to keep you alive. *Remember that.* What else do I have to do to prove myself to you?"

The venomous words stung more than a slap in the face. Tears tightened her throat, cutting off any apology she tried to formulate. The longer he stared at her, the more his anger waned until only his impassive mask remained.

"Andrew, I…"

He stepped back into the room while his eyes focused on the fascinating wall sconce across the hall. "Just go."

"I'm sorry. I—"

"I'll investigate this third party. You've done your job." With that, he closed the door before she could say anything else.

For a few minutes, she stared at the black numbers on the white door in complete shock. *Cohen is right.* She kept lecturing Chance about instigating fights, but in the pivotal moment, she had done the same damn thing.

Lilith could have knocked on his door and asked, given him the benefit of the doubt, but she hadn't. The man didn't always do things the correct way, but he had never given her a single solid reason not to trust him since the meeting with Farren…since his grandfather had executed her dad.

Did she subconsciously hold him responsible for Gregor's murder, or did she simply expect everyone in her life to double-cross her after discovering her father's past? Neither of those constituted a valid reason to treat Andrew like the enemy, not after what he had endured in the medical center and not after coming to her for help now. Once again, Andrew was merely a convenient target for her pent-up anger.

Lilith was still lost in her thoughts, staring at Cohen's door, when a hand brushed her shoulder. At the unexpected touch, she released a startled cry and whirled around, her pulse going haywire.

"Sorry, I didn't mean to scare you, *mon petite cherie.*"

Lilith closed her eyes, took a few breaths, and buried her face in his chest. Chance rested his chin on her head and folded his arms around her. She focused on his heartbeat, trying to steady her own.

"Are you okay, Lily? What happened?"

"Can we go to bed? I'm tired, and it's been a shitty day."

"Can you at least tell me what he said about the evidence's change of custody?"

With a heavy sigh, she pulled back to meet his eyes. "He doesn't know anything."

The argument forming in his head became visible in his strong features, but he let it go. Instead, he slid his arm around her waist and tugged her close. "Let's get some sleep. We can talk in the morning."

Lilith stared down the rough passage of earth and roots that had become far too familiar over the past few months. Since Gregor's funeral, most of her nightmares had started the same way—standing naked in this damn tunnel. No matter how many times she faced the entrance to her personal hell, she couldn't wake up, change it, or turn away. The point of flickering light at the end drew her in, like a mindless moth to a flame, powerless to resist.

Her bare feet moved on instinct, padding along the cold, dank dirt for the thousandth time. Roots and small rocks bit into the delicate soles, and the wet mud squished between her toes, but she ignored it.

The scent of smoke wafted by, rippled over her skin, and left goose-bumps behind. She squeezed her eyes shut, hoping, even praying, that she would magically wake up. *Why does my mind continue to torture me with an endless parade of demons?*

The tunnel began to narrow as it always did, forcing her to crouch at first, then crawl through the slime. Although her hands snagged on roots and sharp things bit at her knees, her eyes remained fixed on the growing light ahead. The walls closed in, the earth nearly swallowing her whole. If only it would, she could escape what came next. *What if I stop and allow it to happen?*

Despite her best efforts, her body continued forward. When the passage ended, she landed hard on the stone floor, causing pain to flare from her shoulder to her fingertips.

Massive stalagmites and stalactites emerged from the cave, like wicked teeth guarding the mouth of hell itself. The stench of death became thick enough to choke on, almost blotting out the smokey scent. Blood dripped from the ceiling, trailed down each ragged spike, and filled the pools below.

Although the sight had become routine, an odd odor infiltrated the blood this time. Beneath the usual copper lurked something else, something tainted, spoiled, rotten.

While she scanned the area, her ears pricked for the slightest sound. The dream always started in the tunnel and ended with Ashcroft, but what happened in between was a fresh torment each time. The core elements didn't differ much, but the timing and interactions varied a great deal.

Something moved up ahead, and she angled toward the soft patter of agile steps until she faced the stalagmite dominating the center of the cavern. The thing boasted a circumference well over twenty feet, and whatever came next waited for her behind the massive stone.

Lilith moved toward it, ignoring the sharp rocks beneath her bare feet. After all, a dream couldn't hurt her. *Well, except for that one time.* She had learned from experience that the only way through was to get to the end. Once she dealt with Ashcroft, she could finally wake up. Nothing else mattered. At least, that's the mantra she'd perfected, not that it worked particularly well.

While making her way around one of the large pools, her bloody foot slid, and she lost her balance. Although her arms flailed through the air to keep her upright, it didn't help. *No, no, no!* With a thick splash, she crashed into the putrefied blood. The tainted coppery substance flooded her mouth, making her gag, and she fought through the congealing liquid toward the surface. As soon as she emerged, she drew in a gulping breath, her lungs burning with the effort.

The putrid blood and clots matted her hair and stuck to her skin, attaching to her like a mob of microscopic leeches. Lilith splashed and kicked in the direction of the pool's edge, but swimming through the syrupy stuff proved difficult.

Then something grabbed her ankle.

She tried to jerk her leg away, but the grip only tightened each time, and her dread soon blossomed into true fear. However, the panic didn't kick in until something began to emerge from the depths.

As Lilith stared in horror, Miriah's mangled face broke the surface, blood gurgling between the slices in her rotten lips. The lidless eyes had decomposed into shriveled spheres, yellow puss leaking down her sallow cheeks. The tattered remnants of skin flaked off and drifted before disintegrating.

Lilith shrieked and thrust her free foot at the horrific face, resulting in a sickening crunch of bone beneath her sole. The restraining hand sprang open, and Miriah's corpse sank back into the rancid liquid. Without a second glance, Lilith swam for the edge, terror ringing down her spine.

After hauling herself out, she frantically wiped at her body. The stench infiltrated her skin, seeping into her bones, contaminating her.

"Breathe, breathe. This is just a dream. It can't hurt you." The mantra didn't work this time, so she sat down, drew her knees to her chest, and took slow, deep breaths, tears sliding down her cheeks.

These night terrors robbed her of more than a good night's sleep. Lilith couldn't even remember what Miriah, her vibrantly happy cousin, looked like anymore. For over forty hours, Ashcroft had forced Lilith's uncle to witness his daughter's agony, listen to her cries, and see her features mutilated until only a hollow shell of shredded flesh remained. Now, all Lilith could dredge up were the mangled results of the monster's handiwork. The smiling face she had known and loved no longer existed in her mind.

When she wiped the bloody tears from her face, she caught a brief glimpse of someone bent over the opposite side of the pool. The figure disappeared in the blink of an eye, leaving an expanding ripple across the surface.

A chill ran down her spine, and she stiffened, scanning the area like a frightened prairie dog. When nothing moved, Lilith swallowed the lump in her throat and slowly stood. She had to keep going. The light still flickered past the stalagmite, beckoning to her. None of this would end until the dream completed its mission.

Lilith hugged the massive rock, taking careful steps, fingers sliding along the rough stone. When an antique lantern came into view, she cautiously peeked around the clearing but only spotted a figure slumped over in a chair. Even without seeing the face, she knew who it was and collapsed against the rock, weeping.

Facing the most painful of her ghosts was never easy. Each time, she forgot the loving face she'd known her whole life a little more. The one that cried while holding her at her mother's funeral. The one that wore a proud smile when she took her first case. The one that brightened every time she entered a room.

A scream erupted from her throat, echoed off the walls, and rattled the jagged spikes above her. Lilith wanted to stay put and avoid what awaited her, but the nightmare wouldn't end until it brought her to *him*.

To steel herself, she recalled the memory of riding her father's shoulders as a girl and wrapped herself up in the moment. The full moon's glow had bathed them both in cool light, like a blessing from a mysterious goddess. The summer breeze kissed their skin before rustling the giant trees in Central Park. When she had reached for the moon, her father laughed and told her to try harder. Gregor's magical smile widened so much, it revealed the subtle dimples in his cheeks.

I'm only delaying the inevitable. After one more deep inhale, Lilith crossed the stone, circled the body, and finally faced it. Once she opened her eyes to the grisly scene before her, the happy memory dissipated like smoke.

Tears flooded her eyes, and she stared at the decayed image of her father. A putrid brown substance oozed from the desiccated bullet wound, and his skin hung loosely from the bones, peeling and splitting. Even his once sky-gray eyes were shrunken to pale marbles lying in the dark sockets.

She squeezed her eyes shut and strained to retrieve the memory of riding Gregor's shoulders, but to no avail. The decomposing face of her father scorched it from her mind. With a defeated sigh, she opened her eyes and mourned yet another loss.

In a sudden motion, the corpse lurched forward, the rotting mouth hanging open in a soundless scream. Lilith jumped backward too fast and ended up flat on the floor with a thud, knocking the air from her lungs. The cadaver came crashing toward her, and she tried to scramble away, but her bloody feet slid uselessly, and her nails scratched the smooth surface without taking hold. Since she couldn't escape, Lilith clamped her eyes closed and concentrated.

Wake up! Now!

Every muscle clenched with dreadful anticipation while she waited for her father's corpse to land on her, but the moment never came. As the seconds stretched into minutes, her pulse slowed, and her chest loosened until she dared to open one eye, then the other.

The cave, along with the horrors it contained, was gone.

Huh. This is new.

Lilith stood and scanned the anonymous room with a mixture of apprehension and excitement. The cold tile floor already chilled her bare feet, but when the air conditioner kicked on, its low hum filling the silence, it sent shivers over her naked skin.

The shapes of desks, computers, and equipment took form from the misty substance hovering in the room, while fluorescent lights flickered to life overhead. Lilith stood there, witnessing her mind create the space, until she finally realized what it was—a lab, but not one she knew. Glass cell doors and workstations lined the circular space with a massive computer dominating the room's center. It wasn't Goditha or Solasta.

The mist continued to recede, revealing bodies and blood spatter everywhere. The place resembled a ghastly massacre from a sci-fi movie, complete with flashing lights and a warning siren. *Where am I?*

She frowned down at the closest person, trying to make sense of the shape. Rich black hair splayed across the face, and the limbs stuck out at odd angles. as if they'd each been broken. After a moment's hesitation, Lilith bent, wiped away the hair, and stumbled backward in shock.

No. No, it's not true. My mind is playing tricks. This isn't right.

She stared into Gloria's milky eyes in disbelief. Only real corpses haunted her dreams, except for Chance. His death had become prominent that first night in Knoxville. *This* was new and somehow more terrifying.

With a sense of urgency, Lilith ran to the other bodies, flipping them one by one—Sophia, Rose, Erica, Nicci, Timothy. Her throat tightened a little more with each bloody corpse until the air in her lungs burned like napalm. *This isn't real. It's just a nightmare. This doesn't mean anything.*

When she reached the final body, her heart dropped.

Lilith hated this moment almost as much as seeing her father's zombie-like remains. She wiped away angry tears and approached the tall figure with chestnut hair sprawled out on the floor. Reluctantly, Lilith rolled him over, knowing what she'd see.

As Chance's head flopped to the side, his once-hazel eyes—now reduced to a milky tan—rolled in the sockets. Her gaze drifted from his lifeless face, searching for the inevitable slice across his neck, but it wasn't there.

This time, his throat was a bloody mass of mangled meat—no careful precision, only raw, savage, animalism. It looked like something had dug its teeth into his neck and shook him like a chew toy. The warm, sticky blood seeped toward her fingers, and she pulled back as if it were poisonous. *What the hell is this?*

Lilith pushed away, shaking her head in denial, her chest continuing to tighten. For almost a year, her nights had consisted of the same core elements—loved ones she failed to save, Chance's slit throat, and Ashcroft. Occasionally, Peisinoe and her frightening talents had made an appearance, but beyond that, the dream didn't differ much, except in minor details and surroundings. *So, why the dramatic deviation? Why now?*

Every nerve trembled with growing trepidation until she turned on her heel and sprinted for the exit. Her hands smashed into the swinging door, and Lilith ran through, only to stop short in the middle of a hotel hallway. Her eyes scanned each end of the empty hall and then landed on the white door with black numbers in front of her—105. *Cohen.*

One question whirled through her mind before she knocked on the door. *Why is he here?* She had never seen Andrew in her nightmares, not once.

The door creaked open with a groan, and Lilith fought to control her rising panic. Inky blackness consumed the doorframe until Cohen's face slowly appeared. His lips curled into a pleasant smile that didn't fit him, like a Stepford version of the emotion-feeding Durand.

Her eyes traveled down his smooth neck to his scarred chest and abdomen. The deep cuts faded to fine white lines, but the names of Clyde and Orrick Ashcroft's victims were still legible—Mary, Finlay, Mirren, Margareet, Bridget, Emma.

Her eyes lingered on Mary's name because her death had been the catalyst. The brutal rape and murder of Gregor's twelve-year-old daughter had ignited the fuse. If she'd stayed home with her brothers instead of going to the market with her parents, none of this would have happened. *None of it.* Six hundred years of tragedy and countless deaths could have been avoided.

Amid the ghostly names, a new one began to form. Thick scarlet blood seeped from the letters as they appeared, one by one.

L-I-L-I-T-H.

Lilith stared at her name sliced into Cohen's skin, cold creeping deep into her marrow. Her blood roared in her ears, and her vision traveled back up the pale, scarred body. When she reached the face, it no longer belonged to Andrew.

Lilith's heart seemed to stop.

Ashcroft's mangled visage stared back at her. His sunken eyes burned hot, his thin lips splitting like a knife gash, revealing stained, crooked teeth.

The motion pulled at the massive burn scar—angry and red with bits of charred black—that dominated the left side.

Although she willed her body into action, her muscles tensed but didn't move. When faced with the monster who controlled her nightmares, Lilith froze for the hundredth time, powerless to stop him.

For a moment, he stood there, unblinking like a statue, his eyes fixed straight ahead. Then they swung down to meet hers, and his gruesome smile widened, which sent her heart racing wildly.

Before she had time to blink, the monster's hand shot forward, and his sharp nails sliced through her skin, burrowing inside her neck. Hot, sticky blood gushed down her chest while she choked and gagged. Ashcroft's mouth hardened into a vicious line. His talons curled around her trachea and squeezed.

Lilith tried to fight back, like she always did. Her hands scratched at his arms, leaving bloody furrows behind, but he never flinched. The grip only tightened, making the world spin. Either blood loss or the lack of oxygen would kill her, not that it mattered which one. The result remained the same regardless.

When his fist slammed closed, the crunch of cartilage echoed in her ears. Her eyes widened in shock seconds before his arm jerked back. Time froze. She stared at the lump of bloody flesh in his taloned hand and collapsed to the floor, darkness consuming her.

Lilith screamed until her throat felt raw. She fell out of the tangled sheets and collided with the thin carpet. Her hands flew up to her throat, rubbing the skin as if unsure it still existed.

"Lily!" Chance leapt over the bed and crouched in front of her. "You kept screaming, but I couldn't wake you!" He grabbed her shaking shoulders, pulled her into his arms, and pushed the sweat-soaked strands from her face. "I haven't heard you scream like that since…Peisinoe."

Her throat still felt impossibly tight, which prevented her from talking, even if she wanted to. With tears in her eyes, she silently nestled into his warm arms.

Instead of pressing her with questions, his hand slid through her hair in gentle strokes, and he whispered in her ear, "You're okay. You're safe. I've got you. I love you."

She melted into him, sobbing against his chest. His strong heartbeat comforted her frayed nerves. Chance was right about one thing—this nightmare *was* different from the others. It rattled her to the core, but she didn't understand its meaning.

Sure, Chance died in a lot of them, but Lilith recognized that as her fear of losing the person closest to her. This time, even his death had been different, and Gloria, Nicci, the girls, Tim, and Cohen had never appeared in her nightmares. Her therapist would say her dreams frequently stemmed from survivor's guilt, but this one…

"Don't dwell on it, *amour de ma vie. Síl vous plaît*…think of a good memory." As he whispered, his fingers traced down her back in soothing circles.

When she closed her eyes and tried to summon another thought, any thought, she only witnessed dead faces until Ashcroft's loomed in her mind. "I can't." The raspy words barely escaped, and tears rolled down her cheeks.

Chance pulled back, curled his finger under her chin, and lifted her gaze to meet his. "Then we'll make a new one." The tenderness in his eyes held her captive, and his hand slid over her neck, sinking into her auburn curls.

The first touch of his lips began to sear away the horrific flashes plaguing her head, so she pulled him closer, drawing on his warmth, basking in its glow, and returning his hungry kiss.

A soft moan escaped when he pulled her onto his lap, and his hands gripped her hips tight in answer. The sudden rush of desire had nothing to do with burying the bodies from her nightmare. Those images were already gone.

The jolt of lightning coursing up her spine and spreading into every cell had everything to do with the man who moved his hips against hers. Lilith needed him in a way she had never needed anyone before in her life. Not to fight her battles, protect her fragile psyche, or inflate her self-esteem, but to share her life, her pain, her grief, her joy, and make her complete.

Plato's mythos of soulmates foretold a feeling of amazement when one discovered their missing half and experienced true love, friendship, and intimacy. That was the only way she could describe the overwhelming emotions flushing her skin as Chance softly bit her bottom lip.

There had been a time when she thought she loved him because he was the only thing left for her in this world, but she had been wrong. Gloria, the girls, Nicci, Tim, even Andrew cared about her. Even if she had lost the center of her universe—her father—she still had plenty of surrogate family. Chance wasn't a last resort or a lone stone to cling to in the raging river of terror that had become her life.

The Lotus Tree

Lilith chose him every day for the man he was to her—a beautiful soul who had loved her from afar for over a decade, the one who never took her for granted, the man who would battle the devil himself if he stood between them, the one who felt he'd be nothing without her.

In that surreal moment of introspection, she realized the ghosts of her past shouldn't taint her future with a man who loved her so fiercely. Chance would never hurt her, especially not like David had during that horrific year in college.

With an unexpected surge that interrupted her thoughts, he wrapped her legs around his waist and stood. A surprised yelp escaped, and she held on tight. They crashed onto the bed, his lips leaving hers with a growl and trailing the tender flesh of her throat. His teeth grazed the surface, and a delicious tremble followed in their wake while he made his way down her body. Every inch clouded her self-reflective thoughts until only crashing waves of ecstasy existed.

Definitely a good memory.

Chapter 12

A thunderous boom woke Lilith from a sound sleep. She opened her drowsy eyes and searched for the clock. Seven a.m. She frowned at the thing, deeply offended by the answer it gave. Another loud slam drew her attention to the door rattling on its hinges.

What the hell?

After detangling herself from Chance's sprawled limbs, she placed a kiss on his cheek and slid out of bed, completely naked. *Shit.* Lilith searched the floor with frantic energy, the persistent knocks growing louder. The nightgown, or rather what was left of it, wouldn't help. Things had gotten a little intense last night, the memory of which brought a delicious grin to her face. She tossed the remnants in a trash can and searched for a fast alternative.

A towel seemed her only option, so she wrapped one around herself, ran to the door, and flung it open.

"About damn time! I've been—"

When Cohen's angry words trailed off, her head tilted quizzically. "You've been…," she prompted.

The man continued to stare.

"Hello?" Lilith tilted her head with a frown and clutched her towel a little tighter.

Cohen shook off the odd trance, and his eyes snapped back up to hers with purpose. "I've been knocking for ten minutes. I'd like to get this interview with your virologist over with and return to *actual* leads. I know you had a *rough* night, but—"

"Wait." Lilith held up a hand and managed to keep her composure. "Before you get snippy, I want to clear the air. I'm sorry about last night.

You were right. I should have come to you and given you the benefit of the doubt instead of hurling accusations."

His face maintained its mask-like indifference, refusing to show any emotion elicited by her apology, if such a thing existed.

"Don't take it personally. My trust issues don't start and stop with you, Andrew. You aren't the only one I've pissed off this week."

He nodded gruffly, and a faint blush crept over his cheeks. "Noted. Let's meet in the lobby and grab breakfast to eat on the way. I don't want to spend any more time in York than necessary."

Something about witnessing the typically composed demon unnerved and rattled brought an impish grin to her lips. "Tired of the local company?"

His face hardened, jaw clenching tight. "It's not the *local* company that bothers me." When she frowned, he hastily amended his statement. "It's the smell. I opened the window this morning to the overpowering aroma of rotten cabbage."

Wrinkling his nose only accentuated the thin, white scars crossing it. Then his eyes roamed the hall, avoiding her and effectually ending the conversation.

"Sorry. We'll meet you in the lobby in a few minutes."

With a curt nod, he turned on his heel and marched away. For a moment, Lilith stared at his back, trying to unjumble their conversation. When her sleep-deprived mind refused to make sense of it, she shrugged and closed the door.

"Everything okay?" Chance propped himself up on one elbow, the sheet draped across his waist—quite an enjoyable view and not one that inspired her to get dressed. In fact, she'd rather slide back into bed, curl up in his arms, and let the world fend for itself.

No. People depended on her. What if Gloria or the girls contracted the virus and she could have stopped it?

With a soft sigh, Lilith sauntered to the bed and tenderly kissed his lips. "Cohen is clawing at the walls."

She turned toward her bag, and Chance slid his arms around her waist, spun her around, and tugged her toward the bed. Lilith crashed on top of him, laughing, and her towel fell away. She quickly became entangled in the sheets with the weight of his body pressed against hers. His lips moved down her neck, drawing a mewling noise from her throat. Although she attempted to remain focused on the task at hand, the shivers tracing up her spine proved difficult to ignore when his teeth grazed her collarbone.

"Chance."

His green-flecked eyes glanced up with devilish delight before he nipped playfully at her skin. "Yes, *mon petite cherie?*" The subtle motion of his hips elicited a surge of carnal desire begging her to shut up.

"Chance, I'd love to let you ravish me right now…"

His lips traveled along her flesh until they hovered over her mouth, just out of reach. "But…"

"But we have to go. Cohen—"

"I don't care what he wants." He cut her off abruptly and nipped her bottom lip. Before she responded, his palms gripped her hips, and his lips trailed down the center of her chest.

"We…uh…still need to see Dr. Thomas." Lilith rested her head on the mattress and tried to sound convincing, but part of her prayed he'd ignore her. *I can't believe I'm really trying to stop this from happening.* "We have to get to the bottom of this thing, and we can't do that holed up in a hotel room. As much as I wish that were possible."

After a sigh that rushed over her stomach, Chance moved up to meet her eyes. Tension once again pulled at the fine lines of his handsome face, and she immediately regretted stopping him. When her palm brushed his cheek, a small smile returned.

"Someday, the world won't rest on our shoulders, and we can run away. There's no one I'd rather disappear with, Chance Allen Deveraux."

The sudden kiss sent another jolt down her spine. Then he broke the spellbinding moment and sat bolt upright as a thought occurred to him. He stared off into space for a few seconds before his eyes drifted back to hers.

"Let's do it."

A bemused frown crossed her face, and she pushed up to rest on her elbows. "Do what?"

An excited gleam lit his eyes, and his fingers slid into her thick curls. "When all this is over, let's just go. Leave the bad memories behind and start over."

Her mouth fell open, her mind balking at the sudden request. "We can't…*I* can't…"

"Why? There is nothing tying you to New York City. Aaron controls Gregor's companies, and your father set up a decent trust fund, so you don't have to work. We could go wherever you want."

"But…Nicci, Tim, Gloria, and the girls…"

"Can get along fine without us."

Lilith slid off the bed to pace the floor, everything rattling around in her brain. When she glanced back at Chance, he was watching her expectantly. The man wasn't wrong. A new city without the memories of dead people and trauma sounded appealing, but somehow, it didn't feel right.

"I don't know. I…" Once again, the right words evaded her, mostly because she didn't know what she wanted. "Can we revisit this another time?"

Faint traces of disappointment haunted his chiseled face, and he nodded. She wanted to take it all back, to erase that expression. He thought she doubted him and their future, but that was the only thing that didn't scare her.

Chance slid to the bed's edge, and Lilith stepped in front of him, cradled his face, and tilted it upward. "I love you more than you know. I…" Words failed her again, but this time, a lopsided grin brightened his face.

"And I love you, *mon amour*. You're right. This isn't the best time." Once he rose to his feet, he loomed over her, slid his hands over her bare hips, and lightly kissed the tip of her nose.

After that, he walked away to gather his clothes and get dressed, while she stood there, consumed with guilt. The man plastered on a happy face, but for the second time this week, she had hesitated at an offer—first moving in together, and then running away for a fresh start.

Lilith loved him more than anyone before, that much was certain. So did her hesitation stem from the ghosts of her past, or was there something more to her gut reactions?

After grabbing a few muffins and bagels from the continental breakfast table, Chance, Lilith, and Cohen piled into the stretched town car. This time, awkward silence replaced the angry tension, motivating them to reach their destination as fast as possible. However, driving through downtown York proved more problematic than expected.

Long traffic lights and spontaneous one-way streets weren't the only issues. Pedestrians crossed without a single glance, walking right in front of moving cars with the insane expectation they'd stop. If that weren't frustrating enough, multiple times, vehicles double-parked next to open parking spots, forcing them to wait for oncoming traffic to clear.

By the time they reached Penn State York, Chance had exhausted every iteration of the word *fuck* and dented the dash. A vein throbbed in his forehead, like it was about to rupture. One might argue that Manhattan rush hour was far more challenging, but at least there he knew the rules. Downtown York appeared to be a vortex of pure chaos that even Lilith found infuriating.

The campus consisted of a dozen or so buildings and athletic fields with meticulous landscaping, no different from a million other satellite campuses across the country. In the courtyard of the main administrative building, they spotted a marble mountain lion, which proudly proclaimed it *Home of the Nittany Lions*, whatever the hell that was. Cohen said it had something to do with a mountain overlooking the main campus in State College, yet another original town name.

The Edward M. Elias Science Center was so unassuming, they drove by it twice. The utilitarian block of brick lay hidden among the trees, by far the smallest building they'd seen on the grounds. Paleovirology wasn't a huge field of study, but science in general seemed to be an afterthought here. Not surprising, considering the athletic fields dominated a third of the campus. The ratio clearly stated the school's priorities.

Still, the small building did provide one benefit. Finding Dr. Thomas's office took no time at all. As Lilith's hand rose to knock, the plain wooden door sprang open. She took a quick step back, almost tripping over Chance and Cohen, when a woman's smiling face appeared.

"Good morning!" Thick lashes surrounded warm brown eyes nearly hidden by long bangs. The woman shoved at her chocolate curls infused with golden-blond strands. Judging by the glowing tan of her olive skin, the highlights probably resulted from the sun rather than a box. Although, a tan virologist seemed contradictory. Most labs didn't provide much natural light, so she either spent all her spare time outdoors or regularly visited a tanning salon. Either way, this wasn't how Lilith pictured the country's leading paleovirologist.

"You're the group from New York City?"

Lilith swallowed her shock, nodded, and pulled on a polite smile. "Yes, we are."

"Wonderful. Come on in." The woman ushered them into an office smaller than their hotel room, packed with books and manuscripts. Most of them centered on microbiology, virology, biology, and anatomy, but a few branched out from the science genre into humanities and history. When

Lilith spotted Joseph Campbell's *The Hero with a Thousand Faces,* she couldn't help but smile. It seemed the virologist and her therapist shared a mutual love of mythological archetypes.

As Lilith perused the books, Dr. Rachel Thomas dragged three folding chairs out of a corner and set them up next to her desk with frantic energy. The woman seemed like one of those people who always moved, kind of like Nicci in workout mode. Lilith found the anxiousness exhausting to be around, but she hadn't slept much last night, so her tolerance level was lower than usual.

"Sorry, the space is limited, and I typically only see one student at a time." The nervous smile deepened Dr. Thomas's already prominent dimples.

"No problem, thanks. This is Chance Deveraux, Detective Andrew Cohen, and I'm Lilith Adams."

Dr. Thomas stopped while unfolding the third chair. "Lilith Adams?" She peeked out from beneath thick bangs with an expression of shocked recognition.

How the hell does she know who I am?

"*The* Lilith Adams from the terrorist attacks in Tennessee and New York?"

Lilith's brow furrowed, and her heart skipped a few beats. The Elders had buried the story, making it a mere blip in the general media. Anyone who wanted to dig would find the cover story they fabricated, but it never flashed across the evening news. "How do you…"

The woman's brilliant smile made her pause mid-question. "I recall your name due to the ironic mythological ties—Lilith being Adam's first wife in the Jewish doctrine. I also consult with the FBI on different things. Two agents came to me about scientific anomalies in those two cases. Your name came up a lot."

Panic lit Lilith's brain, like fireworks illuminating the night sky. *Scientific anomalies and my name? Shit.* Lilith felt both Chance and Cohen eyeing her, but chose to ignore them.

"Plus, I am an avid news hound, and even though the case wasn't common knowledge, some stories mentioned you."

"What sort of *anomalies?*" Cohen shifted the focus away from Lilith with an air of casual intrigue. The man excelled at maintaining his poker face. Of course, he had a lifetime among the treacherous Durand to perfect the art.

Rachel swung her warm gaze to him with the same smile of recognition. "Wait. Cohen. Detective Andrew Cohen. You investigated those cases too, right? Isn't your grandfather in the medical field?"

"In a manner of speaking." The muscles around his right eye twitched for an instant. It was the only indication that the topic made him uncomfortable. The question came as quite a shock to Lilith who hadn't realized Farren was in the public eye, but thankfully, Dr. Thomas was still focused on Cohen.

"And to answer your other question, Ms. Adams and I worked together on several cases, including those two, which is what brings us here today. I am rather curious, though. Why would the FBI consult a paleovirologist?"

The woman frowned for the first time. "I'm not sure I'm at liberty to say…" Bit by bit, the expression melted back into her typical smile. "Of course, since you both worked the case, I don't suppose there is any harm in sharing. You are already familiar with everything in the file."

"Correct."

"Paleovirology is a passion project, but I don't earn enough in grants and private contracts to continue my research. I have a doctorate in virology and master's degrees in both microbiology and biology. I provide consultation services to the CDC, other research programs, and occasionally, the Bureau's Philadelphia office."

"Very prudent." Nothing in Cohen's tone or facial expression indicated that he found any of it impressive, but the doctor didn't seem to notice. "I read every report on those cases, and I don't remember seeing your name."

"Hmm. Odd. Two of their agents approached me about six months ago."

Six months…Over a month after they officially closed the case. *Perhaps Cohen really didn't know anything about the evidence's change in custody. Someone is still digging.*

"They brought me files on a body at Phipps Bend." Rachel tapped a pen against her chin, deep in thought, and lowered herself into the worn chair.

Meanwhile, all three of her guests leaned forward, praying she wouldn't say Ashcroft's name.

"Very tall African American…Coffee, I believe. He had rather unusual features, but since I was unable to study the corpse in person, I wasn't much help. Pictures only tell you so much, and the body was badly damaged. As far as I could tell, he suffered from gigantism caused by an over-production of growth hormone. Unlike most cases, Coffee didn't suffer from cardiovascular issues. He was rather healthy…Well, until he died, that is."

Either the woman had a dark sense of humor, or she didn't understand polite conversation. The snort of laughter seemed inappropriate either way.

"On the New York case, they flew me up to inspect a few different bodies. They thought perhaps a virus could explain the eyewitness accounts, but I found nothing unusual about them. Well, except they weren't still buried in caskets."

"How fascinating."

Although the demon sounded genuine, Lilith knew better. They all felt immense relief that this human was minimally involved and couldn't endanger them.

"I must ask. Someone *actually* dug up corpses and staged them to emulate a zombie attack?" Rachel focused on Lilith with a quizzical stare so intense it bordered on uncomfortable.

"Well, you gotta admit. It's an interesting tactic for creating public hysteria. Thankfully, we kept a lid on the situation and apprehended the people responsible before things got out of control." Having repeated the standard issue party-line for months made the remark sound natural.

"Intriguing." The woman waved her arms, dismissing the conversation, and leaned forward on the desk. "Let's talk about what brought you here." Expectant eyes moved from Cohen to Chance to Lilith, while she wore the same joyful smile.

Are normal people this happy all the time? Perhaps secrets made the difference. This woman didn't have to lie to the world about something as simple as her physiology or spend every waking minute pretending to be something else.

Lilith shoved away the spiraling thoughts to focus on the task at hand. "Dr. Gerald Scott recommended we speak to you about an unknown virus we encountered." The woman's lopsided frown caught Lilith's attention. "He met you at the American Society for Virology seminar…You gave a lecture on a virus found in Siberia."

Rachel's eyes widened, and her smile returned, deeply dimpling her cheeks. "Hefty gentleman with bright red hair and a wicked sense of humor?"

Lilith couldn't help but chuckle at the apt description. "One and the same. We brought a live sample and copies of his research. He's only had eight months but believes it's an extinct virus…possibly related to parvovirus B19." As Lilith spoke, she placed the stack of papers and bio-cooler on the doctor's desk.

"Is that so? I recall him as an exceptionally bright man, so I'm excited to see what you've brought me." Dr. Thomas snatched the first file and immediately flipped through the reports. While she read, her free hand fiddled with a coin-shaped charm on her gold necklace.

"Very interesting," she whispered, setting one folder aside and grabbing another. Then she plucked one page out of the stack and ran her finger down it with growing excitement.

"Hmm…Yes. I see the markers he referenced." With that, she swiveled in her chair and attacked a rusting filing cabinet with furious fingers. After a few seconds, she whipped out a slim binder and slammed it down on the table.

Lilith, Chance, and Cohen watched as the human tornado tore through the pages.

Once Dr. Thomas found the object of her search, she placed it side by side with Dr. Scott's report and ran her fingers down each page in unison.

"Yes, yes…Hmm…I think your friend is correct, but I'll need to finish his genome mapping to be sure." She paused and glanced up at the confused trio. "I believe this virus of yours originated in Ancient Greece."

"You can tell that just by…doing whatever *that* is?" Cohen sounded more than a little skeptical, a feeling they all shared.

Rachel tilted her head in thought, grabbed a hair tie from the desk, and tamed her thick tresses into a ponytail. "I compared the segments of RNA Dr. Scott mapped to my completed maps from various archeological digs. He hasn't completed deciphering the RNA strands, but a few unique markers match ones from a few viruses I found in Grecian excavations."

"Please. Enlighten us on how a virus goes extinct and suddenly shows up again." The strong cynicism in Cohen's voice bordered on hostile, not that Lilith blamed him. The woman's conclusion after thirty seconds of scanning letters seemed as believable as a Victorian seance.

However, Dr. Rachel Thomas appeared all too familiar with derisive doubt. The exuberant smile never faltered as she folded her hands over the strewn papers. "In ancient times, people were spread out. Dozens of miles separated neighbors, if they had any at all. Although my field of study is relatively new, insurmountable evidence suggests specific viruses and bacteria sprang up, attacked a household or small community, and then died out or went dormant when it no longer had a host to invade.

"Now, we have excavated tons of ancient sites, revealing things buried a very long time, Detective Cohen. All the microorganisms I discovered have been inactive or mere fragments, but it is not impossible for a hardy, adaptable virus to survive those conditions. It is equally possible that someone uncovered an inactive one and engineered the thing back to life. There would be little way to know the difference, unfortunately."

"Assuming you are right about the origin, how can this information help us?" Lilith at least attempted to hide her continued disbelief for the sake of cooperation.

Dr. Thomas leaned back in her chair, fidgeting with the charm on her necklace again. and considered the question. "Well, if I narrow down an origin site, you could speak with the excavation's lead, assuming the source is a legitimate project. Finding the dig could help you identify subject zero. It's likely someone involved in the project, who either acted as a carrier or transferred it via an artifact. The knowledge may prove fruitful in isolating those infected and tracking transmission. A complete genome map would also help develop a theoretical vaccine, if such a thing proves possible."

"How long will that take? I mean, Dr. Scott worked this thing for more than half a year, and his map is incomplete."

Dr. Thomas glowed with exuberance as she leaned across the desk. "He provided a wonderful head start. The partial sequences, plus my research, might reveal enough common links to pinpoint a place before finishing the full genome. If it came from any of the official excavations in Greece within the past ten years, I'll have an answer in the next day or so."

Lilith nodded but couldn't match the woman's level of excitement. The whole thing seemed like an insanely long shot, but what choice did they have? No other leads existed.

"Can I ask where you found this virus?"

An awkward silence settled over the trio as the woman glanced at each of them in turn.

"Two cases—one deadly, the other not. A few unconfirmed reports also popped up in the Southeast, but I'm afraid we can't share anything more for now." Flat-out refusing to answer Dr. Thomas's question would make her suspicious, but a vague detail or two couldn't hurt.

"Cases in New York City *and* the Southeast?"

Perhaps I spoke too soon. "Well, yes, but both cases originated from the same area down South. We believe the latest victim traveled to New York *after* being infected."

The Lotus Tree

Cohen cleared his throat, drawing Rachel's attention away from Lilith. "We would appreciate anything you can tell us." He pulled a business card out of his navy suit's breast pocket and handed it to her with a political smile containing zero substance. "My number is on the front, and I've written Ms. Adams's cell number on the back…if you find anything."

The brilliant grin emphasized Dr. Thomas's deep dimples again, and she rose to her feet. "I will be in touch."

The woman's manic energy had distracted Lilith from noticing her clothes when they first arrived. Now, the Dr. Who T-shirt and worn jeans seemed an odd choice, especially with high-heeled pumps.

The trio stood, took turns shaking Rachel's hand, and headed for the door.

"One last thing…" Dr. Thomas waited until she had their full attention before continuing. "What does it do? The virus, I mean?"

Lilith and Cohen exchanged a rather significant stare until he gave an almost imperceptible nod. "It varies, but we've seen encephalitis resulting in impulsive and combative behavior. In others, liver failure occurred. But all of them suffered from bone marrow suppression. One case resulted in transient aplastic crisis, which proved lethal. We don't know much more."

"Does it focus on one specific nationality?"

Lilith frowned, considering the question. So far, all the victims were either vampires or Durand, but she couldn't share that information. "I only know specifics on the two cases I'm handling. One was Austrian and the other either Scottish or Irish." Not a lie, just a literal answer.

"Hmm." The doctor stared off into space, deep in thought while fidgeting with her necklace. Then she glanced up, as if just remembering she wasn't alone. "Let me know if you come across another victim. I'd like to study this bug in its home—see the damage, how it replicates, and spreads."

"Of course." The polite smile Lilith wore was just for show. Unless it struck the human population, the woman had zero chance of joining an autopsy. "Thank you again for your time, Dr. Thomas."

"Please, call me Rachel. *Dr. Thomas* is my ex-husband." With that, she disappeared behind her desk, buried in mounds of paperwork.

Once the door clicked closed behind them, they breathed a collective sigh of relief. Then, before Lilith or Chance opened their mouths, Cohen headed them off, anticipating more accusations.

"I had no clue the FBI consulted with that woman. If it's true, it happened *after* they closed the investigation, and I was not involved in the

New York case, except as a victim. Someone in the Bureau is still digging. Probably a rogue agent working off the clock. If they reopened the case, I would have been called in."

"Must be." Chance kept his tone neutral as they walked toward the small lobby. "Can you make a call or two and see who might want to keep digging?"

Lilith caught the split-second expression of shock on Cohen's face. In fact, the calm, professional, and cooperative demeanor Chance displayed surprised her too.

"Yes. Not a problem."

When they reached the front doors, "Eye of the Tiger" erupted from Lilith's pocket. *Nicci.* She slid her finger across the screen as they navigated a tide of students cluttering the sidewalks.

"Hey, Nicci. Any news on that third party?"

"No…"

Lilith sensed the unease and worry filling that one word.

"Worse. An FBI agent showed up here at the precinct, looking for you. I told him you were out of town, but he insisted on waiting."

A frown furrowed Lilith's brow. Perhaps they didn't need Cohen's help to find the rogue. The FBI asking for her was not a common occurrence. Her contract was with the city of New York, not law enforcement in general, and the timing felt eerie. Of course, if it was the rogue and he already had questions for her, they were in deep trouble.

"Did he mention why he's there?"

"He will only talk to you. The man won't even give me his name. He's been sipping coffee from the crap machine in the break room and staring down homicide detectives for the past hour. Can you swing by before you head home? I don't think he's going to give up."

"Well, if the guy's drinking the coffee, he'll be dead before I get there."

Judging by Nicci's snorting laughter, the joke had at least improved her mood.

"And yes, I will stop in."

"Phew, thanks. This guy is giving me the creeps. Hey. So, how did things go?"

"Well, we are all alive and physically unharmed, so I call that a win."

Chance and Cohen both glanced sideways at Lilith as they climbed into the car.

"I'll fill you in when I get back. Kinda on the fence about consulting an outsider on something like this."

"Especially since outsiders are already investigating the evidence from Phipps Bend, Goditha, and New York. Have you told Aaron anything yet?"

A lump froze in Lilith's throat at the thought of having that conversation. "Nope. I want to know what's going on before I ring that bell. Remember, he wants hard proof, or it didn't happen. In the meantime, dig up everything you can on Dr. Rachel Thomas. I need to know how involved she is with the FBI and if she's a potential problem."

"Wait. She's consulting for the Bureau? This is a whole lotta heat. What did she say?"

"Nothing dangerous. She saw the report on Richard Coffee, including pictures, and investigated Isadora's victims, who were already dead. I don't think she held back, but I want to make sure."

"So, do I send my invoice for overtime to Solasta or directly to your uncle?" Nicci chuckled over the crackly line.

"Pretty sure Aaron will veto that. Sorry."

"Eh, it's worth a shot."

Chapter 13 - *Cassie*

The darkness no longer seemed terrifyingly claustrophobic. Cassie grew used to its endless depths behind the blindfold. So much so, she couldn't be certain she still had eyes, much less ones that worked.

When alone in the dark, pain vibrated through her body until it became her only focus. Without the euphoric effects of the fruit, she felt every broken finger, not to mention her shattered elbow. They constantly buzzed with burning electricity.

At one point, someone bandaged her wounds without setting the bones. They wanted to keep her broken but alive. The cult had more in store for her, that much remained certain. After all, they strapped her to a breaking wheel, and the leader hadn't finished his story yet.

For hours, Cassie obsessed over his monologue, combing through each detail, but nothing sounded familiar. She thought back to every case she could recall, looking for some connection, but if one existed, she couldn't see it. The tale fixated on Greek mythology, a subject she knew nothing about. *Too bad John isn't here. The man is a treasure trove of information and loves Ancient Greece.*

Hours, perhaps days later, Cassie realized knowledge didn't matter. Understanding the crucial bit of information that had made these insane people choose her wouldn't help. She wasn't walking away from this.

Although keeping a hostage blindfolded typically increased the possibility of a safe release, an obvious flaw existed in her situation. The leader had revealed his face, not only to her, but to a building full of dancers. The blindfold wasn't to protect their identities, but to further torment her. If she ever left this black pit of suffering, it would be in a body bag. The simple fact resonated in the very marrow of her bones.

The first time the realization came to her, Cassie went into a hysterical panic attack, and each tiny wisp of air burned like fire until she passed out. Now, the knowledge settled over her shoulders, calming her with its cold inevitability. No one would save her or show mercy. All that awaited her was torment and eventually the peace of death, but why? That was the only question continuing to nag at her.

If they merely wanted information, they would have asked questions and answered her silence with broken bones. No. Extracting information wasn't their primary mission. The violent torment embodied a ritual, a preparation for something exceeding anything she could tell them. *How many more bones will they break before they let me die?*

As Cassie pondered her fate, a parade of footsteps overhead signaled the return of her visitors, and she immediately felt conflicted. Her mouth watered for their mystery fruit despite the torture accompanying it.

The desire stemmed from more than pain relief. The heady substance brought an unimaginable escape. With it, she disconnected from her broken body to float freely in the ether above the harm they inflicted. Perhaps if she ate enough, it would pull her spirit from her body forever and release her from this torturous hell.

Then another question sprang to mind.

Why would they give her an escape if she had to suffer for the truth to be extracted? It seemed counter-productive to drug her, natural or not. A dozen ways existed to prevent her from going into shock without feeding her some exotic, mind-altering fruit. Perhaps it was another way to manipulate her, by making her crave the fruit more than anything else. *In time, would I do anything to taste its bliss?* She already knew the answer.

This time, the woman and overweight man didn't precede the group. Starvation and dehydration made her body conserve everything, which left very little waste. Deep in her mind, Cassie knew it signaled her body shutting down, but that was the least of her concerns. These people were organized—cauterizing wounds, giving her enough water and fruit to keep her alive until they accomplished their mission. The possibility of her organs shutting down before they tortured her to death seemed like a remote possibility, no matter how much she wished otherwise.

"Good evening, Cassie."

Vélos Ambrose. That was the name he had used, though he said to call him Art. The detail snapped into sudden clarity. Although knowing his fake name wouldn't save her, it did provide a reference point, something to concentrate on, a focus for her burning hatred.

"How are you feeling this evening?"

Anger surged through her, but she let it pass. Lashing out would only earn her unnecessary pain. "I…" The rough voice escaping her dry throat was unrecognizable to her. For a moment, her head spun, the disconnected sensation returning.

"I'm in a lot of pain." Her mind flashed to the remedy in response to the admission, and she subconsciously licked her lips.

"You want more lotus fruit?"

Cassie imagined an amused grin to match the cruel taunt in his voice.

"Yes." She cried the word with more desperation than intended.

"Well, you'll have to be a good girl." After a whir of movement, his voice purred against her ear and crept down her spine until her stomach turned. "I will finish my tale, and then *you* will tell me one. If I am satisfied, I may let you have some."

The apparatus she was strapped to tilted backward in a sudden motion, causing an instant sensation of falling into a black abyss. When it stopped with her lying flat on her back, she sobbed in relief. Supporting her weight by her wrists and ankles for days, or perhaps weeks, had taken its toll *before* they started breaking bones.

"A little respite, my dear. I want you to focus on this part of Leto's story."

The parade of footsteps retreated like before, followed by the scuffle of chairs and the click of high heels on concrete. Once everyone settled in, Vélos began.

"When I left off, Leto was pregnant with twins…" His voice sounded slightly faint…He had his back to her, addressing the crowd. "A month before her due date, she returned home to her humble abode to find a monster lying in wait. Not a human with no morals—an *actual* monster, an Empusa, to be exact. Do you know what that is, Cassie?"

Without hesitation, she shook her head. When the silence stretched out, she realized that between the unrelenting darkness and the sudden position change, she couldn't tell if she had truly moved at all. "No."

"I am not surprised. Most think of them as archaic villains, existing only in old myths. Empusa was a stunning demi-goddess born from Hecate and Mormo. She used her wild beauty to seduce handsome, young men traveling the roads into a deep sleep. Once paralyzed, she would drink their blood and tear their flesh, devouring every piece of them.

"As the world grew, guarding Hecate's roads became too much for her to handle alone, so she birthed an entire species, known as the Empusae, to descend upon wayward travelers."

Something in his tone seemed expectant, as if waiting for either questions or recognition. Although she was terrified of saying the wrong thing, saying nothing would be worse.

"Like vampires?" Her voice trembled with fear, and blood pounded in her ears. She waited for his response and braced for more pain.

"Yes." The man's voice brightened with a tinge of excitement.

Relief flooded Cassie's body until it became almost palpable.

"They *are* like vampires. Hard to kill, drink blood..."

He paused, and she anxiously strained to hear what was happening.

His footsteps—she had become adept at separating the sounds of different shoes—moved closer. He strolled at a casual pace until his hand brushed her cheek. The sudden sensation sent alarm bells off in her head. Every time he touched her, something violent followed. The panic made her pant and gasp for each breath.

"Calm yourself." His fingertips stroked her face again before dipping into her brunette curls. "I want to ask you a question. Have you seen one, Cassie?"

She inhaled steadily, willing the air into her chest, and shook her head. "No, I haven't."

The man's fingers gripped her jaw, and his hot breath rushed over her cheek. "Are you sure?"

Tears trailed from the corner of her eyes as she warred with herself. What was she supposed to say? What would make him return to his damn seat? What would make him not hurt her? "I'm not sure. Maybe?"

"Acceptable." He patted her cheek with a rough slap before padding back to his folding chair. "The Empusa who came for Leto was none other than the wife of her former employer and lover. The monster discovered her husband's secret and came to destroy his bastard progeny, just as Hera tried to do. Somehow, by the blessings of the gods, Leto escaped and made it to a hospital. She delivered two healthy twins that very night, and when she gazed into each one's eyes, their names appeared to her in a vision. Artemis and Apollo."

Chapter 14

Lilith had no idea what this agent wanted, but ensuring the smallest audience seemed a worthy precaution. Odds were good it concerned something she'd rather not discuss with Cohen present. She didn't consider it a matter of trust, but prudence. Andrew didn't share every detail of his world, so why should she? They were a far cry from full disclosure.

At first, Chance insisted on going with her, but Cohen refused to drive the "enormous monstrosity" through the city. Lilith pointed out he owned the stupid thing, but he countered with the fact they fired his driver, which was true.

So, in a newfound attempt to be diplomatic, Chance agreed to escort the demon to his hotel and catch a cab back to the precinct. Of course, the Waldorf Astoria was in downtown Manhattan, and with Friday evening traffic, it'd be hours before they escaped the gridlock. In other words, she had to face the music without him.

Lilith stared up at the 19th Precinct with mixed emotions. The gorgeous five-story brick building, with stone accents from the early 1900s, embodied everything she loved about New York City. Among the modern, sleek skyscrapers, vestiges of architectural beauty and history were still revered.

The front entrance was her favorite part, with its vibrant blue doors, gray stone archway, and oversized globe sconces. However, the memories the place conjured haunted her mind, all of which featured her late partner, Detective Felipe Alvarez.

After a cleansing breath, she headed inside and marched up the stairs with purpose. Once she exchanged quick pleasantries with young Detective Boyd and a few others, she made her way to a small glass-enclosed office. Being the liaison for Solasta Laboratories had *minor* privileges. Nicci's desk and three chairs barely fit in the stuffy room.

"How was the ride back?" The petite Italian peeked over the pile of folders dominating her cluttered desk.

"Well, I sat up front with Chance and kept the divider up. Cohen didn't care for the arrangement, but it was quiet. So, where is this agent? Please tell me the coffee killed him and I can go home. I need a nap or perhaps a mild coma."

Nicci chortled and pushed back her chair to stand. "Either that or he got lost on the way to the boy's…" The words trailed away as the smile slid off her face.

"Lilith."

The gruff voice behind her hit like a bolt of lightning. A cold, familiar dread knotted in her stomach, and she turned on her heel despite her entire body screaming for her not to.

"What the fuck are you doing here?" Her heart raced like a frightened rabbit, a cascading flood of memories igniting her fight-or-flight instinct.

Before she decided, the man lunged forward. In the blink of an eye, he grabbed her by the collar and slammed her into the floor, knocking the air from her lungs. Panic seared down her spine as his hand tightened around her throat, reigniting a hundred horrible memories that had occurred nearly a decade before Duncan's disappearance.

"Where the fuck is she?"

He screamed the question in her face, but she couldn't focus on anything but the ceaseless flashbacks and crippling fear. *No. Not again.*

"Whoa!" Nicci shouted.

Dozens of chairs scraped the floor before feet slammed across the hardwood, rushing forward with the thunderous clicks of cocking guns.

"Where is she? Tell me now, dammit!"

The angry words rattled in Lilith's skull, and her air-starved lungs burned.

Focus! She closed her eyes and forced the memories away. *I'm not a helpless college co-ed anymore. I can handle this. This isn't Ashcroft or Peisinoe. He's just a human man. He only has power over me if I allow it.*

As her eyes snapped open, she shot her arms straight up, turning with as much force as possible while her knee struck his inner thigh. The leverage broke his grip, and the surrounding cops immediately descended to snatch him away.

Lilith gulped down air while half a dozen police officers wrestled her attacker into handcuffs. After a few fleeting seconds, the bastard gave up and cooperated, but his dark eyes remained fixed on her.

"Where do you want him?" Boyd hauled him to his feet with a rough yank on his cuffs.

"My office. Secure him to the chair," Nicci growled, stuffing her gun back into the holster.

The officers forced the thick man forward with an elbow to the back and shoved him into a seat. Once they cuffed the assailant to the armrests, Nicci pushed them out of the office.

"Are you sure? I can stay." The young detective kept his eyes locked on the burly man, his chest puffing up with professional pride.

"Out!" Nicci slammed the door and turned her attention to Lilith. "You okay?"

After a painful swallow, Lilith nodded, slowly stood, and made her way over to Nicci, putting the desk between her and the ghost from her past.

"What the hell?" Nicci paced behind her desk and shook her hands, allowing the adrenaline to wear off. "So, I'm assuming you two know each other?"

The broad man flashed a wolfish smile that made him appear far younger, like the one she remembered, which made her less at ease. "You could say that."

While attempting to calm her nerves, Lilith took a long look at her attacker. The years hadn't been kind to him. Fine lines surrounded his dark beady eyes, his full cheeks displayed the ruddy skin of an alcoholic, and grays speckled his curly black hair, which he kept short. The stubble covering his face seemed uncharacteristic, considering his OCD nature. In fact, this disheveled and rattled version barely resembled the man she remembered, which allowed her to reclaim some of her confidence.

"Detective Nicci DeLuca, meet David Boston." She stared him down with an iron will that refused to bend. He might have caught her by surprise, but she would never let him have the upper hand again.

"That's *Special Agent* David Boston." The man's eyes narrowed with an amused glint, and his voice held malicious tones, both of which betrayed his true nature. He wasn't bothering to hide his inner monster.

Lilith snorted in contempt. "No way you passed the psych profile. Did you bribe your way in, or did Daddy do that for you too?"

The amusement disappeared. He jerked at the cuffs, rattling the chair, but she didn't flinch. Instead, Lilith stood stone-still, watching him with nothing but indifference while she rubbed her sore neck.

"Okay. I'm guessing your history doesn't involve rainbows and unicorns. So, *Special Agent*, you thought you could march in here and attack *my* partner in the middle of *my* precinct?"

"Partner?" His black eyebrows shot up in genuine shock.

"Yes, partner. You knew enough to find me here, so why the hell are you surprised?"

David's eyes hardened as Lilith leaned against the desk. Judging by the microexpressions of contempt and fear flickering across his face, women in positions of power made him uncomfortable, which didn't surprise her. They were much harder to manipulate.

"Still as infuriating as ever. You are only a forensic consultant, and as I remember things, you aren't the *partner* type. Doesn't matter. I'm here on business."

"Oh? Is *that* why you jumped me as soon as I walked in the door, like a lowlife thug?" Lilith folded her arms across her chest as her jaw clenched tight. Being this close to the man who had haunted her for years took a great deal of emotional fortitude, and she wasn't sure how much more she had left.

A ripple of tension traveled down his right arm, which ended in a tight fist. "Yes." Then he inhaled deeply and slowly released it along with his pent-up anger. Afterward, he looked exhausted, and Lilith spotted the bloodshot sclera, dark circles under his eyes, and coffee stains on his baby blue tie. "I didn't intend...I saw you and lost control. I'm...sorry. Can we talk in private?"

Lilith gathered her anger and wrapped it around herself like a security blanket to keep from rattling apart at the seams. Recent events had left her in no shape to deal with this part of her past. Besides, she had buried those memories long ago and never thought she'd face them again. That was the agreement, after all.

"Yeah...I don't think so."

The man shrugged as if he expected the refusal. "Look. I shouldn't have jumped you. I'm not myself right now, and things with us...I suppose I could have handled them better."

"*Better*? Seriously? Understatement of the damn century."

The man nodded with a weary sigh, his eyes falling to the stained carpet. Flickers of grief and guilt appeared in his features, but his black eyes held no emotion. They remained glassy and lifeless, like the eyes of a shark. "My partner and I were on the Phipps Bend case."

Dread blossomed anew in Lilith's chest when his eyes lifted with a subtle righteous glint.

Of all the possible enemies...

"Wait." A memory popped into her mind, a recent one. Cohen mentioned the agents he had worked with, and she damn sure would have remembered David's name coming up in the conversation. "The FBI didn't assign *you* to the case. It was..." She fought to conjure the names but came up empty.

"Gorman and Hersch. They worked with a local detective—Cannon, Conan, or something."

"Cohen. So, how are you and your partner involved?"

"I attended the regional debriefing when they gave their final report, if you can call it that. Nothing but a scrubbed mess of total shit. Then your name came up...Well, I couldn't let them shove everything under the rug."

A snort of derision interrupted him.

"Ironic, coming from you. Isn't that your MO, or rather your dad's?"

His eyes honed in on Lilith with open hostility. "Fuck you. You're involved in some weird shit. You always have been." His eyes narrowed to points, and he leaned forward. "There's just something...not right about you. I saw it back in L.A., and I see it now. You don't look like you've aged a fucking day. You act like a person, but something's missing, wrong."

As much as she wished they didn't, the words cut deep, wounding her already fragile sense of self. On some level, Lilith still believed she was marked, cursed as an angel of death, doomed to watch the ones she loved die around her, and his words reinforced that belief.

Somehow, she managed to keep her eyes dry and focus the pain into a rage that ricocheted through every nerve. Lilith didn't realize she was moving forward, with her hand balled into a fist, until Nicci touched her shoulder and broke the spell.

"Do you have a point, or do I have to guess?" At first blush, Nicci didn't appear intimidating at five feet tall, but she was more than capable of taking down a man David's size. The issue was conveying that strength to intimidate people.

Jenny Allen

With David having no first-hand knowledge, Lilith wasn't surprised the man didn't take the petite detective seriously.

He swung his malicious gaze to Nicci, offended by the intrusion. "My partner and I were investigating Phipps Bend off the books. Then this case came in from New York City, with her damn name again." His focus returned to Lilith. "Who are you protecting?"

After shoving her anger aside, Lilith tried to formulate a response. *Come on. Do what you're best at—half-truths.*

"I'm a prominent forensic investigator with Major Crimes. Of course, my name is on the case files. It's also none of your business since you're conducting an *illegal* investigation. Are you here to question my involvement in those cases, or are you looking for something else?"

The man leveled her with a hostile stare, and an awkward silence settled over the room. For a moment, Lilith thought he'd refuse to answer out of sheer spite.

"Six months ago, my partner, Special Agent Cassandra Cappalletty, disappeared." He didn't verbalize the accompanying accusation, but his tone made it obvious.

"And you think I had something to do with that."

"Did you?"

All her emotions disappeared, leaving her face an impassive mask of neutrality, and she leaned over the desk. At least Cohen had taught her one useful trick. "This is the first I've heard of *you* or *your partner*. I haven't thought about you since college, and I don't plan to start now. I don't care about your problem. I had no hand in it, nor would I. Dig all you want. You won't find anything. I have *nothing* to hide."

The brief glimpse of fear and hesitation on his face brought a sense of exhilaration, but it didn't last. David shifted in his chair, reclaiming his confidence, and the malicious glint returned to his shark-like eyes. "I think you're into some scary shit posing as *terrorist attacks*. Cassie's disappearance has *something* to do with you. I know it in my damn bones."

"Why? Because then you can paint me as the villain instead of the victim? Because then you'll feel less like a monster? Go fuck yourself, David. Detective Boyd! Get him out of here!" Lilith gripped the desktop, unsure whether her body wanted to run and hide or throttle the asshole, though the last option seemed more appealing and cathartic.

The young detective burst through the door with two officers flanking him.

"You know something! Either you're behind her kidnapping or you know who is!" As soon as they released the handcuffs, the agent surged forward, knocking them off-balance. Before anyone could react, he hammered his fists on the desk, making it creak with the force.

Somehow, his violent behavior brought a confident calm over Lilith this time. Although it seemed counterintuitive, this version of David Boston was all too familiar. Lilith leaned closer, her face inches from his, and locked onto his malevolent stare.

"You are in the middle of *my* police station. I could have you charged with assault and resisting arrest. I'm sure that would look impressive in your file. Perhaps I'll call your supervisor too, fill him in on this tirade—assaulting multiple members of local law enforcement, obvious day drinking, and illegal investigations. In case you forgot, the FBI frowns on those activities. Now get the hell out here, *Special Agent* Boston."

The cops wrangled him back into handcuffs, and the defiance leaked from his ruddy face. The entire time, his lifeless dark eyes stayed glued to hers, but his expression softened into one of desperation.

"Cassie is a good person. Better than anyone. I just want to find her. If you didn't have anything to do with her disappearance, help me. Please."

"Six months is a long time. Either she saw the real you and ran, or you're looking for a corpse. I can only help you with one of those things. If I stumble across something, I'll send you a postcard. Go home!"

The vulnerable guise evaporated like smoke, and his lip curled, revealing a sharp grin, which shook Lilith's resolve. "Oh, I'm not going anywhere. I'll be seeing you, *Lily*."

"Not if I have anything to say about it, pal." Boyd shoved him through the door, *accidentally* slamming his broad shoulder into the frame. "Oh, man. Sorry. Such narrow doorways in these old buildings."

"Take him to the drunk tank and let him sleep it off." Nicci barked the order while continuing to pace back and forth.

"Yes, ma'am."

"Yes, *Detective*," Nicci corrected the youngster, out of habit.

"Yes, of course, Detective."

As soon as they escorted David through the bullpen and into the elevator, Lilith slammed her shaking fists on the desk with a scream. Her wide-eyed partner came to a halt, inched around the room, and pushed the door closed.

"Who in the holy hell was that?"

"Someone from college. Things…didn't end well." Lilith sank into the seat, every inch of her body trembling with a hundred old emotions. David's reappearance was the last thing her damaged psyche needed.

"Uh, yeah. I kinda gathered as much. How do you know him, *exactly*?"

"It's a long story."

With a dramatic gesture, her partner slid into a chair and propped her feet on the desk, fixing Lilith with an expectant stare.

"It's personal."

"Correction. It *was* personal. The man showed up at the station, attacked you in front of witnesses, and accused you of kidnapping a federal agent. This goes beyond embarrassing stories from your past. I need to know what is going on."

The woman had no intention of letting it go, and Lilith was far too tired for a futile argument. Besides, Nicci had become one of her closest friends after the medical center, and she was the perfect person to confide in. As a detective, she could listen to the story and stay objective, while Gloria would be cloyingly sympathetic and Chance would fly off the handle.

"You're almost as stubborn as I am."

Nicci merely nodded in absolute agreement.

"Look. I've never told anyone about this. Any of it. *No one.*"

"I won't spill the details. Scout's honor." The tiny Italian held up three fingers in an honest-to-God Girl Scout sign.

"I'm only telling you because you're right. David's obsessive and violent nature is an issue." Lilith took a deep breath to organize her chaotic thoughts and rubbed her shaking hands together. After nearly a decade, she was finally going to release the ghost of her past. The very thought made her nauseous.

The image of her father confessing in that Knoxville hotel room suddenly flashed into her mind. He'd held onto his demons for six hundred years, with only his brother sharing that burden. She couldn't imagine caging that much torment in her mind for that long and staying sane.

When the silence went on for too long, Nicci cleared her throat, bringing Lilith back to reality.

"Sorry…In my sophomore year at UCLA, I took a law enforcement class with David. The professor assigned us as partners for a few projects, and we hit it off. Over summer break…we started dating, something new for me. Until him, I never made time for boys. I didn't see the point, being what I am."

Nicci's eyebrows rose sky-high. "*That* David? The one who just left this office?"

Lilith shrugged, unable to offer a convincing defense. "He was charming when he wanted to be…and a clean-cut looker back then. Moving on. During Christmas break, he asked me to move in with him. Thanks to his dad, he had his own apartment, and I was in love."

Lilith shook her head, her jaw set tight. She hated associating the word with *him* and hated herself for having been so naïve.

"I *thought* I was in love. I had no clue what the word meant when I was nineteen. Honestly, I didn't understand what love really was until Chance. Anyway, I didn't think twice about moving in, and everything was wonderful for the first few months. The man leaned toward stringent on the cleanliness scale and organized with enthusiasm, but things worked smoothly."

"Call it a wild guess, but…they didn't stay smooth, did they?"

A sardonic chuckle escaped Lilith's throat. "Yeah, *definitely* not. We went to a party during Spring Break, a typical frat kegger. The rowdy testosterone-drenched crowd already made me uneasy, but a girl he knew started laying it on thick after we arrived. She openly flirted with him right in front of me, so I asked him to get us some drinks.

"The chick followed him, and while he got in line, she sat in the kitchen chair right next to him. I watched from across the room as she ran her bare foot up the inside of his leg, all the way up. The asshole actually turned and grinned at her."

Lilith's fist tightened as an old anger coursed through her.

"I didn't handle things well. I stormed across the room, shoved her out of the chair, and started screaming. The girl hopped up and slapped me, but David pulled me back before I could return fire. Then I went off on him for flirting with her."

"Rightfully so…"

"Yeah, well…I wish that was the end of the story, but it's only the beginning."

Her cheeks burned, and she stared down at her hands, but after a deep breath, Lilith continued.

"David dragged me outside, yelling about how I embarrassed him. I was *nothing but a psycho bitch imaging shit*—his words. Once we got to the car…"

She paused again to clear the emotional lump from her throat. *You can do this.*

"He started hitting me." Her gaze fell to the floor, ashamed to admit her weakness. "Just a few slaps, but his face...I saw something dark there, and it scared the shit out of me. I should have gotten out of the car, ran away, and never looked back, but I didn't." Tears threatened to spill as she thought about the consequences of that fateful decision, but she held them at bay.

"Jesus, Lil."

"When we got home, I figured the fight was over. I chalked it up to a bad night of high tension and alcohol, but he wasn't finished. After he clocked me, leaving a nice shiner, he convinced me I was paranoid. He said he never even looked at her. According to him, I was losing my mind, riddled with insecurities that made me overly jealous, and seeing what I wanted to see. I was young and stupid with nowhere else to go, so..."

"You stayed?" The sheer disbelief in Nicci's voice only deepened Lilith's sense of shame.

"Worse. I believed him."

"But...how? You knew what happened, and you could have come home or moved back to the dorms."

"Coming home wasn't an option. My father enforced a strict rule about living with humans—never do it. I never even told him we were *dating*. By the time things went wrong, I was too ashamed to tell Gregor. Hell, I couldn't even tell my friends at college. None of them liked David much, and I didn't want to hear the endless rounds of *I told you so*. So...I convinced myself that I overreacted and stayed.

"The next six months were like a damn rollercoaster. Either he'd be overly sweet, bringing home flowers and gifts, or he'd be a demon, taking his frustrations out on me verbally and physically. I constantly walked on eggshells, trying to keep him in a good mood by being perfect, but the word didn't exist to him.

"Nothing I did was ever good enough. If I bought sexy dresses and makeup to impress him, I was a cheating whore. If I wore jeans and a T-shirt, then I was letting myself go and he deserved more effort. When I realized that nothing I did helped, I spent more and more time in the Powell Library. Home felt more like a war zone than a sanctuary." Her hands started to shake again as the memories she had tried to bury roared to life in her head.

Keep going. It's important.

"Then one night in October, while leaving the library, I spotted David's car in a vacant lot across the street. Against my better judgment, I walked past my bus stop and crossed the road. I had to be wrong. He had no reason to be at the Astronomy Building, but as I got closer, I realized it *was* his car. No one else in L.A. had a Philadelphia Eagles license plate frame."

"So, what did you do?"

"I stood there for a moment, paralyzed by indecision, but then the passenger door swung open, and a woman I didn't recognize scrambled out, shrieking. After a single step, her platform heel went sideways, twisting her ankle, and she crashed to the pavement. I ducked down, just out of sight, while the woman continued to scream for help. Her shaking hands tried to piece together her ripped shirt while mascara ran down her cheeks. Then I noticed her skin-tight skirt, shoved up around her hips, and the torn panty-hose.

"That's when I heard David yelling from inside the car. He called her a teasing whore and told her she was practice for her roommate…I was so sick to my stomach that I clamped my hand over my mouth to keep from puking."

"Holy shit!" Nicci mimicked the same motion, her skin paling.

"Then the poor thing saw me huddled by the trunk. She cried out and begged me to help her, but I couldn't move. When the driver's door opened, I bolted as fast as I could, but it didn't matter. The only thing David ever earned on his own was a UCLA track scholarship. When he caught me…"

Lilith stared at her hands for a moment, vivid and violent memories replaying in her head.

"Someone must have called campus security because I remember them pulling him off me. I only avoided a mandatory ambulance ride by calling Proteus, our medical facility on the West Coast."

Nicci gasped, but Lilith kept going. If she stopped now, she wouldn't get through the rest of the story.

"When I got out a week later, the police kept me in protective custody, but David's dad is a real estate mogul with his hands in a lot of corrupt pies. The woman he raped that night developed amnesia about the same time someone paid off her student loans. The bastard tried to pay me off too, but I didn't want money. I only wanted his son *far* away from me. The charges disappeared, and David transferred to Temple University in Philadelphia. I moved back into the dorm and haven't seen him since."

"Holy crap, Lil. You never told your dad?"

Lilith nodded, sending tears streaking down her cheeks while the horrible memories washed over her like acid rain. "I never told anyone until now."

An expression of realization slowly crossed her partner's face. "That's why you freaked out when Chance asked you to move in, huh?"

"A big part of the reason. I've lived alone ever since. Hell, Chance is the first man I've let sleep in my bed. I mean, he is *not* David. Chance would *never* hurt me, but old fears are hard to shake, especially after Peisinoe."

Nicci released a long sigh. "Yeah, I understand. I've never lived with anyone. I've been with Alicia for almost three years now, and I love her, but I like my private space and alone time." She let the silence stretch out for a moment before broaching the most important topic. "So, what are we going to do about Special Agent Boston? We can't have him digging around."

When Lilith glanced up, deep in thought, she realized the door wasn't completely closed, and a shadow stood behind the blinds. Her heart stopped, and she replayed the whole conversation in her mind. *Did I say anything incriminating? I don't think so...except for the "living with humans" part. Crap.*

Before she could move, a hand shoved the door open, and Chance's enraged face stared back at her. Pure wrath rolled off his body in nearly visible waves, making her muscles clench in fear. This was so much worse than a random cop overhearing their odd conversation. Lilith wanted to say something, but the lump of tears in her throat prevented her from speaking, even if she knew what to say.

"Where is he?" The deep growl held so much venom, it didn't sound like his voice anymore.

Nicci hopped out of her seat with a jovial shrug. "Locked up in the drunk tank for the night. You can't beat him up until morning." The little Italian grinned and patted Chance on the shoulder without any hesitation, a fearless gesture. Then Nicci wrapped her arms around Lilith and squeezed. "I'm always here if you need to talk, partner, but I think I should give you guys a minute alone."

"Thanks, Nicci."

"And you..." The detective rounded on Chance, pointing a finger at his chest. "Don't fly off the handle like some puffed-up white knight. Listen and be gentle." Once he nodded, she disappeared into the bullpen.

As soon as the door closed, the anger leaked from his skin. "You should have told him, *cherie.*"

Lilith stared at the desk, unable to meet his eyes. "How much did you hear?"

"Enough." A finger curled under her chin and lifted until her eyes met his. "You should have told Gregor, and you should have told me when I asked you to move in."

"You knew my father better than anyone. Telling him would have been the worst thing, more than I even realized at the time. Gregor would have killed him, a real estate mogul's human son. This isn't fifteenth-century Scotland. The ordeal would have ended in disaster. Thank God I was too embarrassed to say anything." Lilith managed a small lopsided smile and thought about the second part of his statement. "And I didn't tell you because…" When she paused, he filled in the gap.

"You don't trust me."

The ridiculous comment instantly caught her attention. "What? No. Why the hell would you think that?"

Chance turned to lean against the desk and stare at the door, avoiding her gaze. "Peisinoe…"

"That wasn't your fault, and she's dead."

"…and your father and I are not that different, *mon cherie*. We protect the people we love."

Lilith frowned at the unbalanced comparison. "What my father did was *not* protection. It was vengeance, which resulted in countless more deaths. You can't protect me from things that already happened. Besides, that is *not* the reason I didn't tell you."

When he still wouldn't look at her, Lilith moved to stand right in front of him.

"These are *my* demons, not yours. I never shared the story with anyone because I thought saying the words out loud would…make them more real, and I was ashamed of being so stupid. Plus, I want things to be uniquely *us* and move at a comfortable pace without the past influencing our decisions. I needed a little more time to let those jitters go."

The stiff posture melted a bit, and he glanced up at her. "I understand. You aren't the only one with demons, but him showing up here—"

"Believe me, I never expected to lay eyes on him again. His father promised me."

Chance reached out, lacing his fingers between hers as he squarely met her gaze. "So, what do we do about him?"

"We can't kill him." She stared him down defiantly. "I mean it. The man is a piece of shit who deserves some karma, but his dad is still a big wig, and David's a federal agent now. Maybe if we find his partner, he'll walk away and leave us alone."

"There is no *maybe*. He *will*. One way or another." With a warning glare from Lilith, Chance held up his hands. "You said I can't kill him. A hell of a lot can happen between nothing and killing someone. Besides, he deserves worse than death."

Warning bells went off in her head when she recognized the same bitter need for vengeance she'd seen on her father's face. Perhaps his earlier comparison wasn't far off. With a sudden desire to deescalate the situation, Lilith changed the subject.

"Wait. How are you here? I thought you were driving Cohen to the hotel."

In the blink of an eye, the blood-thirsty rage dissipated, replaced by a familiar impish grin. "Well, we hit gridlock a few blocks away. I *convinced* him to drive the rest of the way himself." The warm yet mischievous smile ebbed away the longer Chance stared at her. "Can I ask you something?"

"Of course."

"If I hadn't overheard all this, would you have ever told me?"

Her first instinct was to shout *Yes, of course*. Instead, she tried to formulate an honest answer. He deserved no less than the complete truth.

"I'd like to think I would have told you eventually, but I don't know. It's a dark part of my past that I'm ashamed of, and *you* are my future. Not everything buried needs to be dragged into the light."

"I appreciate your honesty, and I understand. I haven't told you much about my past for the same reasons. Still…no one should ever go through what you did, Lily. Humans are quick to villainize anything different, but they are just as capable of atrocities. I'm sorry you experienced any of it, especially alone with no one to turn to."

Tears welled in her eyes but not from bad memories. Releasing her death grip on that secret had left her wide open and emotionally raw. "It was a long time ago." With a heavy sigh, she slipped her arms around him, and he hugged her close, enveloping her in safety and rubbing her back.

"Thinking that someone hurt you like that…made you feel…" His jaw clenched so tight he couldn't finish the sentence. After a moment, he sighed heavily. "I just wish I'd known. I could have…I don't know."

The helplessness in his voice struck a chord, and she wanted to take his guilt away, so she leaned up and kissed him.

"Don't start thinking that way. You didn't know. It was *my* problem, and I dealt with it. It's in the past."

Chance tilted his head with a raised eyebrow. "But it's not. The man is right here, right now, where he doesn't belong." After a second, he reined in his anger again and tried to approach the problem logically. "If we help him, we need someone who appears neutral, with our best interests in mind. He is not to have any further contact with you."

"Okay." Although she rarely liked taking orders, this one she'd happily follow. "But who? It has to be someone we trust to be discreet."

Chance stared at her for so long, she didn't think he'd answer. "What about Tim? He has a P.I. license."

"True. Without any solid leads in our jurisdiction, we can't officially help, but if we offer him a gifted private investigator…"

"I'll call him."

"Woah. The man is your BFF. I don't want you calling in favors to ensure Agent Boston's untimely demise."

The crooked grin on his face was a definite admission of guilt. "All right, I give you my solemn word, but it should come from me. I want you as far away from this thing as possible. I make no promises if I bump into the bastard, though."

"Beyond not killing him?"

With a reluctant sigh, he finally nodded. "I already promised I wouldn't kill him, *cherie*. You're right. His death would cause too many complications. In other news, Charlie called. My package from Goditha arrived at your apartment."

Chance took Lilith's confused expression as reason enough to clarify.

"I knew we were going out of town, and your place has security who can sign for packages. Wouldn't want one of the homeless guys stealing it for building materials."

"Premium boxes are a hot ticket item. Makes sense." She struggled to keep a straight face. "Don't want to come home to a shanty village."

"So, dinner and then stay at your place tonight?" Although he tried very hard to sound normal, his anger lingered in his fine muscle movements. After she nodded, a sudden private smile lit his face with genuine happiness. "So, I'm really the only one you allowed in your bedroom?"

Her cheeks burned hot, and her eyes darted away for a moment. "Yeah, well…" All the smart-ass comebacks evaded her, and when she met his gaze, a newfound bravery emerged. "You make me feel safe enough to be vulnerable, something I never thought possible. Once we wrap up this case, let's do it. I love you, and I don't need my own apartment."

"Seriously? You're moving in?" His hazel eyes widened with shock, his excitement hidden behind guarded caution.

"Yeah. Seriously."

His eyes fell for a moment, as if debating something while maintaining a calm and collected façade. "You don't have anything to prove to me, *mon cherie*. I can wait if you aren't ready."

After taking a step closer, Lilith slid her arms around his neck and angled her head to look him in the eye. "Are you trying to talk me out of this?"

"No, I just—"

"I understand, but I wouldn't say yes if I wasn't ready. Seeing David reminded me how lucky I am. You've seen me at my absolute worst and love me even more for it. Hell, you've sensed every horrible emotion I've dealt with for the past eight months and kept it secret because you didn't want to make me uncomfortable."

"True…" After another pause for an internal argument, he finally met her eyes and swept a stray curl from her cheek. "You are a fierce woman, Lily, one of the many things I love about you. I sensed what you were going through and desperately wanted to help. However, I was also aware of how hard you tried to keep it hidden, and I didn't want to take that strength away from you. Sharing what you're going through should be your decision."

Tears misted her eyes, and she kissed him tenderly for a moment. "I'll never understand what I did to deserve you."

A small chuckle rumbled from his throat. "See, the thing is…I feel the same way." The excitement he'd been holding back erupted to the surface, and he squeezed her tight, lifting her off the ground. "You've made me a happy man, *cherie*."

"Well, we still need to crack this case and shake Agent Boston. Neither of those seem like simple tasks."

"We'll figure it out. We always do." His lips brushed hers in a tender yet teasing touch before he whispered in a deep voice, "Are you sure I can't kill him?"

The unexpected question made her laugh, despite his somewhat serious tone. "Trust me, if it wouldn't ruin our lives, I'd give you a green light, Batman, but we'll have to find another way."

"Okay, but first, food. I'm ravenous." A slow grin curled his lips, his eyes clearly displaying a different sort of hunger.

"You, sir, are trouble." After stealing a quick kiss, she reached for the door handle. "Let's pick up something to eat on the way."

"How about greasy fast food?" Chance followed her through the sea of cluttered office desks with a slight spring in his step.

"Hey, guys!" Nicci's Italian-accented voice boomed from the far side of the room. When they glanced over, she jogged around the furniture to join them. "Can I ride down with you?"

The ancient elevator moved at a frustratingly slow speed, but saving time wasn't her motivation. That much was clear by her expression.

"Yeah, Sure."

Once the doors closed and the behemoth groaned into motion, Nicci turned around to face them. "I did some digging into Doctor Thomas, like you asked."

An all-too-familiar sense of impending doom crept up Lilith's spine. If her partner wanted privacy… "You found something?"

"No. The opposite. She attended the University of Tennessee on a full scholarship, volunteered in Africa when the Ebola virus hit a few years back, and she coaches a woman's volleyball team. She's basically a saint."

"Okay…"

"*But*…all her juvenile records are sealed tighter than a nun's ass. Accessing anything prior to the age of eighteen will require some major illegal hacking. On top of that, no birth certificate, no adoption records, no social security number before she turned eighteen, nothing. It's almost like she didn't exist before college. I don't know. I mean, there are legitimate reasons this could happen—a fire at the records office, a small town that still uses a paper system, but—"

"Your gut says otherwise."

After a moment, Nicci nodded, her long ponytail bobbing with the motion. "Something's not right. I'm gonna keep digging and try to unlock those juvey files."

"Honestly, I hope you're wrong. I think Agent Boston and his partner are the FBI agents who approached her about Phipps Bend. She only had limited access to the peripheral, non-crucial parts of the cases, probably the only things he could get unofficially."

"Yeah, he does *not* need to be swaying people toward his cause. He thinks there's something wrong with you. The man admitted as much."

Lilith felt the tremor run down Chance's arm seconds before his hand balled into a fist.

"They were just words. The man was lashing out with blind insults. He doesn't know anything."

"Let's hope not." Nicci grimaced as the elevator stammered to a stop, and the doors opened on the bustling police lobby.

Agent Boston was dangerous in far too many ways. Hopefully, Tim could find some leverage to get him out of her life again, this time forever.

Chapter 15

Morning light filtered through the blinds, illuminating the floating dust like glitter. Lilith stretched in bed and watched them drift weightlessly, envious of their carefree nature. Things seemed bleak *before* Agent Boston's sudden appearance, and now…Her arm hit empty space, but before the frown formed, the whir of the Keurig accompanied the alluring scent of coffee, which seeped into the room.

She padded blearily into the kitchen.

Chance poured a teaspoon of sugar into a mug that read: "Damn right I shot first." A penchant for quirky Star Wars memorabilia was one of many things they shared.

"I made a fresh cup for you and picked up the sweet Italian creamer you love." He didn't bother turning around as he spoke.

"Guess I won't be sneaking up on you, huh?" Lilith tiptoed up behind him and pressed a kiss against his shoulder before reaching for the fridge.

When he turned toward her, he lowered his mug, an impish grin plastered on his face. "Trust me, I don't need Cohen's blood to know when you're around. You walk on your heels and favor your right leg."

"Hmm, almost sounds like an insult." Lilith snagged the still-steaming coffee and glanced sleepy-eyed at the clock. "Eight? How long have you been awake?" Once she poured enough creamer into her mug to turn her coffee a milky tan, she added a dash more.

"Since four thirty. Couldn't sleep." Chance paused for a moment with a distant stare, then shook it off. "I kept thinking about the computer from Goditha, so I decided to start working on it."

Apparently, he didn't want to discuss the true reason for his insomnia, although she could probably guess. Instead of digging in her heels, Lilith respected his choice and stayed on topic.

"Any luck?"

After releasing a ragged sigh, he raked his fingers through his tousled hair. "I handled the standard security measures fine, no problems, but..." He took a long sip from his coffee, the gears moving behind his eyes. "Dr. Nichols added additional security that is...problematic."

"Hmmm." Excitement prickled over her skin. Added security raised more red flags. Perhaps her gut was right. "Did he encrypt the whole computer?"

"No. I can access most of his files—standard research folders with videos, papers, audio, etc. However, the encryption on the second hard drive is...intense. I tried everything I can think of, but no progress. I understand how these things work, but I'm not a coder."

Chance stared at the doorway to the dining room with his mind still in hyper-drive.

"Anyway..." After shaking his head, he refocused on Lilith and flashed a weary smile. "You should call Nicci. This falls within her realm of expertise. Oh, and speaking of calls, I spoke with Tim this morning."

The cheerful smile she wore melted into a worried grimace of conflicting emotions. "What did you tell him?"

His chuckle filled the sunlit kitchen with a much-needed levity. "Come on, *cherie*. I'm not stupid enough to have a federal agent killed, especially after he's flashed his badge all over town, looking for his missing partner."

"How much did you tell him about..." Her hands shook slightly, and she sipped her coffee, trying to breathe.

"*Mon cherie*, it is your story to tell, not mine. I only said you shared a history, and we need him out of town as soon as possible."

"Thank you."

"Of course, *cher*. Tim said he'd meet with the guy, help him if he can, and report back." As he spoke, his eyes fell, and he held the mug a little tighter. He was holding back something important.

"And?"

"And what?" His attempt at blissful ignorance was not convincing in the slightest. When she still stared him down, he reluctantly continued. "I just asked him for a full sit rep—"

"A what?"

"Situation report...to gauge his threat level."

Chance leaned against the counter with a weight in his eyes.

"Lilith, if he doesn't walk away after this mess with his partner is settled...if he keeps coming after you..."

She sighed into her coffee and nodded. "I know. We can cross that bridge when we come to it."

"And if your uncle finds out about him before then?"

A sudden lump of fear caught in her throat. She hadn't considered that possibility. "Aaron is all the way out in L.A. We just need to be sure he stays put and pray no one tells him."

Before Chance responded to her absurd logic, an intrusively loud chime rang through the room. It took her a few seconds to recognize the sound as her doorbell. Guests always called up from the lobby, and she'd leave the door cracked. She couldn't remember the last time someone had rung the bell.

"Expecting a visitor?"

Lilith shook her head, her mind racing through the possibilities. "No." After pushing off the counter, she padded through the living room and peered through the peephole. *Crap. What day is it?*

She cracked the door open. to see Nicci jogging in place with an overly cheerful smile.

"Ready to run, partner?"

As Lilith opened the door wider, revealing her silky robe, the petite Italian came to an abrupt stop, and her Cupid's-bow mouth formed a disapproving frown. "You forgot, didn't you?"

"Why didn't you call from downstairs?"

"Oh, Al was busy and waved me through."

With that, Lilith trudged back to the kitchen, Nicci following in her wake. "To answer your question, I forgot we pushed our run back to Saturday. Excellent timing, though, I was about to call you."

"Oh, hey, Chance." Nicci flashed a smile when she rounded the corner. "So, what were ya gonna call me about?"

"Want some coffee?" Chance pulled another mug out of the cabinet and started a cup before Nicci answered his question.

"Uh, yeah. Thanks. Black, though." Then she hopped onto the island, her short legs dangling merrily.

"The computer from Goditha arrived, and we've hit a wall. He can tell you more while I get dressed. Regular clothes, though. We'll have to skip our workout today."

"Sex is not a substitute for cardio." Nicci chuckled and winked as Lilith walked toward the bedroom.

"If you do it right it is." Lilith held up her middle finger from the doorway and closed the door while Nicci chuckled.

Chance stared into his mug after Lilith left the room, still stuck on the problematic computer. But Nicci apparently had other things on her mind.

"I'm assuming you two had a productive talk?" The petite detective peered at him expectantly.

"Yeah, we did. Tim will give Agent Boston a hand with his search while keeping him far away from Lilith. Hopefully, he'll give up his obsession if he finds what he's looking for."

"What if he doesn't like what he finds?"

Chance met the petite Italian's stare and shook his head. "A valid question, but I don't have an answer. If the man dies and anything traces back to us—"

"Well, then we'll keep looking for a solution." Her chocolate-brown eyes drifted to the bedroom. "How is she?"

"She's rattled and wants to avoid the subject when possible. What that man did…Not the physical stuff—that she can deal with—but the mental abuse got to her." Chance stared into his mug, pausing to contain his anger and collect his thoughts. "I understand now why she was so quick to take all the blame and label herself an angel of death. Somewhere, deep down, she still believes he's right and there's something wrong with her."

"Luckily, the woman has someone to correct her on a daily basis."

A secret smile lit his face for a moment, but he didn't comment. Instead, he turned to the Keurig, which had stopped making noise, and grabbed the fresh mug of coffee.

"So, the doctor had some hacker friends?" Nicci took the steaming cup he held out to her and inhaled the scent with a happy smile.

"No clue, but there is a separate drive that is encrypted all to hell. I can handle our security subroutines and whatnot, but I'm no expert. Do you wanna take a peek?"

"Sure." As she hopped off the counter, her long ponytail bounced back and forth. "Although, if I need the big guns, I'll have to take it back to my place. I own some anti-encryption programs that can help, but it might take a while."

"How long?"

Nicci shrugged and slid into the dining room chair. "Day or two." Then she turned her attention to the computer, and her fingers flew across the keyboard.

Screens popped up and disappeared faster than Chance could keep track.

"Well, you aren't wrong. The man invested in some heavy security. Weird since this is not a personal computer. It runs on an internal system. The only reason to build a complete partition and *encrypt the hell out of it* is to hide something from your company. Suspicious."

"Perhaps he used it to hide research he didn't want other employees to see. I mean, scientists can be very competitive. That alone doesn't prove he had anything to do with the virus, right?" Chance peered at the screen with a mixture of fear and hope, uncertain which answer he wanted to hear.

"True," Lilith added as she leaned against the doorway in a violet dress shirt and dark-washed jeans. "But he was the head of research for the entire facility."

Dawning realization lit Chance's face while she spoke. "Which means he had top clearance. He had access to everything on his subordinates' computers, but only corporate could view his files. Most of them would never bother unless they had a reason."

"Sounds like Lilith's hunch is becoming more and more plausible. We need to crack the drive. I'll take this back to my place and get started. Like I was telling Chance, it might take a day or two. Maybe more if there's any nasty surprises. Let's hope it's not his porn collection or black market organ deals."

After closing the laptop, she grabbed the power plug.

"Oh, and you owe me a run, partner." The smile held equal parts playfulness and seriousness.

"I know." Lilith grimaced for added effect and walked Nicci to the door. "Let me know when you have something. Tim is meeting Boston, so we should have more details about his partner's disappearance by tonight."

"Yeah, I did some preliminary research this morning. As of now, the Bureau has no official missing persons case, which is incredible after six months."

"How is that possible?"

"Reports indicate that she had a fight with her partner and made comments about needing a change of scenery. There's also an internal memo mentioning a transfer request. Boston is the only one crying foul play, and he isn't very popular. No one is taking him seriously…"

Nicci paused with her hand on the door before she met Lilith's eyes.

"I got the impression from his coworkers that they were more than partners. It's possible she found out about his past, or maybe he did something to her, and she took off. Wouldn't be the first time. After all, people don't change. They just find new ways to lie."

"Thanks. I appreciate you looking into things."

"Well, it's not only for you. I love you and all, but if this guy keeps digging—"

"Chance and I already had that discussion."

"Started that discussion, you mean." A warning hid in his voice as Chance started the Keurig again to refill his coffee.

While Lilith cast an irritated frown in his direction, her unknown caller ringtone—"Who Are You," by the Who—filled the air. She jogged for the kitchen, glanced down at the 717-area code—central Pennsylvania—and answered with her overly polite business voice.

"Ms. Adams, it's Dr. Thomas. You dropped off a specimen with me…"

"Yes, what can I do for you, Dr. Thomas?"

Nicci sidled away from the door, drawn back like a moth to a flame, so Lilith put the call on speakerphone.

"Actually, I'm calling about what I can do for you. I ran through the genome mapping with a bit more detail. Now, I can't guarantee this without a complete map, but I believe I have a match for you."

"A match?"

"Yes, to a location. An excavation about eight years ago explored the deeper levels of Apollo's temple in Northern Greece, along the slope of Mount Parnassus. The lead archeologist, Dr. Kelley Wolfe, brought me biological specimens from various items. Anyway, there are remarkable similarities between the viral fragments I collected and the specimen you brought me."

"Wow. That's fast work. I mean, Scott has worked on this for more than half a year."

"Of course. He did all the heavy lifting so far. I wouldn't be able to make this educated guess without his research."

"I understand."

Both Chance and Nicci echoed her skeptical frown.

"I must stress that this is only an educated guess. I still need to complete the mapping for an antiviral treatment or vaccination to combat this. There is a long road ahead, but I believe I have enough evidence to support my theory."

"Okay, we'll arrange a meeting with this Dr. Wolfe. Can't hurt to ask some questions."

"That is the other reason I'm calling. Dr. Wolfe is speaking this evening at the Museum of Natural History Gala, their annual fundraiser. He is planning a new dig at Ephesus." The enthusiasm in her voice meant either the work or the man fascinated her, maybe both. "I have four extra tickets, and it would be the perfect way to speak with him in a casual setting."

"A gala? I'm not sure I should discuss things this delicate in public." Not to mention, Lilith was less than thrilled by the idea of a richy-rich party full of fake laughter, deep pockets, and false bravado. "We can make an appointment—"

In mid-sentence, she glanced over at Nicci, who was bouncing on the balls of her feet with excitement. The tiny detective resembled an over-enthusiastic teenager as she mouthed the word *Please!*

"Everyone will be asking about his work. You don't need to be specific. The man is not a virologist, but he can tell you more about the artifacts, most of which will be on display. He also uses the same core crew, who will be in attendance. This is the perfect opportunity to ask questions."

Lilith squeezed her eyes shut, and her head slumped forward in defeat. The woman made a convincing case. When she opened her eyes again, Chance studied her face with a quizzical expression.

"All right. What time should we meet you?"

Immediately, Nicci began celebrating with some sort of victory dance.

"Splendid! I'll put you on the list. Arrivals begin at eight p.m. Oh, and don't forget, it *is* a black-tie event."

"I figured as much. Thank you, Dr. Thomas."

After hanging up, Lilith slid the phone across the counter and glared at it as if the thing had somehow betrayed her.

"Do you own a tux?" Lilith sighed the question, but a lopsided grin crossed Chance's face.

"Black tie!" Nicci squealed with excitement. "I have *always* wanted to go, but tickets are thousands of dollars."

Lilith couldn't help but chuckle at her enthusiastic partner. "Yay." The sarcastic quip went unnoticed by Nicci, so she turned back to Chance. "So, do you?"

"Yes. Gregor required me to wear one for several events a year, so I figured it was worth the investment. Why four tickets, though? Only three of us went to see her."

"I guess she figured Cohen would want to bring a date…and by Nicci's exuberant reaction, I'm guessing she's willing to play the part."

"Not ideal, but I can work with it." Nicci's bright grin stretched from ear to ear.

"Wait. Why bring him at all? I mean, you and I can ask questions."

As Chance spoke, Nicci stopped moving, and her crestfallen expression grew.

"True, but you know he'd be offended. Plus, I'd rather keep him within sight while Agent Boston is around. Those two meeting would be a catastrophe on par with him bumping into Aaron. Besides, the demon's silver tongue is an advantage at times, and it *is* his element."

"Okay. Point taken. So, Nicci…I'm assuming your encryption software can run on its own, right?"

"Yep! So, I can go?" The petite woman began bouncing again.

"You might not find entertaining Cohen as exciting as you do now." Lilith chuckled as Nicci waved off her concern with a dismissive hand.

"Worth it. I need a dress, though. Wanna come with?"

"You know…I don't think I've ever seen you in anything but pant suits and gym clothes." Chance grinned, added a spoonful of sugar, and took a long sip of his second cup of coffee.

The detective planted her fists on her hips with a stern scowl. "What? You think because I'm adventurous and gay I can't kick ass at dressing up?" Both Lilith and Chance blinked, uncertain how to answer the question, until Nicci's frown split into an impish grin. "Come on, guys! This is gonna be so much fun!"

"If you say so." Lilith muttered the words into her coffee.

"What? You don't like dressing up?" Chance eyed her with disbelief and leaned against the counter. "I've seen your collection of heels. I'm gonna have to build you a closet just for shoes."

"Smart-ass. I love a great dress, but I'm not keen on the destination. A lot of hollow, pompous hypocrisy wrapped up in fancy clothes and jewels, spending thousands to appear generous and noble. Besides, I've always enjoyed dressing up more than the actual party."

Chance flashed a wolfish smile, placed his mug down, and stalked over to her. "Only because you didn't have the right date."

Her eyes narrowed playfully. "You, sir, have a mighty high opinion of yourself."

The feigned shock on his face was priceless. "You wound me, madam, right to the core."

"Wow. You guys are so cute..." Nicci gagged and then chuckled.

"Don't you have a computer to decrypt?" His growl lingered in the air, and he stared the petite woman down with a slight smile.

"Yep. I know when I'm not wanted. Lil, meet me downtown at noon? I'll text you the address." Nicci grabbed the computer and made a quick exit.

Lilith moved to place the empty cups in the sink, and Chance slid a hand around her waist, pulling her into a proper waltz form.

"Um, what are you doing?" A slight bubble of panic formed in her stomach.

The question made him stop and peer down at her in confusion. "Don't tell me you don't know how to dance."

"Fine. I won't tell you." After the brisk retort, Lilith tried to pull away, but he tightened his hold.

"Oh, no you don't. The cost of accompanying you to the benefit is one dance while we're there."

"A middle school slow dance? Because that's my only move."

"Oh, come on. The waltz is easy. I'll show you."

"My dad made you take dance lessons?"

"Um...not exactly." A bright pink tinged his cheeks, and his eyes drifted elsewhere.

"Okay..." Something about his expression made her uncomfortable, and his lengthy dating history flipped through her mind.

"It's not what you think." His eyes flashed back to hers when he sensed her apprehension. "I told you before that my childhood was...not ideal."

"Yes..."

"Well, the only happy memories I have of my mother are watching old musicals with her—*Summer Stock, The Easter Parade, An American in Paris, Singing in the Rain*. She loved them and taught me some dances."

Lilith's lips stretched into a tender smile, and she slipped her arms over his shoulders. "That explains so much."

Chapter 16 - *Cassie*

The man continued narrating his story with Cassie barely clinging to consciousness. The pain kept threatening to pull her under, but she couldn't endure another shattered joint, so she breathed through the agony and tried to pay attention.

"Leto suffered a nasty bite to her neck and multiple lacerations but had no insurance. Medicaid only covered the length of stay for a normal delivery since doctors determined her injuries were self-inflicted. In fact, they held her for forty-eight hours in a psychiatric ward and recommended mental health services, but Leto refused. She wasn't crazy."

"What about the wife?" Cassie decided to try a bold new tactic. Perhaps she could steer the conversation or at least earn some goodwill. The man seemed to respond positively when she showed interest in his lengthy tale.

The silence stretched out for far longer than she felt was comfortable. As she started to think she'd made a huge mistake, the man who called himself Art spoke up again.

"She returned to her husband without reprimand. No one believed a prominent and wealthy member of the community would sprout fangs and attack a former housekeeper. Even if the woman was pregnant with her husband's bastard children, the story seemed too outrageous to the outside world."

An eerie quiet settled back in, and a suffocating foreboding seized her body.

"I appreciate your interest, Cassie. I don't want you to think this is a reprimand for asking questions, but this must happen."

The apprehension blossomed into true terror, and her limbs shook. Her eyes squeezed shut, and she stretched her other senses to the max, waiting for the inevitable pain.

"Why? Why does it have to happen?" As the words left her mouth, a block of wood pressed against her right knee. Panic and bile burned their way up her throat until she tasted it on her tongue. "*Why?* Explain it to me, *please!*"

Everything came to a standstill. Even the air didn't seem to move.

His footsteps approached, circling her once again. "My sweet, I explained earlier. Your torture serves a higher purpose. Only when you experience agony can you appreciate the gifts the lotus fruit brings, and only then can we learn the truth we seek."

"But I *already* appreciate them. Why continue to punish me?" Tears caused her to choke on the words.

The man's fingers brushed over her lips in a lingering touch. "You've only obtained a glimpse. You are chosen, Cassie. It is an honor, not a punishment. Your pain…your tears…your cries, they are sacrifices to the gods. As we break you down, you will come closer to the divine and bring favor to us all. The fruit acts as a vehicle, allowing your soul to separate from your mortal form and embrace divinity."

He leaned close enough for his breath to tickle over her ear.

"You understand what I mean. You left your body, hovered over it for a time, didn't you?"

"No, no, no. Please!" In between the psychotic babble, Cassie heard the answer—the cult planned to torture her to death. "Why me? I've done nothing to you! I'm a *good* person. *Please.*" Her sobbing pleas died, and the heavy silence stretched on.

"That is precisely why we chose you over others. You *are* a good person and will bring us honor as a sacrifice befitting Olympus. I told you before. You will recognize your part when it comes. Until then, we must continue."

Before she processed his words, a crushing blow slammed the wood into her knee, shattering the joint with a gut-wrenching crack. Her bloodcurdling screams echoed off the walls as sheer agony welled up, like a tidal wave about to drag her into unconsciousness.

A sizzle echoed off the walls, and the scent of burning flesh permeated the air. However, the pain from cauterizing the ruptured skin paled when compared to the torment already flooding her brain.

The wet surface of the lotus fruit was pressed against her screaming mouth. Immediately, Cassie sank her teeth into the sweet pulp and took as many greedy bites as possible before they pulled it out of reach again.

"You did well." Art's hand smoothed through her hair, and she swallowed.

The stabbing pain receded to the distant corner of her mind, or perhaps she was the one pulling away. Once again, the disconnected sensation became overwhelming, and she floated above her body, just as he described. *What if I keep going? What if I retreat until I leave my broken body behind forever? If I could die, they couldn't torture me anymore. I would finally be free.*

Three sharp slaps to her cheek brought her back to reality. She tried to focus her eyes behind the blindfold but only met the same familiar darkness.

"Cassie, I'm going to continue now. Are you awake?"

"Yessss." The word stretched into a long, slurred attempt at speech. "What is it? The fruit."

"I told you. It's the lotus fruit—a piece of divinity on Earth that removes the shackles holding us back."

"No fruit does this…" She giggled as the inky blackness morphed and melted into odd figures, who made happy gestures.

"Are you able to concentrate, or should I crash your high?"

The steely resolve in his voice conjured images of cartoon villains until the meaning sank in, acting like a splash of ice water to the face.

"Yes, I'm okay." Cassie gulped down the sudden lump of fear and prayed for Art to begin speaking again.

"Good. We are almost to the end. Leto knew the Empusa would attack again, so she did the only thing she could—she ran. After adopting aliases, she blended into a quiet community in Spring Grove, Pennsylvania.

"For nine years, they lived in peace. Leto remained devoted to her twins, who proved rather extraordinary. The girl embodied Apollo's sunny essence, while the boy possessed Artemis's dark gift of the hunt. Although the role reversal surprised some, their mother saw their names at birth and understood their destinies. She thanked the Olympians every day for her blessings, and the house overflowed with love."

The happy, reminiscent tone made the story seem personal, as if he lived it. Of course, with the effects still blurring her mind, the observation might have been her imagination, connecting dots where none existed.

"Then what happened?" Although her words came out slightly slurred, he appreciated her interaction. If she couldn't avoid all the damage, perhaps she could at least minimize or delay it.

"Well…the gods are rather fickle in their affection and continually test the loyalty of their followers. They give, and they take…"

The man paused, deep sadness tinging his speech.

"With the aid of numerous private investigators, the wife tracked Leto to her little hideaway. The Empusa struck for the second time on a stormy night. The twins awoke to screams between the cracks of thunder. Apollo proved braver than her brother and dared a peek. The door to their mother's bedroom lay open, and a figure clothed in black tore and slashed at Leto. Apollo snuck back to their room and grabbed Artemis. They escaped through the window and ran for the police station."

"They left her?" The question slipped past Cassie's lips without much thought. A blissful fog still clouded her brain and protected her from feeling the shattered joints and compound fractures.

"They had no choice. The day would come sooner or later, so she trained her children to survive, to do what was necessary. She made the children promise they would leave her behind when the Empusa came and run to safety. After all, her life was inconsequential. The twins had a duty to protect and reform the world as the messengers and vessels of the gods. *They* were what truly mattered."

"But they were only kids." A heavenly warmth seeped through her body, pulling her into the man's story. The answers to all her questions lay buried in his words. Even if she couldn't make the connection yet, it existed, looming just out of view.

"No! Don't you see? They weren't kids!" A heated passion infused his voice, and he surged to his feet. "That is the point!" His shoes slammed against the floor as he raced over to her. "You must see. You *have* to! They weren't even human. They were demigods charged with a divine duty!"

The man's ridiculous leap in logic left her frowning beneath the blindfold. Before she formulated a response, angry fists slammed down on her uninjured knee. The sharp pain seared up her leg as the joint bent back at an unnatural angle. Her ragged cries nearly drowned out his hysterical voice.

"You, of all people, should understand!"

The fists pounded against her naked chest, knocking the air from her lungs. Cassie kept trying to pull in panicked breaths, but his furious hands continued to rain down on her battered torso.

"You've seen one! You saw an Empusa! You *know* it's true!"

"Art!" A sharp female voice rang through the room with commanding authority, and the barrage ended, at least for the moment.

Cassie took advantage of the pause by drawing in wheezing gulps of air.

"That is enough!"

Somewhere in the back of her mind, Cassie recognized the voice but couldn't place it.

"She knows!"

The angry snarl grated down her spine as she continued to draw in ragged breaths.

"We must adhere to the ritual. You told the story, Art. That is enough for now." The woman spoke as if she were talking a jumper off a ledge, which didn't seem far from the truth.

Cassie's entire body ached and throbbed, which worsened with each inhale, and the fruit's divine bliss abandoned her to her agony.

"Art…"

The warning sent chills over her exposed skin, and her brain raced. He was out there, lurking in the darkness, intent on inflicting harm.

A loud huff hitched across her face. "Very well," he said begrudgingly. His shoes receded to the doorway and clomped up the stairs without another word.

"Clean her up. She may take one bite, but not until you are done. Pain is part of the journey." The woman's tone sounded too happy and bright for the context of her words.

The high heels clicked on the stone floor but paused before the staircase.

"Remember, she must remain virtuous. You *know* what I mean…"

"Aye." The sudden grunt emanated from above her head, making her jump.

Virtuous? After a moment, the meaning finally sank in.

"I need your word."

Cassie found the woman's lack of trust disconcerting.

"Yes, I know." The breathy wheeze conjured the image of an overweight and sweaty man looming over her. "I promise. She will…stay virtuous."

When he spoke again, she recognized the voice. This was the same man who had prepared her when she first arrived. Bile rose to burn her throat as she recalled his rough hands slithering over her skin.

Satisfied with his oath, the woman retreated up the wooden stairs, leaving Cassie alone with a lecherous monster. Even before his clammy palms slid down her stomach, she knew he'd stretch the limits of his promise.

Cassie tried to pull away from his touch, but when her legs twisted, the broken knee joints screamed in response. With sudden inspiration, she latched onto the blinding torment and drew it closer. After a few seconds of fighting and writhing, the agony dragged her into blissful unconsciousness, where she could no longer feel his calloused fingers.

Chapter 17

Lilith peered out of Nicci's apartment window, waiting. Bright orange lights warmed the growing dusk, and a light summer rain mottled the sidewalk. Cohen's sleek limo pulled up, followed by Chance's Ford Explorer Sport, both coming to a stop under the streetlamp's harsh glare.

"The guys are here."

When she turned around, Nicci emerged from her bedroom in a vibrant yellow gown. The tropical color complemented her tanned skin, while the sweetheart neckline and bodice maximized her athletic figure. Instead of her signature ponytail, she had braided her mahogany tresses into a queenly work of art that left Lilith almost speechless.

"Wow. I mean…"

"Don't make my girlfriend jealous." Nicci flashed a sassy wink to match her impish grin before she twirled, making the citrine skirts swish with beautiful weightlessness.

When the bell rang, Lilith opened the door, still laughing at her partner. However, when she turned to face their guest, time stopped.

Chance stood still as stone, with an easy smile frozen in mid-formation. His leanly muscled, six-foot-three frame was wrapped in a sharp tuxedo coupled with a black dress shirt and matching tie—very Johnny Cash. Fine stubble graced his square jaw, and he'd tamed his tousled chestnut hair into a sleek style without losing its personality. Somehow, she doubted the rib-cracking corset had anything to do with her breathless state.

"Lily, you…" The sentence faded off as he searched for the right words.

Lilith glanced down at her lavender lace dress, with its sheer overlay of tiny glinting gems, and bit the corner of her lip.

"It's okay, isn't it?"

After clearing his throat, Chance straightened, and his familiar wolfish grin returned when he leaned closer. His warm breath tickled over her ear as he whispered, "The only place that dress could *ever* look better is on my bedroom floor. You're stunning, *mon petite cherie.*"

Before stepping back, he left a soft kiss on her burning cheek. When their gazes met, his eyes sparkled with more meaning than Lilith had ever witnessed, which took her by surprise. The sheer intensity and depth they contained became too intimidating, and she glanced away.

"You, uh, should have seen the hideous thing Nicci put me in first."

"Oh, come on. It wasn't *that* bad." Of course, the woman's inability to keep a straight face destroyed her credibility.

Lilith snorted sarcastically, despite being grateful for the distraction. "The bubble-gum pink monstrosity, complete with horrendous flashy jewels, made me look like a Jersey Shore prom queen."

Nicci doubled over with laughter. "Or a gypsy bride! Oh God! It was sooo awful."

"Did you sneak a picture?" A hopeful grin lit his face, and Lilith swatted his shoulder.

"Of course not!" Nicci exclaimed, but as soon as she thought Lilith wouldn't notice, she nodded and winked at Chance.

"Seriously, Nicci? Delete it!" Lilith narrowed her eyes at her partner.

"Nope. Love you, though." Nicci flashed a smile as she pranced across the room to join them.

"Well, you ladies ready for the party bus?" The sarcasm in Chance's voice indicated Cohen didn't share their jovial mood.

Awesome.

"By the way, you are radiant, Nicci. Far better than your date deserves."

"Why, thank you, kind sir." The petite Italian performed a sweeping curtsy with all the drama and fanfare befitting the eighteenth-century Court at Versailles.

"I spotted old Bessie. We are riding together, right? I don't want to abandon my partner, especially while Cohen's still pouting."

A warm chuckle escaped Chance's lips. "Of course. I drove so we can part ways once we return here. I plan to spend as little time with the demon as possible. Also, Tim called."

"Way to bury the lead. What did he say?" Lilith followed him into the hall while Nicci locked the door.

"He met with…Special Agent Boston." He paused before speaking the name, trying to contain his contempt. "The man isn't happy about you passing him off to a PI, but he's desperate. The story about searching for his partner appears legitimate, but like Nicci said, there is no active missing person's case."

"Did Tim find anything about her disappearance?"

"Witnesses last placed her outside the Fred Astaire Dance Studio in Richmond, Virginia, about six months ago. Boston planned to meet her the next day, but she never showed. Her cell went straight to voicemail and no answer at her apartment. No living family, no boyfriend, and the two friends she attended the dance with haven't seen or heard from her since. They said she escorted them to their vehicles and was unlocking her car when they left."

"What about her vehicle?"

"Bronze Honda Civic with Virginia plates. No sign of it so far. If someone abducted her, they took the car. A suitcase and some clothes were missing from her apartment too. She either skipped town or the perps went to her place and packed for her."

"Okay. So, assuming someone took her…" Nicci nodded to herself as she thought through the scant bit of info. "We are talking about a trained federal agent capable of defending herself. The easiest way to catch her off guard and avoid a scene would be by doing their homework—tailing, surveillance, learning her routines, and researching personal history. If I'm right, they knew how, when, and where to strike to minimize an investigation."

"Tim said the same thing, and Boston agrees. Someone targeted her. Of course, the bastard thinks it's Lilith. He believes you're either seeking revenge or covering up the terrorist attacks." Although Chance remained composed, a wry expression twisted the corner of his lip.

"So, did Tim form an opinion on him? Will he go away quietly, or is he a problem?" Leave it to Nicci to cut right to the true issue.

The elevator came to a halt on the ground floor, and an odd silence filled the confined space. When the doors opened, Chance found his voice again.

"If we locate his partner and convince him we aren't involved…there's a shot. I think it's worth the attempt. As much as I'd love to feed his dismembered body to the gators, Lily is right. The man is an FBI agent from a prominent family, and the Bureau suspended him for investigating Phipps Bend—in particular, *you*. If we take him out, everything leads to us."

"Okay, so we pour our resources into helping him with the missing person's case." Nicci nodded, again in thought. "Tomorrow, I'll canvas cameras in the vicinity of the dance studio."

"Tim and Agent Boston are searching hospital and morgue records in the city for anyone matching her description."

"Why here if he believes someone grabbed her in Virginia?" As soon as the question left Lilith's lips, she realized the answer.

"He's searched for six months and exhausted all possible leads in the Richmond area. The man is desperate, grasping at straws, and you are his last lead. Tim will keep him out of the way while we deal with this virus, but avoid the police station for now."

"Noted."

"His service record might come in handy. If the FBI cited him for fixating on you, we could use the information to obtain a restraining order. We can *make* him go away, if he won't go willingly." Nicci paused with her hand on the outside door, and Lilith almost saw the angel and devil arguing on her shoulders. "If I can't uncover enough for a case against him...I can ensure I find more."

"Let's cross that bridge when we get to it." As much as Lilith wanted Boston out of her life, the thought of fabricating evidence didn't sit right with her. "Besides, do you think a restraining order is gonna stop him? The monster would view it as a challenge. After all, he attacked me in the middle of a police station."

"He did what?" Chance rounded, intercepting her before she reached the glass doors. All his carefully crafted composure scattered to the wind.

Her cheeks blazed when she realized she had never told him the full story. "Sorry. In all the craziness, it skipped my mind."

One eyebrow raised as he stared at her, refusing to move until she explained.

Lilith smoothed the sheer overlay of her lavender gown to avoid his piercing stare and collect her thoughts. "It was nothing—"

A huff from her partner interrupted the casual dismissal. "As soon as he laid eyes on her, the fucker grabbed her by the neck and slammed her to the floor." Clearly, Nicci still harbored a lot of anger and guilt about the series of events.

"He caught me off guard for a moment, but I broke his hold, and the officers restrained him. The whole thing lasted ten seconds."

"*Putain de bordel de merde!*" After the indecipherable outburst, Chance bit down on his anger and swallowed most of it. "He's making it *really* difficult for me to keep my promise."

Lilith stood tall and locked eyes with the six-foot-three wall of homicidal rage. "You can't save me from things that *already* happened. The takeaway here is, I didn't let him beat me for long. Thanks to you, Nicci, and Tim, I'm better prepared." With high heels, she didn't need to stretch to reach his lips with a tender kiss.

"You're trying to distract me." Anger still lingered in his voice despite the playful nature of his words.

"Let it go. The man isn't worth your time or energy and not worth spoiling our evening." With a proud smile, she straightened his tie before patting his lapels. "You are a handsome sight in this tux."

"We could always skip the gala..." A mischievous grin crossed his lips as he spoke. "Nicci and Cohen can ask all the questions while we—"

"All right! Break it up!" Nicci shoved Lilith through the front door, while Chance followed with an amused smile. "God, you two are nauseating sometimes."

They came to a halt on the covered sidewalk. Light patters of rain splashed on the ground, and the taillights of Cohen's town car cast everyone in a bloody glow.

"The demon awaits." Although Chance sounded less than thrilled, he dashed into the night and swung the door open for the girls.

Lilith fell onto the seat across from the Durand, who stared into his scotch glass with all the happiness of a basset hound. The man's fatigue and hopelessness elicited a moment of déjà vu, which jolted Lilith out of her thoughts. Eight months ago, he sat in the same seat, staring into the same glass, while they rode into the mouth of hell—the same night she lost her father. *Now isn't the time. Get it together.*

After smoothing the gem-accented layer of sheer lavender, she glanced up and caught Cohen staring at her with an odd expression.

"Lilith...you..."

When Chance climbed into the seat beside her, the demon's eyes moved to him, and his words trailed off.

"You were saying something?" Lilith prompted while Nicci sat beside him with a jubilant smile.

"Uh…" Once again, his eyes flickered over to Lilith's date. "Nothing." He murmured the last word into his scotch and stared at the floor.

Chance shrugged and slid an arm around her shoulders. "So, do we know anything about this archeologist?"

After a second, Lilith shook her head, knocking the cobwebs and unwanted memories from her mind. "Only what Dr. Thomas told me. She believes our virus came from one of his digs. It's a long shot, but perhaps he can be helpful."

"He worked as a junior professor of archeology at the University of Tennessee for five years before he began organizing excavations with the Museum of Natural History. All his work focuses on Ancient Greece, and he holds a doctorate in World Mythology. Most people describe him as charming, though his pictures don't impress me, not that I'm an authority on male attractiveness." Nicci chuckled and glanced at Cohen, but the man ignored her and continued his abysmal assessment of his scotch.

"You did your homework." Chance smiled as Nicci swung her focus back to the people interested in holding a conversation.

"Yeah. Habit. I do preliminary background searches on anyone I plan to interview…or work with…" The detective glanced over at Cohen's sullen face again. "Of course, some people are off the grid, like Giggles over here, or at least he used to be. Since PMIC began using him as the company's poster boy, he's got a lot more exposure."

When the demon didn't supply her with a reaction, she shrugged and moved on.

"Now, *your* history provided an interesting read." A crooked grin split her lips, and her eyes settled on Lilith.

"That's an outright lie. I doubt you found much more than the Phipps Bend fiasco."

"I have a question." A venomous tone infused Cohen's voice as he interrupted, continuing to stare at his almost empty glass. The abrupt intrusion made everyone freeze, and the pleasant bubble of conversation collapsed into a tense silence. "What is the *point* of all this?" His baby-blue eyes rose to Lilith with heat behind them.

"I told you. I'm hoping Dr. Wolfe can identify the virus's origin. If we discover where the thing came from, perhaps we can figure out who is behind all this."

Andrew slammed his glass into the cupholder with his jaw clenched. "Who cares! The damage is done! The virus is killing my…*our* people. We need an antidote or a vaccine, not a fucking history lesson!"

Chance started to move, but Lilith laid a hand on his arm and turned her attention to the tense ball of anxiety in the car. "Andrew, you're frustrated. I understand. I wish I had more, but this is our only lead."

After a derisive huff, Cohen grabbed the decanter of scotch. "I never should have come here."

"Look. Both Dr. Scott and Dr. Thomas are mapping the genome. Nicci is running decryption programs on Dr. Nichols's computer. There is *literally* nothing else I can do. Even if Wolfe can't help, we are at least *doing* something other than brooding in a hotel room."

Cohen chewed his lip and folded his arms across his chest. "This feels like a waste of time." The anger leeched from his voice, leaving only his tired guilt—a sensation they all shared. "My people are suffering, turning into mindless killers, dying, and here we are…dressed up for a gala to visit an archeologist who might have unwittingly brought a virus back to life."

"I know…"

At the sound of her voice, his gaze snapped up to her again. "I could do more if the Council would listen! After everything with Luminita and Farren, they *still* think I'm a petulant child crying wolf."

"My uncle is no different. The man doesn't want to start a panic. I understand the frustration. It's like trying to break down a brick wall with a plastic spoon, but this is the only move we have."

For a long moment, he searched her face while uneasy silence enveloped the car. "Okay," he uttered as he slumped back, refilled his glass, and resumed his mission to find the bottom.

After waiting in line for two hours, the limo stopped in front of the Museum of Natural History, and the door opened to a red carpet lined with paparazzi. Camera bulbs flashed with the speed of a seizure-inducing strobe light, and journalists shouted questions over each other until they became an unintelligible roar of sound. Lilith sat still, paralyzed by the overwhelming chaos.

Crowds were never her thing, much less ones reporting to billions of viewers across the globe. All those eyes focused on her, even for a millisecond, made her skin crawl and her chest tighten. Why couldn't they find a back entrance and pay a busboy to avoid all the drama?

Someone stepped in front of her, blocking the cacophony, and she peered up at Chance's outstretched hand. As soon as she slid her hand into his, the panic in her chest receded, and she stepped out of the vehicle, keeping her eyes on his.

When she glanced ahead at the long line of celebrities and aristocrats, a bubble of anxiety returned, but Lilith found it manageable this time.

"Perhaps this isn't the best idea. How are we going to find this guy, much less ask him a bunch of questions?"

Chance leaned closer and kissed her cheek. "I've got you." Then he took a deep breath, put on a charismatic smile, and led her into the stream of guests parading through the media frenzy.

"Lilith!" Nicci's voice boomed over her shoulder so loud she nearly jumped out of her skin. "Do you see who's behind me?" The woman's excited squeal of glee reached a higher pitch than Lilith thought possible. "It's Alec freaking Baldwin!"

Somehow, her partner's gushing excitement calmed her nerves, and they strolled past the constant flashes, which left spots floating in her vision. When she turned back, intending to reply to her over-eager partner, an unfamiliar voice rose from the chaotic pandemonium, yelling her name.

At first, she thought it was a mistake. What reporter covering a fluff piece like this would have any clue who she was? To her dismay, the voice only became clearer and louder until she could no longer ignore it.

"Lilith Adams! Ms. Adams!"

She whirled around, scanning the crowd on the other side of the rope.

"Ms. Adams, over here!" Waving hands led her gaze to a man in a plain blue suit with an unimaginative navy tie. "Any comment on the terrorist attacks last October?"

A chill ran over her skin, and the bright lights faded into nothingness. The world narrowed to this one man asking an unexpected and dangerous question.

"Ms. Adams! How can you classify dozens of corpses pulled from their graves and littered across the city as a biological terror attack?"

Chance tugged her arm with a light touch, but she remained rooted to the spot, unable to move.

"How do you explain the bystanders' claims of men decapitating a cab driver in the middle of the street?"

"Ignore him, *mon cher*. Come on," Chance whispered into her ear, urging her forward again.

The noise of the crowd died down. Instead of shouts and demands for photo ops, murmurs and whispers popped up like wildfire.

"He's drawing too much attention! We need to get inside."

The words prompted her into action, and they rushed down the carpet, maneuvering around posing couples and celebrities. However, when Lilith glanced at the crowd behind the ropes, the odd man matched their pace, pushing his way past people, like a bloodhound with a scent.

"Ms. Adams! Can you tell us about the unexpected disappearance of your father? Where is Gregor Adams? Are you hiding him? Is he involved with the coverup?"

Lilith stopped dead in her tracks at the mention of her father, and she wasn't the only one. Rage vibrated off Chance's skin, and his arm slipped away from hers, his hands clenched into fists.

An odd silence settled over the scene. A hundred or more confused faces focused on them, and each passing second made the situation more precarious.

If Chance slugged the reporter in full view of every news camera in the country, the cops would arrest him. As a result, they'd miss their shot at speaking with Dr. Wolfe. Still, if the man didn't shut up, his outbursts could prove equally catastrophic. The last thing they needed was a bevy of investigative reporters all digging for the truth, especially with a virus on the loose.

"Deveraux!" A commanding voice split through the whispering crowd like a blazing knife.

When Chance froze a few feet away from the ropes, the reporter scrambled back into the sea of paparazzi.

"Return to your *date*."

The familiar voice crept over Lilith's nerves like venomous spiders, and she turned to face the source of her recent frustrations. The middle-aged man didn't appear intimidating in his classic tuxedo with gold cufflinks, but he stormed down the red carpet with authority, wearing the scowl of someone who never smiled. His fingers ran over his receding hairline, causing the close-clipped silver hairs to bristle. Meanwhile, his icy gray eyes fixated on Chance.

When Lilith stepped into his path, forcing a sudden halt, surprise wrinkled his angular face.

"What are you doing here, Aaron?"

The man's shock melted into a bored expression before he answered her question. "I attend every year to support the sciences." Then the full weight of his stare bore down on her as he took a step closer. "Why are *you* here, *niece*?" The title held all her uncle's disdain for their shared heritage—the only sentiment they had in common.

Lilith flashed a reassuring smile at the crowd and lowered her voice. "None of your damn business."

Aaron's nose crinkled in distaste. He turned on his heel and made his way to the entrance. For a moment, Lilith stared daggers into the man's back, but sadly, her powers didn't include telekinesis.

Once her uncle disappeared, she grasped Chance's hand and, with a desperate need to escape prying eyes, pushed past the people crowding the final photo-op area. The nosy reporter with too much information bothered her, but Aaron, here…now…

"Whoa, Hurricane Lilith!" Nicci jogged up next to them, holding her dress to keep from stepping on the hem. "I can't run in this thing. Can we slow down a notch?"

Despite the request, Lilith kept a brisk pace. When the door appeared, it became her only focus. The bubble of panic threatened to explode in her chest, and she needed to escape the mad crowd.

Lilith barreled through the doors, and two attendants hopped out of the way. As soon as she stood inside the blue-and-purple-lit hallway, hidden from hundreds of cameras, she clutched her sides and drew in slow, deep breaths to quell the consuming panic.

"Well, your company is a never-ending source of excitement. You attract enemies like flypaper for villains." Cohen's dry tone held a note of irritation that rubbed her the wrong way, but Nicci stood closer.

"Don't be a damn ass!" Her partner swatted the back of his head, and he turned to stare at her with a confounded frown, which she ignored.

"Okay, Lil. Not an ideal start, but remember, we are here for a reason. Don't let anyone distract you. After the gala, I'll dig up info on our mystery reporter, but for now, I need you to pull on your game face and charm the pants off Dr. Wolfe."

Chance's sudden scowl made the color leak from her face. "*Figuratively* speaking, of course!"

The humorous moment helped Lilith regain her composure and kicked her brain into gear. "You're right. We can't do anything about the guy right now…unless…" With a sudden bolt of inspiration, she turned back to Chance. "Is Ray still in town?"

Ray Valinski had served with Chance and Tim on Gregor's security detail. After her father's death, he took security contracts where he found them but always returned to New York City.

"Yeah. I'll call and give him the specifics. Perhaps he can pick up the man's trail." After retrieving his phone from his jacket, Chance stepped away to make the call.

With one situation mostly settled, Lilith turned her focus on Cohen. "I cannot stress this enough. *Stay away from Aaron.* If he figures out who you are, it will cause problems for both of us."

The demon sighed and crooked an eyebrow. "We have larger issues than your family squabble."

Lilith took a step closer. "You want to discuss family squabbles?"

Thankfully, the demon picked up on her subtext and shook his head.

"I didn't think so. Aaron leads the Elders in North America now. He's suspicious of your family's involvement in recent events, and I refuse to give him specifics on the Durand—one of many reasons he despises me. If he catches wind of you working with me on this virus—"

"Ray is on his way." Chance rejoined the group, tucking away his phone. "We need to move, *cherie*. This is not the place for sensitive conversations. Let's do what we came here to do."

After a brief nod, Chance led her through the entrance into an almost unbelievable scene. Dozens of tables dotted the cavernous room, adorned with crisp white linens and elaborate centerpieces of blue and gold. Flickering blue lights created a sparkling underwater illusion enhanced by the life-sized whale sculpture dangling from the ceiling. An orchestra near the stage welcomed them with a spirited sonata to top off the visual feast.

"Names, please?"

Lilith jumped at the unexpected voice beside her and turned to face a man who stood five foot three, perhaps less. The man's shock of red hair peeking from beneath his bell-boy-style hat matched his ruddy complexion. "*Names?*"

"Sorry. Lilith Adams, Chance Deveraux, Andrew Cohen, and Nicci DeLuca. I believe Dr. Rachel Thomas reserved four seats for us?"

The disgruntled man scanned his clipboard with a frown, running his finger down the lengthy list. She doubted he'd spend so much time looking for Alec Baldwin's name, but who would? The man was a legend.

"Follow me." The squat man spun on his heel and took off without a backward glance, forcing them to pick up the pace and shimmy past tables. Ian—as displayed on his shiny name badge—stopped before a table near the stage and waved his hand in a gallant yet hollow gesture. "Your seats."

"Thank you." Lilith turned with a polite smile, but Ian was already gone. After a moment, she spotted him weaving through the crowd with an artistic flourish, but when she pivoted to greet their table mates, her hopes for the evening came crashing down spectacularly.

Shit. Why does the universe hate me?

"Well, this is a small world." The derision dripping from Aaron's words grated down her spine like nails on a chalkboard.

"Uncle." After acknowledging his presence, her gaze landed on the two women sitting on his left, righteous indignation burning in her gut. "Allow me to make the introductions." She squeezed Chance's hand and fixed a plastic smile on her face. "Chance Deveraux, this is Dr. Brittany Price, my shrink, and her girlfriend, Renee."

The doctor swallowed hard before speaking. "Ms. Adams. I'm happy to see you, and wonderful to meet you, Mr. Deveraux."

"An unexpected pleasure. I had no idea my therapy paid so well."

"It doesn't…Your uncle kindly offered these tickets for Renee's birthday." A blush crept over Dr. Price's cheeks, indicating she spoke the truth, but Lilith never met a therapist who didn't excel at lying.

"How uncharacteristically generous." The dry comment hung in the air like an oppressive cloud, and she took the seat farthest away from them.

"What brings you and your *friends* to such an elegant event?" Between the droll tone and his bored expression, Lilith couldn't tell if Aaron expected the impolite conversation to rattle them or merely wanted to complain about their presence.

Of course, Lilith's preoccupation with deciphering his motives left her unable to come up with a plausible answer. Thankfully, Nicci was quicker on her toes.

"I ran into Dr. Wolfe a few years ago in Greece. Fascinating guy. When I spotted his name on the speaker's list for tonight's event, I pulled some strings." Her partner flashed a bright smile, as if a five-ton elephant composed of pure animosity wasn't sitting in their midst.

At least Dr. Thomas wasn't present to add more complications to their train wreck of a night.

"And this is…" Aaron waved a hand in the direction of Nicci's date.

"My boyfriend." The petite Italian squeezed the demon's arm and leaned in to kiss his cheek. "Andy."

Lilith bit back an eruption of laughter at Cohen's shocked expression.

"Are you certain he's aware of your relationship?" Aaron narrowed in on Cohen, studying every line as Nicci chuckled.

"Oh, he's just shy. Personally, I think he's embarrassed that I can still whoop his ass in the gym."

While the rest of the table chuckled at her comment, Aaron remained fixated on Andrew. The laughter died down awkwardly, and his gaze moved back to Nicci.

"Hmm. I thought you were"—the man fidgeted with his napkin until he decided how to end the sentence—"opposed to male company."

To her credit, Nicci crooked a stoic eyebrow and remained calm. "Did you see that in my personnel file? Sorry to disappoint, but my tastes vary."

Aaron nodded with a tight jaw before turning his attention to the rest of the room, signaling an end to the unpleasant chit-chat.

"I'm so sorry I kept you waiting." The cheerful voice made Lilith's heart plummet into her stomach. *No. How can this night get any worse?*

With a deep, steadying breath, Lilith rose from the chair, her mind dissolving into a panicked chaos. Dr. Thomas took her hand and shook it before claiming the seat beside her.

"I come up here all the time, and I'm still not used to the traffic."

The virologist's intricate black lace dress clashed with her minimalist makeup and hasty ponytail, but she showed no other signs of being uncomfortable in the environment, which shouldn't have surprised Lilith. A professor specializing in an under-researched field probably depended on a lot of donor-schmoozing to fund her work.

"I didn't realize you were joining us." Although Lilith kept her plastic smile in place, the tension was impossible to hide. Her brain kept screaming random profanities in an endless cycle of pandemonium. *Can it possibly get worse? I shouldn't even think that question.* Recent history had taught her one firm lesson—catastrophes lurked around every corner, waiting for her to summon them.

"Well, of course." Somehow, Dr. Thomas appeared oblivious to the awkward drama. In fact, her eyes hadn't roamed the table yet. The woman's smile widened, deeply dimpling her cheeks. She settled in and hung her purse from a fancy travel hook. "So, the speeches take place during dinner and dessert. Afterward, I will introduce you to Dr. Wolfe, and you can ask questions."

The last statement drew Aaron's laser-sharp focus to the woman in lace. By implying none of them knew Dr. Wolfe, she had exposed Nicci's lie, a fact Lilith's uncle did not miss. His piercing eyes moved to Nicci, who inspected the floral centerpiece with extreme dedication. The virologist remained blind to the growing tension.

"I'm happy to help with something so interesting. If we are right, this is a landmark scientific discovery! Oh goodness. Where are my manners? Good evening, Mr. Deveraux and Detective Cohen."

Rachel's radiant smile embodied the exact opposite of Lilith's insides as her uncle turned his attention once more.

"Cohen. That's 'priest' in Hebrew, if I'm not mistaken." The thin man's intense gray eyes fixed Andrew to his chair with an unmistakable weight.

"I suppose." The Durand refused to show any signs of intimidation. After a nonchalant shrug, he took a deep swig of water, probably wishing it was scotch.

"My niece has rather ambiguous things to say about you." A brief glare at Lilith drove home his anger at the subject. "So, you are in New York for social reasons?" Aaron's scowl made his skepticism clear, daring the man to scramble for a believable answer under his scrutiny.

However, Andrew decided not to play. Without peering up from his glass, he swirled the water with all the calm indifference Lilith had come to expect from him and uttered, "Yep."

The obvious refusal to interact frustrated her uncle, so he changed tactics and turned to their newest party member. "Aaron Bogdan, and you are?"

"Dr. Rachel Thomas." The woman's brilliant smile made her resemble a cheerful, animated chipmunk capable of breaking out in song. "And you are Lilith's uncle?" Curiosity sparkled in the woman's warm eyes.

"Yes." His ambivalent tone implied his desire to add "unfortunately" to the answer. "So, Doctor, what is your specialty?"

Rachel paused to sip her water, laid a napkin across her lap, and folded her elbows on the table. "I hold several degrees, but my current work is paleovirology." Although the lifeless answer seemed uncharacteristic, she probably answered the same question every day.

The doctor glanced around the table with minimal interest, but her eyes paused on Renee a second longer than the others.

"And what is paleo—"

"Virology, the study of ancient viruses."

When Aaron's eyes swung back to her, Lilith wanted to crawl under the table. "Is that so? Viruses…How fascinating."

The clenched jaw and tightened skin around his steely eyes said it all. First Cohen and now *this*—collaborating with a human. The safety precautions Lilith took wouldn't matter to him.

"And you are working with my niece, Ms. Adams, on a discovery?" A warning lay within his crisp tone, too obvious for anyone to miss.

"Uh…" Rachel frowned as the odd tension finally registered. "Yes. Academic research. Nothing critical. Dr. Scott put us in touch on an old sample he uncovered."

"Well, it sounds cool to me." Renee blundered into the conversation as if she needed to defend the woman's life's work. Her short, ash-blond hair bobbed when she jumped and turned to Brittany in surprise. "What?"

Dr. Price shook her head, trying to quiet her girlfriend.

"I'm only saying her work sounds super fascinating."

"Perhaps Renee and I should get some air."

"That is unnecessary. This is nothing more than a friendly conversation, after all. We don't need to discuss business if it makes you uncomfortable. After the reporter outside, we've all experienced enough unpleasantness for one night, wouldn't you say, Lilith?"

"That is an understatement, you fucking bastard." She mumbled the words under her breath and plastered a fake smile on her face.

"What's that?" One thin eyebrow rose in distaste.

After clearing her throat, Lilith raised her voice over the orchestra's swelling crescendo. "I said he made quite a statement but has running mastered."

Although he did not appear amused, Aaron turned his attention to the stage without another word as the first speaker stepped up to the microphone.

Chapter 18

After two hours of dinner, dessert, coffee, and a parade of speeches packed with forced humor, the formalities ended. The orchestra retired, the DJ took over, and staff moved the tables to make room for the dancing, alcohol, and mingling that led to bigger donations.

To Lilith's immense relief, Aaron disappeared into the crowd without any more questions, but she couldn't shake the dread gripping her stomach. *It isn't over. This is a temporary reprieve. Aaron will have questions, and he'll expect answers.*

"Hey, partner." Nicci slid a champagne glass into Lilith's hand with a genuine smile. "I think Aaron split, so we should be clear to chat with Dr. Wolfe." She gestured toward a thin man with slicked black hair on stage, speaking with a brunette in a lovely blue dress.

When her partner didn't reply, Nicci bumped her shoulder.

"Is it the reporter?"

Lilith frowned at her bubbly champagne. "Part of it. Questioning the attacks was weird, but Dad? The man connected dots that shouldn't exist. I thought we cleaned things up."

"Crackpots are always forcing random pieces into a pattern they want to believe. We will find him and ensure he has no credibility. And the other parts?"

"Pick something. My uncle meeting Cohen, Dr. Thomas outing our collaboration, my worsening nightmares, the virus, my abusive ex with a federal badge, and let's not forget, Dr. Price. I *just* shook the idea of her spying on me for my uncle. Now she shows up with him at this damn gala."

"So, you're pissed you may have been right not to trust Dr. Price?"

"Hell yes. Of course, I am. Aaron has no right to spy on me. None of my crap is his business."

"Actually…"

Lilith rounded with a shocked glare, but her partner remained unfazed, leaning against the table, her eyes roaming the crowd.

"A lot of it *is*. As much as you dislike him, he needs the truth to do his job. The Elders, which include him, should decide how to deal with Cohen and the Durand, not us. The man may be unsupportive of our current investigation, but we should fill him in on our progress. I know he's a fucking bastard—I heard you earlier—but he can't make informed decisions without data."

Lilith's jaw dropped while her partner continued with all the nonchalance of a boring conversation about football or the weather.

"And I think you are more upset about losing someone objective you can talk to about things. After eight months, you bought into Dr. Price's spiel and thought she could help you. Now you feel betrayed and lost."

"Nicci…" A clear warning lingered in Lilith's voice, but the fearless woman paid no attention.

"It's okay! What if things happened the way Dr. Price said? Gala tickets do not mean she's in his pocket, but if she is, we'll deal with it. You still have people to talk to…like me." Then Nicci bumped her shoulder again and disappeared into the crowd.

Dammit. Lilith stared into the mingling throng, Nicci's words repeating in her head. As much as she hated to admit it, the woman wasn't wrong.

Aaron needed details to make decisions and lead their species. The man wasn't an interloper. When her father died, the Elders had chosen Aaron to take the helm. Still, her uncle was callous, ruthless, and unforgiving—the exact opposite of her father…but was he? Gregor didn't show Ashcroft or his family mercy, justified or not.

The Durand posed a legitimate threat. Although they had been aware of vampires for centuries without making a move, things were different now. Lilith and Chance possessed damning information about them, which made them dangerous. Plus, they were responsible—directly or indirectly—for the deaths of prominent Council members.

Although she trusted Cohen to warn them if the Durand planned to retaliate, he no longer possessed reliable access to that kind of information. Before Farren died, no one on the Council viewed Cohen as a threat, which made him invisible and allowed him to discover things in secret. Once he took his grandfather's seat, the other Council members didn't respect him, his position, or how he attained it, but they considered him dangerous and kept him in the dark.

"There are rules about beautiful women frowning in a place like this."

The warm timbre of Chance's voice brought a smile to her lips.

"Is that so? What's the penalty for such a crime?"

"A dance." He stepped in front of her and held out his hand with an irresistibly jubilant grin. "You did promise me one."

"I suppose I did." After setting down her champagne flute, Lilith slid her hand into his and let him lead her into the swarm of twirling bodies littering the dance floor. One arm slid around her waist, pulling her close, and they swayed in a gentle rhythm.

"Are you okay, *cherie*? I know things haven't gone as planned."

"Stop worrying. I'm okay. Nicci gave me a dose of truth—painful but necessary. I have to stop treating Aaron like the enemy."

"You hate the guy, and I understand your reasons. Hell, I share your opinion, but he's the boss man, whether we like it or not."

"I don't like it." Lilith pulled on a playful pout which made him chuckle. "But I get it. We have obligations. However…I understand the situation with the Durand impacts all of us, and he can't make informed decisions without details, but—"

"You don't want him to be the only one with the information."

"Yes, exactly! What if he buries the info or uses it for himself?"

"Simple. We bypass Aaron and present our findings to *all* the Elders at one time. I have Antonio's number in New Mexico. I'll call and ask him to arrange a conference via zoom. If we arrange it ourselves, Aaron will press us for information first. This way, no one has an advantage, and everyone gets all the facts."

"You're brilliant!" With a surge of exhilaration, she leaned up and kissed him.

Once the surprise wore off, he held her close, savoring the intimate moment. When the kiss ended, he spun her in a sudden twirl before pulling her back against him.

"I should give you ideas more often."

The roguish grin still made the butterflies in her stomach flutter after eight months. Then a moment of clarity struck her. "Thank you, Chance."

"For what, *amour de ma vie?*"

"For being here, dealing with my screwed-up psyche, overlooking my trust issues, helping me grieve my father, teaching me strength, putting your problems aside to make me comfortable, asking me to move in…but most of all, thank you for loving me as much as I love you."

For a moment, he couldn't speak. Tears misted his eyes. "*Mon petite cherie*, you mean everything to me. Always have. But I, uh…never thought you'd say anything like that to me, you know, before…Still kinda feels like a weird and wonderful dream I might wake up from, and you'll be gone."

"Come on. I'm not *that* easy to put up with, and I'm sure you didn't fantasize about my PTSD, night terrors, and neurosis."

"Well…to be fair, you didn't have those issues when I first met you."

She swatted his shoulder with an expression of playful outrage. "Wow. Smart-ass."

"One of my many fine qualities." His arm tightened with a tug, drawing her in closer.

"I think I over-fluffed your ego. I take it back."

"No takebacks."

"Are you reverting to grade school rules?"

"You mean, *fundamental* rules? Yes." His lips curved into an impish grin, and he spun her again.

This time, her body collided with his when she completed the turn, and he held her firmly against him to make it appear intentional.

"Seriously, though. I don't *put up with* anything. I love you, Lilith Adams, as you are, spots and all. I enjoy every minute."

One eyebrow raised despite herself. "*Every* minute? Including the stubborn ones that make you punch walls?"

A small chuckle escaped, and he continued to grin. "Yes, even those moments. Most of the time, you're right and I need the push. Plus, it's better than dating a mindless muppet who always agrees. I read something once that stuck with me…"

"What's that?"

"'True love does not ask you to change. It simply invites you into a safe space where you can stop being who you are not.'"

"That's…beautiful." The deep sentiment coupled with the vulnerability in his eyes made her brain freeze. Intense emotional moments always caught her off guard, not because she didn't share the same feelings, but because she never thought someone else would feel that way about her.

"Where's that from? *The Notebook*?" Part of her brain screamed for her to shut up, but the defensive reflex was compulsory.

A sudden grin split his lips, and the affectionate depth of his gaze only deepened after her sassy retort—another one of his fine qualities.

"No, smart-ass. It's a quote from Maryam Hasnaa, a spiritualist Gregor met in Oakland. Although, I've been forced to watch *The Notebook* more times than I can count."

"Never seen it and never intend to. See? An added bonus. You'll never have to sit through that movie again."

"Never, huh? That's a long time…" When her cheeks started to burn, his lips hovered over hers, just out of reach. "I like the sound of that."

His breath rushed over her skin, and she moved to close the gap, lost in the dizzy swirls of warmth the kiss brought.

"Ahem."

The sudden interruption brought them crashing back to reality.

"Well…I appreciate the invite, but dinner was about as fun as yoga on a mat of cactus needles." Cohen drained the last of his champagne with a pained expression and stared in disappointment at the empty glass. "Nicci sent me over. She wants to borrow Chance, while we speak with Dr. Wolfe."

"I'll keep an eye on the two of you from a safe distance." Chance kissed her cheek, stared down Cohen for a moment, and then disappeared.

"I promise, I had no idea he'd be here."

Cohen's hazel-flecked eyes rose to hers. "Who? Your uncle?" A snort of derisive laughter filled the air, and he handed his champagne flute to a passing server. "You aren't that masochistic. It's fine. I wish we'd had a way to warn the virologist, but what's done is done. Let's do what we came here to do and leave."

Cohen turned toward the stage and came to an abrupt stop, a frown creasing his face.

"Wow. He's the emo-punk version of an archeologist." His lip curled at the man's dark black hair styled over one eye and the black-on-black suit with tails. "Is he wearing eyeliner?"

"We aren't here for fashion advice. I don't care what he wears if he gives us useful answers. We can't afford another dead end."

"Are your friends joining us?" Dr. Thomas stepped in front of them, wearing her typical radiant smile, and brushed back her thick bangs. The woman's high level of excitement seemed disproportionate, but it usually did.

"Uh, no. We don't want to overwhelm the man, so it's just me and Detective Cohen."

"Oh." Disappointment pulled at her soft features for a moment but was quickly abolished by a jubilant smile. "Are you ready, then?"

"Yes, thank you. Oh, and sorry about the uncomfortable dinner. My uncle and I are...not close."

The woman waved off her apology, her cheeks dimpling further. "Relatives can be difficult, I suppose. I don't have much family myself. Well...not many blood relatives. All right, let's go."

As they neared the stage, Dr. Thomas rose on tiptoe and waved above the pressing crowd, which seemed more like groupies at a rock concert than donors at a fundraiser.

"Kelley!"

The guest of honor perked at the sound of his name, and his eyes scanned the clambering mass until they rested on Rachel. An instant smile stretched his thin lips into a charming expression, softening his features.

After holding up a finger signaling them to wait, he leaned over to speak with an overweight, balding man to his left and pointed down to the approaching trio. The stocky associate's beady eyes followed the line of sight until he spotted Rachel, and he started pushing his way toward their group.

The man made an effective bulldozer, shoving his three hundred plus pounds through clusters of gossiping celebrities, nouveau riche, blue bloods, and drooling bystanders. By the time he reached them, his labored breaths wheezed with each inhale and his complexion had turned ruddy.

Lilith doubted the man would last long in a zombie apocalypse.

"Ms. Thomas...Always...a pleasure." Without waiting for a reply, the man turned around and marched toward the stage, and they scrambled to follow in his wake.

"Do all archeologists have flunkies? I assumed they sat around, staring at broken pots and playing in the dirt with tiny brushes. I don't understand the appeal. This guy is no Indiana Jones."

Lilith barely stopped herself from chuckling at Cohen's whispered commentary. "Who says he's a flunky? Perhaps he's a mutual friend." She glanced over her shoulder, and Cohen raised an eyebrow.

"I've been around enough flunkies to recognize one. Trust me."

When they reached the stage, they followed Rachel to the small group surrounding their target, which included Dr. Price and her girlfriend, Renee.

As if Lilith had summoned her attention, the therapist glanced up when they approached and intercepted them. "Lilith, can I have a word?"

"I'm here on business." Despite the immense background noise, the hostility was difficult to miss.

"This won't take long. I want to apologize. This looks bad, but when Aaron offered the tickets, Renee went nuts. I had no idea you'd be here." Brittany pushed her horn-rimmed glasses up the bridge of her nose and smoothed her teal slip dress—obvious self-comforting measures.

"The last part, I believe. I didn't take you for a mythology buff, but *The Hero with a Thousand Faces* should have been a hint."

Cohen stood stiffly by Lilith's side while she avoided Dr. Price's stare. Instead, Lilith studied the individuals surrounding the archeologist. Their interactions, body language, and tone indicated close relationships. They even shared a common social awkwardness, except for their focal point— Dr. Wolfe. He possessed all the charisma and power in their dynamic, though she didn't understand why.

"I'm sorry, what are you talking about?"

The quizzical tone caught Lilith's attention, bringing her eyes back to the therapist.

"The book in your office, by Joseph Campbell, on archetypes throughout mythology. I recognized the title from a college class."

"Ah. I haven't read it. Renee gave me the book as a gift on our first official date. She's a professor at Columbia University, specializing in ancient religions. I never cared much for the subject, but it reminds me of her." A blush crept over her cheeks, and she pushed at her glasses again.

"She looks familiar, but I can't figure out where I've seen her. I took a couple of courses at Columbia. Perhaps I ran into her on campus." Movement within the group caught Lilith's eye again. The way Wolfe brushed a strand of Renee's silvery hair from her face made Lilith curious. The affectionate interaction suggested a closer relationship than the others, but how close?

"And she knows Dr. Wolfe?"

Brittany glanced at the people behind her. "Kelley? Sure. She consults on finds from his excavations, and he's been over for dinner. Several times a month, they all take a trip to his place in Midstate New York and work on various research projects. They are all quite close. Kindred spirits and all."

The edge of jealousy in the woman's voice made her seem more…human. Perhaps Lilith *had* leapt to a conclusion she wanted to believe earlier. Aaron wasn't a generous person, but accepting the tickets didn't mean he had succeeded in buying her cooperation.

"How did you two meet?" The vague sense of familiarity nagged at Lilith the more she watched Renee, but she still couldn't place her.

Apparently, Cohen had grown bored with the conversation and stared over at the people surrounding Dr. Wolfe. The man didn't excel at patience, especially lately.

"Well, she attended a lecture I gave on the emotional costs of sexual violence about…five months ago. My speech moved her, and she approached me afterward. We went out for coffee, shared our life stories—most of them, anyway—and before I knew it, we were dating." Brittany's lip lifted at the corners in a dreamy smile.

"Is she aware you don't live here?"

The question shook Dr. Price out of her doe-eyed trance, like a splash of ice water to the face.

"Well, yes…I told her I'm here as long as my primary client needs me. She travels a lot, and…perhaps I'll like New York enough to stay."

Lilith's eyebrow rose in a skeptical arch, which made Brittany frown.

"Besides, you have more than enough issues to keep me busy for years."

Lilith caught Cohen smirking and merely held up her middle finger at him.

"Wow, Dr. Price! Was that a sarcastic jab at my emotional damage? How unprofessional." Whether a result of the witty burn or a sense of comradery over blossoming relationships, a smile crossed Lilith's lips, and her sense of distrust eased. "Am I crazy for liking you more after that comment?"

Dr. Price chuckled and patted Lilith's shoulder. "Sharp humor is your comfort zone, so I'm not surprised. Ever heard of the expression 'Sarcasm is how I hug'? Whoever wrote it drew their inspiration from you."

"That's the damn truth," Cohen muttered, earning himself another middle finger. "If you two are finished bonding, can we get back to business?"

"Yes. Sorry, I appreciate the talk, Dr. Price."

"Right. Of course. See you on Monday." With a slight smile, Brittany moved past the people between her and the stairs, heading for the exit. The quick retreat probably had more to do with Renee grabbing Kelley's shoulder and laughing than a need for fresh air.

"So, that's your shrink?" Cohen's voice sounded bored, but curiosity lingered in his expression.

"Yes, and I'd rather not discuss it. Let's just do what we came here to do, okay?"

Cohen shrugged as they stepped past Dr. Wolfe's admirers. "Good evening. Dr. Thomas sent us to speak to you."

"Detective Cohen and Lilith Adams I presume. A pleasure to meet you." Dr. Wolfe moved forward, with a toothy smile befitting his last name.

Up close, she realized what Cohen had mistaken for eyeliner was nothing more than thick, dark lashes. His hair color, however, resulted from a dye job. The harsh black clashed against the olive undertones in his skin. She guessed the man's natural color was about three or four shades lighter.

"Likewise." Lilith pulled on a diplomatic smile and shook his hand. "Dr. Thomas said you might be able to assist us on a case Detective Cohen and I are investigating."

"Ah, yes. She mentioned you had questions about my dig at Apollo's temple." A casual grace infused his movements, reminding her of Cohen when they first met. Perhaps it was the man's self-absorption and over-confidence. "Would you like to go somewhere a little more private?"

Between the noise from the crowded hall and the sensitivity of their conversation, Lilith eagerly accepted his offer. She glanced into the crowd, spotted Nicci and Chance, and motioned to them. Once she received the nod of approval from Chance, she followed Kelley and Cohen backstage.

The amount of sound drowned out by the thick fabric amazed her. The music, loud chatter, and whoops of laughter from the hall lowered to a manageable level in the background, allowing them to speak at a normal volume.

"Ah, much better. Now, how can I help you?"

"Well, to be honest, I'm not sure." Lilith paused and filtered through their information, aiming to convey the situation while avoiding dangerous territory.

"Did you experience any abnormalities at Apollo's temple? Find anything unusual?" the detective jumped in, with the vaguest questions possible.

As the archeologist tilted his head with a confused frown, his hair slid to reveal both blue eyes. "Every site is different. Unusual how?"

"Any corpses or unexpected finds?" Lilith asked.

"It wasn't a burial site, so no remains. Apollo's high priests utilized the chamber, which meant a lot of ceremonial objects. Are you searching for something specific, Ms. Adams?"

While deciding what to tell him, she glanced at Cohen, who nodded with a slight movement. Still, she hesitated, unable to jump in feetfirst. The Durand didn't suffer the same reservations.

"What about relics capable of harboring a virus?"

"A virus?" Dr. Kelley's thin eyebrows shot up in surprise after a brief hesitation—a poor acting job.

Perhaps Dr. Thomas mentioned our agenda, but why feign surprise?

"Hmm. I understand why Rachel sent you to me now."

"She found inactive viral strains on a few things from the excavation and believes our virus matches them. I realize the dig happened a while ago, but do you know which objects she collected samples from? Or if anything went missing?"

Judging by the appreciative smile Dr. Wolfe wore, Lilith had asked the correct questions.

"I see."

The man leaned against the wall. His blue eyes studied Lilith and Cohen, sizing them up. Although the reaction struck her as odd, most people probably didn't ask such specific questions about his work, outside a classroom.

"I can send you a manifest of the tested items. Nothing was reported missing, though things do slip through the cracks over the years. I arranged the dig to recover the Arrows of Artemis and Apollo. Are you familiar with the myths?"

"No. I spent as little time in world mythology as possible. No offense." Although Lilith wanted to skip the history lesson, Dr. Wolfe seemed to enjoy the sound of his own voice far too much.

"Did you know the first documented account of disease in Ancient Greece appeared in Homer's *Iliad*? Agamemnon insulted a priest, and Apollo punished him by shooting arrows that caused a sudden fever to spread through the camp like wildfire. An amusing tale, but my personal favorite is the myth of Niobe." Kelley peered over at the Durand with an amused half-grin. "What about you, Detective? Any background in mythology?"

The tension in Cohen's jaw stretched down to the clenched fists he shoved into his pockets. The man had been dangerously low on patience *before* the archeologist started story time. "No. Not a hobby of mine. I prefer *actual* history over fairy tales and myths originating from the drug-addled minds of incestuous polygamists."

Dr. Wolfe stiffened as if offended by the comment. Of course, if someone thoroughly dismissed her life's work, Lilith would take it to heart too.

"Not all myths are baseless. Many are rooted in fact, and your so-called *history* is nothing more than stories written by victors and tyrants."

"So, these arrows?" Lilith interrupted before the conversation dissolved into outright war. If they wanted information, they needed to play Wolfe's game, or the entire evening would be a waste.

"Niobe, daughter to the King of Phrygia and wife of Amphion, birthed seven sons and seven daughters. The woman's hubris led to her downfall. She boasted her fertility as superior to Leto's...a tragic mistake."

Before he continued, his shoulders straightened and his chin lifted—indicators of pride.

"Artemis and Apollo were fiercely loyal to their mother. The legend states the twin gods each launched seven arrows carrying a fatal illness, killing all of Niobe's children. Not only did they remove the source of the woman's pride, but forced her to witness her offspring's slow, painful deaths."

The man's storytelling unnerved Lilith. Something about his voice and posture...the conviction and sense of personal pride...

"That's an extreme reaction. Imagine the PTA meetings if people followed their example. All those people do is one-up each other. There'd be a *lot* of empty schools. Might improve funding, though..." Her feeble attempt at humor fell flat, and Cohen stared at her with a horrified expression. *Yep, going to hell for that one.*

"Ancient Greece thrived on brutality, and Leto was more than a woman. She was a goddess, one of Zeus's lovers, and insulting the gods is a grave sin." Beneath Kelley's polite smile lurked a tension Lilith couldn't explain, but it made her wonder how seriously he took these myths.

"Well, good thing they're not around this one." The detective nodded toward Lilith with a stiff chuckle. "She insults people without effort on an hourly basis."

Although an amused glimmer shone in his steel-gray eyes, a subtle undercurrent of truth lingered in his voice. She wondered if her accusations at the hotel still bothered him. In her defense, the man hadn't gone out of his way to create trust in the past. However, since the medical center, he had shared everything—motives, information, resources, frustrations...In truth, this raw version of Cohen disturbed her more than the reserved man with shifting motives.

Kelley's smile appeared both bright and forced. "She isn't the only person capable of insulting others. You are both lucky the gods don't still walk the earth. Imagine if they met the two of you."

An eerie silence settled in as they tried to figure out if the man was serious or cracking a bad joke. The odd grin on his face didn't help Lilith decipher the subtext.

"So…where are these arrows located?" She broke the uncomfortable lull in the conversation and got them back on task.

"Well, that's the easy part—my private lab in Midstate New York. Only me and my direct team have access. I can send you a list. However, Rachel has only found inactive fragments, so the possibility of finding a complete virus is almost nonexistent."

"We need to investigate every possible angle. Can you include a list of everyone at the site and any consults with access to items recovered from the dig?"

"Of course. I should still have records of personnel, though I can't vouch for the accuracy of the contact information after so much time." Kelley paused, his eyes roaming between them. "What is this about? Have you stumbled upon an undiscovered infection?"

"We aren't at liberty to discuss ongoing investigations with civilians." The detective's rehearsed answer held subtle traces of animosity the archeologist didn't miss.

"Perhaps *you* can't, but Miss Adams is not on the police force, are you?"

The man's smooth smile made her nervous. "I'm sorry?"

"I read the newspaper. You're the forensic consultant involved in the attacks last year. The exhumed bodies littering downtown made quite a statement."

"Um, yes, I suppose…" *First Dr. Thomas, then the nosey reporter, and now this guy? Do I have a flashing neon sign over my head?*

"I must admit, I was eager to meet you. I don't often meet someone so…unique and instrumental in stopping multiple terrorist attacks."

Something about his word choices gave her chills, but before she formulated a reply, Renee's silvery blond head popped through the curtain.

"Kelley, we need you!"

"Of course, well." The man pushed away from the wall and brushed his hair back. A ring of brown bled into his cool blue irises, something Lilith hadn't noticed earlier. "You heard the woman." Irritation made his voice emerge in a higher pitch, and he shot a sharp glare at Renee. "I'll ensure you receive the information you require."

"Thank you for your time."

After an apologetic smile, Dr. Wolfe disappeared behind the thick fabric wall.

"What utter bullshit!" The sudden bang of a fist hitting wood made Lilith jump. "A total waste. Magic arrows? The man is a joke!"

"Whoa! Calm down…" She reached for his shoulder, but he rounded on her with a maniacal gleam in his eyes.

"Calm down?!" He closed the distance, anger rolling off him in waves. "Please tell me you aren't buying into his Mt. Olympus bullshit!"

"Of course not. Come on. Lower your voice. I understand your frustration, but we do not want to attract attention."

"All of this is ridiculous!" Cohen's eyes hardened to an icy gray that made her blood run cold. "People are dying, and we are listening to fairy tales from a delirious virology professor and an archeologist who owns far too many My Chemical Romance albums. I came to you for help, and *you* are wasting my time."

An indignant frown formed as she took a step back. "What do you expect me to do? Please, if you have a better idea, share it with the damn class."

The demon opened his mouth to say something but closed it.

"Yeah, that's what I thought. You're upset and want answers, but don't take it out on me."

The muscles of his face only tightened. "Oh, so it's okay for you but not me."

"What the hell do you mean?"

"Come on. You know exactly what I mean. The hotel?"

I knew it.

"Andrew, I apologized—"

"I don't want an apology!"

Lilith frowned, confused by the interruption. "Then what do you—"

"Do you still hold me responsible for your father's death?"

"What? No. Of course not."

"Are you sure?"

Something about him felt…off. *Why dredge all this up now? What is his agenda?* "Do you blame yourself? It's obviously weighing on your mind, if you decided to bring it up."

Every one of his muscles stiffened into a rigid line of defensiveness. *Guess that answers my question, but why is he suddenly so easy to read?* The man perfected hiding his emotions, intentions, and motives, which is why he'd been so difficult to trust at first. *So, what changed? Did the ordeal with Luminita and Farren alter his fundamental personality?*

"Andrew," she spoke softly, touching his shoulder, "let's call it a night. I'm tired, hungry, and itching to escape this lavish hellscape. I'll touch base with you in the morning."

When he continued to stand still, his lips mashed together into a firm line, she released a heavy sigh.

"Okay. Nice talk." When she turned toward the curtain, Cohen's hand on her arm stopped her short.

"I need the truth. Do you blame me for what happened to your father?" This time, the anger in his expression softened into a plea.

For a moment, Lilith stared at the faint scars on his face and considered her response. Part of her wanted to walk away, but something in his eyes told her he needed an answer, closure. After all the times he had saved her life, she owed him that much.

"At first, sure. Gregor was my world, and *your* grandfather murdered him while you stood by and did nothing."

He started to interrupt, but she barreled ahead.

"Let me finish. That's how I *felt*. I was angry and lashed out at everyone, including you. I realize you're not at fault, and his death isn't the reason I've had trouble trusting you."

"Then what is it?" The sheer vulnerability in his voice made it almost unrecognizable.

"Why is this so important?"

"Just answer the question!" The expression on his face evolved from lost desperation back to anger. His brows drew together, and the sudden transition put Lilith on the defensive.

"I told you. My trust issues don't start and stop with you. And what about me?"

"What do you mean?"

"Since you showed up at Chance's place, you've fought me at every turn. Either trust my lead or come up with a better plan." She scowled down

The Lotus Tree

at his hand, still gripping her forearm, until he released her. "I'm not having this conversation again, Andrew. All this animosity between us, as well as you and Chance…Drop it and work *with* us or go home."

Without a backward glance, Lilith turned on her heel, released a deep breath, pulled on a false smile, and pushed through the curtain. She moved across the stage toward the stairs and spotted Renee and Rachel standing a short distance away from Kelley's throng. The two were engrossed in a heated discussion, and according to their body language, Dr. Thomas had the upper hand.

"Lily!" Chance hollered over the crowd a yard or so from the stage and waved his hand.

Giving him a warm smile, she grabbed her skirts and moved down the stairs with a desperate desire to escape the need for false facades and hollow words.

She never understood how people chose to spend their entire lives in a lie, like this gala—always pretending. As a vampire, she had no choice, but she blended into an ocean of humans by avoiding situations, vague descriptions, and omissions, not outright lies.

She approached Chance, and the line he quoted earlier resurfaced in her mind. *True love does not ask you to change. It simply invites you into a safe space where you can stop being who you are not.* The concept seemed simple, but in her nearly twenty-nine years, she'd never experienced anything like it, until now.

With him, she could shed all the pretense, and they could embrace their individuality together. They understood each other, accepted one another as is, and didn't constantly question the other's motives. If that wasn't true love, then she'd never comprehend the abstract notion.

Chapter 19 - *Cassie*

Pain and darkness became Cassie's only companions in the endless silence. The horizontal position they'd left her in became uncomfortable and then torturous. The wide gaps between the wheel's spokes didn't support her shattered joints. Each muscle burned from the pointless adjustments of her trying in vain to lessen gravity's pull.

Somehow, the mental agony disturbed her more. The memory of the sweaty man's lecherous hands made bile rise in her throat. Not even scrubbing with bleach and a Brillo pad would remove the taint he'd left behind. The only comfort she took was knowing she wouldn't have to live with the burden for long.

Although each visit from the cult meant pain and torment, they rescued her from the dark, distracted her from the chaos in her head, and delivered the beloved fruit she craved with every fiber of her being. Besides, one of the visits would be the last, and Cassie embraced the inevitability.

If by some miracle the FBI managed a rescue, her life would never be the same. Eight of her fingers, her left elbow, and both knees had suffered compound fractures and were healing without being reset, not to mention the burns they had inflicted to stop the bleeding. The best-case scenario involved re-breaking every joint to reset them—*which may not be possible at this point.* Worst case, she'd never walk again or be able to care for herself. With no family, significant other, or close friend, who would help her? Not her partner. *He made that crystal clear. No. This is how the life of Cassandra Cappalletty ends—at the hands of madmen.*

Perhaps things are better this way. After all, what did I do with my life?

She had focused all her time on grades no one cared about and exceling at a job where no one appreciated her dedication. Her partner and lover, the one person she should trust implicitly, didn't care about ruining her career and professional relationships. He had merely used her to perpetuate his obscene obsession with his ex and nothing more. *He never loved me. At least here, I'm important.*

"God, this is so fucked up. Stockholm Syndrome at its finest."

Although she poked fun at the thought, it still warmed the distant corners of her mind. What if the horrors they inflicted on her gave her life purpose? Perhaps it was the intoxicating fruit or her mind's attempt to find meaning in the horror, but she couldn't help wondering... *Will my death mean more than my life?*

When the familiar parade of footsteps sounded overhead, an odd mixture of excitement and fear percolated through her battered body. But more followed, bringing the total close to twenty or thirty. *Today must be important.* This time, the excitement overcame her lingering fears.

"Good morning, my dear Cassie."

The affectionate tone took her by surprise after the way their last session had ended.

Footsteps clattered on the concrete—some circling her and others remaining near the stairs. A metal screech followed by a hollow thump indicated someone dragging over a chair and sitting beside her.

"Today, we are going to have a little chat." Art spoke near her right side, confirming her assumption. "But first, I want to apologize for my behavior on our last visit. You do not deserve my anger." A soft palm caressed her cheek in a motion so meaningful, it brought tears to her eyes. "Do you forgive me for my outburst?"

A sudden lump of emotions prevented her from speaking, so she nodded adamantly.

"Thank you, my dearest. And Jerry behaved himself after I left? He didn't...spoil you?"

"Nothing happened before I lost consciousness."

"Such complete honesty. You have come a long way. I'm so proud of your journey." Despite a sliver of logic screaming obscenities in her head, his words summoned a glow of validation and pride.

"Now, we should attend to your needs."

The apparatus tilted forward, raising her head. Gravity pulled at her injuries, forcing a whimpering cry despite her attempt to remain silent. The metal touched her chapped lips, and she attempted to gulp down the water but choked and gagged, sending rivulets of the cold liquid rushing down her naked chest. The second attempt went smoother, and the sips of cool water soothed her parched throat. Then the cup disappeared.

A delicious scent filled her nostrils moments before the peel met her mouth. Warmth rushed through her body and pulled the soul from her skin, allowing her to float above the pain in a euphoric cloud of invulnerability.

"Cassie." He pulled the contraption back into a horizontal position before grasping her chin with a light touch. When she didn't respond, he tapped her cheek. "Can you hear me?"

She nodded in slow motion, like a drugged-up junkie—or at least she thought she did.

"Good."

Art slid back into his chair and started his monologue, but she missed the beginning. Concentrating on his words proved difficult. They sounded strange, like a foreign language spoken through a long metal tube.

"…that is why I told you my story. You saw an Empusa." When the silence stretched out, he grabbed her chin again with less delicacy. "Do you understand?"

She understood the words but didn't grasp their meaning. *I am so tired, so very tired. If I sleep…*

"Tennessee! Do you remember?"

"Tennessee, yes."

"Good. I am going to ask you questions. If you refuse to answer, you will be punished, although it will hurt me to do so. If you cooperate, I will reward you. Understood?"

"Yes, of course." Cassie agreed to his terms without hesitation, not only because she wanted the torture to end, but because his kindness felt like the sun shining down on her and she wanted nothing more than to bask in his glow.

"Why did you go to Tennessee?"

"I…My partner, he…he thought the Bureau closed a case too soon."

"Continue."

A tear escaped her eye as she focused. Understanding his words took so much effort, and finding the answers in her traumatized brain provided even more of a challenge. "He knew someone involved and wanted to tie up loose ends."

"You investigated Dr. Nichols's murder?"

She frowned at the unfamiliar name. "No."

"The doctor who tested the strange blood sample—from the Empusa?"

"I…I don't know who that is or anything about strange blood."

"You never went to Goditha, to the lab?"

She paused, trying to shake the details loose. "We went, but they wouldn't let us in…No warrant. Never got past the front door."

"But you did investigate Phipps Bend, didn't you?"

"What was left." A giggle escaped her lips. *What is wrong with me? The lotus fruit always gives me a weird high, but never like this.* "It was a crater in the ground."

"Yes, yes. But you recovered corpses."

"Gorman and Hersch did. They ran the original investigation."

"Yes, but you went through the files, visited the site, and took the information to a third party. You know what they recovered. One of them was a dangerous Empusa."

"A what?" The strange word made no sense to her drowsy mind, which drifted farther from her body.

Art released a frustrated growl that vibrated through the air and tickled her skin. "We gave her too much." A wicked slap made her left cheek throb, and the sensation pulled her consciousness closer.

"Concentrate! This is vital, not only to me but to the world! You can save them all! What happened to the bodies from Phipps Bend?"

As hard as she tried, Cassie still came up empty. Her brain felt like half-licked cotton candy. "I don't know."

"You gave a file to an expert in York, Pennsylvania. You told her they weren't available for examination. Why?"

"Dr. Thomas? But how—"

"How is not important. If I must, I will pry the truth from your lips. Why couldn't she inspect the cadavers?"

"We never…" The words slurred and trailed off as she lost focus.

"Why?"

Tears spilled from her eyes, and she fought the disorientation, trying to remember. Art placed his hand at the bend of her uninjured elbow and shouted.

"Why?!"

"They were gone!" When the hand fell away, her eyelids fluttered with a woozy sensation. The darkness spun, making her stomach churn and pitch. The thought of more broken bones would have made her vomit if she'd eaten more than a few bites of fruit.

"Gone where?"

"Just gone." Her voice emerged faint and hollow, and she drifted off again.

"Cassandra." A calm restraint replaced his frenzied shouts. "An Empusa attacked my mother, drank her blood, tore her to ribbons, and left her on the bedroom floor." The man paused, his voice breaking, and the vulnerability and trauma drew her in, pulling her closer. "Don't you want justice for victims like her? Isn't that why you joined the FBI?"

Tears cascaded across her cheeks again. "Yes."

"Then help me, my love. The entire race is far too dangerous. We cannot allow their existence," the man pleaded, his breath warming her ear. His fingers moved through her mahogany hair in affectionate caresses, lulling her into a feeling of safety. "You want to help me, don't you?"

"Yessss…" She leaned into his touch and took slow, deep breaths.

"Good. Now close your eyes." He smoothed the hair from her face and lowered his voice to a hypnotic tone. "Think back. You went to the morgue, but the bodies were missing. Why?"

"Someone took them."

"Stolen?"

"No. The FBI gave them away. Most of them, not all."

"Be specific."

Her head tilted toward his voice, but the blindfold kept her from gazing at his face. "One stayed. The rest went away."

"One…The big one? The one you asked Dr. Thomas about?"

How long did he follow me? Before the anger kicked in, an irrational jealousy dominated her mind.

"Did you spy on everyone involved? Was I just the easiest one to kidnap?" Tears infused her drowsy voice, and a sudden anxiety attack left her gasping for air. *My life meant nothing, and they chose me out of convenience. I don't matter, not to anyone.*

"Shh. Cassandra. Breathe." The relaxing yet luxurious sensation as he stroked her hair again elicited a murmur of contentment. "We chose you for a multitude of reasons. *I* chose you. You are special. Now…You and Agent Boston discovered the FBI sent them to someone?"

"Yes."

"Take a deep breath and let your mind go back. Boston told you where they went, didn't he?"

Somehow, she knew he was right. David had told her, but the memory remained disconnected, lost in the chaos. "I can't reach it."

"Relax and allow yourself to remember. What happened when you and your partner went to examine the bodies?"

Cassie sifted through her jumbled mind and brought herself back to that day. "We spoke with the medical examiner in Knoxville. David asked about Phipps Bend, and the doctor said someone shipped them to an expert in New York City before he completed a preliminary exam."

"Excellent. So, you went to New York City?"

"Yes." The mental picture swirled and reformed into a scene in another morgue with a gruff man limping through the room. "The examiner was hostile and didn't appreciate our questions, but he claimed no record of a shipment from Tennessee existed."

"They never arrived?"

Cassie squeezed her eyes shut and focused harder. The images melded into a vague mist, slipping away from her grasp. "No. I don't think so. I thought the man might be lying, but David inspected the manifests personally and found no discrepancies."

"What did you do next?"

"We left the city. David was furious. He kept saying he knew *she* was involved somehow. I'd never seen him so angry, and it scared me. He punched the dash of his car, and the horrible expression he wore when he looked at me…" Tears flooded her eyes again as she relived the moment. It had been the turning point, the catalyst for her transfer, the reason she wanted to disappear.

"Shh…He can't hurt you now. Continue."

"He turned on me…He said *she* was gonna get away with it because I didn't agree to help him sooner. Gorman was right about him all along…"

"She?"

"A woman he dated…in college. She lives in New York City."

"And she took the bodies?"

"No." A frown formed. The car ride came back to her in bits and pieces. "He called someone at the FBI…a friend. They told him the cadavers and tissue samples were rerouted during shipment to a private party for independent research."

Then everything unfolded before her, and she released a moan of relief.

"Pegasus Medical International Corporation. That's where they went."

"Pegasus Medical? Are you sure?" Barely restrained excitement infused his voice as if he didn't dare believe her yet but desperately wanted to.

"Yes…I didn't think the information was important. Boston couldn't get past the automated phone menu, and we couldn't find a physical address…a dead end. 'The woman is the key,' he said. With her name connected to both the Tennessee and New York City attacks, he remained certain."

"Excellent. Do you remember this woman's name?"

"Lilian…No. Um…Lilith! That's it. Lilith Adams."

Lips touched her cheek in a lingering kiss. "You did so well, Cassie." After he stroked her hair again, the blindfold slid away.

Having the cloth removed made her feel vulnerable and exposed. She had worn it for so long, through so much, and now they stripped away her shield of darkness.

"It's okay, my dearest." Art's hand moved in calming strokes through her hair.

She blinked, trying to adjust, but the illumination burned into her retinas like lasers.

"Take your time."

Someone gave her more delicious bites of the mana from heaven, and a drowsy state flooded her body. The lure of unconsciousness waged war on her opportunity to *see* something, but for a moment, a blurry face loomed into view.

"Enjoy your rewards, dear Cassie. They will make the rest easier." As Art caressed her cheek, he smiled, the same enigmatic smile he had worn that fateful night. Thick dark lashes still framed his sparkling blue eyes, with their pop of brown circling the irises.

She had made him happy, and he didn't hurt her…

The delirious high won, dragging her into the unfeeling depths of a deep and dreamless sleep.

Chapter 20

After arriving at Nicci's, Cohen grunted an ambivalent goodbye while Nicci, Chance, and Lilith climbed out into the warm summer night. The stretch town car pulled away the second they stepped into the street, reinforcing Cohen's displeasure at the night's events. Although she understood his frustration, Lilith found his tantrums distracting, irritating, and confusing.

Give him time and space. A lot of things changed in his life too. Losing Luminita and Farren might mean he's free, but it also means he's alone.

She took a deep, cleansing breath, let go of her anger, and started across the street, watching for oncoming cars. A maroon Buick pulled to the curb a half block down and parked with its lights off but the engine running.

"Lil, you coming?" Nicci held the door open for her.

"Uh, yeah." After flashing a tight smile, she caught up to Chance inside, and he pressed the elevator button.

"You okay, *cherie?*"

"Yeah. It's just…Nothing, never mind."

"What is it, Lily?" His voice transformed from concern to business mode, his shoulders tightening.

"A maroon sedan parked down the street—lights off, engine running. Could be nothing, but…God, I sound paranoid."

Chance wrapped an arm around her shoulders and kissed her temple. "I'm sure it's an Uber driver or something. Once you change clothes, we'll head home. We can put on pajamas, snuggle on the couch, watch an episode of *The Last of Us*, and relax."

A warm smile lit her face, and she nestled into him. "Sounds perfect. Hopefully, this episode won't make me cry as much as the last one."

A soft chuckle escaped, and he squeezed her shoulders, bringing her closer. "I even picked up kettle corn popcorn, Orville Redenbacher's, your favorite…"

"Break it up!" Nicci frowned, stepped into the elevator, and held the door for them. "I'm gonna spray you two down with a hose if you don't knock it off." Although her annoyed tone and crossed arms indicated anger, she winked at her partner and cracked a smile.

"We'll be out of your hair as soon as I change."

"No biggie. You can use my room while I unbraid my hair in the bathroom. This complex mess is gonna take a hot minute."

"Thanks, Nicci."

"No problem, partner."

Once they all entered the apartment, Lilith grabbed her bag and headed into the bedroom. Nicci hung back and waited for Lilith to close the door.

"Do you really think it's an Uber driver?" Nicci spoke up before Chance could.

"No. Go ahead and change. I'll keep an eye out."

After turning off all the lights in the room, Chance edged toward the huge window behind the couch, leaned against the wall, and peered down at the street.

The maroon car Lilith had described was still parked half a block down the street with the engine idling. Although he spotted a shadow in the driver's seat, at that distance, Chance couldn't make out any features. Besides, the vehicle sat in the black void between two streetlamps, escaping their harsh orange glare.

The bathroom door closed, and he sensed Nicci's nervous energy begin to dissipate, most likely soothed by the familiar act of undoing her hair, washing her face, and whatever else constituted her evening routine.

While still watching the street below, Chance focused on Lilith and attempted to sort through the tumultuous melting pot of emotions she contained. The sadness and futility she had tried to suppress since October dimmed, overcome by anger, purpose, frustration, and curiosity. Still, somewhere in the mess, she was happy. The deep, intimate moments they shared scared her but also elicited a euphoric sensation, making his heart soar.

Everything he sensed from her should have put his mind at ease, but he still worried. *Eventually, everyone leaves*—the lesson he'd learned from his parents, but he was determined not to repeat their mistakes. Most people blamed the drugs, but they were a symptom, not the cause.

For brief moments, they had appeared happy, but they made each other miserable after a while. They suffered from a fundamental incompatibility they tried to overcome but failed. In the end, they brought out the worst in each other.

I won't let that happen with Lilith.

"Whatcha doing?"

Chance almost jumped at the unexpected sound of her voice.

After clearing his throat, he glanced over at her—now dressed in comfy jeans and a sage sweatshirt featuring a black floral skull. "Keeping an eye on the car you mentioned. Can't be too careful."

Relief and gratitude. She was glad he took her concern seriously.

"Okay. Well, ready to go?" Lilith adjusted the bag on her shoulder as he stepped away from the window. "Talk to you later, Nicci." She raised her voice, strolling toward the door.

Nicci's face peeked out of the bathroom, her brown hair a mess of wild waves. "See ya."

Once they reached his Sport Trac and climbed in, he pulled onto the street, watching the rearview mirror.

Sure enough, the maroon Buick turned on its headlights and followed.

Lilith leaned to peer in the side view mirror. "I was right. Someone's following us."

"One car back on the left—classic FBI formation."

"Shit. You think it's—"

"Special Agent Boston, yes." His eyes narrowed to slits, and he stared daggers at the rearview mirror. *Fuck.*

Their peaceful solution of using Tim as a middleman had apparently failed, but killing Boston would only attract attention from the Bureau and his influential father. *Still. What he did to Lilith…the man doesn't deserve to share the same air as her.*

"So, what's our move?"

"We stick to our plan. Lead him to my place. It's remote, and—"

"Plenty of places to hide a body? No. Plus, the man's an idiot, but he's not stupid enough to follow you into an abandoned industrial park."

"And the downside to scaring him off is?"

"My place. This shit needs to end…"

"No." A mixture of anger and fear roared to life in his chest.

"We can't have him following us while we investigate this virus. It's too dangerous. We need to end it now. Please, just drive to my place."

Lilith's plea made sense, but if the man tried to attack or said the wrong thing, Chance couldn't guarantee he'd control his temper. Of course, none of it mattered. Once Lilith made up her mind, nothing could deter the woman. It was one of the things he loved about her.

"Fine." Chance squeezed the word through clenched teeth before a deep inhale. Once he released the breath in a steady stream through pursed lips, he continued. "I'll drop you off at the door and call you. Stay out front while I circle the block. It's time I talked to this guy." The plastic groaned as his hands tightened around the steering wheel.

"Chance…" The warning fell flat, and he sensed conflicting emotions ricocheting through her mind. Part of her wanted the man dead.

"I said *talk*, not *kill*."

An uneasy silence filled the rest of the drive. Lilith watched the Buick weave through traffic, never more than one car away. After the gala's fun-filled emotional fireworks, this was the last thing Lilith needed, but she couldn't put off confronting her demons forever. She needed to send David a message he wouldn't forget.

When the truck came to a stop, Chance turned to her and stared until she met his gaze. "Stay on the phone. If you are standing out front alone, he might get out of the car. If he does, run inside the lobby. Do not take unnecessary risks. I'm serious." The rigidness in his voice left no room for argument, but she had never dealt well with authority.

"Okay."

"Lilith…"

"I understand!"

He still appeared skeptical, probably because he knew her too well or maybe it was the Durand blood.

She slipped out of the vehicle while the driver behind them blared the horn. For a moment, Chance ignored the noise and watched her walk up to the doors.

After he sped off, the person driving the maroon Buick parked across the street and turned off the headlights, eradicating any doubts that they were following her. *What the hell do they want? Is it David waiting for his opportunity to take revenge?*

The upbeat tone of *The Office* theme song—their current favorite show to binge—interrupted her intense focus.

Before he asked, she answered the question. "He parked across the street. No movement so far."

"Stay put. I'll be back in a few minutes."

The more she stared at the Buick, the more resentment and anger rose to the surface. *Who does he think he is? Attacking me, threatening me, now following me, like I'm the fucking villain.*

"Lilith?"

"What?"

"You *know* what. Don't do it, please!"

The sorrowful plea threw her off balance.

"Does your emotion detector work over the phone now?" The sarcasm emerged sharper than intended, but she was tired of people ordering her around.

"No, but…I know you."

"Then you know I'm not going to listen." She hung up on his protests and marched across the street. Her olive eyes bored holes into the offensive car, and each furious step drove back the remnants of fear. When she closed in, perhaps fifteen feet away, the door swung open, and Agent Boston lumbered out of the vehicle.

"Why the hell are you following me?"

The man's facial features hardened into cruel lines. In college, the familiar expression had made her cower, but she flat-out refused to play the victim anymore. Ashcroft, Luminita, Boston, Farren—all of them had tried to strip away her will, beat her down, and leave her powerless. *To hell with that. It's my fucking turn.*

"You think you can pawn me off to some two-bit PI lackey?" As he spoke, a car blared its horn, and he turned his back on her, clearly refusing to consider her a threat. Once they reached the sidewalk, he rounded on her. "This isn't a joke. Where is Cassandra? What did you do to her?"

Lilith stuffed every submissive instinct into a deep, dark corner and faced him, standing inches away from his anger-riddled body. "Do I need to spell it out for you? *I don't know!* Solasta put me on paid suspension with mandatory therapy eight months ago. I haven't left the city!"

The proclamation didn't weaken his resolve. The fine wrinkles around his black eyes only deepened, and he leaned closer. "Doesn't mean you didn't have a hand in it."

"You stubborn asshole! You *know* I'm telling the truth, but running out of leads makes you feel powerless. How better to reclaim your sense of control and dominance than beating on your old punching bag? It's toxic, abusive bullshit."

His face turned beet-red with either embarrassment or fury, most likely both, but he didn't interrupt her.

"Oh yeah, you're a big, strong man, pushing around a woman to make himself feel important. Did Cassandra realize what a demented, psychotic waste of skin you are and run? Did you take your frustration out on her too?"

The man's left fist clenched a split second before he swung, but she expected it. After all, Boston was easy to bait and had always led with his left. She slammed her forearm into his, blocking the blow. He gaped in surprise.

Before he recovered, Lilith thrust her palm into his Adam's apple, and her heel crashed down on his right shin. The man lost his balance and grabbed his throat, choking on agonal breaths, but she wasn't done.

Lilith took full advantage of his vulnerable state by hooking his leg and shoving her body weight against him. He hit the concrete with a sickening crack, and she perched on top of him, thrusting her forearm into his neck. The man's contorted face turned varying shades of purple, and her glowing sense of pride swelled when he stopped struggling.

"I'm not such an easy mark these days."

When she leaned close, the stench of alcohol almost made her gag.

"You are going to leave me alone and stop following me. If I uncover anything connected to your partner's disappearance, Timothy will contact you. Do you understand?"

Boston gritted his teeth and bucked in a sudden attempt to knock her off, but the predictable move didn't surprise her. At the first muscle quiver, her knees clenched his chest. When his arched back collapsed on the pavement, the momentum sent her forearm crashing against his windpipe, causing a violent coughing fit.

"Lilith!"

Her head shot up.

Chance ran toward her, a mixture of anger and fear on his face.

Although the distraction only lasted a split second, Boston took full advantage. With a surprising burst of energy, he shoved one shoulder up, making her topple, and locked a meaty hand around her neck. Chance accelerated to a sprint as Boston's hand tightened.

Lilith's lungs burned, and panicked memories of David, Ashcroft, Farren, and Peisinoe spiraled through her head.

When Boston glared down at her with a malicious grin, the memories halted, and a clear resolution snapped into focus. Lilith coiled all her strength and shot her palm up against his bicep. The shoulder joint dislocated with a stomach-churning pop, and the man shrieked in pain.

"You broke my fucking arm!"

David jumped back, howling and cursing, but before Lilith scrambled to her feet, Chance tackled him, making the man's face collide with the pavement. Besides losing a button on his dress shirt, his tuxedo survived the brief scuffle. Thankfully, he had left the jacket in his truck.

In seconds, Chance had him subdued—one hand gripping the man's neck, and the other twisting the injured arm behind his back. "Give me a fucking reason."

When David went limp, Chance peered over at Lilith.

"Are you okay?"

She nodded, rubbing her sore neck, and anger replaced his concern.

"What in the hell were you thinking?"

A frown formed as she brushed off her pants. "I don't need you to solve all my problems. You taught me to stand my ground, remember? ...*which I did*. I had everything under control." Then she addressed the asshole on the ground. "And your arm isn't broken—just dislocated—and you deserved it."

Boston struggled while they seemed distracted, but Chance only increased the torque on his injured arm. When the man stopped howling in pain, Chance shot Lilith a significant glance, which meant they'd discuss things later, and shifted his icy stare back to Agent Boston.

"On your feet." Without waiting, he lifted the dislocated arm, giving the man no choice but to clamber awkwardly off the ground.

"Who...the fuck are you? I'm an FBI agent, and this woman is a suspect in a missing person's case! Let me go! You're assaulting a federal officer!"

Chance spun him around, maintaining a tight grip on his elbow, and towered over him, using every inch of his six-foot-three frame.

"I want to be *completely* clear. I don't care about your shield or your father's influence. I promised Lilith. That is the *only* reason you're still breathing, you worthless fucking coward. You will drive away and *never* contact her again. If you so much as look in her direction, you'll beg me to end your life. Tell me you understand."

"I…"

When Boston hesitated, Chance shoved the man's wrist toward his dislocated shoulder, eliciting an agonized scream.

"Stop! I understand!"

As soon as the words left David's mouth, Chance released him with an unnecessary shove and watched the man sprint to his car. After the Buick sped off, he stormed over to Lilith, grabbed her hand, and tugged her toward the road.

"You don't have to hold my hand while we cross the street. I'm not five."

The pitiful attempt at levity fell flat. He arched an eyebrow but didn't speak.

The silence continued as he escorted her into the lobby, waved at the security guard, and ushered her into the elevator. Once the doors closed, he rounded on her.

"That was reckless and stupid! There is a world of difference between self-defense and picking a fight to prove something. I told you to stay put. I'm the pro, remember?"

The words cut deep and dampened the pride she had earned by conquering her personal villain. *Why doesn't he understand how much I needed that moment of victory?*

As the thought crossed her mind, markers of concern and realization appeared on his face. *Stupid emotion-detecting blood.*

"I let the bastard traumatize me…I allowed the ghost of his abuse to haunt my life for over a decade. He made me scared and weak, and I needed to reclaim my strength. I *needed* him to understand that I'm not his punching bag anymore. Besides, I wasn't reckless." When he countered with a skeptical scowl, she stated the obvious. "You were right around the corner."

He opened his mouth, but she cut off his protest.

"I hear you. I understand what you're saying, and I'm sorry. I should have waited for you. Can we stop arguing? I've had more than my fair share for the evening."

After a weary sigh, Lilith leaned against him, and his arm slid around her shoulders without another word. A smile pulled at the corners of her mouth, and he softly kissed the top of her head, drawing her close.

She envisioned stripping off her clothes and curling up in her cozy bed with Chance, but "Eye of the Tiger" broke the comfortable silence.

"What's up, partner?"

"I decided to check on the progress with Nichols's computer. My program decrypted some of his secure files, and it's not a massive porn collection…"

The tremble in her voice raised the hairs on the back of Lilith's neck, and she stiffened.

"This is serious shit."

The words sparked a more than familiar apprehension, and she stepped away from Chance with apologetic eyes. "So, I'm guessing this can't wait until morning. Yeah, okay. We're on our way."

"No rest for the wicked," Chance sighed.

Lilith flashed an apologetic smile and reached for the lobby button, but he grabbed her hand first.

"I need to change clothes."

An impish grin curled her lips. She ran her fingers up his black dress shirt and straightened his tie. "I don't think you do. I'm rather fond of this particular look."

With one finger, he tilted her chin upward, and his lips caressed hers in a sensual kiss that nearly burned away the memory of her partner's call. "Thank you for the compliment, *mon cherie*, but fair is fair. You already changed out of your dress. Besides, I'd like to keep this tux in one piece, and you should really *eat* something before we go."

He didn't mean food, and he was right. In all the craziness, she'd forgotten to drink her daily *supplement*, which might have explained her irritability.

Judging by his expression, the night's events weighed heavy on his mind, and his smile faltered. "When we leave, I'll pull the truck around. I need you to wait inside…Lily." Once he had her full attention, his hazel eyes locked onto hers. "…Please."

"*Aye, aye, mon capitán.*"

"I'm serious. I think the weasel hauled ass to the ER, but I can't guarantee he didn't stick around."

"I get it. I'll warm up some blood while you change. Then I'll stay put in the lobby until you pick me up. I promise."

After she'd proved her point to David, she had zero qualms waiting in the bright lobby while Chance scouted the darkness.

Nicci swung the door open and ushered them inside with urgency. She'd traded the citrine gown for a pair of yoga pants and an oversized NYPD T-shirt that swallowed her petite frame.

"Thanks for coming over. I realize it's late but…"

The haunted tone in her partner's voice made Lilith more than a little uneasy.

"…this is scary shit."

Once she led them into her office, Nicci plopped down in front of the computer and clicked through a few files. "First, I found this."

With one click, a picture filled the screen, and Lilith's jaw hit the floor.

Dr. Nichols was flashing a radiant smile and raising a champagne glass. The sight summoned flashes from Goditha in an instant—Ashcroft's skull reforming after a point-blank shot, bloodcurdling screams, talons ripping through the doctor's body while Ashcroft fed on the fear and agony.

However, the traumatic montage wasn't what left Lilith shell-shocked. On Dr. Nichols's right stood Dr. Rachel Thomas, raising a glass with a conspiratorial grin that highlighted her dimples.

"No way this is a coincidence, guys. The virologist who identified our virus *and* the foremost expert on vampire DNA? Plus, the pic is titled *First Successful Trial.*"

"First trial of what and when?" Lilith stared hard at the screen, wishing it would magically give up its secrets.

"Well, it's dated six years ago, but *what* is the million-dollar question. I'm still trying to open the rest of his files."

"Okay…," Chance spoke up, pacing the small room. "This photo is…compelling, but did you drag us down here for one picture?"

"Of course not. This was the *first* thing I found, not the only thing."

After a few more mouse clicks, an Excel file filled the screen.

"What are we looking at? A database?"

Nicci swiveled around to face them with grave sincerity. "This is worse than the virus."

"How?" Lilith's soft-spoken question lingered in the air like a specter until Nicci continued.

"Did you know Dr. Nichols was human?"

"What? That's impossible!" A deep frown formed, and Lilith crossed her arms. "The man headed every research team. He explained Ashcroft's blood sample to me—vampire markers, phenomenon, and all. Duncan would never..."

"Would never, what? Hire a brilliant scientist to fulfill his dream of an artificial blood supply?" The petite Italian cocked an eyebrow. "Or do you mean, he'd never hide the genealogy of a genius to protect him from the rest of us?"

"But..." Before Lilith could form a sentence, Nicci barreled ahead.

"Dr. Nichols played an instrumental role in every single breakthrough Duncan made for the past two decades."

"Wait." Chance waved his hand, as if clearing the air before paranoia consumed them all. "The Elders put protocols and precautions in place to prevent things like this. They would never approve a human working in such an integral role, no matter the cost."

"Correct. *Protocols* and *precautions* that *Duncan* developed and enforced. He is the only one who could circumvent Gregor, Aaron, and the others."

Nicci's disapproval rang with certainty, but Lilith couldn't wrap her mind around the concept. Each time she opened her mouth to say something, the rebuttal died before reaching her lips.

Over the past year, she'd learned how far Duncan and Gregor would go for revenge and the advancement of their species. As much as she hated to admit defeat, a strong possibility existed that Nicci was right.

"I don't expect you to take my word on blind faith. Here." Her partner spun back to the computer and opened the doctor's health and employment records. "Everything to the outside world says human..."

"As it should. Vampire isn't an option on the race questionnaire."

The woman ignored Lilith's sarcastic jab and continued.

"And internal records pronounce him a half-blood. However..." She pulled the Excel file back up and scrolled. "This database is the doc's pet project. I'm assuming it was a secret since he buried this thing in heavy encryption. Dr. Nichols recorded the DNA sequence of every sample he touched, which includes vampires, human donors, even the Elders."

As stunned silence filled the room, Nicci continued to scroll through the endless file.

"Here: *Lilith Adams, complete sequence, result: full-blood vampire. Gregor Adams, complete sequence, result: full-blood vampire, paternal match to Lilith Adams.*"

"Fascinating and disturbing, but I don't understand how this proves Dr. Nichols's heritage." Chance raked his fingers through his hair, an edge to his voice.

"Because the man recorded his own DNA." She highlighted the doctor's name. "*Result: human, no vampire markings.*" Then Nicci turned her keen eyes on Chance. "He also sequenced you, by the way."

The sudden suspicion startled them both.

"Well, after drinking Durand blood"—Lilith cast a nervous glance at him before continuing—"which is still affecting him, I'm not surprised—"

"No." Nicci interrupted with a firm denial, making Lilith's heart skip a beat. "The sample originated from the children's hospital where Gregor found him and shows abnormalities."

Chance stared at the screen, and his eyes widened. "What *abnormalities?*"

"Your DNA displays the expected vampire and human segments but also something else. You're certain your dad was a half-blood, right?"

He responded with a slight nod, unable to tear his eyes away from the screen.

"What about your mom?"

When he didn't respond, Lilith gently touched his shoulder. "Chance?"

He squeezed his eyes shut, forcing himself to think. "Uh, I don't know."

Nicci quirked an eyebrow and leaned back in her chair with open disbelief. "You don't *know?*"

A tremor traveled along his clenched jaw, and his eyes narrowed in on her. "I was ten when they died, and genealogy lessons weren't a priority."

"They never mentioned—"

"No! My mom came over from France in the 1970s. Léna Vieux. That's the extent of my knowledge, and I learned that from Gregor. Both my parents were junkies who spent their time chasing new highs. They fought a lot…and the violence escalated. She'd reach a tipping point and run off, and Dad always found a way to blame me when she did…"

The haunted expression he wore as his eyes drifted to the floor cut Lilith to the core. Chance had hinted a few times but never spoke in detail about his parents. Now she understood why, and he'd only skimmed the surface.

"Anyway, she'd come home after a few weeks, followed by a week or two of tearful apologies, and the cycle would start over again. The pattern repeated every three or four months for as long as I can remember. So, no, they didn't sit me down and talk about their families."

"Chance, I'm…" Lilith's hand tightened on his shoulder, the words dying in her throat. *What can I say? Sorry seems woefully inadequate.*

He straightened, and the faraway expression dissipated. "When Gregor brought me to Goditha from the children's hospital, they labeled me a *diluted half-blood due to my low need for replenishments.*"

His eyes swung back and forth between them.

"Does it matter?" Chance surged to his feet and paced the floor, scratching at his arms. The only thing he hated more than being the center of attention was sharing childhood traumas. "Dredging up my fucked-up past won't help us! I am not the problem."

Nicci's cheeks reddened, and she nodded. "You're right. Off topic, sorry."

"Okay." Lilith drew in a deep breath, pinching the bridge of her nose. "If Nichols was human, he chose to work in our world, and Duncan must have had reasons to trust him. Perhaps this database is part of their research? All the DNA data would help them synthesize compatible blood supplements."

"But the private encryption?"

"This database is excessively dangerous in anyone else's hands. High security doesn't make it malicious. Duncan would insist on extreme protective measures."

"I'm not done." Nicci's voice exuded sympathy this time, which only made Lilith's heart sink further. "The database is a *share* file."

"Meaning?" Lilith snapped the word in pure frustration.

"Other people have access," Chance chipped in before Nicci answered, and the words filled the air, like brimstone heralding the apocalypse.

For a moment, Lilith couldn't breathe. The anxiety tightened her chest to a painful degree. *No. Keep it together.* "Do we…Can we tell who? I mean, if Duncan and Nichols collaborated, it makes sense they'd both have access."

"I don't have names or IP addresses yet. I'll crack the heavy security in time, but I can tell you there are more than two users."

The information sent Lilith's brain into a self-deprecating spiral. How could her uncle be so careless? *Because he lost his grip on reality, became hyper-focused on science, and alienated the people around him. His own son fell for Ashcroft's hollow promises because of Duncan's emotional withdrawal and indifference. Now he might have doomed us all.*

"When was it last accessed?" Chance leaned in, eyeing the screen with calm contemplation, but then, this was his element—damage control.

"Hmm. Yeah. I should be able to find out…"

Lilith peeked at the screen and silently prayed as Nicci clicked away.

"The last edit occurred…two days ago."

"Can you tell what changed? Typically, share files track changes so other users can spot them."

"Good point, Chance. Let me see…here…" The words trailed off, and the color drained from her face.

Lilith studied the screen until she spotted what had left Nicci speechless—a file named *Ashcroft Orrick*. The sudden surge of terror left her shaking.

"Impossible. Dr. Nichols didn't know his name, and I never told him where I found the blood."

"Someone changed the file name two days ago, and the doc died in October."

"Who else could know? Ashcroft burned up in Tennessee. To identify the sample, they'd need to know his identity, his species, where he died… *and* crossmatch with blood from the crime scene to confirm."

"Hold on. The user changed the content as well." After scrolling past the lengthy DNA sequence, Nicci clicked on a text file. "Looks like a transcript of a voice recording."

Lilith stood over her shoulder and skimmed through the text.

"Shit!" Rage and betrayal coursed through her veins. "That's my fucking therapy session!" With one quick motion, she pulled out her cell and began dialing a number. "I told her everything they needed to know."

"Wait. Who are you calling?" Chance edged toward her like he'd approach a jumper on a ledge.

"I'm scheduling an emergency therapist visit."

"I'm going with you." When she started to protest, he held up a hand to silence her. "You have no idea what any of this means…"

"It means I was right not to trust her."

"Perhaps…If she *is* involved, she won't appreciate you kicking down her door, *cherie*. I'm going."

"Fine." *No sense in arguing.* Then she turned to her partner. "Call Cohen and fill him in on the connection between our virologist and Dr. Nichols. If Dr. Thomas doesn't answer or won't talk over the phone, send him to her hotel. Perhaps he can persuade her to talk with his weird mind tricks."

Although the detective couldn't control people like the evil siren, Peisinoe, he could influence them enough to tip the scales in his favor.

"What about Aaron?"

For a moment, Lilith stared at Chance, weighing her options.

"None of this is definitive proof. We need something airtight."

"What about the breach?" Nicci piped up, on the verge of outrage.

"We don't know the extent or if it's an *actual* breach. Until we do, we say nothing."

"*If?* How could it not be?" The petite Italian surged to her feet.

"The Elders might be the other users. We can't prove the virus or Nichols's choice of friends has anything to do with this database."

"That's no excuse. If it is the Elders, you're only telling them something they already know. If not…Aaron is in charge, not us! These are his decisions to make." Nicci stood up straight, stretching her five-foot frame to its max height in a symbolic ultimatum.

"The transcript from my therapy session could be Aaron's doing. He hired the woman, after all. I don't trust him, and what if he's hiding all this from the others? Give me forty-eight hours to find definitive proof one way or the other. Please?"

Nicci and Chance stared at each other for a long time before nodding, but Chance countered with one condition.

"If we don't find anything in forty-eight hours, we'll go directly to Elder Antonio with what we have. Aaron will be pissed about us going behind his back, but Antonio's a neutral party."

"For the record"—Nicci perched on top of her desk, gloom clouding her delicate features—"I hope you're wrong about Aaron. If he's the enemy—"

"I hate the man, but I don't want it to be true either. Thank you for giving me time."

Her partner nodded before walking toward the door. "I need more coffee…"

As Nicci left the room, Lilith returned her attention to the phone in her hand.

"Lily…"

"I understand I'm asking a lot, but something is off about this entire thing. Please…I need you in my corner."

"*Cherie*, I'm always in your corner. Go ahead and make the call. Hopefully, she can shed some light on this debacle."

"Thank you." After flashing a bright smile, she pressed the call button. "I need to meet with you immediately. It's…Yes. I know what time it is. This can't wait. Can you be at your office in fifteen minutes?…You said you wanted to help on the case…Fine, forty-five."

"Sounds like we have time for a pit-stop. I'm ravenous. A fancy salad and a couple of minuscule beef medallions aren't a meal, no matter how delicious."

Lilith chuckled, and they headed for Nicci's front door. "Too many people watching their girlish figures."

Chance glanced over his shoulder with an appreciative grin. "I prefer a woman's figure."

"I'll take that as a compliment."

"As you should." He held the door open for her, and as she passed, he slid his arm around her waist, tugging her close. "See? Perfect fit." The roguish wink that followed sent a delicious shiver down her spine.

"I agree, and you're very skilled at distraction, but we need to focus. There'll be time for flattery later. Promise." Then she turned and raised her voice. "We're heading out, Nicci."

"Be careful!" her partner bellowed from the kitchen.

"Come on, handsome. We'll grab something quick on the way."

When his grin only widened, she rolled her eyes, but a thrill still raced down her spine.

"Food. I'm talking about food."

Chapter 21 - *Cassie*

Pain dragged Cassie, inch by inch, out of a deep sleep and forced her consciousness back into her broken body. The agony built with each passing second until she opened her mouth to scream, but only a pitiful croak escaped her chapped lips.

Once again, she wondered how much time had passed since her capture. Two days…two weeks…more? *How much time do I have left? Do I want more? After all, death would end my suffering…spare me from more torture.*

A soft rustle of fabric, the patter of shoes, and a slight wheeze told her she wasn't alone. Her panic escalated, and she strained her ears until a sudden touch on her forearm made her jump, a reaction she immediately regretted. The sharp pain from her shattered elbow and broken fingers became so intense, her consciousness wavered, like a streamer in a high wind.

The coarse rope circling her wrist loosened, and a sprig of hope bloomed in her chest. *Is this a rescue? Is someone setting me free?*

The slack restraint slipped away, and her broken arm dropped like a lead weight between the spokes of the wheel. Tears streamed over her cheeks in agony and joy as she envisioned her freedom.

Quiet footsteps moved around her before fingertips brushed her ankle and tugged at the rope. Cassie's hope grew a little more with each limb released. *I might make it out of this bizarre mess alive.*

As her rescuer reached for the rope around her neck, the familiar parade echoed above, and a panicked frenzy consumed her. *No! I am so close!*

"Hurry." The hoarse whisper that escaped didn't sound human, much less hers.

The person untying her didn't share her sense of urgency. The fingers moved at the same steady pace, unchanged by the presence of others. Not hearing her was understandable, but the thunderous sound above was impossible to ignore.

Only the restraint at her waist remained when the crowd reached the stairs. Still, the person moved with calm diligence.

A realization took hold.

This is not a rescue. Melancholy overcame her newfound hope like a riptide, pulling her under, drowning her vision of freedom in the endless darkness. The croak of the door opening confirmed her suspicions, providing the final deathblow to any remaining dreams of escape. Her normal life had ended outside the dance studio, and now, she only prayed for a merciful death.

"Good, you're awake!" The cheerful timbre of Art's voice no longer grated her nerves. Although he caused her pain, each visit brought her closer to freedom and a sense of purpose. "Bring the stretcher."

Shuffling feet echoed through the room with a buzz of activity, and she unsuccessfully tried to decipher their movements. The cover over her eyes vanished in a sudden tug, and the light streaming from the open door blinded her, like red-hot daggers burrowing deep in her brain. Cassie tried to squeeze out the light and return to the darkness.

The rope at her waist fell away. Dozens of hands slid underneath her, lifting her broken body from the wheel. Between the unexpected motion and the agony accompanying it, her stomach lurched, but she had nothing to throw up. Since descending into this pit of darkness, they had only provided the lotus fruit to eat, barely enough to keep her alive.

The pain and nausea reached a fevered pitch, nearly dragging her into unconsciousness. Once they placed her on a soft surface, the hands pulled away. The luscious scent of greenery and lotus fruit saturated the air around her, and Cassie inhaled deeply, drawing its comfort into her marrow.

Once the smell-induced calm settled over her, she tried to look around, still finding the dim light torturous. Tears welled in her blinking eyes, and the weak rays burned into her retinas, like the scorching light from the sun.

"Take your time." Art's voice hovered over her while a hand caressed her cheek. "Bring her water and a lotus fruit."

The order almost brought her as much satisfaction as her release from the breaking wheel. Both were escapes, not to the outside world, but from agony.

When the cool metal touched her lips, she gulped the cold water until she drained every drop. "More." The eerie croak sounded unintelligible, but someone understood.

The cup returned refilled, and once she emptied it, she braved the light again. Her eyes still watered but began to adjust. Darkness, her constant companion throughout her captivity, abandoned her, as all things did eventually, but only shapes and blocks of color greeted her eyes.

"Eat, Cassie."

The delicate scent filled her nostrils, and she took gluttonous bites, consuming as much as possible before it disappeared. To her surprise, a second one was held before her, and she took smaller bites this time, savoring the citrusy pulp.

The sudden pull didn't scare her anymore. Disconnecting from her battered body was true freedom. Escaping her captors couldn't undo the damage they had inflicted. The lotus fruit allowed her an escape no rescue could achieve—one where she left all her physical woes behind to fly above the wreckage as a spectator.

When she opened her eyes once more, a bright glow shone behind dozens of dark faces, glistening off their heads like halos. The angelic imagery caught her by surprise, and she stared in wonder at the golden silhouettes fluctuating like holy fire. *Am I dead? Is this heaven?*

Art's handsome face loomed into view. For the first time since the dance studio, the depth in his sea-blue eyes appeared inviting, and she found the burst of chocolate brown circling his irises mesmerizing. The more she stared, the more the colors pulsated and swirled with an unnatural light, like the impossible eyes of a god.

"So beautiful…" Cassie's melodic voice floated through the air, and a smile stretched her blistered lips.

"It's time, my dearest Cassie." His palm cradled her cheek, and affection seeped through her skin. "Don't be scared."

His face receded into the darkness along with her newfound wonder, leaving behind a vacuum quickly filling with sorrow.

"Proceed."

As soon as he spoke, the stretcher rose and moved forward. The dark rock walls ended at an arched doorway, and when they turned the corner, light flooded the stairway, warming her skin. Joyous tears spilled down her cheeks as brightness filled her world once again. She had survived the darkness, and now the streams of light appeared more beautiful than ever.

The procession moved up the stairs, the stretcher jostling her broken body. The lotus fruit allowed Cassie to disconnect from the pain, but the motion still brought waves of nausea, so she fixated on the wooden ceiling. Remaining focused on something helped.

They rounded the bend and traveled up the final flight of steps.

Once the motion sickness passed, she turned her head and took in the surroundings, her eyes ravenous for stimulation after so much deprivation. The peeling wallpaper featured an Old World design, perhaps turn of the century. That along with the desiccated wainscoting and crown molding indicated a once-posh place abandoned for decades. Matching properties rattled through her head, but dozens of places existed on the East Coast alone.

The stairs led to an endless mahogany-clad hallway. The dark wood conjured a mild sense of claustrophobia interrupted by a few faded portraits clinging to the walls.

When the walls ended, the stretcher paused, and Cassie peered into a massive room with a glass ceiling. The midday sun poured through the dirty panes in glorious fashion, making everything glow.

A familiar scent wafted by, more potent than ever before, and Cassie craned her head, searching for the source. A beautiful trio of trees sat in the expansive room, bathed in sunshine. The twisted trunks intertwined with elegant branches bearing white and purple blossoms and juicy red fruit.

"Take Cassie to the chosen tree and prepare her while we begin." Art's commanding voice boomed through the huge space, echoing with a divine quality.

The stretcher moved forward in a smooth motion, as if floating through the air. The sun's rays seeped into her skin, filling each cell with comfort and brightness. As they approached the center tree, Cassie stared up through the twisted branches, light flickering between the thick, waxy leaves. The quiet tranquility filled with such beauty made the torturous basement seem like a distant nightmare from another life.

Perhaps Art had a point. The torture she had endured made her appreciate the moment in a way she couldn't have imagined before her capture. After all, Richard Evans once said, "It is often in the darkest skies that we see the brightest stars."

Cassie closed her eyes and basked in bliss. Dozens of hands, wet with the lotus juice, anointed her battered body. All her fear and pain dissipated, leaving her to enjoy the reverent caresses that left a glowing warmth in their wake.

"Hear us, Apollo, ruler of the sun, knowledge, and light," a female voice rang clear, with a pleasant lyrical quality.

When Cassie opened her drowsy eyes, the room spun and swirled until her vision rested on the woman who spoke.

Grecian robes of cream flowed to the ground, and a laurel crown sat upon her head. Although the woman's short silvery hair clashed with the mythical ensemble, when she raised her arms to the sky, her chant contained the fervent zest of an impassioned believer.

"Please hear us and aid us in our plight! Our patron defender with music in your heart, your mighty arrows serving their part. To the blessed, they bring healing and new life. To the wicked, they bring plague and strife. True justice you wield with grace and beauty. Never tiring of your duty. Uplift us! Bring us to the light! Uplift us! Prepare us for the fight!"

A sea of voices joined in, and the energy thrummed along Cassie's skin as their words echoed through the room. "All Hail Apollo! All Hail Apollo! All Hail Apollo!"

The crowd faced the tree to her right, so Cassie followed their line of sight to a woman in vibrant yellow robes. A gold necklace glinted off her tanned chest, and golden laurels adorned her rich umber tresses.

They continued to cry out to the woman, and Cassie couldn't resist the swell of emotions. Their conviction and pure belief became intoxicating and inspiring. She wanted to not only believe in magic and myth, but share the calling these people experienced.

"Hail Apollo!"

The shout emerged as little more than a rough croak, but it still roused the crowd. They cheered and repeated her words with renewed vigor until the woman in yellow held out her arms with an adoring smile that dimpled her cheeks.

"I, Apollo, hear your prayers, and I welcome my faithful children."

A vague thought nagged at Cassie's drug-addled brain until it became clear. *Apollo is a woman?* Cassie had never majored in mythology, but she was fairly certain Apollo was a god, not a goddess. However, before doubt infiltrated her new sense of purpose, the woman with the silver bob spoke up again.

"Hear us, Artemis, deity of the hunt, forest, and moon. Divine protector, with you we shall commune. Wild, primordial essence of purity.

Blanket us in your wise and vengeful security. With deadly arrows, your anger flies, poisoning the wicked heart until it dies. True justice you wield with grace and beauty. Never tiring of your duty. Uplift us! Bring us to the light! Uplift us! Prepare us for the fight!"

Again, the people shouted their devout chant, renewing Cassie's doe-eyed belief as she joined them. "All Hail Artemis! All Hail Artemis! All Hail Artemis!"

This time, they faced the tree to her left, where Art stood in grand robes of indigo blue adorned with a silver belt and matching laurels. He held his arms out to the reverent crowd and closed his eyes to drink in their melodic adoration.

As she studied him, he transformed into something more ethereal. His pale skin glowed like a precious moonstone with glittering currents of light running beneath the surface. The prominent nose appeared more majestic, and his pitch-black hair shimmered with accents of purple and teal…Then, he opened his eyes, and she gasped.

Cassie had considered his eyes godly before, but now they shone like the cosmos dancing into life. Eternity swam in their depths, and she wanted nothing more than to embrace it.

"I, Artemis, hear your prayers and welcome my faithful children."

"The anointing of the innocent is complete!" the woman with the silver bob proclaimed, picking up a fresh laurel wreath and proceeding up the hill, like a bridesmaid marching down an aisle.

The people surrounding Cassie lifted her from the stretcher and placed her fragile body against the center tree with gentle care. Her consciousness floated above, watching them weave coarse ropes around her limbs, but this time, they weren't a prison.

Pride burned in her chest, not despair. Two gods stood on either side, thrumming with power, and they had chosen *her*. People waited their entire lives to uncover the reason for their existences. They climbed mountains, visited exotic lands, spoke with religious leaders, dedicated themselves to charities, studied meditation techniques, and pursued higher planes of existence, but most never caught a peek of true divinity.

Truth stood before her, the shimmering connection to the cosmos. Any lingering doubts evaporated like a drop of water in the Sahara. *This is my reason for being, my purpose.*

After the silver-haired woman smiled and placed the floral crown upon Cassie's head, she kissed her forehead. "The blessings of Apollo and Artemis are with you."

The woman stepped aside, and a heavyset man approached. The wheezing breath and body odor betrayed his identity, and Cassie flinched when he reached forward to place a delicate purple flower in her hair.

"The blessings of Apollo and Artemis are with you." When his devout lips touched her skin, her uneasiness bled away, replaced by the warmth of a kindred spirit.

A sea of endless faces followed, one by one adorning her with flowers and blessings. Each person added to her euphoria until Cassie drifted above the mundane needs of her physical body and transcended into a higher plane filled with warmth, light, and love.

When the goddess clothed in vibrant yellow and gold stepped forward, Cassie's breath caught in her chest. Apollo's olive skin glowed as if she'd swallowed the sun and infused the star's essence into her corporeal form, and in her palms, she carried a plump, red fruit with a familiar fragrance.

"I, Apollo, bless you. Your sacrifice serves the greater good and will rid the world of an ancient evil. I honor your life and death, Cassandra Cappalletty." The deity's dimpled smile brightened, and she kissed each of Cassie's cheeks, leaving the lotus fruit at her feet.

As Apollo stepped aside, Art appeared, and an overwhelming swell of adoration grew in Cassie's chest.

"Artemis blesses you. Your sacrifice serves the greater good and will rid the world of an ancient evil."

His mesmerizing eyes locked onto hers, and he cupped her face with gentle hands.

"You have come so far, my dear sweet Cassie. You are a beacon of truth heralding a new age. The entire world will know what you sacrificed in our names. They will understand your pain, your joy, and your beauty but also your heroism and purpose."

When he kissed her cheek, his lips lingered, and his breath rushed over her skin.

"I honor your life and death, Cassandra Cappalletty." The god's smile burst with pride, and he kissed her opposite cheek.

The ceremony left her so enthralled, she didn't feel the knife cut into her wrist. She existed beyond something as trivial as pain, but she sensed her essence ebbing away.

As her drowsy eyes drifted from the deity's handsome face, Cassie glimpsed a silver blade slice up her other wrist. Hot, crimson blood welled in its wake and trickled down her broken fingers into an old copper pot.

Somewhere deep inside, she waited for the panic to kick in, but it never came. Whether caused by her newfound purpose, the lotus fruit, or embracing the inevitable, a quiet calm settled over her shoulders. *It will be over soon.* Not the pain and torture, which no longer touched her, but the constant struggle to achieve mediocrity and pretend it made her happy.

"You will never be ordinary again. Your life, your death, it *means* something now. You will never be forgotten." The god spoke as if he had glimpsed inside and plucked the words from her mind. "This is my gift to you, a symbol of all you accomplished."

A joyful tear slid down her cheek when Cassie glimpsed the iron collar sitting in his hands. The Greek letters engraved in the metal glowed with an unearthly beauty, distracting her from the ancient mechanism on the side. With a gentle touch, he fastened the thing around her neck and turned toward the group.

"Today, we complete our manifesto. One we will reveal to the world on the sacred festival."

Art nodded to his counterpart, who lifted a bronze pot to her lips.

"With the blood of the innocent, we gather strength to defeat our enemies."

While he spoke, he picked up the matching pot. Then together, they drank until the blood trickled over their chins and stained their robes.

"*Níki í thánatos!*"

Artemis and Apollo both released a war cry Cassie couldn't understand but felt deep in her marrow. When the entire group echoed their cries, the fevered pitch made her tremble.

The chanting grew louder as the numbness took hold. The grandiose room swirled in hazy streaks, and her body became impossibly heavy. The iron tightened around her throat, but her focus narrowed to the impassioned voices roaring over the weakening thump of her heart.

A black vignette slowly invaded her vision, and bit by bit, Cassie returned to the familiar comfort of the darkness she once loathed. The war cry of *her* people still filled her ears, honoring her death. Each breath came in slow gasps. Finally, she surrendered to the cosmos, escaping the cruel world and embracing divinity with her life fulfilled.

Chapter 22 - *Cohen*

A persistent buzz from the bedside table made Cohen groan. After the evening's fun-filled events, he wasn't in the mood to speak with anyone who had this number, especially since that list only consisted of Nicci, Chance, and Lilith.

His thoughts paused on the last name until he rubbed his face in frustration. *No. Stop.*

The phone fell silent, and he released a sigh of relief before sitting up in bed. An arm draped over his hip, but it summoned more annoyance than warmth.

Feeding on sexual energy didn't hold the same joy it once did. It was an irritating necessity, or perhaps it was merely the women he chose. He couldn't tell if his recent preference for redheads was helping or making things worse.

None of them are her, the voice in his head reminded him for the thousandth time.

A frustrated growl rumbled from his throat, and he gripped the pale wrist between his thumb and forefinger, setting it on the bed. A soft moan escaped the woman's mouth, and she cuddled into her pillow, thankfully still asleep.

Andrew's eyes lingered on her fiery red hair spilling over the pillow. *A few shades too rich to be natural.*

The phone vibrated again with annoying tenacity. He snatched the infernal device, walked into the bathroom with purposeful strides, and softly closed the door before glancing at the screen.

His brow wrinkled. Cohen was uncertain if he was more disappointed or relieved. After concentrating, he pulled his impassive mask over his emotional wounds, collected his calm, and answered.

"Good evening, Nicci. What can I do for you?"

"Oh, good! You're awake."

"I am now."

As usual, Nicci ignored the clipped words and barreled ahead. "Well, Lilith asked me to call…"

"Of course, she did. Too pissed at me to call herself?" He sighed heavily, unable to contain his irritation after the argument they'd had at the gala.

"What? Uh, no…Her and Chance are heading to her therapist."

"A little late for couple's counseling, isn't it?"

"It's business-related, asshole. Someone's been recording her therapy sessions."

A jolt shot up his spine, and his entire body stiffened. "What? What sessions?"

Nicci audibly sighed. "She's been in *mandated* therapy since the medical center. You'd know that if you'd bothered to keep in touch. She's kept her mouth shut this entire time, but earlier this week. Dr. Price threatened her job."

"Dr. Price…From the gala?" That explained the well of anger, hatred, and betrayal he had sensed from Lilith when she spoke to the woman.

"Yeah, keep up. Anyway, Lilith finally opened up and started talking."

Andrew swallowed the sudden lump in his throat. "What did they record?"

"Information about Phipps Bend—Ashcroft, to be specific."

Fuck. "What exactly?"

"Nothing about the Durand, if that's what concerns you." The disapproving tone in the petite detective's voice grated his already frazzled nerves.

"Detective DeLuca, I realize we don't know each other well, but that is *not* my only concern. I would appreciate you not making assumptions about my character when you have nothing to base them on."

The stunned silence further deteriorated his calm.

"I assume you're calling me for a reason, so why don't you skip to that?"

"Uh, yeah. Do you remember the scientist at Goditha? The one Ashcroft carved up?"

"Dr. Frederick Nichols. Yes. Why?"

"Well, Lil had a hunch, and we got ahold of his laptop." The woman paused, and Andrew leaned against the sink, waiting for her to continue.

"Once I got through all his extra security, we found a photo of him and Dr. Thomas celebrating. She knew him, and we need to figure out how."

"So, you think Dr. Nichols was responsible for the virus?"

"We don't know for certain. I'm still decrypting stuff, and I outsourced some background searches, but there's enough evidence to suggest that he was involved in…some shady shit."

Andrew cleared his throat, an all-too-familiar irritation itching under his skin. Once again, they were keeping him in the dark, limiting information. "If we are going to be partners in this investigation—" he started.

"Oh, I'm sorry. You want to be partners now?" the fierce woman interrupted. "Because from where I'm sitting, you've done nothing but dump your shit on us and fucking pout."

He clenched his jaw and stood up straight. "Nicci…" A clear warning saturated the angry growl, but the petite detective ignored it.

"No. You fucking listen to me. You might be some freakishly strong, well-connected, emotion-sucking parasite, but for some fucking reason, Lilith insists on keeping you involved, despite the fact that you've done nothing but bitch and brood more than an overdramatic teenager. Why don't you suck it up, pull on your big-boy pants, and actually do something? Or do I not know you well enough to say that?"

Dozens of emotions surged to the surface along with his rage, but he swallowed them all because she was right. "You've made your point. What do you want?"

"Lil wants you to get ahold of Dr. Thomas. We need to know her relationship with Dr. Nichols. There's a possibility that she could be connected to all this."

"That would be a hell of a coincidence. Are you certain the scientist that recommended her isn't involved?"

"Lilith has known him a long time. She's worked with him since she came home from college, and she's *usually* a good judge of character."

Somehow, he felt that was a dig at him, not that he blamed the detective. He definitely hadn't been at his best lately.

"Yeah, okay. I'll give her a call."

"If she doesn't answer—"

"I'll go to her hotel," he interrupted. "I am a detective, you know."

"So, that's not just a cover?" The question sounded more accusatory than inquisitive.

"No. I attended the academy and worked through the ranks, like everyone else. Did you?"

"Of course," she bit back defensively.

The woman's unease made him smile, but making her uncomfortable wasn't particularly productive.

"I'll get in touch with Dr. Thomas and get to the truth."

"Thanks… and…"

"What is it?" A sigh accompanied the question.

"I'm sorry for going off on you."

"No, you're not. Lies don't become you, Nicci." He hung up and stared at the screen, the woman's words ringing through his head.

Absolutely vicious, but true.

After sliding his phone on the counter, he turned to face the mirror. His olive eyes—*of course, they are fucking olive*—glared at the faint scars marring his face, and he released a weary sigh.

Eight months and he still didn't have a grip on things. After the medical center and Luminita…Those events had ripped him open emotionally, and nothing he did could stop the bleeding. The scars were a cruel reminder of the unhealed damage inside. *Will it ever heal?* Despair seeped into his bones, bringing a chill with it.

Cohen turned on the faucet and splashed cold water over his face. *Get it together, asshole.*

A few deep breaths later, he snatched up his phone, pulled up the picture he'd snapped of Dr. Thomas's business card, and dialed the number.

"You've reached the voicemail of Dr. Rachel Thomas. Please leave—"

His thumb jabbed the end call button. "Of course. Nothing is ever easy anymore."

Andrew closed his eyes, steeling himself. Eventually, the constant anger, frustration, self-loathing, and jealousy faded into a manageable hum. He smoothed his hair to his scalp, then exhaled, cracked the bathroom door open, and peered into the hotel room.

The woman was still asleep, the sheets twisted around her.

At least one thing is going right. He didn't have the energy for another fight. Getting them to leave was always the difficult part. *Well, not so much difficult as repetitive.*

Andrew crept into the room and carefully retrieved the folded slacks from the dresser, the dress shirt, jacket, and tie from the chair, and inched toward his suitcase, which sat dangerously close to the bed.

As he slowly pulled back the zipper, he kept his eyes locked on the woman's face. *The woman. Fuck. I can't even remember her name.* He shook off the self-deprecating thought and grabbed a pair of socks. *Does it matter? No. Of course, it doesn't. She's not her, so she doesn't matter, right?*

The intrusive inner voice summoned a sinking pit of jealousy in his very core. *She belongs to Chance. That's where she wants to be.* His lips pressed into a firm line as he attempted to quell the sickening sensation squeezing his chest like a vise. No luck.

His shoulders drooped. Cohen carried everything into the bathroom and softly closed the door. After placing his clothes on the counter, he leaned in to stare at his reflection again.

"Stop this," he whispered firmly. "You are pointlessly torturing yourself over an impossibility. You saw them at the gala..."

The pep talk didn't help. All it accomplished was summoning painful memories.

He'd stood in the swirling crowd of the gala and watched Nicci walk away from Lilith. Cohen had taken a few steps toward her, fixated on the lavender lace gown she wore and the tiny gems shimmering on the thin overlay. The woman was an absolute vision, and he couldn't focus on anything else.

Sadness had lingered in her face, her olive eyes studying the crowd. He knew that haunted expression, that feeling of helplessness and desperation. It echoed everything he held inside.

A woman had stepped into his path with an intoxicated smile a few feet from his destination. With a frown, he guided her out of his path and spotted Chance approaching Lilith.

Within seconds, her entire demeanor transformed. Light danced in those olive eyes as he pulled her close, leading her in a waltz.

He didn't need to hear their conversation. Even past the chaotic sea of emotions emanating from the crowd, he felt their connection. She loved him with every fiber of her being, and he returned that love in equal measure. It was an undeniable fact cutting him deeper than Luminita's scalpel.

Cohen hung his head again and fought back the stomach-churning envy. He trusted Lilith, and to him, that was worth more than anything else she could offer. Besides, if he truly cared about the woman, what right did he have to rob her of happiness on that level? What right did he have to interfere? None.

It's not like you can offer her anything like what she has with him. You're an emotionally crippled, selfish piece of shit for even thinking about it. She deserves better.

He swallowed the last bitter remnants of jealousy, and cold acceptance settled over his shoulders. *Being her friend is enough. It has to be. If you can manage not to fuck that up.*

After a sigh and one last glare at the scars carved into his face and torso, he quickly pulled on his clothes. Nicci's chastising words repeated in his head while he straightened his tie.

"Focus on the case," he told himself. With that, he squeezed his eyes shut and concentrated, pulling that familiar mask of indifference over the raw emotional wounds. Slowly, the olive hue gave way to a crisp sky-gray and calm trickled through his body. It was nothing more than a bandage on a festering cut, but it worked…temporarily.

The man straightened and cracked the bathroom door open, peeking into the room again. The redhead's eyes were still closed, and a gentle snore that sounded more like a purr filled the air. He grabbed his shoes when he crept by the bed, laid a twenty on the nightstand for cab fare, and quietly exited the hotel room.

B y the time Cohen maneuvered the limo into valet parking at the Muse Hotel, every shred of calm had evaporated, like water in the Sahara. He threw the vehicle in park, white-knuckled the steering wheel, and glared sightlessly through the windshield, trying to reclaim some sliver of dignity. Driving anything more substantial than a coupe in New York City was sheer madness.

A sharp knock on the window made his jaw clench. After a slow exhale, he exited the car, dropped the key in the valet's palm, and stalked toward the entrance.

"Did you want your ticket, sir?"

Cohen held up a dismissive hand and continued toward the hotel. "I'm pretty sure you'll remember which one is mine," he barked over his shoulder, shoving through the door.

The lobby sat vacant, not a surprise at nearly eleven at night. The marble floors, modern lines, and austere decor didn't capture his attention. He had spent far too much time in hotels to be impressed. Just another facade promising impossible standards but failing to deliver.

Kind of like you, right? the intrusive voice retorted.

After a sharp exhale, Cohen stormed up to the expansive front desk and the cheery young blond behind it. *Blond, pity.*

Stop! For fuck's sake. Irritation and anger always made that inner voice more powerful.

"Good evening, sir. How can I help you?" The woman's tone was annoyingly happy, *unlike…*

Stop! he growled internally, cutting off the thought.

With a frustrated frown in place, he dug into his breast pocket, pulled out his badge, and flipped it open. "Detective Andrew Cohen. I need the room number for one of your guests—Dr. Rachel Thomas." He hurried through the request in his Southern accent while glancing around the lobby.

"I'm very sorry, but I'm not allowed to share client information. We have a strict privacy policy."

The detective whipped his head around, and his eyes narrowed in on her. "I'm a police detective here to question a material witness. I need the room number."

The woman—Jillian, according to her name badge—straightened, and her youthful face pinched. "I understand, but as I said, we have a strict privacy policy."

The icy tone made Andrew realize he'd taken the wrong approach.

After releasing a soft sigh, he leaned against the counter with an apologetic smile. "I am sorry, miss." The smooth Southern accent became more pronounced, and he peered at her from under his brow.

Pink tinged the woman's cheeks, and the glow of attraction lit the air around her. *It's not even a challenge,* the inner voice complained, but he ignored it.

"I've been workin' a difficult case." His eyes fell to the counter for a moment and slowly rose to meet hers again. "I understand how important privacy is, but…"

Andrew leaned in closer, and Jillian's pink cheeks flushed crimson. His eyes locked on hers, utilizing every ounce of his influencing ability, and his voice dropped to a velvety whisper.

"I really need that room number, darlin'. Can you help me out?"

Jillian shoved a strand of hair behind her ear and swallowed hard. "Umm…"

Jenny Allen

The rate of her breaths quickened, and she glanced at the screen and then back at him. Desire infused the air and tickled over his skin. Once upon a time, that sensation had brought him a thrill, but now, it all felt hollow.

"I mean, I'm not supposed to, but…" She peered around the lobby before leaning close to whisper, "If you don't tell anyone…"

"Jillian." A squat man marched toward them from the back office. "I'll take it from here."

The woman straightened and stepped aside with a pained expression. *So fucking close.*

Andrew glanced up at the surveillance cameras focused on the counter. Flashing his badge had probably summoned the balding little office troll. He managed to keep his sigh of disappointment internal before standing straight and flashing a professional smile.

"Detective Andrew Cohen with the Knoxville PD. I'm here to question a material witness—Dr. Rachel Thomas. She's a guest here."

"A little far from your jurisdiction, don't you think?" The squat man raised one bushy eyebrow.

"I'm working the case with Detective DeLuca with the NYPD and her partner CSI Adams."

"Ah," the man responded, his pinched face softening a touch. "I understand your position. My name is Patrick Gladfelter, and I'm the hotel manager."

Cohen's mood lightened when the man smiled. About time something went right. "Well, the Knoxville PD appreciates your cooperation, Mr. Gladfelter."

"Unfortunately…"

Fuck. I spoke too soon.

"Unless you have a warrant, I'm unable to comply with your request. Our policy is rather stringent." Something in the man's energy read as enjoyment. The little troll craved control and relished any opportunity to flex his power.

"The doctor is a material witness, not a suspect."

"Hmm. Yes, well. Then I would suggest contacting Dr. Thomas and getting the room number directly from her." Mr. Gladfelter rested his chubby hands on the counter, a saccharine smile splitting his doughy face.

Anger licked at Andrew's insides like flames, but he kept it buried. He refused to give the asshole the satisfaction of reacting. "Well, thank you for your time, sir." His eyes swung to Jillian, and heat infused his smile. "And a definite pleasure to meet you, Jillian."

Her cheeks flushed again, and she nodded in reply.

"I think I'll sit at the bar and try her number again...Perhaps I'll even have a few drinks." Cohen kept his mischievous gaze locked on Jillian's soft blue eyes with a clear invitation. "Y'all have a good evenin'." He didn't bother glancing at Gladfelter before he walked away. The man wasn't worth his attention.

Hopefully, the young woman would take the bait and come to see him when her shift ended. Until then, alcohol would help quell the emotions still writhing under his skin and perhaps silence the demon in his head.

Once again, he ignored his surroundings to focus on the only thing that mattered—the bar. The long slab of black marble sat next to a rather impressive wine fridge running from floor to ceiling. Of course, wine didn't fit his current mood.

Andrew slid into a vacant seat between an intoxicated businessman celebrating his freedom and an escort scouring the bar for her next client.

"What can I get you?" A middle-aged woman dressed in a crisp white shirt and a black vest paused in front of him.

"Johnnie Walker Blue, neat."

His eyes hesitated on the red strands that weren't tucked behind her ear. "Make that a double." His gaze fell to the black marble, and he focused on the hypnotic swirls of gray.

When the bartender walked away, he turned to survey the area, ignoring the mid-century aesthetics as he concentrated on faces. None of them looked familiar.

"Did you want to start a tab?" The clink of a glass followed the question, and he turned back around, digging out his wallet.

"Yes, please." Cohen handed the woman his credit card, stowed his wallet, and took a long swig of his scotch. The familiar burn was comforting.

Andrew stared into the liquid's golden depths, a barely restrained flood of memories churning beneath the surface. He had survived horrific events at the hands of his grandfather—the murder of his parents, beatings, isolation, the assassination of anyone who came too close, the emotional neglect and abuse. He had lived through all that without losing it, and two women undid him—Luminita and Lilith—for very different reasons.

Being betrayed by another Durand shouldn't shock him. The lack of loyalty seemed to be a racial trait. *Are we incapable of it? Is it something we're missing? Some essential part of the soul we are born without?*

No, that can't be the case. I had several opportunities to save my skin and abandon my new allies, but I didn't.

You didn't abandon her. You would have left the others to die. You're mistaking selfishness for nobility. The vicious retort of his inner voice made his hand tighten around the glass, and he drained the last of his scotch before slamming it on the counter.

The bartender reappeared, and he tapped the marble. She poured another four fingers of scotch with a tight smile.

"Detective Cohen?" a feminine voice emanated from the crowd behind him, and he paused with the glass halfway to his lips.

When he peered over his shoulder, he spotted Renee, the therapist's girlfriend, from the gala.

"It is you! I thought so. Are you staying here too? What a coincidence." A jubilant smile lit her heart-shaped face, and she smoothed her silvery bob.

"No, actually." Cohen drained the scotch in one gulp and swiveled to face her with a raised eyebrow. "Don't you live in the city?"

Renee chuckled and rested an elbow on the bar. "Yes. I was visiting with some friends from the gala that are staying here."

"Friends like Dr. Thomas? Someone mentioned that you know her and Dr. Wolfe."

"Yes, actually." Curiosity sparked her emerald-green eyes. "Is that who you're here to see? She didn't mention anything."

Hmm. Perhaps I don't have to wait on Jillian. "Yes. I tried to call, but she didn't answer. I just have a few questions for her. Do you happen to know her room number?"

The petite woman's lips spread wide. "Of course, but I can do better than that. I'll take you to her. We just finished our post-gala meeting."

"Your what?" He arched one blond eyebrow, and the woman giggled.

"Our collective. We work on a lot of projects together, including some of the gala planning…Well, for the exhibits we displayed this year anyway."

"Collective? Sounds like a cult." An amused yet skeptical expression crossed his face, and the woman giggled loudly, her hand brushing his knee.

"Oh, no. Not at all. It's just a group of intellectuals from different specialties working together on projects."

"So, the entire collective is upstairs?" A brief dart of apprehension struck him for some inexplicable reason.

"No, silly. Most of them turned in for the night. It's okay. Come on." The woman grabbed his hand and tugged, but he remained seated. "What's wrong?" Renee frowned when Cohen's eyes narrowed.

He carefully considered her for a moment, confused by the excitement vibrating over her skin. If Dr. Thomas was involved with the virus, Renee might be too in some way. She could be leading him into a trap. Unfortunately for them, they didn't know who and what he was, and a few humans didn't scare him. "I need to close my tab."

"Oh, of course." A warm smile spread her lips again, and he slowly swiveled back to the bar.

He held up a hand, signaling the bartender, and then smiled back at Renee. "So, how long have you belonged to this…collective?"

"Hmm." The woman's eyes darted up and to the right as she thought, indicating the recollection of a memory and not a fabrication. "At least five years for me, but Kelley started the group back in college."

"Besides creating exhibits, what does your group do?" Cohen leaned against the bar with a casual air of curiosity, pulling out his wallet.

"We do a lot of research, plan excavations, perform detailed tests on artifacts…A lot, really." This time, her eyes sliced to the bottom left a few times, and her energy shifted from excitement to nervousness.

Cohen's inner demon practically purred with satisfaction. This Collective was up to something. No doubt about it.

"Like testing for viruses?" he asked nonchalantly.

Her gaze snapped up to his, and a hesitant smile appeared. "That's Rachel's area of expertise."

You're pushing too much. Back off.

The bartender slid his credit card and receipts on the counter, and he nodded appreciatively.

"Of course. So, Renee…" Cohen wrote in a generous tip, signed, and retrieved his card. "What is *your* area of expertise?" The roguish grin he wore elicited an undeniable response. *Apparently, she isn't only attracted to women.*

"World mythology and urban counterculture."

"Counterculture?" One eyebrow rose, and he slid the card back in his wallet.

"Fringe societies that rebel against cultural norms. I spent years in the Gothic scene for my doctoral thesis."

"How fascinating." To his surprise, he meant it.

"Yes, well..." Sadness and pain hovered in the air, and her gaze fell to the floor momentarily. "That scene can be dangerous."

Before Cohen responded, the woman pulled on a smile.

"Anyway. Are you ready?"

Andrew tucked his wallet into a pocket and studied her. The brief glimpse of darkness had intrigued him. *Only because you want to know you aren't the only one who's broken.*

"Are you sure Dr. Thomas won't mind? I'd hate to intrude." *Isn't that what you're here to do?* The voice refused to be ignored, but he did his best to suppress it.

"No. Not at all." Renee's jubilant energy returned, and a sudden dart of fear struck him.

I thought you weren't scared of a few humans? Or are you just scared of women? The taunt hardened his resolve.

"In that case..." Andrew slid off the stool and smoothed his tie. "Lead the way."

"Wonderful." The exhilarated tone seemed disproportionate, but perhaps his gut reaction stemmed from his unfamiliarity with the emotion. Perhaps normal people were simply...happy. Maybe this collective was simply what she claimed, and he was reading too much into things. *Don't make assumptions. Follow the evidence.*

When they walked through the lobby to the elevators, Cohen noticed the front desk was vacant. *Perhaps Jillian is on break, and you aren't as charming as you think.*

He pinched the bridge of his nose and concentrated on silencing the fucking demon on his shoulder.

"Are you okay?" Renee peered up at him with wide eyes.

"Yes," he replied wearily. "It's been a long few days." The honest answer surprised him, and he quickly pulled on a smile.

"Oh..." Renee clearly appeared uncomfortable and struggled to find a new topic while they waited.

"You are dating Dr. Price, correct?" He knew the answer, of course, but was curious about her reaction.

"Brittney? Yeah. It's pretty new." Pink tinged her cheeks, and she pressed the up button again.

"My apologies. I didn't mean to bring up a sensitive subject." The unpredictable shifts in her emotional energy fascinated him.

"No. You're fine. It's just…all new to me still."

Nope. Don't touch that landmine. Change the subject.

"I'm guessing you know Lilith, then." *Why the fuck are you bringing up that subject, you masochist,* the inner demon shouted.

"Not much. I've only talked to her twice. Once at Brittney's office and then at the gala tonight. I mean, I read about the terrorist attacks, so I knew who she was and what she did for a living, but that's about it. Have you known her long?"

A sharp ding announced the elevator's arrival, and the doors opened.

"A little less than a year but…we went through some things together."

"Right. You were there in Tennessee during the first attack. The one at Phipps Bend?"

"I was," he stated as they stepped inside. "And at the medical center here in New York City."

"The reports sounded pretty brutal, and the media typically sugar-coats things. So…"

Andrew raised an eyebrow and slowly turned to stare down at her. "Did you have a question?" The cold tone suggested only one reasonable answer.

"No, I suppose not." Renee quickly glanced away and smoothed her hair.

After several awkward seconds, she found her bravery again.

"I just wondered how bad it really was."

Andrew stared at her from beneath furrowed brows, his eyes narrowing. "Do you care to share your experiences in the Gothic scene?"

The woman paled and shook her head.

"Then I politely decline to answer."

The elevator doors opened as the tension became stifling, and Renee moved quickly, leading him to Rachel's room.

"Here we are." She smiled nervously over her shoulder and knocked three times.

When the door swung open, Renee rushed inside, and Cohen followed at a leisurely pace. Dr. Thomas sat in an armchair by a lamp—the only light source in the room. As soon as she saw him, she stood with a radiant smile deeply dimpling her cheeks.

"Detective. How wonderful to see you. I apologize for not answering your call. I was in a meeting."

His eyes shifted to Renee standing next to the doctor. "I heard. Would you mind if we spoke in private? I have a few questions."

Rachel's head tilted, and her smile dissolved into a frown. "Renee is one of my closest friends, and I have nothing to hide. Ask your questions."

He hesitated, surprised by the response, then shrugged and moved further into the room. "CSI Adams and Detective DeLuca found a photograph of you and another scientist."

"Well, I know a lot of them and work on many group projects, especially with the collective. It's not uncommon."

The obvious deflection raised his suspicions, and he focused on the woman more closely. An odd mixture of satisfaction and triumph with a hint of fear emanated from her.

"How did you know Dr. Frederick Nichols?"

Shock widened her warm eyes before she could deny it. "He was one of my mentors back in college. Why?"

"Have you kept in touch?" Cohen stepped forward again, focused on her energies as they shifted more toward fear.

"We have corresponded a few times."

Formal language. You've struck a nerve. Keep pressing.

"About what, exactly?"

Andrew focused intently on reading the woman's reactions.

A swell of triumph overtook everything else when Rachel's lips curved into a sudden smile, once again displaying the deep dimples in her checks. "You'll see soon enough."

Cohen frowned at the odd response seconds before blinding pain rang through his skull. He crumpled to his knees, the world spinning. Cohen instinctively felt the back of his head, and his hand came away wet with blood. He stared at the sticky warm liquid on his palm in confusion before another strike made the entire world go black.

You fucking idiot. You didn't even check the room, the demon voice taunted one last time before he slid into unconsciousness.

Chapter 23

"Okay. I'm here. What is this all about?" Dr. Price pulled her strawberry-blond hair into a hasty bun. The woman's horn-rimmed glasses sat slightly crooked on her nose, she'd hastily thrown on mismatched clothes, and she definitely was not happy about being dragged into her office after hours. However, the woman's perturbed expression faltered when Chance marched in behind Lilith.

"Save it. How the hell did you know Dr. Nichols?"

"Who?" The shrink shook her head at the sudden question. "Wait. The lab tech from Goditha who died?" The shock and confusion appeared genuine enough, but therapists made excellent liars.

"You know *exactly* who he is."

The therapist ran a hand over her frazzled hair. "No, you are mistaken. I'm only aware of what *you* wrote in the report. Why?"

"This is why!" Lilith slammed a handful of papers on the desk. "Do you recognize these?"

The woman frowned at the pile before grabbing one of the scattered sheets. She scanned the page, and her brow furrowed. "These are transcripts of our therapy sessions...I don't understand. Why would you—"

"I didn't!" Lilith cut her off with a venomous glare.

"But I don't record—"

"Really? Because this is word for word. Guess where I found it."

"Lily..." Chance shot a warning glare. "Are you sure you want to—"

"Yes." She spun on her heel to face him, a firm set to her jaw. "I need to know."

When she turned back to the doctor, Lilith inched closer. "Guess you aren't Aaron's lackey, after all. I found it in Dr. Nichols's database."

"He died over eight months ago. You aren't making sense."

Pointing out the logical error instead of claiming innocence only solidified the answer in Lilith's mind. *She is part of the conspiracy.*

"It's a shared file," Chance interjected.

A dawning realization blossomed over Brittany's pointed face. "You think I…" She glanced from Lilith's cold glare to Chance's impassive face. "No. I did *not* record our sessions! There must be another explanation."

"Don't lie!" Lilith leapt forward, but Chance swung an arm around her waist and pulled her back with little to no effort.

"Calm down." He whispered the words into her ear and didn't let go until she stopped fighting.

Chance turned his attention back to the therapist, while Lilith stewed in the corner. "If you didn't supply the information willingly, it only leaves two options—either someone coerced or compromised you."

Brittany regained her mental footing, her chest rising in defensive pride. "I don't know anything about this!"

"Okay…"

"What?" Lilith gawked at him as if he'd grown a second head. "You believe her?"

When he turned toward her, his face held a mixture of fear and compassion. "Look at her, *cherie*. You read people better than anyone, and even *I* can tell she's not involved." Chance lowered his voice to a bare whisper. "What's more likely? A reputable therapist betraying her patients, or someone hellbent on uncovering the truth bugging her?"

"But…"

Chance leaned in close and held her gaze, willing her to cooperate. "Let me handle this. You aren't thinking objectively."

"Fine." Lilith pushed the word past gritted teeth, and when he continued to stare her down, she waved a permissive hand.

"We shouldn't take up any more of your time." As he spoke, he moved to the desk, grabbed a pen, and jotted something down. "This must be a misunderstanding." He turned the note toward the therapist and jerked his head in the direction of the waiting room.

The woman nodded and strolled around her desk. "It's all right. I understand Lilith's mistrust, and I'm not offended. I hope you uncover how someone recorded our sessions."

Both of them followed the doctor to the door. "We're sorry we bothered you so late."

Price reached for the door and held it open for them. "I understand the urgency."

All three filed into the waiting room, and Brittany firmly closed the door.

Once they reached the front, Chance broke the silence but kept his voice soft. "If someone is listening, we don't want to provide more ammunition. Now, I'm going to explain, but this is confidential. You are not to breathe a word of this to *anyone*. Do we have an understanding?"

Dr. Price straightened and pushed her glasses back up her nose. "Absolutely. Client confidentiality. Lilith is my client, as are you by proxy."

"Nichols created a database share file with DNA sequencing and information on everyone he came across. It is *extensive*. We found these transcripts inside, which means other people are contributing. We are trying to ID the users, but the encryption is intense. Who has access to your office?"

While Chance delivered the news, Lilith studied Dr. Price—the dilation of her eyes, the curve of her mouth, the sudden tension ricocheting through her body. *He's right. She doesn't know anything.*

"My assistant...but we've worked together for over thirty years...A cleaning lady comes in twice a week for this floor, but she's never alone in there..."

"What about clients?" When Lilith rejoined the conversation, an almost imperceptible ripple of relief ran through the therapist.

"I can't divulge names, but I have fourteen human clients and three vampire ones, yourself included. I never leave them alone in the room for *any* reason."

"Okay, so the assistant or the maid. Sounds like a game of Clue." Lilith chuckled, but no one else found it funny.

"Not necessarily," Chance countered, glancing at the door to her office. "Any recent gifts? Flowers, pottery, anything like that?"

Brittany frowned, deep in thought. "No...not that I recall."

The *Police Academy* theme cut through the tense silence, and Lilith scrambled for her phone. "It's the precinct."

"Hey, it's Boyd. I'm not supposed to call you on cases, but the higher-ups are requesting you at a crime scene in upstate New York."

"That's quite a hike."

"Yeah, but the locals aren't equipped to handle this, and the state police requested NYPD Major Crimes Division because of our connection to Solasta, which includes you."

"That's never happened before."

"The weirdness doesn't end there. They requested our best ME…"

"Don't say it."

"Frank will meet you there. He's already on his way."

"Of course." Lilith released a deflated sigh.

"Considering the incident at the station, there's something else I should tell you. Locals found a badge on the scene that matches the victim's height, hair color, etc. They tentatively identified the body as the missing fed, Cassandra Cappalletty."

Her heart leapt into her throat as he relayed the worst possible scenario. "Did anyone contact Agent Boston?"

"I called you first, but I can't vouch for the local or state cops."

"*Do not call him.* He is a suspect and is to be treated as such. Can you call Upstate and pass on the information?"

"Sure, but they also reached out to the FBI. I doubt they'd call Boston, but expect to see a few suits on site. And Lilith?"

"Yeah?"

"Judging by the preliminary report, it's bad. Worse than bad… Horrific…"

The haunted tone made goosebumps fly over her skin. "Thanks, Chris."

"What's going on?" Chance moved closer, concern flooding his eyes. Of course, he experienced the fear rolling off her as if it were his own, thanks to the Durand blood.

That's how he knew Price spoke the truth.

"It's Agent Boston's partner."

"She's dead?"

Lilith nodded.

Dr. Price stared at them in confusion. "Who is Agent Boston?"

"*That* is a subject for a whole slew of sessions, Doc. I need you to reinstate me. Solasta isn't giving me a choice." As much as she wanted her badge, this was the last case Lilith wanted to work. A horrific end to Boston's partner? It didn't bode well. "We need to go. The place is at least two hours away."

"Wait!" Dr. Price disappeared into her office and returned a few moments later. "Here."

Lilith caught her badge with a flurry of conflicting emotions, none of which she wanted to explore. "Thanks."

"What else can I do?"

"Search every square inch and figure out who bugged your office."

After Chance and Lilith passed Poughkeepsie, they navigated dark winding roads reminding her of Madisonville, near Duncan's country home.

That fateful night seemed like a lifetime ago. So much had taken place in the months since she started the search for her uncle, most of it horrific and life-altering. Now they raced toward a grisly crime scene that promised to bring more suffering into their lives. Sooner or later, Boston would be a problem she couldn't ignore.

Lilith tried to shake off her melancholy and enjoy the scenery. A full moon bathed the countryside in pale blue light and revealed a handful of homes half-hidden by trees. The world appeared so tranquil, but they knew better.

Gloom settled so heavily on their shoulders, neither of them spoke. Apparently, they both preferred silence to pointless speculation and hollow reassurances.

When the truck crested a hill, revealing a sea of flashing lights, the apprehension only intensified. Local cops had closed the road with a barricade, and a long line of vehicles sat parked in knee-high grass leading to a circular grove in the distance. Bright rays from floodlights peeked between the trees, but the thick foliage prevented them from seeing anything else.

Chance slowed the vehicle to a crawl and rolled down his window as a uniformed officer waved at them.

"Sorry, sir, ma'am, but the road is closed. You'll have to turn around."

"We're with NYPD Major Crimes. This is Forensic Investigator Lilith Adams. I believe you're expecting us." He conveniently left out introducing himself since he didn't have an official role.

"Right…" The burly man paused, rubbing his receding hairline. "You can pull in here, park behind the others, and walk from there. Officer Kinney can check your credentials and fill you in. He's a statey parked near the tree line." The man shoved a stubby finger toward a navy cruiser with yellow markings parked up front.

"Thanks, Officer." Chance nodded and turned the truck into the wild grass.

"Man...I haven't seen this much activity since...the hotel fire."

Chaotic images raced through Lilith's mind as he spoke—a dozen ambulances, twice as many cop cars, multiple firetrucks, blaring sirens, a roaring inferno, ash-covered people wandering in shock, children crying for their parents, a desperate mother begging for help. This was nothing compared to the pandemonium in Knoxville, but she understood the sentiment.

"Yeah. I'm not used to working with an audience." As soon as the words left her mouth, anxious energy clawed at her insides. Investigating a scene in front of local, state, *and* federal law enforcement—all of them human—made her more than a little uncomfortable.

Fine trembles made her hands shake, and anxiety gripped her chest. So many things could go wrong. Lilith reached into her pocket, grabbed the two blood capsules she had stashed, and knocked them back, hoping they'd help her breathe easier.

"We'll manage. We always do." When Chance spoke, the words sounded hollow, as if he harbored doubts but wanted to reassure them both.

The truck came to a stop behind the NYPD Coroner's van, and they hopped out to a warm breeze rustling the tall grass.

"Looks like Frank beat us here. Too bad Nicci stayed behind. I could use her charm, even if she earned it with bribery." After grabbing her forensics kit from the backseat, Lilith started toward the grove.

"Bribery? How does that work?"

Chance fell in step beside her with a curious smile she didn't buy for a second. Although he was more interested in distracting her than in Nicci's work ethic, she still answered.

"She buys his cooperation with homemade lasagna and red wine."

"Sneaky but effective."

Lilith came to an abrupt stop, her chest still tightening. Playful banter wouldn't cut it this time. "Shit. What are we doing here?"

"What do you mean? I thought you'd want the case, and they did ask for you."

She rubbed at the goosebumps on her arms and stared at all the vehicles. "We should be focused on the virus, not investigating the corpse of David's partner in front of three branches of law enforcement."

"You could have said something earlier and avoided the drive."

The attempt at humor only made her raise an eyebrow.

"*Cherie*, I understand this is a lot for you, but if we can help, it gets Boston out of our lives faster."

"Hopefully..." Her tone indicated strong disbelief in that outcome. "I...have a bad feeling about all this."

"Of course, you do." Chance wrapped an arm around her shoulders and guided her forward. "Boyd said the summary was horrific...Did he give you any details?"

"Nope. Only the vic's ID, which the killer left at the scene. Most criminals try to obscure the victim's identity, not advertise it, and why leave her here in the middle of nowhere?" Then she spotted a black sedan with government plates. "The feds. Hey, maybe they'll take over and we can split." *Wishful thinking.*

If the FBI claimed jurisdiction, they would have sent Frank home and called off the reinforcements—herself included. They either hadn't decided or wanted the help.

"I don't think you want that outcome. Boston and his partner were investigating you before she disappeared..."

The implied concern hung over her like an ominous cloud.

"I know." A heavy sigh escaped, and she stared at the light blazing between the trees. "I'm tired. It's been a long night and this..."

Although it wasn't the entire truth, Chance didn't push for more.

"Can I help you?" A short African American man dressed in a state police uniform stepped away from his car and strolled toward them. Nothing in his body language indicated concern. The man probably didn't expect anyone outside of law enforcement to make it this far—a naïve presumption made by most new-bloods. A seasoned officer would never make that mistake.

"I'm Lilith Adams, Solasta forensic investigator on retainer with NYPD Major Crimes..."

A warm smile curved the officer's lips, and a hint of surprise lingered in his almond-colored eyes when he glanced down at her aluminum case—a familiar yet irritating reaction. "And this is Security Expert Chance Deveraux, also from Solasta."

This time, a frown furrowed the man's brow. "Security expert? He's not affiliated with law enforcement?"

"Not officially. He consults on cases, provides personal security, and carries a PI license but isn't overseen by the NYPD. I've experienced too much excitement this year to visit a crime scene alone."

Chance pulled out his wallet and passed over his license, which the man inspected with care before handing back.

"Appears legitimate." Despite standing a foot shorter than Chance, the policeman straightened and puffed his chest, clearly expecting an argument. "I can let you in the outer perimeter, but you can't set foot past the tape."

Chance visibly relaxed and flashed an appreciative smile, while the state cop all but sighed with relief. "I understand, sir. Not a problem."

"I'm Officer Kinney with the New York State Police, by the way." After reaching an understanding, they shook hands with a professional nod of comradery.

However, when he turned to Lilith, his smile transformed into one of attraction. "Ma'am, I'll need to see your credentials before I let you inside."

"Of course." She shifted her kit to the other hand, pulled out her bifold, and handed it over with a hollow smile. "So, were you the first to arrive?"

The man studied her badge longer than necessary before answering. "No. Locals called us in. I'm only the gatekeeper."

"Waiting for the Keymaster?"

Although Lilith appreciated Chance's humorous comment, the *Ghostbuster* reference was lost on Officer Kinney.

"I'm sorry. What?"

"Nothing." She flashed a quick frown at Chance before returning her attention to the state cop. "Do you know who arrived first?"

"Officer Linebaugh. He's still on scene if you have questions. Sergeant Hayes is running things, at least until the FBI decides what to do. Special Agents Gorman and Hersch arrived about fifteen minutes ago."

The familiar names summoned conflicting emotions. The agents had run the official investigation of Phipps Bend, but they also worked well with Cohen and had closed the case without issue. They didn't even insist on in-person interviews with Chance, Gregor, and herself. They allowed Cohen to obtain their official statements and didn't feel the need to question them. *This could either be a stroke of good fortune or a huge problem.*

"Everything appears legitimate." The tone in his voice came across as too flirtatious when he handed Lilith her badge.

"So…" Chance interrupted the awkward silence with a slight edge of impatience. "We just head through the trees?"

Kinney's eyes bounced between them for a moment as if he had finally picked up on something. *Took long enough.*

"Uh, yeah. Follow the trampled grass, and once you're in the clearing, ask for Sergeant Hayes."

"Thanks, Officer." Before he had an opportunity to reply, Lilith marched forward, following the trail left by dozens of boots.

"For a minute, I thought he was gonna ask for your number." The jovial tone wavered enough to reveal the irritation in Chance's remark. "An odd place to pick up women."

"Not all men possess your level of *game*, Mr. Deveraux."

"Hey now." When she glanced over her shoulder, his pout appeared genuine. "That's no longer a part of my life." The exaggerated Southern drawl caught her off guard, and she laughed. He cracked a grin and winked.

"Better not be." She nudged him with her shoulder as they continued along the makeshift path.

"*Tu es tout ce don't j'ai besoin, mon petite cherie.*"

"And in English?"

Chance grasped her hand and came to a stop. When she turned back, he tugged her close and held her gaze. "You are all I ever need, my little sweetheart."

The unexpected sincerity made her cheeks flush, and she scrambled for something to say. A smart-ass remark about not being small at five foot nine sprang to mind, but she suppressed the glib comment.

"You're all I need too." Saying the words out loud made Lilith feel vulnerable and exposed, neither of which added to her comfort. "However, …we are at a crime scene, so…"

"Right. Best behavior." With a roguish grin, he stole a quick kiss before letting her go.

"Best behavior…You do know what that is, right?" A smirk crossed her lips, and they forged ahead.

"I tried it a time or two. Can't say I care for it much."

She chuckled as they turned into the grove, but once they passed the trees, her amusement evaporated.

At first, the multitude of uniforms milling around distracted them from everything else. The buzz of their chaotic energy worked her frayed nerves.

She found it difficult to concentrate past the flashing cameras, barked orders, and hollers for evidence tags.

They waded into the fray, and she caught glimpses of police tape surrounding an odd tree in the far corner of the clearing.

Everyone avoided looking in the tree's direction, and a cluster of green-faced cops stood to one side, their backs to the secured area. Not all of them were young rookies either. Even the seasoned officers appeared queasy—not a great sign.

Lilith grabbed a local cop when he passed them. "Hey, we're looking for Sergeant Hayes."

The young man's face paled, and he glanced toward the ominous tree. "He's searching the secondary perimeter with the local forensic team, but the feds are around here somewhere." The man moved on before she could thank him, eager to put distance between himself and the corpse.

"Okay. Well, at least we have a direction."

Roughly halfway to the police line, Chance came to a complete stop.

"Are you okay…" The words trailed off when she turned around.

He stood perfectly still, every muscle tensed. His dilated eyes stared off into the distance, and the color drained from his face.

"What's wrong?"

At first, he didn't answer, but then he shook his head and closed his eyes with a pained frown. "I can't…" When he opened them again, they jumped from one person to the next, and his breath quickened. "This is too much. They're all…Everyone is…"

Before he forced the words out, Lilith dropped her kit, rushed up, grabbed his face, and made him meet her eyes. "Ignore them. Focus on me. Breathe."

The tension leaked away the longer he stared at her but never vanished.

"You can't cross the tape, so there is no reason to come any closer. You have nothing to prove."

Chance nodded, still taking slow relaxing breaths.

"Why don't stay near the tree line? I need to find Sergeant Hayes."

Before either of them moved, two people stepped into view, both wearing cheap black suits and unimaginative ties—FBI. "CSI Adams?"

"Yes?" Lilith stepped away from Chance, her heart beating a little faster.

"Special Agents Gorman"—the tall African American man with an old boxer's body and tawny eyes gestured to himself—"and Hersch." He jabbed a thumb at his female partner, who stood at least six inches shorter with a modest, athletic frame and a medium brown pixie cut that accentuated her heart-shaped face.

"You're the ones who worked the Phipps Bend case with Detective Cohen."

"Yes, ma'am." Hersch's face split into a friendly smile that put Lilith at ease, allowing her pulse to return to normal.

A cough over her shoulder served as a reminder to introduce her companion. "Sorry, this is Chance Deveraux, my...security specialist." Although reducing him to such an impersonal role seemed wrong, she realized people didn't typically bring their boyfriends to crime scenes.

"A pleasure to finally meet you both." Unlike his partner's obvious Tennessee accent, Gorman's voice contained an odd mixture, making him difficult to place in a geographic sense.

"Where are you from? If you don't mind me asking." Chance broached the subject before she did, probably as a distraction from the chaotic and horrifying emotions swirling around him.

"Bryson City, North Carolina, originally, but I worked in multiple offices before landing in Knoxville."

"I didn't realize Knoxville qualified for an FBI branch. It isn't a very large city," Lilith chimed in, keeping the focus off Chance until he got his bearings.

"You'd be surprised. Tennessee has a long criminal history from "Machine Gun" Kelly—the gangster, not the millennial punk with pink hair—to the formation of the Ku Klux Klan. Did you know Tennessee is home to one of the oldest serial killer cold cases? The Night Marauder assaulted or killed more than forty people between 1919 and 1926."

"Yeah, uh, he's a huge history nut, if you can't tell." Hersch cast a disapproving frown at her partner, which the man pointedly ignored.

"All things history...it's a passion. Anyway..."

An awkward silence stretched out until Lilith broke it. "So, you two arrived in record time. I'm guessing you weren't in Tennessee when you got the call?"

The two exchanged a look containing an entire conversation before Gorman answered. "No. We were nearby, following up on another case."

The rather vague response from someone who appeared to over-share made her uneasy again, especially when neither of them decided to clarify. "Well, I'm not sure what your plan is, but the locals requested me. I'm more than happy to walk away if you plan on handling this internally."

"Did they request Mr. Deveraux too?" Hersch nodded toward the Cajun towering over Lilith.

"No. I'm sure you two understand why I keep extra security around when possible."

"Of course." Gorman straightened his baby blue tie, visually switching to business mode. "Hersch and I discussed this on the way here. They requested the FBI for the same reason they called you in—the severity of the crime. We were assigned because of our...proximity."

A ripple of tension crossed the man's broad features as he paused.

"We are well acquainted with agents Cappalletty and Boston, and..." He glanced away, struggling with his words again.

"So, you are aware of their illegal investigation?" Chance cut to the chase before the agent recovered.

"You know?" His tawny eyes widened, and he needlessly straightened his tie again. "Did Agent Boston contact you?"

"He assaulted me in the middle of a police station. I'm pretty sure that counts as contact."

"Is he locked up?" Hersch wore a guarded expression Lilith found difficult to interpret.

"No."

Disappointment flashed across both their faces. "So, he's still a suspect." As Gorman spoke, the agents exchanged another look that held volumes.

"Still?"

This time, Hersch adjusted her suit jacket, which didn't quite fit her lean frame, and took charge. "Agent Boston had a...less than sterling record before he began his vendetta investigation. When the FBI uncovered it, they asked us to question him since we ran the initial Phipps Bend case and consulted on the New York fiasco."

Lilith swallowed the nervous lump in her throat while she waited for Hersch to continue. *Were they polite and friendly earlier to throw us off guard? Is this where the other shoe drops?*

"We recommended he be declared mentally unfit for duty. The Bureau was about to fire him, but the guy's dad is some real estate mogul with deep political ties, and..."

"I'm aware," Lilith added, and the woman's cheeks turned red. "This isn't the first time his dad bailed him out of trouble."

"He did mention you two shared a history."

"That's a story for another day. So, what do we do here? There're four different agencies here, and no one seems eager to take lead."

"We spoke with the Knoxville director. He wants us to stay in the loop but suggested someone else take point. Given the nature of the crime, you and your team have the most experience."

Lilith didn't know if she was more relieved or dismayed at the prospect. Although heading the investigation would allow her to minimize the involvement of her personal history, it also meant more interactions with Agent Boston—the last thing she wanted.

"So, here's my idea," Gorman spoke up as the rest of the group fell silent. "I'd like to help with the initial investigation, if you don't mind, and perhaps Mr. Deveraux can assist Agent Hersch in gathering statements from the first cops to arrive." The man appeared genuine and gave them no reason to mistrust him and his partner.

Lilith glanced over her shoulder with the silent question, and Chance nodded, so she turned back with a friendly smile. "Divide and conquer."

Chance leaned in, whispered, "Be careful," and squeezed her hand before following Hersch away from the police tape. A sudden sensation of vulnerability swept over Lilith as he walked away, but she steeled her nerves, picked up her kit, and turned back to the FBI agent.

"Have you seen the body yet?"

Gorman shook his head as they moved past a cluster of state cops. The tension in his arms and shoulders said it all, but he still clarified, "I wasn't in a hurry, if you know what I mean."

"Can I ask how long you've known the victim?"

"Cassie…Cassandra Cappalletty transferred to the Knoxville office about four years ago."

"Wait. Boston and Cappalletty worked in your branch?" The thought of them being assigned to Phipps Bend instead of Gorman and Hersch made her stomach lurch.

"Yes, but they investigate financial cases, with very little fieldwork. Anyway, Cassie is…was quiet, consumed by the job, but a good egg. Her first partner died in the line of duty, and she didn't take it well. Work became her entire existence. She was on her way to an early burnout when they paired her with that animal." The disgust rang clear in Gorman's voice, and he wrinkled his nose.

"I take it you aren't in his fan club?"

"I'm pretty sure Cassie and Boston's father are...were the only two members." Twice, he had corrected himself, trying to adjust to the murder of his colleague and friend, a painful task Lilith had experienced too many times lately.

"So, she didn't have problems with him?" Although she couldn't hide the surprise in her voice, Gorman shared her reaction.

"I know. Shocked. Me too. For about a year, they appeared...more than close. The man is adept at manipulating vulnerable females, but being partnered with Cappalletty calmed him down. They made a decent team until last October."

"The Phipps Bend case."

The man nodded again. "We consulted them to track Phipps Bends' financial and real estate records. As soon as he read the full report...Cassie kept trying to make him drop it, but the guy is obsessed with...well, you." The man stared at her, expecting an explanation.

"We...dated in college. Things didn't end well, and his dad transferred him to Temple University in exchange for me not pressing charges."

"Charges for what?"

For over a decade, Lilith had kept the story to herself, and now it seemed she had to tell everyone. Exposing the secret still felt unnatural. "He put me in the hospital...Almost killed me and another woman."

"Holy crap." The agent stared off into the distance, continuing to stroll at an easy pace. "I mean, I suspected, but...How did he make it into the FBI?"

"Like you said, his father has a lot of juice, and no one ever pressed charges. So, Boston refused to drop his witch hunt, and Cassie gave in?"

Gorman either didn't notice her anxious desire to change the subject or overlooked it. "Not willingly. When the local director hauled him in, Boston insisted Cassie helped him with everything, in the hopes it'd make him more credible. The director transferred them both to Richmond, to put physical distance between them and Phipps Bend, but Boston still wouldn't give up his investigation, so the Bureau suspended them both."

"Well, that would definitely put a strain on a relationship."

"Between that and the suspicious bruises. Cassie always told me he had a temper but a good heart. Damn fool." Gorman gave an indignant snort. escaped "The mantra of battered women everywhere.

"Then, about a week before Boston claimed she went missing, Cassie applied for a transfer back to Knoxville…without him. I figured she finally wizened up and dumped the asshole."

"I have to ask…Why was there no official missing person case? Six months? The FBI *had* to suspect something."

"We did, but Boston's dad pulled strings before, and he's the chief suspect. Two IA agents were discretely looking into it but found nothing to tie her disappearance to him or anyone else. There's no CCTV in the plaza where we believe she disappeared, and once authorities found her car, they ran out of leads."

"They found her car? I thought it still hadn't been spotted?"

"As I said, the IA agents were being discrete. They didn't want anything leaking back to Boston, not that it helped. The car was wiped down—no prints, blood, DNA, or anything else."

"Well, we'll see what the body can…"

As Lilith spoke, they stepped around three state cops, and both came to a dead stop.

Chapter 24

Spotlights converged on a gnarled tree, providing a harsh contrast Lilith found off-putting. At first, that's all her brain interpreted—an odd tree with thick, waxy leaves, tall grass trampled into a circle around the trunk, exposed roots sitting atop fresh dirt, and yellow police tape fluttering in the light breeze. A chill ran down her spine at the beautiful yet unsettling imagery.

Then features began to pop out, like the 3D image hidden in a *Magic Eye* picture from her childhood—nasal cartilage, zygomatic process, clavicle, iliac crest, ribcage…Someone had merged the body into the tree by force, breaking and arranging the corpse until the feet melded into the roots and the hands ended as gnarled twigs. The rotting lips were parted in a breathless sigh of pleasure, making the twisted limbs appear more abhorrent, and flowers graced the desiccated corpse, like tokens of profane worship.

"Oh God…" A sudden lurch of her stomach sent bile searing up Lilith's throat. She turned away, squeezed her eyes closed, and doubled over, concentrating on her breathing.

While she managed to keep her dinner down, the FBI agent wasn't as lucky. Once he stopped retching, she gave him a way out and prayed he'd take it.

"You don't have to go with me. I'm used to working alone, and you knew her…"

The man wiped a hand across his mouth and shook his head. "No. If I can help somehow, I owe her that much."

"All right, but get it out of your system now. You can't puke on my scene, and it's only going to get worse, I promise you."

The harsh comment also served as a personal pep talk. The brief glimpse told her this one rivaled Mariah's cadaver—more fuel for her nightmares. *At least I'm not related to this one.*

"Are you ready?" Lilith placed a hand on Gorman's shoulder, hoping the gesture might help him focus.

After pushing a slow breath through pursed lips, he nodded and stood up, straightening his tie, but avoided looking at the body.

"Okay. Have you worked with a CSI on-site before?"

"Once or twice. The forensic crew is usually done before I start."

"We are going to walk in a straight line. Until we reach the site, keep your eyes on the ground and scan for anything out of the ordinary— impressions, shoe prints, anything the perpetrators left behind."

After setting her aluminum case down, Lilith clicked it open, pulled out two pairs of nitrile gloves, and handed him a set.

"When we reach the body, we will start at the top and work our way down. No pacing and only minimal movement. Don't touch anything. The gloves are only a precaution. If I'm the only one handling evidence, it keeps the chain of custody clear, and gives the defense attorneys less ammunition, especially since you knew the victim."

While speaking, she slid on a wrist holder for small instruments and loaded it with various supplies.

"Focus on fine details. It will make compartmentalizing easier. Always refer to the corpse as the victim, not *she*, and never by name."

"Got it."

"Can you hold on to these for me?"

Once Gorman nodded, Lilith passed him a selection of small paper and plastic evidence bags to keep him busy.

"Last thing, put these on."

The man stared at the blue paper booties in her outstretched hand, and a frown wrinkled his face. "But…we're outside."

"They will lessen impressions of our footwear and keep us from contaminating trace evidence with the gunk on our soles."

"Understood." As he pulled them on over his black dress shoes, his eyes wandered upward.

"Focus on the ground until we're close. Judging by the yellow markers, they've already done a sweep, but avoiding the whole picture until you've adjusted to the fine details helps." After closing her case and slipping the booties over her black Converse, Lilith took a deep breath and glanced at her makeshift partner. "Ready?"

Although his dark complexion had lost some of its color, he nodded with grim determination.

When they crossed beneath the yellow police tape, it felt like stepping into another world. The noise from the milling crowd dulled, the warm breeze stopped, and the bright floodlights stripped the area of color, all of which made each fine hair stand on end.

Lilith kept her eyes locked on the ground, following alongside a trail of trampled grass. The chaotic layered impressions made individual footprints impossible to discern, and at least half of them probably belonged to law enforcement.

"Many people came through here, but…" She started, but Gorman finished her thought.

"No signs of heavy equipment. From the brief glance, it appeared the tree was moved here, but if that's true, they did it by hand…Lots of hands, I'd say."

"They warned me you were coming."

The gruff but familiar voice startled her so much, she lost her balance, but Gorman caught her arm and kept her from face-planting into the grass.

"Nice to see you too, Frank." Lilith glanced up long enough to spot the old man leaning on his cane.

"This is a bit of nasty business, this one." A subtle Old World London undercurrent snuck into the medical examiner's voice, something she'd never noticed.

"What can you tell us?"

"You look ridiculous, staring at the ground. The photographer's taken pictures of the tracks and obvious evidence. The local and state cops can comb through the grass all they want. Hurry and get over here so I can take these hair and tissue samples to the lab."

"Keep your eyes on the ground or Frank until we are closer," Lilith whispered before picking up the pace.

A few feet out, the stench hit her like a physical force—far worse than Miriah's scene. Of course, from her quick glimpse, this corpse was well into the process of active decay. Most of the organs and muscle were probably liquified, oozing from every orifice or opening in the skin and mingling with the air. Miriah's corpse had been fresh, with only the odor of urine, feces, and blood.

For a moment, Lilith put the back of her gloved hand to her nose, trying to adjust. Then she paused to pick apart the scents. As expected, decomposition dominated the horrific bouquet, but underneath... something fragrant yet citrus. *Odd.*

"Decomp places the time of death at anywhere from a month to five months depending on..."

"That's an extremely wide range," Gorman interrupted.

Frank turned his cold stare on him.

"Yes, it is. The environment a body is in after death affects the rate of decay, as you should know, *Special Agent*. Someone moved the tree here...recently. I cannot make a more educated guess on the time of death until I know where they kept the body. I *can* tell you the victim has been...on the tree for quite a while. None of the attachment sites show fresh disruption of the phloem or inner bark."

"Any thoughts on the cause of death?"

When Lilith finally reached Frank, the expression he wore reflected more sadness than animosity. "Asphyxiation or exsanguination are the most likely culprits. I'll narrow it down during the autopsy."

"Thank you, Frank. I'll send you a report with anything we find and ensure they transport the body to you as soon as possible."

For once, the gruff man didn't roll his eyes or make an abrasive remark. He merely nodded, grabbed his bag, and left.

"Okay." After a few steady breaths, she turned to her improvised partner. "Are you ready?"

Every microexpression on his face said no, but he nodded anyway.

They both faced the trunk as she clicked the voice recorder on her phone.

"NYPD Forensic Consultant Lilith Adams and FBI Special Agent Gorman on-scene in Millbrook, New York. The victim is an adult Caucasian female with long brown hair, tentatively identified as Special Agent Cassandra Cappalletty."

After glancing over at Gorman to ensure he was ready, she continued.

"The victim's body is in an active state of decay, with the soft tissue beginning to liquify and the skin darkening. Some areas of bone are exposed, which could indicate injuries. There are no obvious signs of insect activity, so the body was kept in a controlled environment after death."

Lilith inhaled through her mouth to minimize the stench and moved closer to inspect the scalp through the thinning and brittle hair. The leathery skin made bruising difficult to discern, but there were no breaks in the skin or dried blood.

"No immediate signs of head injuries, although foliage and flowers in various states of decay are present in the hair. Someone visited the body regularly...paying tribute. So, most likely a climate-controlled environment capable of sustaining a tree but accessible...A greenhouse or something to that effect..."

Lilith moved on to the black pits of the orbital sockets, bile rising in her throat. Although it was common with a corpse in this state, the sight was still disgustingly haunting.

"The...eyes are gone, most likely liquified during decay. No tool marks or trauma to suggest otherwise."

Gorman peered closer and chimed in, "The thick metal collar around her...the victim's neck is iron, Old World stuff, and the mechanism on the side...I've seen this before..."

"In another case?"

"No." The man's brow furrowed, and he poked at the crude components. Then his eyebrows rose. "It's a crucifixion collar."

"A what?" Lilith hadn't darkened the doorway of a church in quite some time but didn't remember a collar on the crucifix.

"I have a thing for the Archaic and Classical periods of Greece. One of the finest yet most horrific civilizations in history. Schools teach a lot of common misconceptions about crucifixion. Executioners fitted many of their victims with collars like this, which are slowly tightened until the victim dies."

"Ancient Greece is the topic of choice lately. Can't seem to get away from it."

"How so?"

For a moment, she forgot who she was talking to—a rookie mistake. *Sloppy.* "Oh...another case I'm working."

"Any possibility they're connected?"

"No."

However, the more she thought about it, the more likely it became. What were the odds of two separate cases with strong ties to Greece? Still, their only other connection was her involvement.

"Moving on. The darkened skin and loss of soft tissue make discerning the bruise patterns difficult, but these breaks..." Lilith traced the unnaturally twisted and contorted limbs, her stomach churning. "The only visible breaks are on the extremities—elbows, wrists, fingers, knees, ankles."

Lilith pulled out her penlight to closer inspect the exposed bone fragments, ignoring the rest of the body. If she honed in on small details, it helped. She might not have been related to this victim, but the woman had suffered...more than anyone ever should.

"Hmm...this elbow shows hemorrhagic staining, and the surrounding skin is burnt"—she moved to the next split in the decimated skin and used a blunt probe to expose the bone—"but the wrist doesn't have the same damage."

Then she crouched down and poked through the strings of muscle, ligaments, tendons, and skin clinging to the legs.

"Same here. The knees show hemorrhagic staining and burns, but not the ankles. Some fractures occurred antemortem, like the knees...Mostly likely from an anterior blow..." Lilith paused again.

The scenario sprang to life in her head. Someone had shattered the woman's knee while she was alive...hitting it with such force that the bones punctured the posterior skin, and then cauterized the wound.

After clearing her throat, she continued, "...and others postmortem."

Gorman observed her moving from limb to limb, confirming her suspicion. "The pattern..." He spoke as she prodded the desiccated tissue around the neck. "It's circular."

Lilith paused and took a step back, reluctantly taking in the entire picture. The shoulders and hips remained in place, but the legs twisted around the trunk, and the outstretched arms twined through the branches, like a twisted Vitruvian Man. *Who could do something like this?*

"Does that mean anything to you?"

"Well, it could be anything, but..." The man paused, his head cocked to the side and his focus fully restored. Perhaps the historical angle allowed him to view the corpse as research instead of a colleague.

It appeared as if the FBI agent was more adept at compartmentalizing than Lilith was, and she'd never met the victim, much less worked with her.

"The crucifixion collar got me thinking. If this was pre-Christian Greece, I'd bet money they used a breaking wheel."

"Well, that sounds ominous."

"As it should. The breaking wheel is an old torture technique. The Greeks believed testimony given during intense pain revealed the absolute truth. Crucifixion was a popular execution technique after they got what they wanted. This…is different, though. They didn't use live trees, and this species doesn't appear common to the area. Then there's the date…"

"I'm guessing it's significant somehow?"

"July is seen by some scholars as the Grecian New Year. On the seventh day of the month, Ancient Greeks celebrated Apollo in a festival called *Hekatombaion*. Although the festival fell out of popular favor, the name survived as the month of their New Year. Today is the seventh. It could be a coincidence, but…"

Lilith peered over at him as if he'd grown a second head. "Are you serious? How the hell do you know all this?"

The man shrugged and lowered his eyes to the ground. "I minored in ancient civilizations in college. My parents weren't thrilled with that decision, but I always loved history, and the Greco-Roman empire embodied the quintessential fall of an advanced civilization. Plus, I have an exceptional memory for odd facts. I could tell you some wild stories about the Spartan festival of Karneia."

"No thanks. I've seen *300*."

Judging by the tight-lipped smile, Gorman had a lot to say about the movie, but they had work to do.

"Okay, so a ton of clues pointing to Ancient Greece…" Lilith scanned the body again, and a thought occurred to her. "Whether you're right about the date's significance or not, they held onto the corpse and kept the tree alive until tonight. They wanted someone to find it, for us to see it, *now*. Do you know who called it in?"

"Anonymous tip from a pay phone downtown."

"I bet one of the perps made the call. They are saying something, but what?"

A puzzled expression pulled at Lilith's features while she studied the overall pattern and tried not to envision the once-lively woman who'd inhabited this broken body.

"It looks like they tried to make her part of the tree." Even the dark pallor and wrinkles in the decomposing skin blended into the bark with sickening accuracy. Lilith stood on tiptoe for a better look at the shattered and molded hands. "They shoved twigs under her nails for a more seamless transition."

A dark shiver crawled down her spine, making her blood run cold. Torture involving the eyes, teeth, and nails bothered her more than anything else.

"And…" As she started to step back, a glint in the body's open mouth caught her attention. "Hold on. I saw something."

Lilith gently pried the mouth open wider and extracted a rough silver coin with her tweezers.

"Huh." The crude shape sported the profile of a man wearing a helmet on one side and an owl on the other. "This looks old."

Gorman peered into her hand, and an expression of wonder brightened his face. "I've never seen one in person…An obol coin."

When she flashed a vacant smile, he explained.

"Greeks placed an obol coin in the mouth of loved ones who passed so they could pay Charon, the ferryman, to transport them across the River Styx."

"I thought they put them over the eyes."

"Common misconception. Celtic and Hungarian cultures put coins over the eyes, primarily to keep them from springing open. In life, Greeks sometimes put coins in their mouths for safekeeping. In death, they placed them there so only Charon could retrieve them and their loved one wouldn't be caught between worlds as a restless spirit haunting the riverbank."

"So, someone tortured her but cared enough to grant her peace in death. Then they molded her into a tree and brought her flowers on a regular basis until revealing their handiwork? None of this makes sense."

"Perhaps they are two separate messages. What if the torture was necessary but not their grand statement? If you remove the breaking wheel and collar…Dyrope." The odd word escaped his lips in a soft whisper.

"What?"

"A woman from Greek mythology…"

"Of course." Lilith sighed, unable to hide her annoyance at the topic that refused to go away.

"I, uh…can stop if…"

"No, no. Continue. It's relevant to the case. I'm sorry."

"Okay." Gorman's tawny eyes narrowed a bit before he continued, speaking in a tentative voice. "One day, she took a flower from a lotus tree. However, this was no ordinary tree, but a nymph in disguise. When she plucked the flowering bud, the tree bled. As penance for her crime and tribute to Artemis, the gods transformed her into a lotus tree. I wonder…" Gorman reached up and plucked a few leaves and a flower.

"Wait. I thought you said the festival honored Apollo. Why display a tribute to Artemis?"

"They were fraternal twins, and their stories frequently intertwined."

Dr. Wolfe's story about the arrows of Artemis and Apollo suddenly sprang to Lilith's mind. Perhaps the two cases were connected, after all.

"I'll have someone analyze these, but if I'm correct, this is an actual lotus tree. They're nearly extinct in Greece, so someone either transported it from overseas or grew it here in a carefully controlled environment over decades."

"Well, I'm no botanist, and I live in New York City, so I'm no help, but this eliminates *one* suspect."

"Who?" Gorman frowned, tucking the foliage into a paper evidence bag and sealing it.

"Boston. I'm the first to admit the man is violent, but this is too...cerebral for him. Assuming you're correct about everything—and you sure know your stuff—this is a statement...a manifesto, not a crime of passion."

"Yeah, but about what?"

Lilith peered at the twisted and desiccated body, trying to unravel the mysteries it contained but came up empty. "I have no idea."

"Where the fuck is she?" a voice boomed over the chaotic crowd behind them.

Lilith froze in horror. "No. Shit. This is bad." She backed away from the body, removing her gloves, and scanned the area. Boston seeing his partner like this was one thing, but her investigating the body...

"No, Hersch! I know she's here! I *need* to see her!"

Lilith rushed for the tape's edge, hoping to cut David off before he saw the body.

"You can't be here!" Hersch snatched Boston's wrist as he burst into view but couldn't hold on.

David shook her loose, and when his eyes traveled up to the police tape, they landed on Lilith, who stopped dead in her tracks.

"*You!*" In the blink of an eye, Boston drew his gun—a surprising feat, considering Lilith had dislocated his shoulder a few hours ago—and the entire grove went silent. "Why are *you* here?" Venom oozed from his voice, thicker than ever before, and his gun shook. Sweat ran down his forehead into his thick brows and his red-rimmed eyes hardened. This was a man on the edge One slight touch might send him over.

"They requested me." Lilith tossed her gloves on the ground and slowly raised her hands, her pulse racing.

Dozens of cops drew their weapons, and silence settled around them again.

The man had hated her for years, blamed her for everything, then she humiliated him. Now, she stood on the scene of his partner's brutal murder.

"Tell me she's not dead!" Pure animosity and violence burned in his dark eyes. His brows drew down and together, followed by a lip quiver and flared nostrils.

Shit. He had every intention of shooting her, regardless of the consequences.

"David, wait!" Fear screamed through her head like an air-raid siren. "Shooting me won't bring her back."

"What? No lies? No sarcastic, passive-aggressive bullshit, Lily? If she's dead, you don't deserve to live."

"Drop your damn weapon, or we'll open fire!" Hersch bellowed, inching closer.

Lilith silently screamed obscenities in her head while her arms quivered, and sweat ran down her spine.

"Special Agent David Boston! I *will* shoot you. Holster your fucking weapon!" Hersch moved into his field of vision, her voice booming with unexpected authority.

The violent rage in Boston's eyes cooled into something scarier as they remained locked on Lilith, but he holstered his weapon. Officers cautiously advanced, their guns aimed, but Chance surged through the crowd and tackled him with a loud thud. In an instant, he wrestled Boston into submission and tossed his gun to the shocked cops.

"Stand down, everyone!" Hersch barked the order and moved in, shielding Chance as best she could.

One by one, the men lowered their guns but stood at the ready.

"Damn it! How did he find out?"

Gorman joined Lilith at the scene's edge, posing an excellent question, but she still couldn't control her pulse or catch her breath. Every muscle trembled. The man had wanted to shoot her...and would have if Hersch hadn't interfered. Boston's sense of self-preservation was the only reason she was still breathing at all.

"Hey, are you okay?"

Lilith blinked back the tears threatening to spill and nodded. "Yeah." She inhaled deeply and focused until her hands stopped trembling. "Let's go ask him some questions." She marched over while Chance and Hersch got Boston to his feet.

To her surprise, he didn't fixate on her this time. Instead, he stared at the tall man beside her. "Is it true, John? Is it Cassie?" Tears flooded his eyes, and for once, they appeared genuine.

"Found her badge on the scene...Hair, height, and body type are a match, but...we need DNA to confirm." A guarded expression clouded Gorman's face. Although he didn't like Boston, admitting they couldn't visually identify someone's partner was a difficult task.

"I need to see her."

"Come on, Dave. You know you can't be here."

"John, she's my"—his dark brown eyes darted to Lilith for an instant before he continued—"partner."

After a heavy sigh, the agent stepped forward and put a hand on Boston's shoulder. "That's why I'm telling you to walk away. I helped inspect the body, and...you don't want to see her like this."

All the anger leaked from Boston's face, and his eyes drifted to the yellow tape rustling in the breeze. Although she and Gorman blocked his view of the body, the man's words seemingly struck Boston to the core.

For the first time, Lilith felt sorry for him. Losing her partner, Detective Felipe Alvarez, had devastated her. She understood the pain and guilt more than most.

With the situation deescalated, officers strolled away and returned to their tasks, and a quiet hum of activity returned to the grove.

"Come on, Dave." Gorman broke the silence while patting the man's shoulder. "I'll tell ya what I know, okay?"

Boston's eyes remained fixed on the police line. He stood still, ignoring the agent's invitation. Awkward tension surrounded their group, which put Lilith on edge again. *He isn't done.*

As the thought occurred to her, Boston shoved his weight backward with a sudden burst of energy, knocking a sleep-deprived Chance off his feet. Before anyone could move, David sprinted past them with the same speed that had earned him a college scholarship.

Everyone except Chance tore after him in quick pursuit, but no one reached him in time.

David ducked under the tape and came to a dead stop before the ominous lotus tree. They circled him with caution, but his gaze stayed locked on the gruesome display. Tears streamed down his reddened cheeks, and he stared in horror at what remained of Cassandra Cappalletty.

Then he collapsed onto his knees, flickers of guilt pulling at his angular features. "What have I done?"

Chapter 25

David clutched his stomach and rocked back and forth, weeping. "This is all my fault. God, what did I do?"

After a silent conversation of head nods, Gorman moved forward, while Hersch, Lilith, and Chance hung back. He rested his palm on David's shoulder again and kept his voice gentle.

"Dave…did you hurt Cassie?"

With a sudden jerk, Boston pulled away and scowled up at the man. "No! I didn't do *this*!"

"Then this isn't your fault."

Boston found no comfort in the man's matter-of-fact statement, and Lilith understood the impulse. People had spouted the same party line at her a hundred times after Felipe died. Although sympathizing with Boston felt fundamentally wrong, part of her wanted to offer some comforting words to a fellow law enforcement professional. Of course, the outcome of her internal debate didn't matter. The last person he wanted advice from was her.

"Of course, it is! I dragged her into this mess…"

"Phipps Bend? Nothing here suggests any relevance. How do you know—"

"Because I know!" The agent surged to his feet, both fists clenched. The man's grief and sorrow hardened into rage. For a second, he stared Gorman down with open hostility, then he turned his hateful glare on Lilith. "This is *your* doing!"

He started forward, but Chance intercepted him, shielding her from his wrath.

"Okay, Dave. I think that's enough." Gorman sighed wearily as he approached the crazed man. "I want you to take a walk with Hersch, catch your breath, and cool off. I'll ask her some questions."

Skepticism flashed in Boston's eyes as he turned around. "Don't patronize me."

"And don't make me call the director. You aren't assigned to this case. Hell, you aren't on active duty, and you pulled a gun on law enforcement personnel at a crime scene. Give Hersch a statement while I figure out what to do with you."

"Come on, Dave. Let's go." Agent Hersch stepped forward and grabbed his arm, but he pulled away with a scowl.

"Okay. I'll go." After one last death glare at Lilith, he allowed the female agent to escort him off the scene.

"I apologize for that." Once again, Gorman straightened his tie and avoided eye contact.

"How did he find out?" Chance narrowed his eyes and stepped up to the agent.

"No earthly clue. I'd say through someone at the bureau, but…the man doesn't have friends, for obvious reasons."

"And I doubt he knows anyone local," Lilith chimed in, racking her brain for an answer. "Detective Boyd sent us, but I told him *not* to contact Agent Boston, and he would never disobey the order after David attacked me at the station."

"What if he knew because he's involved?" Both Gorman and Lilith frowned at Chance's question. "I understand he was close to the victim, but what's stronger? His attachment to her or his hatred for you? I mean…it's palpable."

"Wait. What?"

"Think about it. The man spent months investigating you and got nowhere. May he snapped and figured if he couldn't catch you, he'd frame you."

"No. I don't think so. This is…involved, intricate, and the evidence points elsewhere with roots in ancient history. David flunked humanities in college, and none of it implicates me. This is ritualistic with many people involved…perhaps a Grecian cult."

"Greek?" Chance immediately picked up on the common thread, and Lilith nodded with a wary expression, darting her eyes to the FBI agent.

"So, we have a dilemma," Gorman interrupted, ignoring their current conversation. "At the very least, Agent Boston is a person of interest in this case. I don't believe he's involved, but only he knows what Cassie was up to before she disappeared."

The man began to pace as he talked out the problem.

"If we take him in for questioning, his father will send an army of suits before we start the paperwork, and everything will disappear. I think you're right, Miss Adams. This is a manifesto that implies catastrophic things in the works. Why make a statement of this magnitude if you don't intend to supply the exclamation point? We need information from him...and fast."

"What are you asking, Special Agent Gorman?" Lilith lowered her voice and moved closer, her eyes searching the clearing.

A few people watched them in the distance, but no one stood within earshot.

A heavy sigh passed the man's thick lips. "This goes against every oath I've taken, but we can't sit here and wait." When his tawny eyes met Lilith's, they held a significant weight. "I want you to question Agent Boston."

"We aren't cops. He doesn't have to go with us, and I guarantee he won't cooperate."

"I'm asking *because* you aren't cops. You can make him cooperate."

The implied subtext hung in the air and made Lilith's stomach queasy. *Is he really suggesting we torture him for information?*

"I have a place." Chance crossed his arms over his chest as his gaze drifted to the ground. "He'll tell me what we need to know."

Lilith's jaw dropped. She stared at Chance as if he were a stranger, but they both ignored her reaction.

"What kind of vehicle do you have?"

"Ford Explorer Sport Trac with a hard tonneau cover. We parked close to the road."

"Um, guys?"

"I can't believe I'm doing this." Gorman talked right over her. "But I don't see any other way."

"Wait."

Chance turned toward her and stepped close. "Do you have another solution?"

Although she ran through each scenario, no alternative emerged. If someone had tortured Cassie for information, Boston was the only person who might understand why.

Chance took her silence as a no and glanced back at Gorman. "We're good."

The agent studied them for a moment before pulling out his cell phone. "I hope I'm right about you two. We *never* had this conversation."

Once they both nodded, he dialed his partner.

"He still with you?...Good. There's a Ford Explorer Sport Trac parked at the back of the line. Meet us there with Boston in five."

"You know this could bite you in the ass, right?" Lilith felt the need to warn him as they walked. "When his father finds out you handed his son off to civilians for...enthusiastic questioning, he'll go after you."

A grimace formed on Gorman's broad face, and he nodded while side-stepping a few cops. "What happened to Cassie is the most extreme thing I've seen. If that is their opening statement, I'll brave Boston's dad to stop what they've planned next. All I ask is you fill us in as soon as you have something." He handed her his card, which she tucked in her pocket.

"You have my word."

"You're a good man. I'll ensure Boston's dad doesn't know about your involvement." Something in Chance's tone and choice of words conjured an ominous feeling that left Lilith frowning, but he barreled ahead before she could comment. "You and your partner distract him. Start a conversation with his back to the truck. I'll do the rest."

"Shit. What am I gonna tell Hersch?"

"Do you trust your partner?" When Lilith echoed the words of her therapist, she cringed a little inside.

"With my life."

"And she trusts you?"

"Of course."

"Then tell her the truth."

The agent rubbed his wiry black hair and sighed. "You're right. I'm gonna owe her, though."

"Lilith, go with Gorman. Your presence will keep him distracted and off-balance, but for the love of God, please, don't provoke him. The man was dangerous before, but now...he's unhinged."

Lilith peered up at him and smiled warily. Staring down the muzzle of David's gun while his finger flexed on the trigger had made her realize survival was more important than proving herself.

"I promise."

His hazel eyes locked onto hers, studying them.

"Seriously, Chance. I'm not looking for trouble."

Once he appeared satisfied, he split off from the group and vanished into the dark. A silent prayer repeated in her head, and she faced forward, continuing to walk beside Gorman. A lot of things could go wrong...

Two silhouettes cut across the field about a hundred yards away—Hersch and Boston.

"You're sure about this?" Lilith double-checked as they neared the point of no return.

"If you have a better idea, now's the time to speak up."

No matter how much she wracked her brain, nothing else came to mind. "Nope."

"You know, Detective Cohen spoke highly of you."

"Oh?" Although she welcomed a subject change, the unexpected comment caught her off guard. "How was it, working with Andrew?" She harbored a certain curiosity about his demeanor with others, especially humans.

"Eileen, my partner, took a shine to him, at least at first. She has a...complicated view of most men, though. Seems like a decent enough detective. He told us how you went down in the Phipps Bend basement alone, armed with a pistol, to face the terrorist and save everyone."

A blush crept across her cheeks, not from the flattery, but from the embarrassing inaccuracy of the statement. "That's kind, but I didn't save everyone...or anyone, for that matter. I got caught, and *they* had to rescue *me*."

"Which they couldn't have done if you didn't patch up Chance and set free one of the hostages."

"I suppose. We still lost people." Her voice trailed off, the images flashing through her mind for the thousandth time—Alvarez with blood gushing down his shirt, Duncan gnawing at his own shackled limbs, Coffee howling in pain as Ashcroft clawed through his abdomen.

"Well, if you didn't feel any responsibility, I'd be worried, but you're not to blame. The killer is the only one at fault."

"You sound like my therapist."

The man's sudden hearty chuckle brought a smile to her lips. "They do have a way of stating the obvious with annoying clarity."

"I'm assuming you know from experience?"

"Yeah, a few times. The first time I shot a perp, after my partner died in 9/11, but the worst was marriage counseling with my second wife."

After raising a skeptical eyebrow, she smirked. "Seriously?"

"Oh yeah. By a mile! I can talk about work all day, but discussing chore charts, date nights, and scheduling sex to fit between soccer and karate classes? There's a reason I've had three failed marriages."

Despite the evening's gloom, the unexpected confession made Lilith chuckle. "Let me guess. You tend to ramble when you're anxious?"

"Is it obvious?"

"Not at all." Lilith winked at him and braced herself as they approached Chance's truck.

When they walked up, the two agents turned to greet them. A malicious snarl contorted David's face when his eyes landed on her.

"Why is *she* here?" He growled the question between clenched teeth.

"Because I asked her to join us, Dave. What is your problem? The woman is a prominent forensic consultant with NYPD Major Crimes. She has the country's foremost lab at her disposal. Don't you want the best?"

"We were investigating *her* when Cassie disappeared! Why isn't she a suspect?"

Lilith held up her palms and took a step back to ensure she kept her promise. "I had nothing to do with this. The locals requested me. That's the only reason I'm here, but if this is an issue, I'm more than happy to leave."

"Bullshit! You're the fucking devil, the angel of death. I was closing in, so you took my partner for information—"

"Wrong." Keeping her temper reined in proved harder than she thought, but after a deep inhale and slow exhale, Lilith continued. "You blame me for having to leave L.A., but you almost killed me. I was in the hospital for a week, David. You did that to me...the person you lived with and supposedly loved."

"Love?" A maniacal cackle filled the air. "You like to play the victim, don't you? Went crying to the college and got me expelled. If you had any evidence, you would have gone to the police."

"That's not what happened. Your father tried to pay me off, like he did the others, but I didn't want money. I agreed to drop the charges if he transferred you back to Temple and promised I'd never see you again. That is *all* that happened. I let things go, and afterward, you only existed in my rearview mirror."

The man's angular features hardened. Nothing she said would ever penetrate the man's armor of hatred. Perhaps he needed it to survive. Letting go of the anger and blame meant examining himself and facing the horrible things he'd done.

"Oh, I think you thought about me more than that, *Lily*."

Before the malicious grin fully formed, an arm circled his throat. In one swift move, Chance pinned him to the ground in a sleeper hold, his legs locked around him.

David's face turned bright red, and he tugged at Chance's arm, thrashing his legs. The activity dwindled until the man's eyes rolled back into his head and he finally went limp.

"What the hell is going on?" Hersch drew her weapon and jumped back quicker than Lilith thought possible. Her deep blue eyes traveled from one face to the other in search of an explanation.

Chance released David's unconscious body and slowly got to his feet with his arms raised. "I only put him to sleep."

"Eileen, put your gun away." Gorman's tired tone reminded Lilith of a parent chastising a child who had overreacted.

The long awkward moment stretched out—Chance stood still with his hands in the air, while Hersch stared at her partner. Silent tension weighed on everyone's shoulders until none of them took a breath.

"Fine." The woman holstered her gun, and everyone released a sigh of relief. "Are you going to explain?"

"Of course, but not here." Gorman strolled over to his partner and patted her shoulder. "Come on, Eileen. I'll buy you a beer."

Her confused frown remained fixed in place, and she turned to Lilith and Chance. "Um…it was nice meeting you…I think." A slight blush graced her cheeks before she turned away and followed her partner to their car.

"Lily, can you open the tailgate?"

Everything had happened so fast, her sleep-deprived brain had trouble catching up.

"Lil?"

Once she tore her gaze away from the retreating FBI agents, she shook her head and turned back around. "I'm sorry. How can I help?"

The slight millisecond twitch of his lips showed irritation, but he kept his voice calm and slung David over his shoulder. "Tailgate."

"Right."

After rushing over, Lilith popped open the back, and he slid the unconscious man into the truck bed.

The guy almost appeared peaceful without the typical snarling expressions. A time had existed long ago when she found him charming and funny. *Was it all an act? A manipulation to pull me into his control?* Whatever happened in the years since college, he had changed, devolved, became less able to contain his monster.

"Are you okay?" Chance's hand on her shoulder brought her out of the spiraling thoughts and back to the task at hand.

"Yeah. What *is* the plan, by the way? You said you had somewhere—"

"Stop a minute," he interrupted, closing the tailgate and taking a deep breath before meeting her eyes.

Whatever he is about to say, it isn't good.

"I need you to listen and trust me."

Her brow furrowed deeply when he implied that she didn't. "Of course."

For a moment, he scanned the area, ensuring no one else was around. "I have not been one hundred percent honest about the work I did for Gregor."

The confession sent her brain racing in a million directions as he searched for the right words.

"Yes, I worked on the labs' security systems, and I led Gregor's personal security detail, but…I also acted as his…enforcer, for lack of a better term."

Lilith cocked an eyebrow, her arms crossing her chest. *Enforcer?* The word burned in her mind, but she owed him the opportunity to explain without peppering him with questions.

"A few times, we encountered threats to our privacy. A human got too close, a rogue vamp drawing too much attention…That sort of thing. On rare occasions, we required information from those threats to properly assess the damage…info they would not give freely…"

His eyes remained locked on the ground, pink tinging his cheeks, and she could no longer keep the questions at bay.

"You tortured people for him?"

The revelation shouldn't have shocked her. Chance had proved he'd do whatever he deemed necessary to protect the people he loved. Still, the thought of him inflicting pain with calm indifference, like what had happened to Agent Cappalletty…

"Only as a last resort and only until we got what we needed. I swear it."

Lilith nodded, mulling over the subject. The logical side understood the necessity when lives depended on information, but…

"I'll be honest, because...well, what's the point of lying when you're an emotional litmus test? The thought of you hurting people in that way..." When she glanced up at him, his shameful expression deepened, making her resolution to remain truthful more difficult. Of course, she wasn't entirely certain she knew what the truth was. "We can talk more about this later. I'm guessing you brought this up because it pertains to our current situation?"

"It does."

"Continue."

"To conduct these interviews—"

"You mean, interrogations?" When he glanced up at her with his jaw clenched, she backed off. "Sorry. Go on."

"We needed a secure place—out of the way, minimal traffic—where construction equipment and building supplies wouldn't be unusual..."

"Shit. You have a torture chamber at your place?"

When crimson flushed his cheeks, she released a heavy sigh and began pacing.

"Where?" The word snapped with authority, and she kept her gaze on the ground, letting it all sink in.

After swallowing the lump in his throat, he answered, "First floor."

"Makes sense, given the hobo aesthetic you've cultivated down there." Under normal circumstances, the comment would have made him chuckle, but the anger infusing her words cut deep.

"It's more like a hidden, sound-dampening room. Sensory deprivation is a highly effective technique."

Lilith spun on her heel and stared him down. "So, mental torture is more humane than physical?"

"Well, no." Chance balked and took a step back. "I was only clarifying."

"God...and I joked about you having a cage downstairs."

"It's not a cage, *cherie*."

She came to an abrupt stop, her back tensing. The flat attempt at humor merely worsened her mood.

"Okay." After taking a firm stance in front of him, she held his gaze with fierce determination despite the six-inch height disparity. "This is *not* the place to continue our discussion. We are going to get in the truck and drive away before someone overhears us."

"Yes, *mon cher*."

"I am not done. We we *will* revisit this at a better time. Agreed?"

"Of course."

His crestfallen expression made her heart ache, and despite her anger, she felt compelled to erase it.

"Hey." Lilith stepped forward and pulled his chin up until he met her eyes once again. "I love you, and I, of all people, understand why not every secret should see the light of day, but *this* you should have told me."

"I know, *cherie*, but I…" His arms circled her waist, drawing her closer. "After years, we're finally together, and it's better than I imagined—"

The sharp swat on his shoulder caught him off guard.

"Stop sucking up. I'm not perfect, but go on."

A grin cracked the gloom lingering on his face. "Well, I didn't want to lose you already."

The sincerity of his comment dispelled the brief lightheartedness. "We have to lie to the world every day about who we are, what we do…We shouldn't have to lie to each other, even by omission. If you don't want to lose me, be honest. Now let's go."

As she turned away, he pulled her back for a tender kiss and cupped her face, his hands sliding into her hair. Giddy shivers trickled down her spine until he rested his forehead against hers and exhaled.

"I love you too, *mon petite cherie*."

Chapter 26

Forty-five minutes into the drive back to New York City, pounding fists and muffled screams echoed from the enclosed truck bed.

"Since Sleeping Beauty is awake, what's the plan?" Lilith peered over at Chance.

The cool blue lights of the instrument panel illuminated the chiseled lines of his face while he calmly stared at the road before them.

"Well, we have a full tank of gas, and I confiscated his gun. He won't be a problem until we open the tailgate, and I plan to hit every pothole on the way. Maybe one of them will knock him out again."

"Okay…and then what?"

Chance flashed a tight smile and dug out his cell. "I was waiting to call until we got closer." After he chose a contact, the phone rang through the truck's speakers.

"Hello? That you, Chance?"

Lilith recognized the drowsy voice right away.

"Hey, Tim. I need another favor."

"Yeah, of course. What's up?" The sleepy quality abandoned his deep voice, replaced by concern.

"Meet me at my place in an hour, and come armed."

"Is Lilith in danger?"

"Aww. So gallant. I'm okay. Thank you, though."

"Glad to hear it." She heard the man's smile in his voice. "I'm sorry the fed is giving you trouble. I hope to find something soon—"

"That's why we're calling," Chance interrupted, swerving around an SUV pumping its brakes. The accompanying thump from the truck bed made his smile widen. "We found the guy's partner. She's dead, and the FBI

Jenny Allen

believes he knows why. Trouble is, they can't question him without Daddy showing up to bail him out."

"Do you need me to find him?"

"No, the feds unofficially gift-wrapped him. I *do* need your help to secure him and stand guard. Lil and I need some shut-eye."

Once Chance mentioned sleep, Lilith realized how tired she was. So much had happened—the gala, the fight with Boston, Nicci's place and the database, confronting her therapist, driving nearly two hours north, investigating a grisly crime scene while entertaining the FBI, and Boston almost shooting her. Mentally reciting the list alone exhausted her.

"No problem, boss. Happy to help. What sort of info do you need from him? I can work on him while you sleep."

"Thanks, but the guy needs to stew. He is all about instant gratification and shirking consequences. Plus"—his eyes darted to Lilith for a brief instant—"I want to handle this myself."

She arched one eyebrow and stared him down. The implied warning didn't need to be voiced.

"All right. See you both in an hour or so."

Once Chance ended the call, Lilith decided to voice her concern anyway. "Letting Tim take the lead might be a better idea. He isn't as… emotionally invested."

"Only because he isn't aware of the full history."

"Why would that matter? I mean, Tim is a close friend, but he's not the one I'm dating."

Chance glanced at her, trying to decide something. In the end, he faced forward in silence for so long, she took it as a refusal. However, when she opened her mouth to say something, he started talking.

"Tim's sister is in a group home. He visits her every week with daisies— her favorites. We all knew Jill's husband was a controlling guy. He constantly corrected her, chastised her for wearing the wrong thing or being clumsy, but no one knew he abused her, at least not at first."

He paused briefly, as if unsure of his decision to tell the story.

"She stopped attending family dinners, made excuses during the holidays, and canceled plans at the last minute. A year passed and Tim hadn't seen his sister once. Then he got a call…"

Lilith waited patiently as he swallowed hard and forced himself to continue.

"Jill's husband beat her into a coma. They arrested him and called Tim since he was the next of kin after their parents passed the previous year."

"Oh my god. I had no idea." Her mind flashed back to the night at the hotel, when Tim had left to make an important phone call. She'd guessed he was calling a woman, but not a romantic interest.

"He doesn't like sharing the story. Jill suffered a hemorrhagic stroke, and her entire left side is useless. They prosecuted the husband, but…the judge reduced the sentence to time served due to a technical error by the police."

"Fucking justice system."

"Yeah, well, here's the point to my story. The man never made it home, and they never found the body. You've become like a sister to Tim. If he questions Boston and the abuse comes up…"

"Why the hell did you suggest him as a middleman, then? Jesus, Chance."

"He's the only one I trust."

Then everything clicked into place with sudden clarity. "Holy shit, you wanted him to find out."

"What?"

"You wanted Tim to find out so Boston would die by someone else's hands and you could keep your promise to me on a technicality."

"That is a gross exaggeration. I had no intention of telling him, and he was helping Boston find his partner, not digging into your past."

"But you knew the possibility existed."

Chance stared at the steering wheel for a long time before his eyes darted to her. "I won't lie to you. I saw the possible outcome."

"Damn it." Lilith sank into the seat, her arms crossing her chest. "You do realize the FBI and Boston's dad would be hunting Tim if your plan worked?"

"It was not a *plan*, just a"—he shrugged his left shoulder—"possibility, like you said."

"I thought you weren't going to lie to me."

He death-gripped the steering wheel, his knuckles turning white. "I am not lying. I didn't plan—"

As he spoke, Lilith continued to study his body language and microexpressions, reading the truth right in front of her. "No. Not a plan, but you wanted it to happen."

After a deep sigh, he glanced at her again. "You are infuriating sometimes."

"Oh? You mean, when I'm right?"

"I will do *anything* to keep you safe, *mon cherie*. I won't apologize for that."

"You're willing to sacrifice your best friend to rid yourself of an annoyance?"

The deep frown indicated that the question offended him. "Not an annoyance—a threat. If it means protecting you and our species, then yes, I'd make the call, and so would Tim."

"But he isn't a threat...or wasn't at the time."

Confusion clouded his features, and he stared at the dark road ahead. "How can you say that?"

"Gorman told me everything. The man only has a job because of his dad. No one takes him seriously."

"Yeah, but he knows you're different and is already digging. Do you think anything we do or say is gonna make him stop?"

She mulled the question over, giving it sincere consideration. "Well, since we kidnapped him and intend to torture him for information, I'm guessing no." The sharp tone made her dislike of the situation difficult to miss.

An uncomfortable silence settled over the vehicle until a huff passed her lips as she stared out of the window.

"When did life become so complicated?"

"Pretty much starts at puberty, but sometimes, it takes a while for things to catch up to you. Every choice has a consequence, *cherie*."

"Yeah, remember that when you come clean with Tim." Her gaze remained fixed on the moonlit scenery passing by. If only she could capture some of that tranquility. "I'm too tired to talk about this anymore." Between the lack of sleep and the mind-numbing problems with no solutions, the exhaustion became overwhelming, and her eyelids fluttered.

"We have about forty-five minutes left. Why don't you get some sleep."

While keeping his eyes on the road, he reached into the backseat, grabbed his tux jacket, and handed it to her.

"Thanks."

Although the summer air was warm, Chance kept the car at a chilly seventy degrees, so she happily snuggled into the jacket. When his rich scent surrounded her, it conjured memories that left a smile on her lips despite their arguments. *One problem at a time. Right now, my issue is sleep.*

Lilith gazed out at the silvery trees flickering by as they gave way to brightly lit gas stations and diners. The sky changed to a medium blue, the sun hovering below the horizon.

A new day…better than the last. Wishful thinking again.

Lilith woke when the truck slowed to a crawl. After wiping the sleep from her eyes, she blinked a few times, attempting to survey their surroundings, but couldn't make her eyes focus. *Forty-five minutes was* not *enough.*

"Hey, sleepyhead." A smile stretched Chance's lips, but when he glanced over at her, they curved into a frown. "Are you okay?"

"Yeah, just thoroughly beat. I need more than a power nap. I need a temporary coma. Perhaps a day or three."

His rich chuckle filled the cab. "Soon, I promise."

The sun barely broke the horizon, leaving the buildings of New York City in an early morning twilight. After pushing past the sleep deprivation still clouding her brain, Lilith recognized the area—about a block from home. *Home. Seems like I've mentally moved in with him already.*

"It's awful quiet back there. You didn't crack the guy's skull hitting potholes, did you? The whole point is to question him. Otherwise, all the shit you told me is meaningless."

"Calm down. He's fine. I avoided the bigger ones for that very reason. He gave up banging and yelling about fifteen minutes ago."

Chance turned the corner into a vacant industrial park, and Lilith spotted a tan Honda sitting outside the warehouse. Tim hopped out and shoved open the loading bay door with a wave.

He stood two inches shorter than Chance and had broader shoulders, more bulk, and lighter curly hair. Still, some people mistook them for brothers since they appeared close in age, an illusion they didn't work hard to shatter. Of course, when they spoke, people typically changed their minds. Chance's subtle Cajun-French accent didn't match Tim's Bronx accent.

Tim signaled Chance, guiding the truck into the warehouse, and closed the bay door behind them. As soon as the vehicle came to a stop, Lilith stumbled out of the front seat and struggled to get her bearings. *I seriously need sleep.*

"Lil." Tim's voice was a bit higher than Chance's deep baritone. The man rounded the truck and picked her up for a hug.

"How's the new place?" After rustling his sandy blond curls, she wiggled out of his embrace.

"In desperate need of a woman's touch. Know anyone?"

"Oh, come on, Tim. You know I don't have friends." They both chuckled at their running joke.

"Can't blame a guy for trying. You missed our session at the range."

"Sorry. It's been a crazy week."

"So I hear…Well, some of it." The pointed glare he threw at Chance made it clear he wanted more information.

"And we'll get to it, man. I promise." Chance stalked around the truck, grabbed Lilith's hand, and tugged her away from Tim before locking eyes with her. "*You* need to sleep. We can handle this. I'll crawl into bed once I'm done."

For a moment, she frowned at him, studying his features. Then she peered past him to Timothy.

"Please don't let him do anything stupid, and make sure he doesn't stay up to question him." Once the man nodded, her steely gaze returned to Chance. "You need sleep too."

"Fair enough, *mon cherie.* I'm sorry about—"

"Stop. I don't want to discuss it. I only want sleep." Lilith turned away, attempting to ignore the heartbroken expression on his face. "Tim. I'm serious. Once Boston's secure, send him to bed."

"I always look out for him, even when he doesn't want me to. You have my word."

"Thank you for all your help. I appreciate it."

"Anytime, doll."

"I'll be up shortly. Promise." No signs of deception appeared on Chance's face, but his earlier confessions had made her wary.

No. I either trust him, or I don't.

"You better." Before he could respond, she retreated to the lumbering elevator.

"Thanks again for coming over so early." Chance muttered as Lilith lowered the gate and pressed the button.

"Of course. She seems in decent spirits, considering…," Tim said, joining Chance.

"She puts on a brave face." His eyes stayed on Lilith until the freight elevator lurched into motion and disappeared. "I had to tell her some things…" The words trailed off as he turned back to Tim.

The burly man nodded and patted him on the shoulder. "I figured as much. Told her about the holding cell?"

"Yeah, and why I have it. No details, but they were heavily implied."

"How did she take it?" Tim leaned against the truck while Chance paced the concrete.

"The logical side understands—she told me as much—but—"

"That demon-blood shit is telling you something different?"

"She wants to be okay with it. That's a good thing, right? God, if I lose her because I was hiding shit…"

"Chance. Calm down. You're spiraling out over nothing. Lilith is a smart woman, and she loves the hell out of you. No way she's dumping you over something like this. The girl is sleep-deprived and dealing with a lot. Give her a minute."

"Yeah." As much as Chance wanted to tell Tim the full story of their argument in the truck, he couldn't for a multitude of reasons. If he explained Lily's history with Boston and all the decisions he had made because of that discovery, he wouldn't be able to leave Tim alone with the bastard.

In every other aspect of life, his best friend demonstrated immense self-control—ex-military guys typically did. However, domestic abuse against women, especially ones he cared about, turned the man into a powder keg with a short fuse, one Chance had been fully prepared to light.

Lilith was right. Putting Tim in that situation without any warning was unfair, but he couldn't come clean yet. Full disclosure had to wait.

"Okay. Let's get this show on the road, *mon ami*. Stand back, gun drawn with a clear line of sight, and I'll open the tailgate. The man's gonna come out swinging."

Tim rolled his shoulders, stepped away from the truck, and drew his gun. Once his friend moved into position with his berretta aimed, Chance stalked over to the truck bed. He stayed to the side and reached for the latch as if releasing a coiled snake or an angry alligator—both fitting metaphors.

Chance gave a silent count. *One...Two...Three.* The tailgate slammed down, and David thrust his body forward, but Chance was ready for him. He used the man's momentum to send him crashing into the filthy concrete with a crack.

Before Boston had time to scream, Chance grabbed his injured arm and forced the man to his feet.

"You broke my goddamn nose!" Blood gushed and splattered David's rumpled shirt and coffee-stained tie.

"You're lucky I haven't broken more. Now, you see the nice gentleman with a gun?" Chance waited until the agent turned in Tim's direction. "He won't hesitate to shoot you any more than I would."

"The PI? What the fuck is going on? I told you before, I'm a *federal agent!*"

"I'm aware of who you are. We simply need to chat." Chance twisted the sore arm enough to guide the man deeper into the warehouse's bottom floor.

"If this is about that lying, murderous bitc—Ah! Fuck!" A sudden vicious torque of his arm stopped Boston in mid-sentence. The bastard had someone reset his shoulder, but the muscles were still tender.

Chance leaned close, keeping his voice low and menacing. "I know what you did to her, how you put her in the fucking hospital. Do you remember what I told you outside her apartment? Keep it up, and you'll beg me to kill you."

"You can't hold me here! You're not even a cop!" The confidence had vanished, replaced with something closer to pleading.

"You are correct. I'm not, which means I'm not bound by the rules and regulations of law enforcement." Chance continued to guide the man forward, while Tim approached the back corner.

The area seemed vacant, but with a flick of a switch located halfway down the corner seam, a door opened in the corrugated metal. The "hidden" door would have been obvious if the place had been brand new. However, the layers of rust, chain link, decay, and miscellaneous trash had made the edges challenging to detect.

Tim leaned in and turned on the fluorescent lights before stepping back.

Boston came to a halt, his muscles seizing with a fear Chance relished. "What is this place?"

"Somewhere your dad can't find you." A yelp of pain escaped when Chance twisted Boston's arm further, nearly dislocating the joint again. "Move!"

"Hey, look...uh, I think we got off on the wrong foot—"

Chance spun the man around, grabbed his collar, and stared him down with open contempt. "Are you fucking serious?"

Panic widened the man's nearly black eyes, and he struggled with a response. When he came up empty, Chance turned him back around and urged him forward.

Once they reached the doorway, he shoved Boston inside with too much force. He stumbled, wildly scanning the space.

The light fixture hung about twelve feet off the floor, thick, plush carpet covered the walls, and the concrete was clean with a drain in the center—no chairs, tables, or other fixtures.

"You'll have some private time to—"

The man's nose wrinkled, and his lip curled. "I won't tell *her* or her lackeys anything."

Chance closed his eyes for a moment and sighed, his jaw clenching. "I figured as much, but a few hours in here might change your mind." Chance leaned against the doorway, admiring his handiwork. "The room isn't entirely soundproof, but close enough out here." Then he flashed a sinister smile and turned to leave.

"Wait! You can't leave me in here!" The frantic man spun around the ten-by-ten room, and his breathing became erratic. "I...can't handle small spaces."

Chance turned back, leaned in the doorway, and peered around. "This? It's bigger than most elevators." Then he locked eyes with Boston, his expression darkening. "And I don't give a *fuck* about what makes you uncomfortable. After what you did—"

"What did I do?" Boston moved forward with a newfound bravado. "Defend myself when she came storming over to my car, screaming like a banshee? What else did the psycho tell you? I hit her? She's a liar! She's the crazy bitch who attacked a random girl in college for flirting with me at—"

Before Boston finished the sentence, Chance seized the man by the throat, lifted him off the ground, and slammed him against the carpeted wall. "Say one more goddamn word about her," he growled through gritted teeth, fixing the bastard with a deadly stare.

Boston choked and gagged as his hands flew up, trying to break the iron-clad grip to no avail.

I could squeeze a little harder...It wouldn't take much. A few more pounds of pressure, a mere flex of my hand, and we'd be rid of this asshole. Only a few seconds more...a little tighter. The asshole deserves this.

"Chance." Tim's voice held an unmistakable warning that almost broke the murderous trance.

After a moment, Chance peered over his shoulder without making eye contact.

"We can't question a corpse, man. Come on. Let him go."

Chance's gaze swung back to Boston's reddened face and panicked eyes. *He hurt her, cheated on her, destroyed her self-esteem, and nearly killed her...the woman I love.* All the reasons to tighten his fist swirled in his head, intensifying his anger. "This man doesn't deserve to live."

Tim moved close enough to touch his shoulder. "I'm sure you're right, but *you* told me we need information only he can give us."

As he spoke, the hatred began to ebb away, as if Tim's calm demeanor had seeped into his skin, at least enough to temporarily restrain his thirst for vengeance. Chance searched the bastard's face as it turned from red to ruddy purple. Then he shoved the man to the ground with brutal force and stormed out.

Tim followed, securing the door behind them, with Boston coughing and gasping for air. Once the door shut, the place fell silent.

"Okay..." Tim holstered his gun and stared down Chance, crossing the distance between them. "You said they had a bad history, but what the hell? Was he talking about Lily?"

One raised eyebrow answered his question, but Chance focused on the night's events.

"The guy's following her. Tonight, we led him to Lil's apartment...I told her to stay put." His jaw clenched until he reigned in his anger. "Instead, she storms right over and picks a fight with Boston. He almost...I almost didn't get there in time. Then the fucker shows up at the crime scene while Lilith was investigating the body of his partner. All hell broke loose, and he came close to shooting her in front of three different branches of law enforcement."

"Shit..." Tim fell silent for a few moments before broaching the obvious subject. "That level of animosity starts somewhere. What exactly happened between them?" The tone of his voice indicated he had no intention of letting this go.

"This is a bad idea. I can call Ray. He's checking on something for me, but he can drop it and play babysitter."

"Why?" Tim straightened, his chest puffing with defensive pride.

"I shouldn't have involved you in any of this. Lilith's right. It wasn't fair."

The man's brow furrowed, and he took a slow step forward. "What are you talking about?"

"It's her story to tell. I shouldn't—"

"Nope. You lost the right to play that card when you implied it affects how I do my job."

When Chance still hesitated, Tim took another step closer.

"Spill it now, or I'll go wake her up and get the story myself!"

After a heavy sigh, Chance leaned against his truck. *What choice do I have? I should have ignored Boston, but no. I let him get under my skin, and now…*

"They dated for a while in college, out in L.A. She lived with the guy for a while." He paused again, wishing he'd kept his mouth shut.

"Go on."

"He was abusive, Tim."

The man flinched and then frowned as if he had misheard. "What?"

"Controlling, manipulative, intimidating, physically abusive, all of it."

All of Tim's features hardened, and his hands curled into fists, but he remained silent, waiting for Chance to continue.

"He put her and another woman in the hospital the last time. She never told a soul until the other night. He attacked her in the precinct, and she had to explain everything to Nicci. I only know because I overheard them."

Tim turned and stared at the isolation room, his whole body tensing. "She could have ended up like Jill."

"I know. That's why I'm having a difficult time remaining calm and why I didn't tell you."

The man's nodding motion stopped as something dawned on him. He glared back up at Chance. "You made me the middleman without warning me. Why would you do that? You know my history with this shit."

Chance hung his head and stared at the concrete, unable to assemble a believable lie or tell his best friend the truth. At the time, he had felt confident he made the right call, but now…

Despite his indecision, his body language said all the things he couldn't, and Tim picked up on it.

"You *wanted* the guy dead and didn't care who you hurt in the process." Tim shoved his fists onto his hips and inhaled deeply. "I don't know what offends me more—that you think I'm dumb or that you don't care if I go down for murder. Of all the stupid, idiotic—"

"I'm sorry, man. I didn't think…"

The burly man stormed up and thrust a finger into Chance's chest. "No! You didn't think!"

"I just…He's a problem. A fed with a personal grudge, investigating her. He will not stop digging, and he won't walk away."

"So, your solution is to pair me with him, hoping the emotional trauma I have from my brain-damaged sister will turn me into a homicidal maniac?"

"I didn't think of it like that at the time."

"I sure as fuck hope not, or this will be the last favor I ever do for you." Tim's fist slammed into the truck with brutal force, leaving a dent in the quarter panel. "Go get some damn sleep."

"You shouldn't have to watch him."

"Oh, *now* you care about my fucking feelings? I'm a professional with multiple tours overseas. I can handle my shit. Taking care of Jill's husband was no accident. I refused to let that waste of skin ever touch my sister again. I ensured he couldn't. I acted with a clear and decisive purpose, which is why I'm not in jail. *You* are the one that can't think clearly. Go!"

With that, Tim turned his back on Chance and stalked over to the holding cell door, signaling a definitive end to the conversation.

Well, that went about as well as expected. Fuck.

Chance walked toward the freight elevator with a heavy heart, angry at himself. The only thing he could do now was sleep and try to fix things later. Lilith hadn't reacted as strongly, but sleep deprivation dulled the senses. At best, he expected a thorough lecture from her later.

When he reached the loft, he came to a stop in the bedroom doorway. Lilith sprawled out on her stomach, fully clothed, including her sneakers. For a few moments, he leaned against the door and watched her smile in her sleep.

What wouldn't I do to protect her? Tim's right. I wasn't thinking clearly, but how could I…with what he did to her?

Before the blind rage returned, he crossed the room, kicked off his shoes, and sat on the bed's edge. With nimble fingers, he untied her

Converse. The woman was so exhausted. She didn't move a single muscle while he slid them off her feet and placed them on the floor.

After draping a blanket over her, he slid into bed. Lilith changed positions when he settled in and threw an arm over his chest, cuddling closer with a tiny moan of contentment. Chance kissed her forehead, which summoned another smile, and let the exhaustion take over.

Chapter 27

Lilith woke to the early afternoon sun streaming into the room and glanced over her shoulder at Chance, who was still fast asleep. When she peered down at his arm draped over her hip, she remembered the first time they had shared a bed after her nightmare at Miriah's. It had felt so alien at the time, but now, the gesture was warm and familiar.

With a dreamy smile, she cuddled into his warmth, unwilling to crawl out of bed. Then last night's conversation resurfaced—acting as Gregor's enforcer, a hidden interrogation room, gaining info through brute force, taking advantage of Tim by using his sister's situation against him. It all left a sour taste in her mouth despite his noble intentions.

After sneaking out from under his arm, Lilith crawled out of bed, grabbed her robe, and stumbled toward the bathroom. "I need a hot shower and coffee before tackling complex emotions."

Although the hot water did nothing to quiet her frazzled brain, the scent of coffee brewing eased her nerves enough for her to focus on necessities.

Once she grabbed a bag of blood from the fridge and slid it into a sink full of warm water, she sent Tim a quick text: *I'm up. Want me to bring you anything?*

In a matter of seconds, he replied: *Coffee black two sugars. Thanks doll.*

While waiting for the blood to warm and the coffee to brew, Lilith popped a couple of English muffins into the toaster. Then she got the butter and searched the cabinet for honey. The adventurous evening had left her ravenous, and she figured her friend wouldn't mind a snack.

Between pouring coffee and buttering muffins, she unceremoniously guzzled the warmed blood and immediately scrunched her nose. The stuff still tasted awful, but the warm glow in her stomach felt overdue. In a matter of seconds, her breaths became deeper, and her sensations grew more vivid.

She couldn't argue with the results, even if the stuff tasted like copper pennies coated in molasses.

Once everything was ready, Lilith balanced the plate on top of two coffee mugs and navigated the monstrous elevator with minimal spillage. When the beast rattled to the bottom floor, Tim was there to greet her and open the gate.

"Aww. You brought food too. You're an angel!" He grabbed the plate and reached for his coffee, but Lilith pulled it back before he touched the handle.

"Hey. One of those is mine." She held out her hand expectantly and didn't pass him the mug until he placed an English muffin in her palm. "Thanks. So, how's the prisoner?"

He stuffed half the muffin in his mouth as they walked. "Haven't had any trouble."

"Everything went okay getting him out of the truck?"

"Yep." Tim shoved the rest of his snack in his mouth and kept his eyes locked on their destination in the far corner.

"Something's wrong." Lilith stared at him as they walked, watching the tension in his jaw travel through his shoulders. "What happened?"

"Nothin'. Stop reading me with your weird voodoo tricks. It's creepy."

"Microexpressions and body language are not *voodoo tricks*. Believe me. I've seen real ones firsthand. What's wrong?"

After a deep swig of coffee, he cast a sideways glance in her direction. "It's Chance...I'm worried about him."

"Any specific reason?" She had plenty of them but figured it best to let him vent without her adding to things.

"He has never been reckless, never used people. He stays cool, handles the crisis efficiently, and is always truthful." Tim took another big gulp while collecting his thoughts. "But when he asked me to be a neutral party between you and your abusive ex without telling me the full truth, hoping I'd snap and kill him..." His hand tightened around the mug's handle until his knuckles turned white. "Who does that?"

"I'm sorry. If I'd known about Jill, I never would—"

"It's not your place. *He* is the one that asked me to do this. *He* should have told me."

"You're right. I had no idea until last night, and...I was too exhausted to really react. Everything with Boston, the crime scene, dealing with the FBI...It's been hard on both of us."

"This goes beyond that, and I think you know it. Last year, I almost died helping you both, but you were upfront, and I knew the risks. Come on, Lil. He used Jill against me to get his way."

"I don't know if that's accurate."

The man's harsh black-and-white assessment didn't sit well with her.

"What would you call it then?"

Lilith stared into her mug, trying to wrap her head around things, but everything blended into a chaotic mess. She'd have better luck trying to separate the cream from her coffee.

"Lil, you know I'm happy as hell for you two, but the boy isn't making smart decisions."

"I'm not following." Perhaps it was the exhaustion still lingering in her bones, but she didn't understand the correlation between their current conversation and her relationship.

"He almost killed the bastard this morning for saying shit about you. Don't get me wrong, I wanted to break his face for the crap he spouted, but Chance...The boy comes unhinged when it concerns you."

"Okay." She frowned and took a bite of her English muffin, conflicting emotions battling inside her head.

"This is nothin' against you, doll. The boy needs to get a grip, or he'll spiral out. Losing Gregor on his watch messed him up, but almost losing you..." The man shook his head and slowly exhaled. "He's desperate, acting out of fear instead of using his head."

"So, what do we do? How can we help him?"

"You can start by not seeking trouble."

Tim leveled her with a firm stare, immediately putting her on the defensive.

"I don't."

"I'm gonna stop you right there." He held up a hand with an impatient expression that clearly stated he had expected that response.

"Picking fights with Aaron is one thing, but I know about last night— that waste of skin following you, you guys trying to lure him out, abandoning the plan to prove yourself, and almost getting killed."

She started to protest, but he kept going.

"I get it, better than most. If Jill had the opportunity to prove her ex couldn't control her anymore, she'd take it. But this isn't about just you anymore. You already won. You escaped, moved on, made a life—one that includes Chance."

Her defensive pride evaporated as the words sank in. He was right. The memories haunted her, but ultimately, she had nothing to prove to David. His opinion would never change, and it didn't matter. The realization made her cheeks burn hot, and she rubbed her temple.

"Shit. I didn't—"

"Of course, you didn't. Hey, this is not about blaming you or making you feel bad. Chance is a strong guy, and sometimes we forget he isn't invincible. I'm pissed as hell at him, but I understand, and I'll help him through this. I just need *you* on board."

"I am." After a firm nod, Lilith's eyes drifted to the corner behind him, where she presumed the door existed amid the junk gathered around it. "So, how do we handle this? As much as I'd love to throw the guy in the Hudson River and call it a day, we need to know why someone tortured his partner."

"Well, first off, you shouldn't come anywhere near this. You're nothing but a catalyst between those two. Boston will clam up, and Chance won't be able to focus."

"Understood." The tension in her body lessened a bit. Lilith had no desire to spend more time with David than necessary. "Can you give me your word that you two won't kill him? The FBI might not care what happens to him, but his dad is a pretty influential guy."

"Done. I think you should tell me everything you know." He held up a hand when she opened her mouth to protest. "Not about your history with him. I know the type and can fill in the blanks myself. Tell me what you know about him now—his relationship with his partner, how the FBI views him, his illegal investigation, and anything else I can use as leverage."

After a nod, Lilith compiled her thoughts and told him everything she'd learned from Detective Gorman, Dr. Thomas, and the info Nicci had discovered. The man took everything in with a thoughtful frown. When she finished, Tim stared at her with a puzzled expression but didn't voice a question.

"What?"

The man's brows squeezed together. He wet his lips and turned away for a moment, like he wanted to ask something but felt he shouldn't.

"Tim. Just ask."

He turned back around, his eyes studying her with an obvious frown. "Can I ask one personal question?"

"I have nothing to hide."

"How did you fall for a guy like this?"

Her body went rigid, and she chewed the inside of her cheek. Behind the defensive pride, she felt just as clueless as Tim. After a slow exhale, she met his eyes again and tried to answer.

"In college, he was…charming. I was away from Dad's strict oversight, and David was relentless. He kept flirting, no matter how many times I told him I wasn't interested. It was new, exciting, and forbidden. Teenagers aren't well known for thinking things through."

"How long did you—" The rumble of the freight elevator interrupted him. "Never mind. Put on your game face and remember what I said."

Lilith nodded and took a long gulp of lukewarm coffee as the elevator rattled into sight.

Chance lifted the gate and strolled toward them, dressed in a classic black T-shirt and well-worn jeans that hugged his hips. The man's signature look summoned delightful shivers despite the awkward circumstances.

"You guys having a clandestine meeting?" One hand held a coffee mug that read: "World's Best Boss," while the other raked through his disheveled chestnut hair.

Tim merely frowned in response, which erased the drowsy smile from Chance's face.

"I can't tell you how sorry I am, *mon ami*. I—"

"Stop apologizing and get your head on straight. I love you like a brother, but if you ever pull something like that again, we're done."

After a deep inhale and a long sip of coffee, Chance nodded. "I'm trying."

When Tim gave a gruff nod in return, Chance glanced over at Lilith.

"And I'm sorry for not being—"

Before he finished the sentence, "Eye of the Tiger" erupted from her pocket, and Lilith hurried to answer the call. Not only could it be important, but she'd take any opportunity to avoid the current conversation.

"Hey, Nicci. Find something?"

"Quite the opposite. I'm worried about Cohen."

"Cohen? What's wrong?"

As soon as the name left her lips, Chance tensed and sidled closer.

"Well, I asked him to question Dr. Thomas at her hotel last night, like you suggested, and he still hasn't checked in. His phone goes straight to voicemail."

"Shit. Did you call the hotel?"

"Seriously? Of course, I did." A huff escaped before she continued. "Dr. Thomas checked out. They wouldn't tell me anything else."

"Perhaps they will in person. We need to know if something happened to him."

"Okay, partner. Do you want me to pick you up?"

"Yeah, but give me about an hour."

Once she hung up the phone, she realized both men were staring at her.

"Cohen's missing. He went to talk to Dr. Thomas last night and hasn't returned."

"Maybe he got pissed at our lack of progress and bailed. The man's been on the edge of splitting since we left York." Chance attempted a casual tone but failed.

"No." Lilith shook her head. "He was frustrated, but he wanted to help his people, and he can't do that without us."

Chance took a step forward, his brow furrowed. "Are you sure? Why do you have so much faith in the guy?" Flashes of anger and other emotions flickered across his face too swiftly for her to interpret.

"This is not about faith."

He searched her eyes for a moment and then stood straight, using every inch of their height difference. "I don't want you to go."

The sudden declaration caught her off guard, and her eyes moved from Chance to Tim, who shook his head. The silence settled in while Chance braced for an argument.

Instead, she padded over to him and met his eyes. "Nicci wants me to go with her to the hotel and poke around. That's all. I promise on the lives of Gloria's children that I won't make a move without you, but...if you still don't want me to go, I won't."

His face softened, and the tension rushed out of his body. Then his gaze fell to the floor again. "No. You're right. If something happened, we need to know. Tim could—"

"Absolutely not. I am staying right here. There's no way I'm leaving you alone with him. Nicci and Lilith can handle a little recon."

She stood on tiptoe to peer over Chance's shoulder at Tim. "Thank you."

"Not a single move without me. You promised."

"And I meant it. I know none of this has been easy on you. I'm sorry for making you worry last night."

Chance leaned his forehead against hers and closed his eyes. "*Merci, mon amour.*"

"Okay, love birds. We all have work to do."

"I need to get dressed before Nicci gets here."

His lips hovered inches away, and normally, Lilith would close the gap with a smile. However, the recent secrets summoned uncomfortable feelings, so she kissed his cheek and slipped away.

Then she walked over to Tim and gave him a hug while whispering, "Thank you for keeping an eye on him. I owe you."

"Be careful, doll."

"I will."

Her eyes darted to Chance, whose expression darkened while he stared at the ground. On her way to the elevator, she paused to place a tender kiss on his lips. Secrets or not, she loved the man and knew he loved her too.

Before he recovered from his surprise, she stood back and flashed a small smile. "We'll talk more later, okay?"

"Of course, *mon cherie.*"

Once she disappeared into the freight elevator, Chance turned toward the door in the far corner with a heavy heart.

"We best handle this quick." After releasing a huff, Tim rubbed his curls. "Do you have any bottled water?"

"Yeah, in the truck." Chance strolled over, pulled a bottle from behind the passenger seat, and tossed it to his partner.

"I know you usually take the lead in these situations, but I think we'll make more progress if you stay out of the room."

"Are you sure?"

"I'm not interrogating him about his past with Lilith. Besides, I'm a professional, and I'm not the one dating her."

"True."

"I'm gonna play the good cop and give him some water. Maybe he'll cooperate. If I need you, I'll ask for help. Until then, let me handle this, okay?"

Chance opened his mouth to argue but stopped. He could use a breather, time to settle his rattled mind, and his friend made an excellent point. The odds of Boston giving up the info they needed were better without him there.

"You're the boss, *mon ami.*"

Chapter 28

As Lilith shimmied into a fresh pair of jeans, movement outside the window caught her attention. A flashy white sedan she didn't recognize rolled into the lot. Random vehicles rarely ventured into the industrial park northeast of Port Morris, except for starving artists in search of edgy shots.

After snatching her gun and holster, she tugged on a plum-colored Pink Floyd T-shirt while jogging down the stairs. On her way out, she grabbed a pair of Converse off the shoe rack, hopped into the elevator, pulling them on. The metal beast lurched to life and caught her off balance as she tugged on her last shoe, sending her tumbling to the floor. *Super graceful.*

When the elevator stopped, she threw up the gate, pulled on her gun holster, and edged toward the open bay door.

"Lily…What are you—" Chance strolled toward her with a confused frown.

She held up a hand, put her finger to her lips, and pointed outside.

He paused mid-stride, nodded, drew his gun, and crept toward the wall. Meanwhile, Lilith snuck to the door's edge and peered outside at their uninvited guest.

The white sedan crawled to a stop a few feet away. The unfamiliar driver wore a blank expression, probably a chauffeur, but the tinted glass prevented her from seeing his employer. For a wild moment, she thought about Cohen. He certainly enjoyed someone driving him around, but he exclusively used black stretch town cars.

The rear passenger door popped open, and a head of close-clipped gray hair rose into view. *Shit. This is the last thing I need, especially with an FBI hostage in the back.*

Lilith inhaled deeply, straightened while holstering her gun, and strolled through the bay door. "Aaron..." She spoke the name loud enough for Chance to hear. "This is a surprise."

The man's eyes narrowed while he adjusted his unimaginative black suit. "You don't leave me much choice, *niece*." Once again, the title oozed with distaste, making his hatred for their biological connection clear.

Her uncle gazed past her and studied the derelict building with open disdain. Chance had preserved the warehouse's outer aesthetic for security purposes. From outside, no one would suspect the second floor hid a stunning apartment with warm hardwoods, a spacious kitchen, and a tasteful loft master suite.

"You have...strange taste when it comes to domiciles."

"Yep. I'm guessing this isn't a welfare check, so why are you here?"

"Quite perceptive."

The patronizing tone grated her nerves, but Lilith merely flashed an overly sweet smile and waited for an answer.

"I came to check on the progress with your little *virus*." Although the last word held a derisive intonation, the tightened skin around his eyes and the shift in his posture revealed something else.

"Why are you suddenly taking an interest?"

"Yes, well. After the gala...Detective Andrew Cohen happened to visit while you're working your first case in eight months? Bullshit..." The curse word sounded too modern for his aristocratic tone.

"I'm not his damn travel agent, and I have no control over his itinerary."

"And he is here visiting his girlfriend? A lesbian in a committed relationship? I am not an idiot. I do my research. What is he doing here?"

Her first instinct was to lie and storm off, but Lilith remembered her conversations with Chance and Nicci at the gala. Despite her personal issues, Aaron was in charge, and he needed information to perform his job. Besides, if she stonewalled him now, he'd keep showing up, keep pressing, but perhaps a morsel would appease him for a while.

"He came to me for help. He's looking for the same thing we are."

"What do you mean?" His eyes narrowed to slits, and he took a step closer.

"Do I need to spell it out? This virus is affecting more than us. If you'd let me test—"

"The Durand are affected?" Aaron recoiled, and his eyebrows flew toward his hairline.

"Not all of them, but cases have popped up across the Southeast, centered on Goditha."

"Perhaps *they* are the source, not our supply."

After considering the idea, she shook her head. "I don't think so. Miriah and Malachi had no interaction with the Durand. So far, the cases only show transmission by sex or blood."

"Again, no *actual* evidence, so you decided to consult a human—"

"Dr. Scott isolated the virus from the vampire medium and scrubbed his notes before I passed them on. The woman is a pioneer in her field, and Dr. Scott thought she'd be helpful."

"And has she?" Every muscle on his face displayed doubt and anger. He clearly thought she was wasting her time with the human.

"She gave us a possible origin, which is why we attended the gala." Lilith thought it best to omit their recent revelations about the virologist until they found more than speculation and circumstantial evidence.

"To speak with Dr. Kelley Wolfe, Detective DeLuca's *friend*." The man couldn't resist pointing out their obvious lie from the awkward dinner, but she refused to rise to the bait.

"Yes. We asked some harmless questions about his dig site in Greece."

"And those answers led you to a source?"

"In theory. We are still working on it."

"So, you have made no progress."

The irritating statement triggered her defensive pride, and Lilith took another step forward. "I didn't say that. I may have found a link to Goditha."

"How so?" Aaron raised one graying eyebrow, continuing to stare down his nose at her.

"We secured a computer and found circumstantial evidence to confirm my theory. We'll know more once Nicci finishes the decryption."

"Whose computer? I didn't give you authorization!" Tension rippled across his features for a split second.

"I thought you wanted evidence. I'm doing my job. Chance filed a proper requisition form as the current Security Specialist. The computer belonged to Dr. Nichols, Head of Research."

A slight purse of his lips, eyes widened, nostrils flared—the entire expression lasted less than a second but spoke volumes.

"Is there something I should know?"

Aaron's cold eyes hardened. "Nothing concerning your case."

A truthful statement, or at least he thinks it is.

A million scenarios whirled through her brain while Aaron straightened his tie and regained his calm indifference.

"Well, niece. If that is the extent of your investigation…" The man possessed a gift for making any comment sound condescending.

"Solasta put me on a second case, and since I don't have your authorization to test the blood supply—"

"No! I am not inciting a panic to indulge your speculations." He locked eyes with her a moment and leaned closer. "You have a narrow perspective of the world, Lilith. You see the stone in your hand, not the ripples it makes when you toss it in the water. *That* is why the board put me in charge of Gregor's holdings, not you. Perhaps one day, you'll see the bigger picture and the sacrifices made to achieve it."

Before she responded, he turned away and slid back into his car. While the vehicle backed up and disappeared down the road, she stared sightlessly into the distance, his words echoing in her head.

"Lily. Everything okay?" Chance holstered his weapon and strolled out of the warehouse toward her.

After glancing back at him, she gazed out across the lot, combing over the conversation with her uncle and gathering her thoughts.

"*Cherie?*"

"I think I was right not to trust Aaron."

"Why? What happened?"

"He showed up to ask questions about the virus case but didn't seem at all interested in my answers. However…"

Chance circled to stand in front of her, and she raised her eyes to his.

"When I mentioned the computer from Goditha, he was…nervous and asked who it belonged to. When I told him, he showed markers of guilt and surprise."

"You think he's involved with the virus?"

She frowned, still processing her thoughts. "No. When I pressed, he truthfully replied that it didn't concern the virus."

"The database?"

"Perhaps…"

"Did you tell him where the computer is?"

"No, but…" She stopped for a moment. "I told him Nicci is decrypting it."

"Good."

Lilith frown at his sudden grin. "Um, why?"

"She's on her way here to pick you up. I'll call Ray and ask him to watch her place. If Aaron makes a move—"

"It'll prove there's something he wants on the computer, nothing more. What the hell is he hiding?" A bubble of anxious panic bloomed in her chest, and she rubbed her face. "Fuck all these people and their secret agendas. I'm sick of playing games."

Chance moved closer, running his hands up her arms until he pulled her against his chest. "*Cherie*, we will figure this all out."

"We always do." She finished his new favorite mantra with a half-smile but didn't feel so certain. Then she relaxed into his arms, letting his warmth seep into her skin.

"I love you, *amour de ma vie*. You are my *paradis*. I am so sorry for keeping things from you. I just…"

He breathed deeply and tightened his arms around her before continuing.

"I almost lost you with Spencer…twice. Then again with Ashcroft, Farren, Peisinoe, Luminita…And these past few months, I've felt you rattling apart at the seams, trying so hard to pull things together. I couldn't bring myself to add to that."

When his voice broke slightly, it brought tears to her eyes. "I'm sorry."

"No. Don't apologize, *cherie*. You have nothing to apologize for. I'm the one spinning out, not you."

A soft sigh escaped his lips and ruffled her hair.

"Hearing what happened to you in L.A. was bad enough, but sensing your fear, anger, self-doubt, insecurity…all stemming from this one insignificant man…I lost it. I felt things slipping and kept grasping, trying to find a way to set things right, to regain control. I stopped thinking and merely acted on instinct. And nothing in my past taught me healthy instincts."

Lilith pulled back enough to meet his misty eyes. "It might be time to form new ones."

A tiny smirk lifted the corner of his lip for an instant, and his gaze fell to the ground.

"Hey." She lifted his chin until his eyes met hers again. "You are not in this alone. We are partners, remember? You always say, 'We'll figure this out,' so stop trying to do it on your own. I'm not my father. I don't need you to clean up my messes. We have to work together and trust each other."

"I do trust—"

"You *want to*. I understand, but you need to trust that I will fight for you as much as you do for me."

As she spoke, a frown formed on his face, and his eyes fell to the ground again. "I'm sorry, *cherie*. It's just..." He paused, unable to put his thoughts into words.

"What is it?" She caressed his stubbled cheek and met his gaze.

"Not a single person has fought for me. My parents never wanted me, and when they died, I was only worth a foster check. When I became too much work, they dumped me in a hospital. Even Gregor—"

He stopped when she bristled at the mention of her father, but after a slight nod of encouragement, he continued.

"The man rescued me, and I will be forever grateful, but..." He stared past her, lost in thought, and sighed. "Never mind. I shouldn't dredge all this up."

"Chance." Once again, she forced him to meet her gaze, and his eyes misted. "Don't shut down. Talk to me."

For a moment, he shifted, clearly uncomfortable with opening up, but eventually continued. "Gregor groomed me, provided a place to stay, sent me to college, and gave me a life, but when I talked to him about you and how I felt...he made it clear that I was expendable. If I overstepped my bounds, he had no trouble cutting ties and leaving me to die. Timothy was the first person who honestly wanted me around."

In the blink of an eye, his expression transformed to something darker, and his jaw clenched.

"And now I've fucked that up."

Chance turned away, ran his hands roughly through his hair, and stared up at the early evening sky. "I have no idea what I'm doing! I don't know how to do any of this!"

Lilith swallowed the swollen lump of emotions lodged in her throat and refused to let her eyes tear up while he began pacing. She wanted to run to him, wrap her arms around his waist, and comfort him like he always did for her, but she knew better. Chance didn't need her to solve this problem. He needed to vent, release his pent-up frustrations, and work things out on his own.

As she battled her compulsion to make things better, he came to a stop, released a deep breath, and walked up to her, still misty-eyed. "I only know two things—Tim is my best friend who deserved more from me, and I love you with every fiber of my being. I was so terrified of losing you. I acted without thought and may have lost you both."

Lilith tried to speak without her voice breaking. "Chance, you have not *lost me*. I'm not going anywhere. Do I love you hiding things from me? Of course not, but my love is not fickle or conditional."

His chin fell to his chest. Tears streaked down his cheeks, and his breaths escaped in rhythmic sighs.

"And you haven't lost Tim. He's mad, but he loves you too. You just need to be honest with us and let us help."

He nodded, swallowing hard, but still couldn't speak.

"Life wasn't fair to you. It taught you not to rely on people, that you didn't matter and weren't worthy of love, but it's all lies! You are a warm and compassionate person with so much to offer. I…"

She hesitated as her own insecurities resurfaced, bringing with them a flush of heat. After closing her eyes and focusing, she tried again.

"Sometimes, I feel unbelievably lucky, like this is all some cruel joke because I don't deserve you."

He moved forward, folded his arms around her, and held her close. The rapid thump of his heartbeat began to slow, soothing her, and she pressed her cheek against his chest. Fingers smoothed through her fiery curls while he rested his chin on top of her head.

"You deserve everything I have to give, *mon petite cherie*."

Lilith pulled back enough to peer up at him and stared at his hazel eyes flecked with green. "No more lies. No more secrets."

"I pr—"

"Wait. Before you swear, is there anything else I should know? This is the time to come clean."

As she spoke, the elated emotions leaked from his face, leaving an impassive mask, and her pulse raced. An awkward silence settled in, pushing between them, separating them more with each passing second.

He took a step back and shoved his trembling hands in his pockets. His shoulders curled forward. "There is one thing."

Whatever it is, it's bad. Shit. Her stomach rolled, and a sour taste flooded her mouth. She didn't want to know but had no choice. *I asked for this.* "Go ahead."

"My problem with Cohen…I wasn't completely honest when you asked. The side effects aren't the primary reason I want to snap his spine."

The unexpected answer left her feeling disoriented. "Okay…" Possibilities raced through her mind at break-neck speed.

"The night in the medical center, both you and Cohen endured horrific things. You depended on each other and formed a bond…"

"Of friendship, at most! Where is this coming from?"

His eyes snapped up to hers with a significant weight. "That's true…for you."

"What do you mean?" A chill crept up her spine, raising each tiny hair in its path.

For a moment, he merely stared at her, hoping she'd come to the obvious conclusion without him having to say it out loud, but her brain refused to understand.

"Cohen. He has…" Chance paused again, raked his fingers through his hair, and cleared his throat. "He has feelings for you."

"I'm sorry. What?" Her mind seized like an engine with no oil, grinding to a painful halt for a few seconds. *No. I must have misheard him. He did not say what I think he did.*

The man's head lowered until his chin almost touched his chest again, and his hands slid back into his pockets. Once he released his breath in a slow exhale, he met her eyes. "The man loves you, *cherie*. At least his version."

Lilith stood still, stunned into silence. She thought back through every interaction—the disproportionate anger, the uncharacteristic selfless acts, the curiosity about her early life, the woman at the hotel who resembled her.

"Oh my god!" Her hand flew up to cover her gaping mouth, the horrifying realization finally sinking in. "When did you figure this out?"

"I didn't *figure out* anything. In Alabama, after Gregor…That's the first time I recognized his jealousy."

Then it hit her. "You sensed his emotions." Logically, she knew he had the ability, but understanding what that entailed still came as a shock.

"Yeah." Chance leaned back against the wall, his arms folded across his chest. "Knowing another guy has a thing for your girl is one thing. Sensing every moment of adoration, sexual desire, jealous rage…is an entirely different animal."

Her cheeks blazed white hot, and she tried to wrap her mind around everything. "No wonder you wanted to tear his head off…"

"It's also part of the reason I jumped at the opportunity to go to Goditha after your nightmare last year."

Once again, her brow furrowed, so he elaborated.

"You were so skittish. I couldn't even touch you. You recoiled every time I tried. I felt like someone snatched away *paradis*, heaven, after mere moments. I had no idea if you'd ever recover...if we'd ever be the same, and that alone terrified me. However, experiencing Cohen's internal gloating every time you turned away...It was more than I could handle." A tear trailed down his cheek when he leaned his head back to stare into the sky. "I didn't want to leave you with him, but I can only take so much."

"I can't even imagine how painful it was...I am *so* sorry I..." Her voice broke, preventing her from finishing.

Chance pushed away from the wall and strolled toward her. "*Mon amour*, you have no reason to apologize. You experienced trauma, and your brain tried to protect you. I understand. Also, you can't control someone's emotions, no matter how much you want to. Trust me."

After clearing her throat, she tried again to speak. "Why...didn't you tell me?"

His gaze fell to the ground again, pink tinging his cheeks. "At first, I thought it would pass with time. He doesn't seem like a guy who grows attached to things or people. Then I didn't want to admit I still had these side effects."

"And after that?"

His shoulders sank, and a sigh escaped. "Honestly? Your bond with him scared me. Telling you meant facing the possibility of losing you."

"To Cohen?" Lilith cut him off as anger surged to the surface, and heat flushed her body. "This is *not* some teenage love triangle bullshit! Seriously? You think I care so little about you I'd throw myself at any man who showed an interest?" The more she spoke, the more outraged she became until her blood boiled and her muscles quivered.

With a brisk motion, she turned away, swallowing the sour taste in her mouth as she paced.

"Of all the idiotic reasons to keep this secret."

Chance audibly swallowed. "When you put it like that..."

She swerved and marched up to him, still vibrating with rage.

"Chance Allen Deveraux. I love you and *only* you. I did not fall for you because you professed your love. I'm not an airhead starving for affection! What we have is *real!* Don't you see that?"

For a moment, he stood there, unable to form words. Despite every passing second cutting like a knife to her heart, she allowed him time to assemble his thoughts.

"You are the love of my life, *mon cherie*. I'm sorry. I should have told you, trusted you, had faith that what we have is special."

"Because it is! You are the love of my life too. Use that stupid, infernal demon blood and believe me, please!"

"I do believe you." His fingers interlaced with hers, and he stared down at their interlocked hands before biting his lip for a half-second.

"But?"

"Nothing. *Pour l'amour de Dieu*, I'm trying, *mon cherie*. I've never been in a relationship, and my parents weren't a shining example of a healthy couple. I'm still trying to get used to this." Fear lingered in his eyes despite everything she had professed.

"Perhaps we should wait to move in together. Maybe we're rushing things."

"What? No. *Arête!*" His shaking hands gripped her shoulders, and a feverish sweat broke across his brow. "Lily, *mo laime toi...*"

"You don't trust me or my feelings despite more evidence than any man could ask for...You literally *know* how I feel about you and still can't trust me. That's why you didn't say anything about Cohen."

"No. That's ridiculous. I don't need the demon blood to know you love me."

"Then why do I have to keep proving I do?"

"*Cherie*, that's not what I meant earlier."

"Three times you hid things from me because you thought I'd leave you, as if I ever could! You are a part of me, the lynchpin keeping all my pieces together!"

His breathing became rapid, and he stood there, too shocked and overwhelmed to speak. Then the crunch of gravel broke the spell, and he glanced over her shoulder at the approaching headlights.

"Nicci's here." A dismal tone infected his voice.

Lilith grabbed his chin and forced him to meet her eyes. "I'm serious, Chance. I will not move in with you if you can't trust me."

"Lily, I—" He swallowed hard on the rising panic before continuing. "I don't know how to trust someone like that, but I *am* trying. No more secrets, I promise."

She searched his teary eyes and saw only the truth. "That's an honest start." Lilith wrapped her arms around him and leaned into his chest.

At first, he didn't move a muscle. When she didn't pull away, his arms tentatively settled around her shoulders, and he finally pulled her tight against him with a sigh of relief.

"Hey, Lil. You ready to go?" Nicci hopped out of her red Fiat parked next to Tim's Honda.

"Yeah. Give me one minute." Lilith peeked over her shoulder to see Nicci nod, straighten her navy pantsuit and vibrant yellow blouse, before leaning against her car.

When Lilith's gaze drifted back to Chance, the sadness still lingered on his face. She hated leaving things like this, but they both had things to do.

"I'll text or call if we find anything. I won't make a move without you, as promised. In the meantime, try not to let Boston get to you."

After he gave a brief nod that left her unconvinced, she arched an eyebrow and waited.

"I'll do my best."

"Chance..."

"Look. I get a front-row seat to every flicker of satisfaction he gets from causing you pain—every violent impulse, all his rage and hatred. Sometimes, I can't separate it from my own. All of that on top of knowing what he did to you. I'm trying to get a grip on all this, I really am."

"That's all I ask. I have faith in you. Let Tim lead, and I'll be back soon, okay?"

"Yes, *mon amour*. Be careful." Only a small smile broke through his misery, but she couldn't think of anything truthful to lift his spirits.

After placing a kiss on his stubbled cheek, she reluctantly turned away and jogged over to her partner.

"Um, why does Chance look like he swallowed a cockroach dipped in sour mix?" Leave it to Nicci to sum up everything in one colorful metaphor.

"Let's get to the hotel. I'll fill you in on the way." *When in doubt, ignore the question.* Without waiting for a reply, Lilith climbed into the cramped Fiat.

A few seconds later, Nicci hopped into the driver's seat, placed her key fob in the cupholder, and twisted to face Lilith. "What is wrong?" The woman continued to stare at her, demanding an answer.

Uncomfortable silence flooded the car. The tension kept building until Lilith broke, and everything she'd been suppressing came roaring to the surface while tears filled her eyes.

"Everything is fucked! Some Grecian cult tortured Boston's partner to death, hung her on a tree, and waited for tonight to display their masterpiece.

The FBI can't question Boston because his father has deep pockets and connections, so they gave him to us. Oh, and Chance used to torture people for my father, so he has a handy dandy holding cell on the first floor of his place."

"What the—"

"I'm not done." Lilith cut her off with a pained glare. The woman had insisted on an answer, so Lilith was going to give her a full report. "Also, Cohen is…in love with me, according to Chance. That's why he has zero tolerance around him…And Chance didn't tell me because he was—get this—scared I'd leave him for Cohen!"

"Wow! That makes so much sense!"

"What? How in the hell does that *make sense?*"

"Well, not the last bit. Chance has irrational fears that stem from his abandonment issues."

Lilith raised an eyebrow and peered at her partner. "Stop sounding like my shrink."

Nicci put her hands up for a moment before starting the car. "Andrew's behavior makes a lot more sense now. The man is a master at masking emotions unless you *and* Chance are around. I always thought the animosity was uncharacteristic. At first, I figured it was a feeding technique, but it seemed too…personal."

"So, what the hell do I do about it?"

Nicci peeked over as they exited the industrial park and pulled onto the Bruckner Expressway. "You mean, about Andrew?"

"Yeah."

"Well, you only have two options—either confront him, which could blow up in your face, or do nothing."

"Nothing?"

"His feelings are only an issue if you make them an issue. He hasn't made a move, so he obviously doesn't wish to share how he feels, so let him have them. Continue life as you have and ignore Andrew's…fantasies or whatever."

"Still doesn't solve my issue with Chance. He doesn't trust me. How am I supposed to be okay with that?"

Nicci continued down I-278 onto Randall's Island, toward the Robert F. Kennedy Bridge, frowning. "Seriously? Girl, I love you like a sister, but don't read too much into things."

"I'm not…"

"The boy's parents constantly rejected him and did the ultimate disappearing act by dying right in front of him when he was ten years old. No one wanted him. *You* are the one who told me all this, so why are you surprised it's taking him longer than eight months to get over a lifetime of rejection and abandonment?"

A long sigh escaped Lilith's lips, and she sank as far as possible into the tiny seat. "You may have a point."

"You didn't break up with him, did you? Is that why he looked like he sucked down an entire bag of lemons?"

"No! I just told him I couldn't move in if he didn't trust me…" The words drifted off, and her confidence in them waned. "Shit. Tim warned me Chance is spinning out, losing control, and I just made things worse."

"Hey! You're only human…"

Lilith raised an eyebrow as they passed the toll gate.

"Relatively speaking. You have issues too, especially when it comes to secrets. You reacted, but you can fix things later. For now, shake it off. We need to find your other boyfriend."

"Not funny!" Lilith leveled her partner with a hostile glare, but Nicci merely shrugged and flashed a wide smile.

"I think it's hilarious!"

Chapter 29

The legs of a metal folding chair scraped across the concrete with an eerie screech. The chair twirled with a flourish before Tim's broad frame settled onto the backward seat. His eyes lifted to the man huddled in the corner, and he draped his arms over the back.

"Where am I?" The demanding tone Boston used didn't fit his situation. *False Bravado. How original.*

Tim continued to stare with calm detachment, which unnerved his captive. Boston loosened his stained tie, and his square jaw clenched.

"Are you a real PI?"

"If you think I'm a liar, why ask?"

A huff escaped Boston's parched lips. "Fair point."

"Here. I'm sure you're thirsty." Tim tossed him the bottled water, which Boston caught with a frown. "We didn't lace it with anything. The seal is still intact."

The man still inspected the bottle thoroughly before cracking it open and gulping down half the water. After setting the bottle on the floor, he stared up at Tim.

"What do you want? Money?"

Tim arched an eyebrow and straightened his shoulders. "I think you already know this isn't about money."

After a second's reflection, David's chin jutted out, a sneer distorting his features. "It's about Lilith. She sent you to babysit me when I showed up, and now…" His thoughts rambled on, his confidence lessening with each word until he loosened his tie a bit more. "She wants me to back off? Was Cassie…" The man swallowed hard, and tears misted his red-rimmed eyes.

Hmm. Genuine emotion.

"Was she a warning?"

"Not from us," Tim stated in a matter-of-fact tone. "I'm gonna be straight with you. I'm aware of your history. Enough to want you dead, at least. Men like you think the world owes them everything. You use and abuse until everyone turns their back on you. Then you obsess, fixate, and recreate until every memory turns poisonous so you can justify your actions."

The same unemotional, almost bored tone infused his voice, and David's face flushed bright red.

"Fuck you. That bitch—"

Tim held up his hand. A darkness seeped into his eyes, halting his captor mid-sentence.

"Her name is Lilith. You want her to be the villain because it's convenient and familiar, but we *both* know she is not responsible for Cassie."

David opened his mouth to protest, and all the remaining warmth leeched from Tim's eyes, his features displaying a threat of violence. The malicious expression kept the man silent.

"Nothing we need to discuss involves your past with Lilith. I advise you to choose your words carefully from this point on if you wish to leave this cell alive."

"I have nothing to say to any of you." Boston folded his arms over his chest and stared at the far corner over Tim's shoulder.

Suddenly, a smug smile cracked Tim's imposing glare, drawing Boston's attention. "Whether by logic or force, you will tell me what I need to know. Someone tortured your partner for days, perhaps weeks. You're gonna tell me why, or you'll share her fate."

"Bullshit. You are out of your depth! My father—"

"Isn't here to protect you," Tim interrupted quickly. "David Elias Boston II will not find you here. I think you are the one out of their depth."

Boston's dark eyes narrowed to slits. "You looked up my dad's name. Congratulations. You can use Google. I am still a federal fucking agent!"

Tim's eyebrows rose, and a smile crossed his face. "Who do you think handed you over to us?"

The shocked expression didn't last long, and he didn't argue the point. He knew the truth.

"Yeah. You burnt that bridge when you dragged your partner into your mess." Before continuing, Tim leaned forward on his elbows and fixed the man in place with a sharp glare. "Being someone's partner is sacred, more so than any relationship you'll ever have. You depend on each other in life-and-death situations. You look out for each other. And you abused that."

"Save the lecture."

"The truth hurts. Whoever took Agent Cappalletty wanted information. The most likely reason is her most recent case…the unofficial, illegal one you dragged her into."

"I was investigating Lilith Adams! You and the lunatic she's fucking work for that psycho bitch, so I don't understand how I can tell you anything new!"

Tim's gaze fell to the floor, and his jaw clenched. He took a deep breath and released in one slow exhale.

Boston frowned, confused by the sudden silence.

In one swift motion, Tim stood, swung the chair to knock David back, and used its rung across his neck to pin the man to the floor. David coughed and gagged, his dark eyes widening.

When Tim finally spoke, his voice remained calm. "I told you before to choose your words carefully. You are wrong about her. If you want to keep things civil, you will refrain from making any further disparaging remarks about her or Chance."

Boston's face turned a violent shade of red while panic and fear filled his eyes. Although he pushed at the bar across his throat, the full weight of Tim's six-foot muscled frame pressed down on him.

"Blink twice if you understand."

The man squeezed his eyes shut twice, and Tim stood, taking the chair with him. While David sat up, coughing and wheezing, Tim settled backward on the chair again and waited.

"I…What am I…supposed to tell you?" Boston cleared his throat a few times as he spoke. "The Phipps Bend report was complete shit, so I started my own investigation."

"Ah. See? Cooperation is much better, don't ya think?"

The sour grimace on the man's face deepened, and he guzzled the rest of his water.

"You cared about Agent Cappalletty?"

"Of course, I did."

"Then why drag her into your illegal activities?"

"I needed help. Cassie is…was always better with people."

A slight huff escaped along with his sarcastic response. "You don't say."

A scowl wrinkled David's face, and he leaned back against the wall, rubbing at the angry red mark across his throat. "Funny. I convinced the guy in evidence to let me access some things from the case, but I needed an independent scientist to evaluate them. Someone pulled some huge strings to wrap everything up with a pretty red bow."

"So, Agent Cappalletty had connections?"

"A biologist she worked with back before her first partner died. She is a professor at a university in Pennsylvania."

"Penn State in York? Dr. Rachel Thomas?"

Boston's eyebrows flew up, and his body went rigid. "How do you know that?"

"Not important. Continue."

After a wary stare, Boston started speaking again. "We took her what we had, but she couldn't help much. She said she needed access to the bodies, which were not at the FBI, so we went back to the coroner in Knoxville." Then he paused, lost in thought.

"What did you find in Tennessee?"

David shook his head and focused on the question. "All the bodies and biological specimens were gone, except for one. The coroner said federal agents confiscated them before he started his preliminary exams. He never even took fingerprints or blood samples."

"Did he say where they went?"

Boston's eyes narrowed, and his lips pressed into a tight line.

"Now is not the time to make a stand. Don't you want to catch your partner's killer?"

"I'm still not convinced you aren't involved."

Tim rolled his eyes and leaned forward again. "If we were the killers, you'd be dead, and I wouldn't be questioning you. How the hell did you become an FBI agent?"

"Maybe you want to find out how much I've discovered and how dangerous I am because killing me is a definite risk. Maybe you didn't get what you needed from Cassie, so you turned her into a gruesome spectacle, hoping I'd join forces to track down the killer."

"Wow. You sincerely overestimate your value. In truth, we didn't know about your investigation until you showed up...months *after* someone kidnapped your partner."

"So you claim."

Tim leaned back, re-evaluating his strategy. What the guy lacked in intelligence, he made up for in stubborn bias.

"Consider your options. If you're right and we are the bad guys, we will torture you until you talk and then kill you. However, if you're wrong, we'll try to intimidate you, perhaps get what we need, waste time, and hope we let you go, but Cassie's killer will still be on the loose. Your best option is to talk."

David leaned back against the wall, mulling over Tim's words.

"Look, I shouldn't be telling you this, but…"

The man glanced up, clearly enticed.

"We think Cassandra's death is connected to another case."

"How so?"

"I can't give you specifics, but a lot of lives are on the line. Did the Knoxville ME tell you where the bodies went?"

"Major Crimes in New York City."

The man's voice still held suspicion, but Tim didn't care, as long as the guy talked.

"Cassie and I drove up to the city and spoke with the coroner, an old man with a cane. We asked to see the bodies from Phipps Bend, and he appeared surprised. When we pressed him with the testimony of the Knoxville ME, he claimed the shipments never arrived. He said they were re-routed."

"Re-routed where?"

The captive's eyes narrowed again. "There's something weird about those bodies, isn't there?"

"This is my interrogation, not yours. Where did the bodies go?"

"Why the fuck should I tell you? How the hell will the answer help find her killer?"

"It might establish motive, which would narrow the suspect pool."

"So, you have suspects? Who?"

"Where did the bodies go, David?"

"Fuck you."

Tim rose from his chair, using every inch of his six-foot frame to loom over Boston. "Answer the question."

"Not until you tell me why you want the bodies."

Anger surged through Tim, and his hands curled into fists. "You small-minded asshole. Are you going to let the people who tortured and killed your partner walk so you can hold on to a grudge?"

David turned and stared at the opposite corner, his arms crossing over his chest, making his decision clear.

"Fine. Have things your way, but don't say I didn't try the diplomatic route first."

The color drained from the man's face as he peeked at Tim, who spun on his heel, stormed out of the room, slammed the door, and locked it.

"You okay, *mon ami*?" Chance stopped his pacing when his partner blew through the door.

"Fucking infuriating idiot. How that man ever graduated the academy is a fucking mystery." Tim rubbed his knuckles into his palm.

"What happened?" Chance jogged over and matched Tim's stride.

"He chose the hard way. I should have known appealing to his humanity was a waste of time."

"It was worth a shot. Everyone cares about something."

"Yeah, but the asshole only cares about painting Lilith as a villain. He refuses to see reason. He told me the New York coroner, the old man with a cane, told him the bodies from Phipps Bend were rerouted mid-transit. The fucker knows where they went, but he clammed up. I'm gonna let him stew for a bit, and then I'm going back in…"

Tim walked up to his Honda, opened the door, and reached under the passenger seat.

"…with my knife." He clipped the sheathed tactical knife to his belt and turned back to Chance. "I will make him talk."

"Maybe I—"

"No." Tim shut him down. "He knows you and Lilith are an item. The second he sees you, he has a visceral focus for his hate, which will make him harder to break. He may think I work for Lilith, but he's never seen us together. There are no memories he can summon up to steel his will through hatred."

Chance nodded while his head hung low, searching for some useful purpose. "How about I make dinner instead?"

A brilliant grin split Tim's lips, and he followed Chance to the freight elevator. "Now you're talking my language!"

"What about…" Chance thrust his chin toward the isolation room.

"He won't starve for another three or four days. I gave him water." Tim shrugged and stepped into the metal beast with Chance. "Please, tell me you have steak."

Chance chuckled, pulled down the gate, and hit the button. "I picked up some thick sirloins the other day. I planned on cooking them for Lilith." The humor drained from his face, and the night's earlier discussion played through his head. "Shit. I really fucked things up with her."

Tim squeezed his shoulder and pulled him into a side hug. "You messed up. It happens to the best of us. What you do next defines who you are. Either suck it up and do better, or keep spiraling out of control until you kill someone."

"Yeah, but she thinks I hid things from her because I don't trust her."

"Well, do you?"

"I want to, more than anything."

"Then give it time. You don't have to rush things and stuff your relationship into a perfect little box. Marriage, two-point-five kids, a dog, and a picket fence—that's the norm dictated by a human society who values consumers over authenticity."

Chance cocked an eyebrow and lifted the gate. "You're venturing into conspiracy theory territory there, Tim."

"You know I'm right. We may not be human, but we are still trained to breed, buy, and die."

"Very optimistic of you. Still...I get what you're saying."

Chance grabbed two juicy steaks, butter, and bacon while Tim reached around him for two Miller Lites.

"Grab a third one. I need one for the steaks."

Tim put two cans next to the stove and cracked open a third before settling onto a barstool. "Things will be all right. Once the dust settles and these cases are solved."

"What if we never solve them?"

His friend frowned and took another sip, contemplating the question. "You are freaking out over hypothetical situations. Stop, take a fucking breath, and rebalance."

"Yoga is not the answer," Chance countered, coating the searing cast iron pan with butter.

"This isn't a damn joke." The half-empty beer can groaned as Tim tightened his grip.

After meeting his eyes for a moment, Chance sighed. "Believe me. I know."

"Then take the advice and stop being an asshole...Whoa!" Tim hollered.

Chance paused with a steak hovering over the pan.

"You gotta season those first."

He chuckled at the unexpected change in topic and settled the meat into the searing hot pan. "Trust me."

Tim raised a dark blonde eyebrow and drained the last of his beer but didn't comment.

After sprinkling Worcestershire sauce on top, Chance cracked open a Miller Lite and passed it to Tim. "If you put the seasoning on too soon, it burns. Too late and it falls off. Timing is everything."

"If you say so, bud."

An odd silence settled over them. Chance seasoned the steaks, poured some beer in the pan, and flipped them. Then Tim broached the subject neither of them wanted to discuss.

"Once we get what we want from Boston...what's the plan?"

Chance exhaled slowly and stared into the pan. *That is the million-dollar question.* "I don't have one. The man is a problem in more ways than one, but if we kill him, his dad will—"

"No. If we murder him...If he dies in an accident—or better yet, in the line of duty—his father won't have a reason to come after us."

"Okay. How do we pull off something like that? This isn't Hollywood, and Boston isn't some low-level reporter. He's a federal agent and the son of an influential real estate tycoon."

"Better than Hollywood. It's real life, where the percentage of closed murder cases is a hair over fifty percent."

"Yeah, well...I still don't have a plan."

Chance slid the juicy, medium rare steaks onto plates and passed one to Tim.

"What? No sides?"

After a brief frown, Chance nodded toward the fridge. "Help yourself to some potato salad, but don't touch Lilith's coleslaw. You think she's mad now..."

They both chuckled, and Tim clapped Chance on the back with a broad smile. "Maybe there's hope for you yet."

Chapter 30

Lilith gazed up at the nineteen-story boutique hotel on Forty-Sixth Street. The early evening sun blazed behind the building, giving it an eerie glow. The Muse Hotel was considered by most to be the premiere accommodations in Manhattan's Theater District, which made it an odd choice for a scientist in an underfunded field. Of course, the woman probably chose it based on the name, considering the recurrent theme of Greek mythology.

"Pretty posh for a low-level professor working on a satellite campus." Nicci echoed Lilith's thoughts, planted her hands on her hips, and shook her head at the Renaissance Revival architecture. "Can you believe this place was originally used by a jewelry manufacturer?"

The weird reference made Lilith turn to her with a quizzical expression. "How old are you?"

Although Nicci's eyebrows shot up, her mouth pulled into a frown. "You aren't supposed to ask a lady how old she is."

"I'll remember that when I see one. Answer the question."

With a mischievous smirk, Nicci strolled toward the entrance.

"Oh, come on!" Lilith jogged to catch up with her as she reached the doors.

"I'm really surprised you haven't asked before now," Nicci countered, still avoiding the question.

"Age is such a weird concept for purebloods. I guess I don't think about it much."

The petite Italian turned on her heel and opened the door. "You're my partner. That's the only reason I'm telling you this. Alicia's human, so not even my girlfriend knows. My driver's license says I'm turning thirty-four next month, but I spent time abroad in Italy, the old country. I'm actually turning seventy-two."

"Damn. How did I not know this?" Lilith gaped at her, but the woman shrugged and strolled inside.

"Like I said…you didn't ask. Now, don't blab to anyone, including Chance. It's private."

"Promise." Lilith shook off the surprise and focused on the mid-century modern lobby.

Vertical lines of alternating light and dark marble embedded in the diagonal hardwood floor led the eye straight to the main desk. Three rough stone pillars held up a concrete ceiling covered in horizontal panels of rich mahogany wood, which hovered over the marble-edged reception area.

The high thin wooden table seemed an odd touch. The thing ran the length of the counter and featured curved legs that clashed with all the clean, straight lines. Perhaps it was added as an afterthought, a place for women to put their purses down while rummaging for their wallets.

They strolled forward, and an art feature on their right caught Lilith's attention. Five white barren trees stood within a glass enclosure. Their ghostly skeletal limbs reached toward the bright lights illuminating them from above, which amplified their already austere appearance.

Images of Agent Cappalletty's broken corpse flooded her mind in a barrage of increasingly grotesque flashes. She stopped and squeezed her eyes shut, her stomach churning. *Come on! Keep it together! You can fall apart later.* The inner pep talk didn't help much.

"Hey, you okay?"

When Lilith doubled over and focused on her breathing, Nicci patted her back.

Once she had everything under control, she stood up and nodded. "I'm all right. The severity of the crime scene and my sleep deprivation aren't a good combo, but I'll manage."

"I can question the staff solo. Why don't you have a seat?"

"No, really…I'm fine." Lilith straightened, flashed a soft smile at her, and continued toward the counter.

"Good evening." A cheery young blond greeted them from behind the desk. "Do you have a reservation?"

When Nicci unclipped her shield from her belt and held it up the woman's expression dimmed.

"Not that kinda visit…" She paused to read the golden name tag. "Jillian. Were you working last night?"

The young woman's wide-eyed gaze bounced between them as she considered her answer. "Yes. I worked the second shift. How can I help you…" The woman faltered without a name to complete her scripted verbiage.

"Detective DeLuca, and this is my partner, Lilith Adams. We are looking for a colleague—Andrew Cohen. He came here last night to question a person of interest." She scrolled through her phone and clicked on a professional headshot of Cohen.

Weird.

"I remember him." A disappointed frown curved the young woman's lips. "He came in here, demanding a room number. I told him we don't give out client information. Then the guy changed, like flipping a switch."

As she spoke, the frown slowly lifted into a smile.

"He apologized for being abrasive and asked me to forgive him."

A blush crept over her tanned cheeks, and her gaze drifted away. After a moment, she shook off the obvious daydream and smiled apologetically.

"He was really charming. I almost gave him the info anyway, but my supervisor came out of the back office before I could tell him."

"Did he leave after that?"

"No. He went to the hotel bar. I suppose he hoped to bump into the doctor there."

"Dr. Thomas?"

The girl glanced around to ensure they were alone and nodded.

"Did you see him leave?"

"No. When my shift ended at ten, I went to the bar, hoping to run into him, but he wasn't there. Danielle worked after me, but she didn't see him leave either."

"What about Rachel Thomas? When did she check out?"

Again, the woman's nervous eyes darted around before she answered. "Late last night. And according to Danielle, she left with a large group of people."

"Has the room been cleaned yet?" Lilith interjected.

"Yes. Our housekeeping staff is efficient, and all our vacant rooms are cleaned before check-in times begin," the woman proclaimed proudly, but the glowing smile faded when Lilith sighed in frustration.

"What about video footage? You have cameras all over, right?" Nicci cut in with a side glance at her partner.

"Uh, yes, but…" The young woman turned and peered at the hall behind the desk several times before drawing in a deep breath and exhaling. Finally, she leaned over and lowered her voice. "Mr. Gladfelter has a strict policy on—"

"Can I help you?" A squat man with a pinched face and a ring of hair around his bald spot appeared, as if summoned by uttering his name. Of course, his presence probably had more to do with the surveillance cameras and Nicci showing her badge. "I'm the manager, Patrick Gladfelter."

Nicci flashed a tight smile, her patience beginning to wear thin. "Detective DeLuca and Ms. Adams. We're investigating a missing person case and would like to see your CCTV footage from last night and today."

The smug grin made the man's chubby cheeks pinch his eyes into slits. "We have stringent policies on clientele confidentiality. I'm afraid you'll need a warrant."

The petite Italian stood on tiptoe and leaned on the desk's lower ledge. "I appreciate your commitment to privacy, but the guy who's missing is a detective. We know he came here to see Dr. Thomas, a person of interest in several murder cases. Time is of the essence, and we'd appreciate your cooperation."

Mr. Gladfelter's bushy eyebrows fell, and his mouth sagged into a frown. "I am so sorry. I wish I could help." Something in his beady eyes said he enjoyed turning them down.

"Come on. We're wasting time here. This man doesn't give a crap about public safety or the life of a cop." Lilith grabbed Nicci's arm and started for the front door, while the manager released an indignant huff.

"I'll be sure to tell my buddies in the Health Department how helpful you were!" Nicci hollered as they stormed across the lobby, then she mumbled, "*Testa di cazzo*," under her breath.

"Maybe I should pick up a second language so I can curse people out with impunity." Lilith flung the door open for her feisty Italian compatriot with a chuckle.

"Well, the guy is a dickhead. Shit." She stopped on the sidewalk to compose her thoughts. "Do you think Cohen took a cab here?"

"No. He's pretty attached to that stupid limo."

Nicci glanced at the attendant leaning on a wooden stand beside a metal lockbox. "And without his driver, the stuffy bastard probably used the valet. I doubt he could park that monstrosity."

Before Lilith responded, she stalked over to the gangly teenager and held up her shield.

"Where do you park the cars?"

The guy peered up from his phone with a grumpy expression, but his bloodshot eyes widened when they landed on her badge. He was probably scared they'd discover his recreational drug use, but they weren't interested in his pot habit. Still, the awkward kid stood up straight and smoothed his red jacket before answering.

"Uh, yes, ma'am...Officer. The um...parking garage around the corner there."

As soon as he pointed, Nicci stormed off, leaving Lilith to catch up.

"Whoa. Slow down." She jogged up to her partner as *The Office* theme erupted from her pocket. Thankfully, her partner slowed to a reasonable pace when she answered the phone.

"Hey, Chance." Those two words alone felt incredibly awkward after the way they left things.

"*Cherie*, any luck?"

Apparently, she wasn't the only one who felt that way. The stiffness in his voice pulled at her heart, but there were more important things to discuss, so Lilith stuffed all her conflicted feelings into a dark hole and stuck to business.

"The manager refused to let us access the CCTV without a warrant. We're heading to the valet parking to see if his car's still here. Did Tim get anything useful from our guest?"

"Yeah. Some. The last thing they worked on was tracking down the bodies and biological samples from Phipps Bend. They questioned Frank, and he said the shipment never arrived."

"Well, we know they went to a third party, but I assumed he processed them first. Of course, he might have lied to the FBI. I'll call him when we're done here."

"Okay, *cherie*."

An awkward quiet set in when Lilith and Nicci turned into the garage, and each passing second made her heart ache a little more. She opened her mouth to say something, but he broke the silence first.

"I...uh. I'm sorry about everything, Lily. I just—"

"We can talk about this later, all right? I apologize for losing my temper, but I need a little time to process things."

"Of course. I love you, *mon cher.*" Sadness infused his deep voice, and he hung up before she could respond, leaving a swell of emotions lodged in her throat.

"Well, that sounded incredibly uncomfortable and cliché." Nicci had an annoying talent for summing up a situation with glaring clarity.

"Yeah." Lilith stared at her phone for a moment, debating whether to call him back, but her partner tapped her arm.

"There it is!" The petite detective jogged over to the black stretch town car, and Lilith shoved her cell back into her pocket.

Nicci tried the door first—locked, of course—and then peered into the driver's side window with her hands cupped around her face. "Ya know"— she maneuvered to the darkened back windows but couldn't see through the extreme tint—"we should get the key from the valet."

"Which will help us how?" She didn't intend to snap at her partner, and when the woman raised an eyebrow, Lilith apologized. "I'm sorry, but Cohen went into the hotel, and the doors are locked. They didn't snatch him from here. He would have made the valet bring the enormous thing around front. So, I don't see how getting inside is helpful. The town car is here, which proves he didn't run home. That's all we needed to know."

Her partner's lips pressed together in a tight line, and she rested her hands on her hips. "Yeah, I suppose you're right." Nicci continued to stare at the limo, her eyes narrowing, and then she peered up at Lilith. "Why take him, though? Why not avoid him and sneak off?"

"I don't know. Maybe he confronted them. Did you try pinging his cell?"

"First thing I tried. It went dark somewhere near here."

"So, they knew enough to destroy it or remove the SIM card."

"Yep." Nicci released a breath in a long huff. "What's our next move?"

As if on cue, the ominous tones of "The Imperial March" emerged from Lilith's pocket, and she fished out her phone again.

"Frank. Just the person I wanted to speak to." She smiled at Nicci, and they strolled back toward her Fiat.

"If you say so." The man's gruff voice rumbled over the speaker with an irritated edge. "I rushed the toxicology results on the Cappalletty vic. It shows an unusual combination of fentanyl, ketamine, and a hallucinogenic

I'm not familiar with…However, I recall seeing this odd mixture in a previous case recently."

"Which one?"

A drawn-out huff crackled through the speaker. "I handle a lot of cases, unlike you. I gave the results to Boyd. He's cross-referencing them with all the bodies I've autopsied in the past year."

"Thanks. Hey, while I have you, can I ask a few questions?"

"Of course, you have questions." The irritated sigh that followed didn't surprise her.

They approached the Fiat, and Lilith squeezed into the passenger seat.

"Well, go on. What do you want to know?"

"Do you recall speaking with two FBI agents a while back? They were looking into Phipps Bend. One was our vic, Cappalletty, and the other was Special Agent David Boston."

"I thought the name sounded familiar. What of it?"

"Did you tell them anything?"

"Nothing of use. I am a professional, regardless of what you think. They were humans conducting an illegal investigation."

"So, they didn't see the cadavers?"

An irritated growl emerged before he answered. "No. I would never allow a human access. How reckless do you think I am? Besides, it's a moot point. The evidence from Tennessee never arrived."

"You told them the truth? You never received the bodies?"

"That's what I just said. God, woman. Pay attention!"

"Do you know where they went?"

"No. When they didn't arrive as scheduled, I tried to find out, but I only learned the shipment was rerouted from Atlanta on Aaron's orders. I asked him, but he said it was council business, not mine."

"Aaron?" Apprehension buzzed down Lilith's spine, and Nicci glanced over at her.

"Yes." The word was accompanied by an irritated huff.

"When was the order given?"

"Perhaps two or three days after your Phipps Bend fiasco."

Although Frank's statement held a heaping dose of implied blame, something else bothered her.

"Thanks for the info." She mumbled the words while staring sightlessly through the windshield.

Frank grunted a goodbye and hung up before she snapped out of it.

Then she dialed Aaron's number—straight to voicemail. *Fuck.* She tried again with no success.

"Damn it!"

Things can always get worse.

Chapter 31

"**W**hat's wrong?" Nicci frowned at her partner while waiting at a red light.

"The evidence from Tennessee was rerouted during transport on Aaron's orders days before Gregor died. How would my uncle know anything specific about what happened? I didn't turn in my report until after the incident at the medical center. Why does he want it, and where the fuck did he send it?"

"Seriously? Damn. This is bad."

"Shit. I didn't tell you. Aaron showed up at Chance's place this afternoon."

"What for?"

"To check on our progress—or so he said—but when I told him we had Dr. Nichols's computer, he suddenly became interested in the conversation. He knows something. It could be the database or some other secret we haven't stumbled across yet, but the man is nervous."

"Did you tell him where it is?"

"Well, no...Not exactly."

Nicci swerved into an empty parking spot, threw the car in park, and glared at her partner. "What do you mean, *not exactly*?"

"I mentioned you were decrypting it, so..."

"He'll correctly assume I have it. Shit! Why the hell didn't you tell me earlier?"

"I'm sorry. It's no excuse, but I was...distracted."

"So, the tiff with your boyfriend outweighs my safety?" Nicci shook her head while Lilith chewed the inside of her cheek, staring at her hands, unable to come up with an answer. "We need to head to my place!"

"Shit. I really am sorry. I was upset and didn't think..."

"That's the problem with both of you—not thinking." The woman glanced at her watch. "Shit. Alicia will be there any minute with dinner."

"Chance sent Ray over to guard your apartment."

"Great. My girlfriend is gonna show up and find a strange man in my place. I'm sure she'll love that."

Nicci pressed a button on the steering wheel and said, "Call Alicia." After the robotic voice confirmed her request, the phone rang a few times before someone answered.

"Hey, babe."

"Are you at my place?"

"No. Sorry. I got held up at work, and now I'm stuck in traffic. I haven't even made it to IL Cortile yet."

A rush of air escaped Nicci's lips. "Oh, thank god."

"Um, why?" The woman took offense to the odd reaction.

"I…can't explain right now, but my place isn't safe. Head home and I'll call you later."

"Are you okay?"

"Yeah, I'm fine. Promise. I need to take care of some stuff, but do not go near my apartment until I tell you it's safe."

"Is this because I picked *Avatar 2* for tonight?"

Lilith tried not to chuckle at the question, but Nicci still glared in her direction.

"No. This is serious! Bad people are after something I have. This isn't about a stupid movie."

"Okay! I'll go home and watch it myself."

Nicci scratched at her scalp as her face turned red. "Alicia, come on! I'm trying to keep you safe."

"Fine." The woman's tone ushered in a tense silence that made everyone uncomfortable. Then Nicci's girlfriend sighed heavily. "You'll fill me in later?"

"Absolutely." The tension in her shoulders eased, and she relaxed into the driver's seat. "I'll call you as soon as I can."

"All right. I love you and be safe."

Nicci side-glanced at Lilith and rushed her response. "Love you too, babe."

After she hung up, Nicci stared through the windshield for a few moments before speaking.

"I think we should still—" A chirp over the car's speakers interrupted her, and she tapped the console's screen to display the message. "Boyd got a hit from the tox report."

Lilith remained silent while her partner debated their next move. Alicia was safe, but it was still Nicci's call. Lilith owed her that much, after putting her and her girlfriend in danger.

"You're sure Ray is watching my place?"

"I can find out." Instead of calling and inviting another awkward conversation, she sent Chance a quick text, which he answered almost immediately. "Ray's patrolling the hall outside your door," Lilith relayed.

"And you trust him?"

"He worked for my father for over twenty years, and he's good friends with Chance and Tim. A bit of a loner, but he's dependable and loyal. I trust him."

After a deep inhale, Nicci nodded and put the car in gear. "Okay. Let's see what Boyd dug up. I'll check to see if Jeff made any progress on the list I gave him, including Dr. Thomas's juvenile records. With everything going on, I had to outsource a few things."

As promised, Lilith sent Chance another text. Now wasn't the time to discuss their trust issues, but the update at least provided some peace of mind.

Lilith decided to wait in Nicci's office while her partner ran downstairs to speak with her contact in the records department. She was also waiting on Boyd to dig up the hard file for the case matching Cappalletty's tox report.

All the shady implications surrounding her uncle swirled in her head, forming an endless list of questions. *Is he part of all this? Where did he send the evidence? Another lab? Why? How did he know what happened at Phipps Bends? Did Gregor tell him? Is he working with the council or plotting against them? What is his connection to the database, if there is one?*

A knock on the door interrupted her spiraling thoughts. "Yeah, come in."

She turned in the chair, expecting to see Boyd, but Chance poked his head inside.

"What are you doing here?" Lilith didn't intend for the question to sound abrasive, but all her underlying frustrations leaked into her voice.

He hesitated in the doorway, unsure whether to stay. "Uh, sorry, *cherie*. I'm not trying to interrupt."

"No. You aren't interrupting." She surged to her feet with an apologetic smile. "I was expecting Boyd, and you surprised me. I'm sorry. Come in."

One corner of his mouth lifted slightly, and he stepped into the room with a large bag of Chinese takeout, closing the door behind him. "I thought you two might want some dinner."

When her gaze fell to the carpet, he slid the food onto the desk. "Are you okay?"

A defeated sigh rushed past her lips, and she rubbed at her face. "No. Nothing makes sense."

"I saw your message about Aaron. So, Frank has no clue where the evidence went?"

"Nope."

"You think Aaron is involved in all this?"

"All of it? No. He wouldn't torture an FBI agent for information he already knows. If he suspected Boston and Cappalletty were too close, he would have had them both killed. He's up to something, though. I just don't know what." She inhaled slowly, and tears misted her eyes. The weight of the world seemed to rest on her shoulders again.

"*Cherie…*" Chance crossed the short distance between them and wrapped his arms around her. When she snuggled into him, his tensed muscles relaxed, and he pulled her closer. "We'll figure it out…"

"We always do," she finished with far less conviction. "When is this shit going to end? When do we get our lives back?"

He searched her face and pushed a stray curl behind her ear. "I don't know, *mon amour*."

"I wish I could go back to that Goth kid's apartment eight months ago and take it back?"

"What do you mean?"

"Before I met you and Gregor at the creepy Italian joint, I was at a crime scene. I stood there, bored to tears with my pointless job, and wished for a real mystery, a purpose for my life. I might as well have been holding a fucking Monkey's Paw. I got exactly what I wished for, and now, I only wish I could make it all go away."

"All of it?"

Lilith frowned at the tentative question. "I don't know if I'm making the right decisions anymore. The life I knew guttered out, like a candle wick drowning in wax. I keep trying to relight it, to reclaim some semblance of normalcy, but perhaps it's naïve and selfish to think that's possible."

With a sigh, she stepped away and crossed the tiny room, which didn't put much distance between them. When she turned around, Chance leaned against the door and stared at the ground. Judging by his downtrodden expression, he remained fixated on one thing.

"I don't regret us, if that's what you're thinking."

He peered up with a million questions but couldn't voice one, so she stormed up and glared at him until she had his full attention.

"I love you, but please don't be a fucking idiot." He frowned and opened his mouth to say something, but she barreled ahead. "I am not going anywhere!" She emphasized each word, hoping they'd penetrate his thick skull, but wasn't encouraged by the guilt and sadness still lingering in his half-smile. "Stop acting like I've already left and give me the benefit of the fucking doubt."

"Lily—"

"No. Listen to me. You kept secrets. You lied to me. I have valid reasons for being upset, so why am I the one reassuring you? You keep saying that 'we'll figure it out…we always do,' but that applies to us too! Stop assuming it's over and fight for me. Show me why I'm right to stay."

His hazel eyes searched hers, and he swallowed hard on the lump caught in his throat, but before either of them said another word, a loud knock boomed from the other side of the door.

"Umm, Lil? Can you let me in?"

While Chance attempted to process Lilith's words, he slid away from the door and into a chair.

Nicci hustled inside with three thick folders. "Why was the door locked?"

Lilith nodded at the opposite corner, and the detective followed her line of sight to Chance, who held up his hand in a brief greeting.

"Technically, I didn't lock it. He was leaning against it."

When Nicci arched a quizzical eyebrow, he clarified, "I thought you two might be hungry. Besides, Tim refuses to let me help. I keep pacing the floor, sensing all the anger and hatred from that room, and it's driving me nuts." Toward the end of his explanation, his eyes drifted back to Lilith with an apologetic expression.

"Hey, the more the merrier, especially if you brought crab rangoons." Nicci shrugged and maneuvered around her desk before dropping the folders with a dramatic flourish. "Jeff came through for us. I've got records on Dr. Thomas, Dr. Wolfe, and everything he could dig up on Dr. Nichols."

"Have you flipped through them yet?"

"No, I was waiting to go through them with you, partner." A sudden knock interrupted Nicci as she reached for the first folder. "It's probably Boyd. Can you grab the door?"

Lilith leaned over and opened the door. "Come on in. Join the party."

Detective Chris Boyd peeked inside, his eyes roaming the room before he entered. "Hey, didn't mean to interrupt anything." He rubbed the short black hairs on the back of his head and stared down at the manila folder in his hand with an uncomfortable expression.

"Is that the case connected to Frank's tox results?" Lilith prompted him.

"Uh, yeah. Sorry." Boyd handed her the case file, nodded respectfully, and escaped the room, closing the door behind him.

"That boy's scared of his own shadow." Nicci chuckled, but it didn't lighten the tension in the room.

While flipping open the file, Lilith relaxed into the chair beside Chance. The victim's morgue photo sat on top and immediately conjured a flood of memories.

"Holy shit…" Lilith felt the blood drain from her face as she turned to the crime scene photos.

"What's wrong? Do you know the case?"

Chance gazed at her with genuine concern, but her eyes remained fixed on the familiar surroundings displayed in the pictures: the sloppily painted black walls displaying murals of pentacles and fangs; the once-grand hardwood floors covered in paint, splatters, scuff marks, gouges, water damage, and wax; the candles and fishnet clothes littering milk crates and mismatched furniture; the garbage pile infested with bugs and mice; the tower of stacked Anne Rice novels; the ever-pleasant stench of blood and early decomp…

"Know it?" Her eyes finally rose to meet his. "I worked it."

Without the rice powder makeup and globby mascara, Lilith didn't recognize him at first glance, but the gaping wound in his chest was difficult to miss.

"Who is it?" Nicci inquired, peering over the desk.

"Vincent Colmar."

Her partner recognized the name, which was no surprise. She freely admitted to looking into the cases assigned to Lilith and Alvarez before his death. Of course, Chance had no clue what she was talking about.

"My last case in New York City."

She stared at the photos, a million emotions racing through her brain. The pale corpse lay on the hardwood floor, wearing black pants two sizes too small with chains hanging off one side, glittering in the large blood pool. The black button-up shirt was torn open, and a rough stake protruded from the center of his sunken chest.

"Gregor called me after this scene to arrange the meeting about Duncan's disappearance."

"Well, that's one hell of a coincidence." Chance frowned at the folder in her hands before glancing up to study her shell-shocked expression.

After forcing herself to take a deep breath, she dug out the toxicology report and skimmed through it while the others watched anxiously. "Hmm. I think Frank's right. This case is connected to Agent Cappalletty's. As I recall, the victim showed no signs of restraints..."

"But you said the FBI agent was restrained," Chance chimed in with a confused frown.

"Yes, but that was a necessity. They wanted information. Colman was personal...Most likely revenge, and he was alive when someone pounded a stake into his chest. They must have drugged him...I remember telling Alvarez that."

Her throat tightened when she mentioned her late partner, and she swallowed hard before continuing.

"They, uh...both had a highly unique blend of ketamine, fentanyl, and an unknown organic hallucinogenic in their systems. Do you have Agent Cappalletty's tox report?"

"Yeah." Nicci dug through a few papers and passed her the report. "Frank faxed it over."

Lilith placed the two side by side and ran down the list. "The same compound, the same ratio of components. However, the levels in the liver tissue suggest they gave Cappalletty multiple doses, perhaps daily. Vincent only had one high dose, enough to knock him out, at least."

"Okay, but what's the connection?" Chance leaned back in his chair, raking his fingers through his hair.

Nicci shrugged and made a half-hearted suggestion. "Maybe he knew the FBI agent?"

"I doubt it. He was just some guy with a serious vampire fetish, including crappy dental implants. They didn't run in the same social circles. The man has no criminal record. Hell, he's a janitor at the Natural History Museum."

"Well, Dr. Wolfe spends a lot of time there, and the virus targets vampires..."

"Yeah, but he wasn't one. He merely pretended to be one. If Dr. Wolfe had access to the database, he'd know that."

"Assuming he's involved with Dr. Nichols..." Nicci pointed out the tenuous thread of logic. "We don't know who the users are."

"Aaron." Lilith tossed her uncle's name out there, her jaw clenching.

"We don't know that for sure either," Chance interjected. "He hasn't made a move."

"Yet," she added.

"Let's get back on track." Chance rose from his seat and paced the small space until he leaned against Nicci's bookshelf. Then he crossed his arms while still fixating on the floor. His lips pressed together several times, indicating he was holding things back. Understandably. He still had a lot to say about their personal conversation, but they both knew it had to wait.

After a few moments, his hazel eyes lifted to meet hers.

"Were there any suspects in the emo janitor's murder?"

Lilith scanned the pages until she stumbled across the answer. "One, a girlfriend—Veronica Salt. She had a heated argument with the victim at a local Goth club the night before he died. The police brought her in for questioning but never charged her because she had an iron-clad alibi. They found no other leads. The case just went cold."

While flipping through the photos, she suddenly went still.

"Oh my god..."

Nicci stood and peered over the desk to catch a glimpse of the picture. "She looks familiar. Where do I know her from?"

Lilith stared at the photo, pieces clicking into place. The thick black eyeliner smeared around her emerald eyes wasn't enough to disguise her. After all, the heart-shaped face and sharp silver bob were distinctive. She had known the woman seemed familiar the moment she met her, and now she knew why.

Chapter 32 - *Cohen*

T he distant thump of footsteps echoed through the darkness, rousing Cohen from an uneasy sleep. The throbbing in the back of his head only worsened when he opened his eyes. A thin line of light shone from under a door on the other side of the room, providing the only break in the inky blackness surrounding him.

His body began to wake up. Rough ropes held him in position with his arms spread wide as well as his legs, like DaVinci's Vitruvian Man. His eyes squeezed closed, and he let out a heavy sigh. *Fuck. How long have I been out, and where the hell am I?*

The footfalls continued overhead, and he concentrated on them. Cohen sensed three people, all exuding the same excitement and anticipation. *Well, that's not a good sign.*

The last things he remembered were questioning Dr. Thomas and someone attacking him from behind. *Seems Lilith's hunch was correct, but what does she want?*

Lilith or Dr. Thomas? The inner devil wasn't finished tormenting him, not that he expected anything different. *What if she sent you to Dr. Thomas, knowing the outcome? What if she knows about your little obsession and decided you weren't worth the trouble?*

No. He shut the thoughts down with adamant confidence. Lilith wouldn't purposefully place him in danger. He summoned up the memory in the medical center, with Luminita's blade slicing into his skin. The tears in Lilith's eyes had been real as she begged the woman to stop. When that didn't work, she locked onto his eyes, telling him to breathe and refusing to let him go through it alone. *Lilith would not betray me,* he thought resolutely. *It's not in her nature.*

But it is in yours, isn't it?

Cohen gritted his teeth at the intrusive thought while his captors moved down a wooden stairwell, heading for the door.

Get it together. You have more important things to focus on.

The door creaked open with a rusty groan, and light flooded the room, making him blink until a silhouette filled the doorway.

"Detective Cohen." Dr. Thomas's voice was unmistakable but they typically cheerful tone had turned sinister. "I apologize for the accommodations."

Rachel flipped a switch, flooding the room with light. She was followed by Renee and the heavyset minion from the gala. Over thirty folding chairs filled most of the space.

He peered down his body. Ropes held him against something wooden...something circular...like a giant wagon wheel. *What the hell?*

"Somehow, I doubt that. Since you have me at a distinct disadvantage, perhaps you can do me the courtesy of not lying." Cohen kept his voice flat, as if this were merely a conversation between two acquaintances over coffee.

"Hmm." Rachel's head tilted, and she considered him. "That's a reasonable request."

"In that case, why am I here?" The hostile undercurrent couldn't be helped, but the woman smiled, dimpling her cheeks.

"You'll understand that soon enough. All things in good time, Detective."

"If you intend to torture me for information, the least you could do is use my name."

"Fair point." Rachel strolled up to him at an easy pace, her warm brown eyes dancing with excitement. "By the end of this, we will know each other quite well." The smile that stretched her lips went beyond joyful into the territory of sadistic glee.

Just like Luminita. Fucking wonderful.

"I already know who you are," he replied blandly.

"Oh?" Her eyebrows rose above her bangs. "Do tell?"

"You're a zealot. I know the look. You believe what you are doing is right, for the better good, but you're blind to everything else. You're willing to do whatever it takes to achieve your goal, no matter the consequences."

This time, only one eyebrow rose, and her grin faltered. "And what is my goal?"

Cohen huffed with a grin. "It doesn't matter."

The woman's eyes narrowed, and for the first time since he met her, she appeared...angry. "You'll see my point of view eventually."

"I doubt it," he said with a sigh. "Others have tried to teach me through pain. These scars are evidence of that, so I strongly doubt you will succeed where they failed."

"We will see about that." The skin above her lips quivered, and she tried not to sneer.

Finally, a true peek behind her mask.

After an intense stare down that made him more uncomfortable than he would ever admit, she turned away. *Come on. It's not like she can do any worse than Luminita, and I survived that.*

But did you? the inner demon coaxed. *Can you honestly call these last eight months living? Fucking women and pretending they're her...avoiding her for months but running to her for help as soon as you have an excuse...tormenting yourself while envying what she has with Chance...None of that is living.*

Andrew swallowed the lump of emotions in his throat. *The demon is right, but it doesn't mean this woman will break me.*

How can she, when Lilith already has?

He gritted his teeth against the disparaging thought.

When he refocused on the room, the overweight man stood in front of him, his forehead still slick with sweat and his breath escaping in wheezy huffs. The man's emotional energy was...muted, almost nonexistent. *The porch lights are on, and nobody's home. The man is a minion in every sense of the word.*

"What is this all about, Dr. Thomas?" Cohen tried to shift his focus from the man in front of him, and a slight tremor infused his voice. The lack of emotions was unnerving and made the man unpredictable. Neither of those things made him comfortable.

"Like I said before, you'll understand soon enough." Rachel took a seat and crossed her arms over her chest with an appraising expression. "Let's start small. Jerry, two fingers of your choice."

Andrew's eyes narrowed, and he furrowed his brow until the man gripped his right ring finger in his sweaty paw. An instant of understanding flashed through Cohen's body right before the sickening crack. He bit down on the sudden flare of pain, refusing to entertain them.

Cohen drew in a slow breath through gritted teeth, and his eyes fixated on the woman in control. Jerry gripped his right middle finger next and yanked down with such force, he nearly tore off the digit. This time, bile burned up Cohen's throat, and his eyes pinched, but he kept from screaming.

It will heal...This is nothing more than a few broken bones. This is nothing compared to Luminita's blade.

"Usually"—the sharp throbbing made him draw in another quick breath—"people ask questions *before* they start breaking bones."

An eerie smile slowly stretched the woman's lips. "Andrew, there is nothing usual about us."

That sentence echoed in his head, shaking his confidence for some reason. *What if I can't take what they have planned? What if they want me to betray her? I've already proved that I'm willing to die for her, but am I capable of enduring things worse than death for her?*

He wanted to say yes more than anything, but the darkness emanating from Dr. Thomas made him hesitant.

And that is why you don't deserve her, the demon replied.

Chapter 33

Lilith stared down at the woman's familiar face. There was no mistaking it. "It's my therapist's girlfriend, Renee. You met her at the gala. She's part of Dr. Wolfe's tribe."

"Oh yeah…" Nicci's eyes widened, and she peered up at Lilith. "Crap. Do you think that's how your sessions wound up in the database?"

"I can almost guarantee it. If Dr. Price is innocent, she's in real danger." Lilith grabbed her phone and called Brittany's cell, wishing her hands would stop shaking.

Thankfully, the woman answered on the third ring. "Lilith, I haven't found anything—"

"I don't care," she interrupted, a tad more irritated than intended. "Are you at your office?"

"Yes," the woman replied tentatively.

"Are you alone?"

"My assistant, Hank, is in the waiting room, but otherwise, yes." A nervous tremble infected her voice as she spoke. "Why?"

"You are in danger. I can't explain yet, but you have to trust me. Do you know where Renee is?"

"Renee? She's on her way to pick me up for dinner."

"Call her. Tell her there's an emergency and you can't do dinner tonight. Then, get in your car and drive. I'll text you the address."

A memory of Price's office flashed through her mind, followed by their conversation at the gala. "Bring the book she gave you…the one by Joseph Campbell."

An exasperated sigh crackled over the phone. "You have to give me something to go on here."

"Renee is part of Dr. Wolfe's close-knit group, right?"

"Yes…"

"I can't prove it yet, but they're implicated in at least two murders and a possible epidemic. You aren't safe. I think she used you to spy on my therapy sessions. They're looking for something from Phipps Bend."

A lightning bolt of realization struck Lilith to the core while the words left her mouth.

"I have to go." She hung up on Dr. Price's loud rant of endless questions. "Ashcroft's blood." She mumbled the words, and her lungs constricted.

When she finally glanced up, both Chance and Nicci stared at her in confusion.

"If the virus is deadly to half-bloods, damaging to purebloods, and causes encephalopathy in the Durand, what would it do if they used Ashcroft's blood as a carrier?"

An uncomfortable gloom filled the room, like a suffocating cloud of mustard gas, as the implications sank in. Combining vampire blood with Ashcroft's rich Durand blood had given the monster insane abilities that made him damn near unstoppable. They weren't virologists, but they couldn't shake the feeling that if Wolfe's tribe succeeded, horrible things awaited them all.

Finally, Nicci broke the silence. "There's something I still don't understand. Why kill the vamp imposter? Nothing ties him to the virus."

Lilith pondered for a moment, dredging up everything she knew about Renee and the case. "Hold on…" She paused to flip through the pictures and slid one onto the desk. "I found this at the crime scene." She pointed at the picture of Vincent and Renee, torn in half.

"Still." Nicci raised an eyebrow and peered up at her partner, unconvinced. "It's a pretty dramatic way to break up with someone."

"I think it was more than a breakup…I was talking to Dr. Price at the gala about how they met. Renee approached her after she gave a lecture on the emotional costs of sexual violence."

"But if the group sent her to spy—"

"No," Lilith replied on sheer instinct, but she didn't continue until her thoughts caught up with her gut. "How would they know that she's my therapist? It's not common knowledge."

"What are you saying? I'm confused." Nicci flopped into her chair and rubbed her temples.

"What if Vincent did something to Renee? If we're right about them taking Boston's partner, their group is tight-knit and not squeamish about inflicting violence. Renee...Veronica...whatever her name is, had an alibi, but what if the group killed him *for* her?"

"And she just happened to start dating your therapist? That is one hell of a coincidence." Chance hopped into the conversation with a skeptical frown.

"I think them meeting was a coincidence, but I believe Renee figured things out before they started dating. Brittany mentioned that Renee gave her the Joseph Campbell book when they officially became an item. I think that's how she bugged Brittany's office."

"I guess we'll know for sure when she gets to my place. Speaking of which, you should text her the address."

With a curt nod, Lilith typed out directions while Nicci flipped open the folder in front of her.

"Done."

"Perhaps we should head there and see if Tim's made any progress."

"Yeah. If this group is responsible for Cappalletty's murder, they wouldn't have risked abducting a federal agent on a hunch. They must be thoroughly convinced she knew the answer."

"Um, guys?" Nicci spoke up as Lilith rose from her chair and Chance reached for the door. "I know why Dr. Thomas and Dr. Wolfe are so close."

They both peered at the open folder and sat back down.

"They're twins."

"What?" Lilith and Chance almost reacted in unison.

"Fraternal twins, of course. Rachel's maiden name is Wolfe. She's still using her ex-husband's name, which is pretty common in a profession like hers, where their name is their reputation. They became wards of the state when they were nine, which is when the foster home changed their names..."

"That's odd. Some permanent foster families will change a child's name, usually the younger ones, but group homes don't do that." Chance leaned back in the chair with his arms across his chest. As much as he hated discussing his past, he would know more about the orphan world than they did. "Was their mom a threat? Perhaps they renamed them for protection."

"No. She died, and she's the only parent on the birth certificates. Oh, hell..." Nicci stopped and shook her head. "Their birth names are Artemis and Apollo Lykaios. Their mother, Leto Lykaios, was killed in an animal attack…Well, according to the police report and coroner, at least." Doubt trickled into her voice as she continued reading.

"You don't believe them? Why?" Goosebumps flew up Lilith's arms. She already knew the answer but couldn't say it out loud?

"See for yourself." Nicci passed over a small stack of photos. "Animals don't bust through a kitchen window, run down the hall, and shred a sleeping woman's neck."

Lilith peered through the crime scene photos and stopped at the grisly bedroom scene. The victim's milky eyes stared into oblivion, and the pale translucent face was splattered with blood. However, the true horror was what remained of the woman's neck.

Fine shreds of skin and muscle clung to the bloody, ragged mess. Half of the trachea was missing along with the right side of her neck. Something sharp and thin had shredded through all the muscles, the thyroid gland, and cricoid cartilage, exposing areas of the spine.

The blood and unidentifiable bits of flesh made the wound difficult to decipher, but it appeared to result from hundreds of strikes, if not more. The thin lanes of cast-off blood splatter overlapping one another supported her theory.

"You're right. This isn't an animal attack."

"What did the kids say?" Chance peeked over at the photo but quickly redirected his gaze across the room.

After a few moments of reading, Nicci supplied the answer. "In their statements to police, both children claimed a monster murdered their mother. They used a Greek term, *Empusa*, whatever that is. Apollo, the girl…Wait. What? That must be a mistake…Nope. The woman named her daughter Apollo. Anyway, she said their mother used to clean for the monster's husband. God, this is weird."

"Did she mention a name?"

"Uh, yeah. Calista Nephus. Wait…I know that name."

Lilith nodded, her heart sinking further into the deep mire of helplessness in her chest. "The most famous vamp case we kept out of the public eye. It was before my time, but Alvarez used to talk about it a lot. He used to say, 'You never know when a seemingly normal case is gonna turn into a Calista debacle. You cross every T and dot every I, *bonita*.'"

She swiped at the tears burning her eyes as she chuckled.

"He used it as a cautionary tale. The Solasta investigator down South almost handed the whole case over to the human authorities. He didn't recognize Calista as a vampire, and the rapid blood tests didn't exist back then."

"What happened?" As soon as Lilith started her explanation, Nicci caught on, but Chance was still lost.

"Calista Pantazis, her maiden name, was a pureblood from the most prominent family in Greece. To her parent's dismay, she moved to America and married a human financier for the money. One day she just…snapped. On October twenty-second, 1993, she killed her children, her husband, and every staff member in the house—a grand total of twenty-three people."

"Holy shit." The blood drained from Chance's face, and he swallowed hard.

"The cops responded to a possible domestic violence complaint and found her carving her husband's body on the kitchen counter. They opened fire, but she killed two cops before they put her down for good."

Chance cleared his throat a few times, and his face took on a sickly pallor. "And this monster killed Kelley and Rachel's mother?"

Nicci consulted the file, flipping through the pages until she froze. "I think the kids were telling the truth."

"What makes you so sure?" Lilith studied her partner's horrified face until Nicci finally met her eyes.

"Leto was murdered in Spring Grove, Pennsylvania, on October twenty-first, 1993, the night before Calista slaughtered her family."

"Lily, you said Calista carved up her husband, but how did she…" Chance paused, struggling with the context. "How did she kill the kids and the staff?"

"A single slice to the carotid. All her fury went into…dismantling her husband."

"And Leto, it seems." Chance nodded toward the bloody photo in Lilith's hands.

"Huh. You're right. Sounds like Mr. Nephus was dipping his pen in the company ink, so to speak."

"And only the mother's name was on the birth certificate. I bet Calista's husband was the father."

"Well, I guess we have a motive, although I still don't see the connection to Dr. Nichols." Lilith sighed heavily and leaned her head back to stare at the stained drop ceiling.

"I may be able to help there. I asked Jeff to dig up everything he could on Dr. Frederick Nichols and any connections to Rachel and Kelley." Nicci pulled the third file from the pile and cracked it open. "He worked as a professor of pathology with a focus on hematological abnormalities and bloodborne viruses."

"Explains why my uncle recruited him."

"Yeah, well. Dr. Thomas was a student and T.A. for him…" Nicci scanned farther down the page, stopped, and dug through the papers.

Lilith sat up and peered over the desk. Her partner laid out several photos and news clippings. One headline caught her attention first, and she skimmed the first line.

"*Local woman found dead. Juliette Nichols, daughter of Professor Frederick Nichols, was brutally murdered and dumped outside her father's research facility on the University of Tennessee campus.*"

"This is awful, but—" Lilith started, but Nicci interrupted her.

"Look at the picture from the funeral." She pointed to an image taken at the gravesite. Rachel and Kelley flanked the victim's distraught father. Then Lilith's eyes roamed the other photos—scenes from Juliette's life— and Rachel appeared in all the ones after high school.

"They were best friends in college and stayed close."

"Did the police ever solve her murder?" Chance stood and leaned over the desk, studying the smiling faces while Nicci continued flipping through the info from Jeff.

"Doesn't look like it."

"Any suspects or crime scene photos?"

"No. We'd have to get those directly from the Knoxville PD. Too bad Cohen's missing."

"He'd actually be useful for once." As soon as he muttered the comment, his eyes darted to Lilith, who frowned. "Sorry."

"Anyway…" Lilith focused on the newspaper clippings. "You think there are any details in these stories?"

Nicci shrugged. "Probably all unreliable fluff. I'll have Boyd call and ask for a copy of the official police report."

"This one has a quote from the lead detective…Detective Whitmore." Chance chuckled and shook his head. "Huh, small world. He described the crime as a torture execution and suspected mob or drug involvement. Do you think it's connected to the database?"

"Perhaps…Two years after his daughter dies, Rachel and Dr. Nichols posed with champagne for their first successful trial of what we assume is the virus." Lilith sank back into her chair, theories racing through her head.

"So, you think his daughter's murder drove him to create the virus?" As Chance spoke, he settled into the chair beside her.

"I mean, the timeline fits…"

"But the virus targets vampires…and the Durand, it seems…" His words trailed off, as if waiting to see if she'd come to the same conclusion.

"If we're right, Dr. Nichols had reason to believe vampires killed his daughter."

"Yeah, but why?" Nicci tossed the file on the desk in frustration. "He worked with Duncan for over a decade before her death. Why would we torture and murder his daughter?"

"Leverage, domination, ensuring his silence by inducing fear. It sounds to me like someone was trying to keep him quiet."

Lilith rubbed her face and groaned. "This is all wild speculation built on tenuous theories. I've seen dust-bunnies with more substance, and we have no way to confirm any of it. We need are facts. We need Boston to—"

Nicci's phone vibrated loudly on the desk, followed by the *Police Academy* theme erupting from Lilith's pocket. *Well, that's not good.*

As they both reached for their phones, someone knocked on the door.

Both Lilith and Chance turned in their chairs as Detective Boyd peeked his head in again.

"Uh, Detective DeLuca?" Although the man was usually shy, his voice sounded more tentative than usual, which didn't bode well. "I know you're busy with a case, but—"

"What is it, Chris?"

"I thought I'd warn you about the 187 call that just came in. It's in your building."

A frown wrinkled the woman's youthful face, and she rose from her seat. "Who's the vic?"

"Unidentified white male found in the hall on the fifth floor, and they're reporting forced entry into a few apartments."

Chapter 34

"I'm going with you," Chance insisted, surging to his feet.

Nicci grabbed her keys but paused, holstering her gun, to stare at him. Then she turned to Lilith.

"Do you want to handle this or should I?"

"Nicci, can you give us a minute?" As Lilith spoke, Chance's brow furrowed.

"If you aren't downstairs in five minutes, I'm leaving without you." The woman's typically jubilant nature turned stern, and she marched out of the office, slamming the door.

"I'm going—"

This time, Lilith interrupted him with a firm, "No."

The man's frown deepened, and his jaw clenched, but she continued before he said anything.

"I understand why you want to be there, but you can't go."

"You took me to Cassie's scene," he countered.

"If Ray is the victim, I can't have you on-site. You'll react, like anyone in your situation would, which will invite a slew of inconvenient and dangerous questions. I didn't know Ray as well. I can mask my feelings and focus on the case. We need to know who is behind this—Rachel and Kelley's cult, or Aaron."

His gaze fell to the carpet, and he released a drawn-out sigh.

"I'll be surrounded by cops, and I'll update you when I know something. I can't let you get dragged in for questioning or held as a suspect. Things didn't turn out so well last time."

"I remember." Chance muttered the words and sighed again before he met her eyes. "I'll check in with Tim. You better go, or Nicci will leave you here."

Jenny Allen

"Thanks." After placing a quick kiss on his cheek, she raced out of the room, feeling guilty.

Everything between them felt off, like they'd fallen out of sync, but she didn't have time to fix it now, especially with this new development and Cohen missing.

She prayed the vic wasn't Ray, but her gut burned with certainty. Either the Grecian cult had tracked Nicci down because of the database, or Aaron made a drastic move. The last option scared her more for a multitude of reasons.

If her uncle was involved with the database off the record, it meant he had bypassed the elders, and it opened the possibility of his involvement with Rachel and Kelley's radical agenda. The only thing she couldn't understand was why.

Why align himself with humans who wanted to eradicate vampires? Aaron was an elitist snob and an asshole, but he had never showed signs of an anti-vamp agenda, and self-loathing didn't exist in his vocabulary.

As soon as she stepped outside, Nicci flashed her headlights and honked the horn, interrupting Lilith's thoughts. She picked up the pace, jogged over to the red Fiat, and crawled into the cramped passenger seat. The second the door closed, her partner put the car in drive and sped off.

"I almost left you," Nicci grumbled, swerving around a taxi. "Did you set the boy straight?"

"Yes. I explained why he can't be at the scene. He's going to check in with Tim instead."

"Good. Your ex needs to start talking. At this point, I don't care what they do to him if he gives us a lead."

Lilith frowned and gazed at her partner. The glow from the instrument panel made her stern expression more severe. "Uh, Nicci? This doesn't sound like you. I mean, usually you're the chipper voice of reason."

The woman's jaw clenched, her mouth set in a firm line. "An FBI agent was mutilated, Cohen is missing, Ray is dead, my girlfriend would have died if she was ever on time, and someone broke into my home. We need answers!"

"I agree, I just…"

A slow sigh escaped Nicci's lips, and her hands tightened around the steering wheel. "I'm angry. I don't like people making me look stupid. Dr. Thomas and Dr. Wolfe played us. They knew who we all were and chose to toy with us. Plus, I'm the one who lectured *you* for not reporting things to

Aaron. You were right not to trust him. We may not understand the extent yet, but he's involved in some shady, underhanded shit."

"I understand, and I'm sorry for dragging you into all this."

"No," her partner snapped as they pulled up to a red light. Once the vehicle stopped, she locked eyes with Lilith. "I'm the one who dragged you into this. I brought you the virus case while you were on paid leave. I pushed for your therapist to reinstate you early. I should be the one apologizing."

"We are partners, and you needed help. I'm glad you came to me. I mean, could you imagine Boyd investigating all this? Things could have been so much worse."

"It's still early," she muttered quietly, sharply turning a corner.

Flashing lights and uniformed officers greeted them when they arrived. Nicci led the way through the milling crowd while holding up her badge. She stormed through the lobby, past the doorman typing feverishly on his phone—sharing everything on Facebook, most likely—and marched over to a small cluster of cops guarding the elevator.

"Evening, Detective." One of them tipped his hat in an oddly ancient gesture before pressing the up button.

"Thanks." After a curt nod, her gaze bounced around the room, her palm tapping her thigh.

Lilith didn't need Cohen's emotion-detecting blood to pick up on her partner's anxiety.

A loud ding echoed through the lobby. The doors opened, and Nicci quickly hopped inside, repeatedly pressing the fifth-floor button. Lilith managed to slip inside before the doors closed.

The level of tension permeating the confined space became stifling in seconds. Nicci bounced on the balls of her feet, and her head nodded in time with the elevator music, a nervous tick that made her long ponytail bounce.

Lilith chose to remain silent, unwilling to give her partner false hope by saying everything would be okay. In her gut, she already knew things were only going to get worse.

The elevator doors opened to a chaotic scene—camera flashes, uniformed officers running yellow tape, forensic techs dusting for prints, detectives from Robbery interviewing residents in pajamas, and techs running paper and plastic bags to their designated boxes. The flurry of activity made Lilith's already elevated pulse race until blood pounded in her ears.

"Okay. You find the body and ID it. I'll talk to the other detectives and find out what they know. We'll meet at my place in twenty minutes." The petite Italian didn't wait for confirmation. She just disappeared into the crowd.

After a deep breath, Lilith ventured into the fray. She stood on tiptoe to peer down both ends of the hall and spotted more yellow tape to the right. Being five foot nine had some advantages.

She worked her way down the corridor, dodging techs, cops, and sleepy residents. But Lilith realized her forensic kit was still in Chance's truck. If she hadn't been so distracted, she could have grabbed it before they all left the station. Although, she wasn't here in an official capacity anyway, so it was probably for the best.

The sea of people finally parted, and she glimpsed a covered body at the end of the hall. The sheet meant a forensic team had already taken pictures and gathered any obvious evidence.

I guess I don't need my kit...

A cop with broad shoulders bumped into her hard, and she stumbled into the wall.

"Uh, sorry, ma'am." The man uttered the apology without turning to her and hurried toward the elevators.

Rude.

Lilith shook her head, slid past two plain-clothes detectives, and stepped up to the yellow tape. A young policeman with strawberry blond hair stood at attention on the other side of the body, near an exit door.

"Excuse me? Officer? Are you in charge of the murder scene?"

A frown furrowed his smooth forehead, and he gave a curt nod but didn't step forward. He probably thought she was another nosy resident, but an odd nervousness pulled at his features. Perhaps this was his first scene.

"I'm Forensic Consultant Lilith Adams with Solasta Labs." When she pulled out her ID, the cop reluctantly strolled over to inspect it.

"A CSI already examined the body. We're waiting on the coroner."

"I understand, but the precinct asked me to give it a cursory glance. Can I take a look at the body? Then you can point me toward the CSI."

The young man nodded again, but his face remained stern as he stepped back. When she ducked under the yellow tape, she noticed his hand resting on his gun holster. The rambunctious scene might be enough to put a newbie on edge, but hopefully, he wasn't trigger happy.

Lilith approached the white sheet, and the cop retreated to his corner near the stairwell, his hand still resting on his gun. *Come on. Don't let him rattle you.*

She tore her gaze away from the officer and peered down at the rust-colored stain on the fabric. *Please don't be Ray.* She mentally recited the prayer several times before squatting, grabbing the sheet's corner, and peeling it back. The congealed blood from the exit wound clung to the white cloth, so she lifted it higher until the face was visible.

The fist-sized hole had left splatters of brain, bone, and blood on the victim's face, ranging from a fine mist to sticky clumps. It also obliterated a sizeable amount of forehead and hairline but left the prominent facial features intact.

A soft sigh escaped her lips, and tears misted her eyes as she stared at Ray Valinski's pale face. She might not have known him as well as Tim, but the man had guarded her father for over twenty years. He deserved better.

Dread churned in her belly. She lowered the sheet and wiped her eyes. *A single shot to the base of the skull with an upward trajectory—execution style if Ray was standing and the perp was shorter than him. It's clean, efficient, impersonal, professional.*

"Thank you, Officer." Lilith stood, but her eyes remained locked on the ghostly sheet. When her gaze drifted up to the young cop, he appeared more relaxed. "Where can I find the CSI?"

The man thrust his cleft chin toward the stairwell behind him. "He's logging evidence in there." He stepped to the side and held the door open for her.

"Thanks again." She flashed a smile and ducked through the door.

Detective Vincent Peters sat on the landing with a notepad, a box, and various bags scattered around him. She peered around the space but saw no one else.

"Hey, Vince. I was told the CSI that investigated the body was in here."

The man glanced up with dark bags under his eyes and a cigarette hanging from his lip.

"He ran down to the lobby to take a leak. I'm running the homicide, so I'm giving him a hand with the evidence."

Completely against protocol—breaking the chain of custody, not that I'm surprised. Peters isn't known for clean work.

"What are you doing here?"

"Nicci lives on this floor. We came to check her apartment and see if we could help. Can you tell me anything about the victim?"

"Phillip gave me a rundown. Single gunshot, point-blank to the base of the skull. Gunpowder burns and residue in the hair to confirm. No other obvious marks. Seems like one of two scenarios. Either someone snuck up on him and *bam*, or he knew his attacker and trusted them enough to turn his back on them."

His eyes narrowed, and he peered up at her again, taking a long drag off his cigarette. "Did you know him?"

Whenever the police asked her questions, she stuck as close to the truth as possible, especially with colleagues.

"Not well. He worked for my father before he passed—security detail."

"Does he live in the building?"

Lilith frowned at his suddenly inquisitive mood. The man was five years from retirement and only cared about clearing cases, regardless of the means. "I don't think so, but like I said…I didn't know him very well."

"Hmm." Vince grunted and squashed his cigarette on the concrete step. "Seems like a mob hit. Was your dad in the mob?"

She quirked an incredulous eyebrow at his question. "Uh, no."

"Any idea why he was here? Visiting Nicci perhaps?"

"As far as I know, Nicci and Ray never met. He took security contracts all over the country after my dad died. I heard he was in town, but that's the extent of my knowledge."

"The guy must have had friends…"

"Look, Vince. If you have more questions, we'll have to do it some other time. I need to check on Detective DeLuca."

The man's bloodshot eyes narrowed again, and he dug in his pocket for another smoke. "I'm not trying to ruffle feathers. You're the first lead I have on this thing. No one else in the building recognized him so far. I don't suppose you could get me a list of his former coworkers?"

"I'll see what I can do." Lilith flashed a tight smile while alarms went off in her head. *I should have kept my damn mouth shut. Shit.*

"I appreciate it." After lighting another Camel, he grabbed his pen and jotted down the number of the next evidence bag.

She took that as permission to leave and quickly slipped back into the hall. This time, she headed straight for Nicci's apartment. It had been less than twenty minutes, but the conversation with Peters spooked her. Any preliminary search would show Ray worked for her dad. The information would have come out eventually. Still, she wished she hadn't given him a head start.

Another uniformed cop stood outside Nicci's splintered front door—definitely forced entry.

"CSI Adams. I'm looking for Detective DeLuca."

The clean-cut man nodded toward the apartment but remained silent with his arms crossed over his chest.

Of course, she didn't interact with these guys routinely, even before her suspension. The cops typically cleared a scene, called it in, and posted one officer to stand guard until she arrived. Maybe having the chick who inspected mutilated remains for Major Crimes show up had made them uneasy.

Lilith ducked under the tape and stepped into the familiar living room. The couch and chairs were tipped on their sides, the cushions slashed. Stuffing littered the hardwoods alongside the shattered remnants of knickknacks and a crystal vase. The built-in shelves were bare, but a chaotic pile of books and frames was scattered on the floor before them.

She moved past the kitchen, where the cabinet doors hung loose on their hinges and over-turned drawers sat on top of silverware, utensils, and random junk. The perps even tore apart her fridge and stove.

"Nicci? You in here?"

"Office." The voice sounded muffled and strained.

Lilith hurried down the hall with a hundred scenarios whizzing through her head. "Nicci? Are you okay?"

"Yeah…" A loud thud preceded a string of cusswords.

As Lilith burst into the room, Nicci crawled out from under her desk, rubbing the back of her head.

"What are you doing under there?"

"Grabbing my secret stash. Thank fucking god they didn't find it." The petite woman dragged out a moderate-sized safe, still intact. "I stowed Nichols's computer in here before I left. Call it a gut feeling, but it felt too dangerous to keep out in the open."

Lilith gazed around the wrecked office—photos and frames torn off the walls, holes punched in the dry wall, monitors smashed, computers beaten into twisted lumps of metal, CDs snapped, desk splintered, drawers ripped apart.

"How did they miss your safe?"

A sly grin curled the detective's lips. "I keep it inside the wall behind a fake air return below the desk." After she punched in a few numbers, the safe popped open, and Nicci pulled out passports, money, birth certificates, two laptops, and a huge file stuffed with papers. "Thank you, Dexter."

"Who?"

"I got the idea for my safe from watching that serial killer show *Dexter*. I mean, he used an air conditioner, but still..."

"What is all that stuff?"

"Important papers, emergency cash, Nichols's laptop, the backup laptop with all my decryption programs, and the file Cohen gave you at Gregor's funeral...You know...all the info the Durand had on us. I've been slowly combing through it."

"Anything interesting?" Lilith bent down and grabbed the bundle of papers.

"I've only scratched the surface, but did you know Aaron still owns property outside of Bucharest?"

"Not surprising. He moved there when he parted ways with Gregor and Duncan almost seven centuries ago. All I know about his past is that he was a boyar—nobleman—who sent serfs to fight the Turks and Vlad the Impaler. At the last family reunion, his son, Michael, bragged for an hour about his dad battling the supposed *father of vampires*. Personally, I think Mike read way too much Bram Stoker."

Nicci chuckled and stuffed everything into a backpack. "Sounds like a real piece of work. Does he live in L.A. too?"

Lilith nodded and handed her partner the Durand file. "Yeah, he's never far from his dad. They're practically attached at the hip..." She paused as the thought sunk in. "Now that I think of it...it's odd. Aaron's been here for at least two days. I'm surprised Michael isn't with him."

"Maybe he is. He's probably reading *Dracula* in a hotel somewhere." Nicci shrugged and hoisted the backpack over her shoulder. "I need to grab some clothes and necessities before we head out. Can I crash with you?"

"No need to ask. Pack some stuff, and we'll head back to Chance's place. It's safer than my apartment."

"Thanks, partner. Hey, what's your lease like? I'm officially looking for a new apartment, and you're moving in with Chance, so..." Her mouth curved into an impish grin when Lilith glared at her.

"Just get your stuff."

"Sure thing. Back in a sec." Nicci bounced out of the room with her ponytail swinging back and forth. Now that her valuables were secure, she seemed to have shed her crippling anxiety and irritability.

While waiting, Lilith picked through the shattered frames and pulled the pictures from Nicci's trophy wall out of the wreckage, but her mind remained fixated on her cousin Michael. What she had relayed to Nicci was the sum of her knowledge. Could he be here in Manhattan? And if he was, why stay hidden? He hadn't had any problem showing up at her father's funeral last year.

Aaron never got his hands dirty. Just like the war against the Turks, he sent others to fight his battles. Could he have sent Michael to ransack Nicci's apartment? He never seemed like much of a fighter, and she didn't know if Ray ever met him before the funeral. Could he have taken Ray out? She doubted it.

Wolfe's cult had proven their capabilities when they kidnapped an FBI agent without a trace. Of course, her uncle could have hired a professional. Either party was capable of this.

They needed answers, and the only card she had was Agent Boston. If he could lead them to the cult—and hopefully, Cohen—she could find out who killed Ray. Perhaps she could prove once and for all if Aaron was trustworthy or not.

The universe must truly hate me. Everything hinges on my abusive, piece-of-shit ex who wants nothing more than my total destruction.

With an exasperated sigh, she dug out her phone and sent Chance a text: *"Any luck?"*

When Nicci strolled back into the room a few minutes later, a ding notified Lilith of a new text.

"Shit. We should get going. Tim's out of civil options. He sent Chance upstairs for bleach."

Nicci raised one eyebrow and smiled. "So, you're saying I should drive slow?"

Lilith rubbed the bridge of her nose with a heavy sigh. "No. We need answers from the bastard, but—"

"You don't think the ends justify the means?" Nicci interrupted, tossing her a duffle with a little too much force.

"You do?" Lilith slung the bag over her shoulder and stared down her partner.

The woman shrugged and fearlessly met her stare. "Do I think it's wrong to do what is absolutely necessary to a woman-beater in order to save Cohen and the rest of us? No."

When Lilith didn't respond, she continued.

"That man brutalized you and countless others. He put you in the fucking hospital. His *only* value is the information he has. I don't generally condone torture, but in this case, I thoroughly encourage it. The real question is, why are you defending him?"

"I'm not." Lilith bristled at the accusation, but Nicci raised both her eyebrows and huffed, making her disbelief crystal clear. "David isn't my concern. Tim and Chance are…Crossing those lines take a toll, and neither of them should pay that price. They deserve better."

"Well, shit." Nicci grinned with renewed appreciation for her partner. "You got me there. Let's get moving then."

Chapter 35

David Boston glared up at Timothy with one bloodshot eye. The other was swollen shut, a mass of purple and red oozing droplets of blood.

"I'm not telling you shit!" He spat a blood-streaked blob on the concrete floor and bared his teeth.

For a moment, Tim stood perfectly still, locking eyes with the beast. Then he reared back and slugged the man's jaw hard enough to split his lip.

Boston's smile only widened as he rocked back and forth, sending a rivulet of blood trickling down his chin. "Hit me all you want. I'm not talking."

Tim's jaw clenched. The tension ran across his shoulders and down his arms. He slammed his fist into the carpeted wall and growled in frustration. The man kneeling on the concrete laughed, which turned into a coughing fit, and more blood splattered the floor.

Without a backward glance, Tim stormed out of the room, slammed the door, locked it, and almost ran over Chance.

"Shit. Sorry." Tim stepped to the side and rubbed both hands through his dark blond curls.

"Are you okay, *mon ami?*" Chance set the bottle of bleach by the door and peered at his friend.

A heaving sigh preceded the man's answer. "I swear to God, the man thrives on misery and pain, even his own. Every time I slug him, he becomes less cooperative. Shit!"

"Do you want me to—"

"*No!*" Tim interrupted, whirling around to glare at Chance. "*You* are not to go in there under any circumstances! The asshole will goad you into killing him. How many times do we need to go over this?"

Chance shook his head and exhaled slowly. "What am I supposed to do? You aren't getting anywhere with him, and Lilith doesn't want my help. I can't stand around and do nothing!"

"Yes, you fucking can. We all need one thing from you right now—for you to get your head straight. I don't care how you do it—yoga, Pilates, meditation, an intense workout, comfort movies…whatever it takes. Nothing in that room will help you!"

Chance watched helplessly as Tim turned his back on him, snatched the bottle of bleach, and ventured back into the interrogation room. For a moment, David and Chance locked eyes through the crack in the door, and malice burned there brighter than ever.

Tim is right. Even if I controlled my temper, the man is less likely to talk to me because he can't let go of his hatred.

"Um, excuse me?" A timid voice with a terrified tremble echoed through the vacant area, and Chance whirled toward the door with his hand on his gun.

"Mr. Deveraux?" The confused woman stepped forward when she recognized him. "Oh, thank goodness! I thought Lilith sent me the wrong address."

The woman's strawberry blond hair was pulled into a frazzled bun, and she had traded her business suit for a blue T-shirt featuring a floral triple moon and a pair of yoga pants, but he still recognized her as Lilith's therapist.

"Dr. Price." Chance mentally shook off his dismal thoughts and smiled warmly. "I'll escort you upstairs. I promise, it's a lot nicer on the second floor."

The doctor's gaze darted around the dark and dingy warehouse. She followed him to the freight elevator while clutching her oversized purse, but when they arrived at the metal beast, she came to a halt.

"Is that thing safe?"

When Chance lifted the wooden gate, the entire thing groaned. "It makes a lot of noise, but it's perfectly safe." He continued to hold the gate open while the skittish woman frowned. "I use it every day."

After a deep inhale, the doc ventured into the elevator, holding her hands close to her chest and peering around as if the thing could bite her at any second.

Chance lowered the gate and jabbed the up button. The thing lurched, as it usually did, and Dr. Price latched onto the railing, like a cat afraid of falling.

When they arrived at the second floor, her eyes lit with wonder. It still felt weird letting people into his home. For years, he had kept this place private, except for Tim and Ray.

"Lilith wore the same shocked expression when she saw this place for the first time." He smiled softly, opened the gate, and led her to a barstool in the kitchen.

"I imagine! It is quite a hidden gem." Brittney gazed at the warm hardwoods, serene black and white photos, the spiral staircase leading to the loft, and the plush leather couches. "A lot like you, I suppose."

Chance paused with a hand on the fridge and glanced back at her. "I'm sorry. What?"

"This place." Brittney settled onto the seat and smiled, clearly more comfortable than she'd been in the elevator or downstairs. "From what Lilith told me, you're a bit of a hidden gem yourself."

At first, a warmth flushed his cheeks, but then the day's events sank in, and the glow dulled. He tried to shove the uncomfortable thoughts away and peered into the fridge. "I have Miller Lite, water, apple juice…"

"Anything stronger?"

He closed the fridge with a smile, reached into an overhead cabinet, and placed a bottle of Jameson in front of her.

"Perfect."

He set two shot glasses on the counter and cracked open the bottle while the doc studied him. "Did you bring the book Lilith asked about?"

"Oh, yes." After opening her huge bag, she pulled out a hardcover book and placed it on the table. "I didn't open it. I…uh…"

The woman froze, her gaze locked on the black and white cover.

"Are you all right?" He slid the shot across the counter.

Tears welled in the woman's eyes and her hands trembled. "I didn't have the heart to find out if Lilith's right."

"May I?"

Dr. Price quickly downed the shot and nodded but couldn't tear her gaze away from the item in question.

Chance opened the book near the midway point. The woman breathed a sigh of relief until he bent the covers back to loosen the glue, peered down the spine, and stopped.

"What? Do you see something?" Brittney stood, her anxiety reaching a fevered pitch.

Chance pinched a small black object and pulled, the doc watching in horror. When he set the mic on the countertop, Brittney's hands flew up to cover her mouth, and tears flowed down her cheeks.

"Oh my god…"

"I'm sorry. I know this isn't what you wanted to see."

"No…but…I thought we were happy. I thought she loved me."

Chance poured another shot and slid it toward her. "At least you know the truth."

"But I'm supposed to see past shit like that. I'm a fucking psychiatrist."

"Sometimes people blindside you. It doesn't mean you're bad at your job. It means you tried…You put yourself out there, made yourself vulnerable for someone you trusted. It happens to everyone."

Brittney knocked back the whiskey between laughing sobs. "It's not supposed to happen to me…Not anymore."

Chance poured himself a generous shot, drained the glass, and forced a smile. The last thing he wanted to do was discuss relationship problems with his girlfriend's therapist, especially when his own relationship was on shaky ground.

"I think everyone says that at some point in their lives. Well, there are blankets on the couch if you need to rest. The bathroom is next to the staircase, and the TV remote is on the coffee table."

"Thank you for your hospitality." Brittney wiped at her cheeks and flashed a teary smile. "And thank you for talking with me. You're a good man. I understand what Lilith sees in you."

"Thanks, Doc." His gaze fell to the floor, and the arguments flashed through his brain again. "I should…get back downstairs. Make yourself at home."

The odd conversation rattled around in his head as the elevator reached the first floor. After the metal beast ground to a halt, he heard voices in a heated discussion but didn't see anyone inside the warehouse.

He drew his gun, keeping it loose at his side, eased the gate up, and snuck over to the open bay door. Without the echo effect from the walls, the voices became recognizable, so he holstered his weapon and strode around the corner.

"Was it Ray?"

Lilith spun on her heel with a startled expression that quickly softened. When her gaze fell to the ground, he glanced over at Tim, who rubbed at his tear-streaked cheeks, and realized the answer. Before he could say anything, however, Tim growled in frustration.

"Someone executed him! The cops think the attacker either surprised him or was someone he knew. The guy was highly trained, one of the best in his field. What the fuck is going on?" The man paced back and forth with anger and frustration bubbling under the surface.

Chance peered over at Lilith, who nodded, verifying Tim's account. "Aaron?"

"Possibly…If we can get Boston to talk, perhaps we can figure that out."

"I told you! I beat the shit out of the guy, and he isn't talking. He screams like a girl, but everything makes him more uncooperative. I could go Guantanamo on him, but honestly…I don't think it'll work. The guy doesn't care what happens to him. He only cares about taking you down."

Lilith stared off toward the interrogation room, and a thought occurred to her. "I should talk to him."

"No!" Tim shouted. Then he frowned at Chance, who remained oddly silent.

Lilith took her gun from her holster and handed it to Nicci. "I'm only going to talk. It can't hurt."

"What makes you think he'll talk to you?" When Chance stepped in front of her, barely restrained fear rolled off him in waves.

"He doesn't care about taking me down…not really. He wants the truth from me and justice for Cassie. That's what I need to offer him."

"The truth?" The skin around his eyes tightened, and he stared at her. He was trying to be understanding, trying to work with her and not fly off the handle.

Although she appreciated the effort, his grip was paper-thin.

"A version of it he can accept."

For a moment, he stood still, each muscle tensing. He didn't want her going in that room. That much was obvious. "You're going to do this regardless of what I have to say, aren't you?"

"I have to try. It's my fault we're in this mess."

Although his jaw clenched tight, he nodded. "Then I'm standing guard outside, in case he tries anything."

Lilith's gut reaction to the ultimatum was to say no. However, the conversation with Tim made her think twice. Asking Chance to wait upstairs while she had a one-on-one conversation with her abusive ex was probably pushing things too far, and she needed to gain his trust somehow.

While she tried to formulate an answer, Nicci patted Tim's broad shoulder. "Come on, big fella. You need a break, and I need a drink. Let's raid his liquor cabinet. I can't reach it. Only a six-foot-three recluse keeps his Jameson in the top cabinet."

Once the two disappeared into the elevator, Lilith found her voice again. "Fine. You can stand outside, and I'll leave the door cracked, but please…do not interfere. I know you're concerned, and I appreciate it, but this is something I have to do on my own."

"You have my word, *cherie*."

After a deep sigh, she started toward the holding room. She couldn't tell if her hands were shaking because she was about to play nice with her ex or because Chance once again didn't trust her to handle this alone. Of course, the man was an emotional litmus test. He could sense her apprehension and uncertainty, so why was she surprised that he insisted on being her backup?

When they reached the door, she stopped. "I can do this." Although she wanted to reassure him, she needed to hear the words as much as he did. Maybe he was right. Maybe she needed him there after all.

"I know, Lily. I'll be right here."

After exhaling slowly, she slipped inside the interrogation room, closing the door until only a sliver of Chance remained.

For a moment, she stared at the carpeted door, taking small steady breaths, preparing herself. Standing up to Boston was one thing. Giving the bastard what he wanted was something else entirely. *You can do this.*

She turned to face her enemy and found him kneeling in the middle of the room, staring at the floor. Tim had done a number on him, but still not as bad as he had beat her that last time. The monster deserved violence—Nicci was right about that—but it wasn't what motivated him to cooperate.

"David."

As soon as she spoke, his head snapped up. One bloodshot eye focused intently on her, and his muscles clenched.

"I'm not here to hurt you."

"I'm not talking to you either." The beaten man spat on the concrete near her feet with a snarl of disgust.

"This isn't about me…or you. This is about Cassie."

Boston surged to his feet and screamed inches from her face. "Don't speak her fucking name!"

Lilith remained calm, staring him down like she would a petulant child. "We don't have time for games. I'm here to give you what you want."

He took a step back, and his swollen face contorted into a frown. "What do you mean?"

"The truth. That is what started all this, isn't it?"

The man recoiled and openly stared at her for a long moment before shaking his head. "Yeah, right." A huff escaped his mouth, and he turned away, shuffling over to the opposite corner.

"I lost my partner last year. Detective Felipe Alvarez…"

"I read the report."

"Shut up and listen. I ate dinner at his house every Friday night, had coffee with his wife, Gloria, every Sunday morning, babysat his three daughters when they went out of town. Felipe was more than my partner. He was family." Tears misted her eyes as the memories flooded her mind.

After clearing her throat, she continued.

"My father sent me to Tennessee to find my Uncle Duncan."

Her words finally caught his attention, and he turned back toward her as she spoke.

"We are a very close-knit, private family, and my Uncle Duncan worked on top-secret medical research. Dad didn't want the police involved, so he sent me and his head of security. When I got to Knoxville, I found my cousin Miriah Sanders tortured, murdered, and displayed on her desk, like a Jack the Ripper victim. I've worked with Major Crimes for six years and never saw anything like it before."

As she continued to speak, his hostility melted away until he merely listened. It gave her hope she could make him see reason.

"The killer's name was Ashcroft Orrick, an old enemy from my father and uncle's past. He turned my cousin Spencer against the family, and together, they kidnapped my uncle, tortured his daughter in front of him for over thirty-six hours, and slaughtered her husband, Malachi. When they tried to kill me—and nearly succeeded—Felipe and my father flew down to Knoxville."

Jenny Allen

"Why was Ashcroft's name left out of the report? Why blame everything on terrorists?"

"My friend Detective Cohen made the call. He knew someone with a lot of power bought the Phipps Bend property…Someone was bankrolling Ashcroft, but we didn't know who. He felt it was best to keep things… anonymous."

The man's eyes narrowed for a moment while he thought over her answer. "Okay. I got the same impression when Gorman brought us the property records. So, what really happened in the basement?"

"Ashcroft had my father, Alvarez, and Duncan. Cohen was missing, and my…backup was seriously wounded. I was on my own. I went down there to save them and nearly got caught. My partner saved me by distracting the psycho, but he paid with his life. The monster slit his throat, and all I could do was watch."

Once again, she paused, tears threatening to spill. *Come on. Bring it home.*

"The worst part was not seeing Ashcroft die. I never had the chance to avenge Felipe. That is what I'm offering you. I know who killed your partner. I just need your help to find them."

"Who?" The abrupt skepticism returned, and he took a step closer.

"I'm going to be one hundred percent honest with you, David. The virologist you consulted, Dr. Rachel Thomas, and her twin brother, Dr. Kelley Wolfe, tortured and killed Cassandra."

His frown deepened, but he didn't interrupt, so she continued.

"They created a virus I've been tracking. There's only been a few cases so far, but at least one victim died from the infection. Something from Phipps Bend interests them. I don't know if it's real or if they're delusional, but they think it will help spread their virus."

"Why?"

"Why do they think something from there—"

"No. Why create a virus?"

"Their mother was old-school Greek. She named them after gods and filled their heads with insane stories of monsters and demons. Their father's jealous wife murdered their mother. The evidence from Cassie's remains points to an entire cult of devout worshippers. She was their manifesto, heralding their plan to make the world suffer, like they did when they lost their mother."

He sank to the floor while processing all the information. Then he peered up at her, and for the first time in nearly a decade, no malice lingered in his face. "How do you know all this?"

After a deep breath, Lilith assembled random bits of information into a concept he could understand. It might not be the complete truth but contained a condensed version.

"We stumbled across a computer file they all share. Inside, we found info on the virus—which mimics the parvovirus B19—as well as info on their cult and transcripts of my therapy sessions. They were spying on me to get more information about Phipps Bend."

"And you're sure they took Cassie?"

"I swear on my life."

He stared at her for a long silent moment, studying her with his one good eye before he spoke again. "What are you proposing?"

"Work *with* us. Tell us where the biological evidence from Phipps Bend was sent, and you can confront her killers face-to-face, something I never got the chance to do."

"Why should I trust you?" The man stared at her without hatred or even suspicion. He merely wanted a reason.

"Because without me, you'll never find them. You have a name, but if you'd been able to find the place, you'd have made a move months ago. You and Cassie kept the name under wraps, didn't you?"

The man's gaze fell to the floor, providing the answer.

"If you want the opportunity to confront her killers, you have no choice but to trust me. Lucky for you, I'm telling the truth. Too many lives hang in the balance to play games or hold grudges."

Once again, he studied her in silence for a long time, weighing his limited options. "If you double-cross me…"

"David, I won't. My only concern is finding these psychos before they unleash a pandemic. As far as I'm concerned, our past is just that…the past. I'm not interested in rehashing it. I want to focus on the future." For a brief second, her gaze moved to the cracked door, but Boston didn't notice.

"Pegasus Medical International Corporation. I couldn't find a physical address, but it's somewhere down south."

Although the name wasn't familiar, an enormous weight lifted from her shoulders. "Thank you. I'll have Tim patch you up, and I'm sorry. I should have been honest with you from the start."

The shock on his swollen face was oddly satisfying, perhaps more so than slamming him into the pavement outside her apartment. "Yeah, well...I'm sorry for pulling a gun on you."

Instead of listing all the other times he attacked her, she plastered on a smile and stepped out of the room. One apology was better than none, and she had meant what she said. She wanted to focus on her future.

"Wow. You did it!" Chance picked her up and hugged her close before putting her back down and brushing her curls away from her face. "You were amazing!"

"Um...thanks." Lilith shied away from him and took a step back. "This isn't the reaction I expected from you." She raised an eyebrow and watched him as they strolled toward the elevator.

"Why? I'm proud of you! You made peace with a fucking monster, made him trust you, and got the truth. I mean, offering to take him with us...brilliant!"

"You think so?" This time, she stared at him in utter disbelief.

"Of course." The expression on her face snuffed out his ecstatic mood, leaving behind a smoldering frown. "You were serious?"

"Yes." She bent down and lifted the gate, while he stared off into the distance, trying to wrap his mind around that one little word.

"Lily, no..."

"I'm gonna stop you there. Everyone's going to object, call me insane, and insist Boston stays in the cage. I have my reasons, but I only want to explain them once, so can we just get upstairs?"

Chance searched her eyes for a long moment before giving a slight nod. "You better have one hell of a compelling argument, *cherie*. I love you, but this...is a lot to ask."

She knew he wanted to say more but appreciated his restraint.

When the elevator reached the second floor, they found Dr. Price, Tim, and Nicci sitting around the island. The group's despair showed in their slumped shoulders, tired expressions, and the nearly empty bottle of Jameson sitting in their midst.

"I'm guessing you had no luck either?" Tim muttered the question after draining his shot glass, but when he glanced at Lilith, his frown turned to an expression of hope. "You got something?"

Lilith flashed a bright smile. "I got a name. I didn't recognize it, but I know where the bodies went."

"Well, don't keep us in suspense, partner. What is it?" Nicci pulled her laptop out of the bag and cracked it open, eager to start researching.

"Pegasus Medical International Corporation."

As she spoke the words, Nicci's expression changed. The hope deteriorated into an all-consuming dread which escaped in one word. "Fuck."

"You know it?" Lilith frowned and wandered over to her partner, who was furiously typing away.

"Yeah, so do you. Do the initials PMIC mean anything?"

Memories of shimmering green countertops, an ebony-tiled wall, and brushed aluminum letters flashed through her mind, and she turned to stare up at Chance. He wore the same shell-shocked expression.

"No," Lilith whispered, refusing to believe it.

"I told you we couldn't trust him." Chance growled the words, his hands clenching into fists. "You kept defending him, buying into his wounded-guy-with-a-heart-of-gold crap. I knew he was up to something."

"Who are we talking about?" Tim peered at each of them in turn with a confused frown.

Nicci turned the laptop around so everyone could see the screen. "Pegasus Medical's CEO, Andrew Farren, grandson of founder Andre Farren." Cohen's stoic face peered out from the screen, wrapped in an expensive suit—the same headshot she'd flashed at the hotel.

"No. I don't believe it. When I confronted him, he didn't know anything. I saw the surprise, the shock...No." Lilith shook her head, refusing to accept the most obvious conclusion.

"You saw what he wanted you to see. The man spent his entire life perfecting the art. You've seen it firsthand." Chance turned her toward him, locking eyes with her. "Lily, this is proof. Why can't you see that?"

"No! Something is wrong."

"Cohen is wrong! He probably took off, ran home to clean up his mess, and left just enough evidence behind to make you think Dr. Thomas kidnapped him."

"Chance, no! I'm telling you, they took him. Think about it! The cult believes that PMIC has what they want, and the CEO waltzes in to ask them questions. He is the *only* person who can get them inside."

"Lilith is right." Nicci hopped into the conversation before Chance could respond. "The website doesn't list a physical address. Checking the internet in general reveals nothing. The place isn't on Google Maps. The facility is covert. It took me months to find the address, and I'm a damn amazing hacker. I doubt anyone on their crew has my skills. If they did, they would have acted sooner."

"Fine." A tremor ran through Chance's clenched jaw, and he took a breath. "That doesn't mean he didn't double-cross us. He saw the value in Ashcroft, and he worked closely with the FBI."

"Yeah, but you're forgetting something. Aaron arranged the transfer. Do you seriously think Aaron and Cohen even knew each other before the gala?"

"Then Aaron knows about the Durand, more than he's letting on. He may not have met Cohen, but he knew someone in the organization. Christ, Lily, Andrew inherited the company. You really think he doesn't know everything that happens under that roof?"

Lilith shrugged, refusing to give in. She knew in her gut that Cohen was innocent. The man wouldn't betray her, especially if Chance was right about how Cohen felt. "With the Council treating him the way they are, I think there's a lot he doesn't know."

Chance sighed and hung his head for a moment. "He's the one who told you about the Council. Don't you see? There's nothing to prove he wasn't lying."

Lilith tilted her head, and a frown furrowed her brow. "Just stop…This isn't about him. It's about stopping a pandemic." She stared into his hazel eyes, willing him to see the truth. "*If* Cohen lied to us, he'll pay for what he did."

"*If?*" He shook his head and stepped away, wandering into the living room.

Tears misted her eyes as she watched him, but Tim still had questions.

"Wait. Why were you trying to find the address, Nicci?"

"They kept Lilith and Chance there as prisoners, assassinated Gregor there…I figured it was a pretty important place to the Durand, especially if they went through so much trouble to keep it hidden."

"So, what do we do now?" Tim looked directly to Lilith for the answer.

"We pool our resources and go there."

"What?" Chance turned on his heel. "You want to go into the viper's den, a Durand stronghold, to chase down Cohen and a group of fanatics?"

Lilith straightened and lifted her chin, refusing to back down. "Yes. We can't let Thomas and Wolfe get Ashcroft's blood. We have no idea what that would do to the virus."

"And you expect them to just let us in?" Chance stepped closer, every muscle still tensed.

"No. I don't. That's why I intend to call Agent Gorman and ask for backup."

The room filled with the sound of chair legs screeching across hardwood. Everyone rushed to their feet with a variety of dismissive exclamations. Meanwhile, Chance stood perfectly still, staring at her with an expression that bordered on horror.

Lilith straightened her shoulders and held up a hand, waiting for them to quiet down. Once Tim, Nicci, and Dr. Price fell silent, Lilith shifted her gaze to Chance. The others were important, but he was the one she needed to convince. She couldn't do this without his help. Well, perhaps she could but she didn't want to.

"Hear me out. The Durand won't refuse an official FBI presence, and they won't make a move on us in front of human law enforcement."

To his credit, Chance thought over her statement for several nerve-wracking moments before he answered. "*Cherie,* I get your point, but...you're making strong assumptions, and even if you're right, they will respond in force afterward. We have a tenuous truce with them now. If we traipse into their headquarters with human FBI agents, we'll end up like Gregor, or worse. It's too risky."

"No, Chance. Doing nothing is too risky!"

"Why not call and warn them?" Tim ventured into the conversation with what sounded like a reasonable suggestion.

"We can't. I only have Cohen's phone number. Besides, there is no way that clan of pompous vipers would believe a cult of humans could infiltrate their building."

"She's right about that," Chance admitted.

Although she was grateful for the backup, it was short-lived.

"Tell them the other part of your plan." He tried to keep his face neutral, but Lilith saw the anger and frustration lurking in his eyes.

"I...uh, promised Special Agent Boston we would take him along."

"What? Why the hell would you do something so stupid? Please, tell me you aren't keeping that promise?" Tim's hands clenched into tight fists, and the blood vessel in his temple throbbed.

"Boston is a problem. We can't let him go as things are now. If we take him along, he'll either get to avenge his partner and be grateful, or he'll die in the line of duty."

"Again…you are assuming too much, Lily!" Chance stepped closer, his suppressed anger roaring to the surface. "I am not giving him a fucking weapon! You honestly think he won't kill you the second he has one?"

Lilith swallowed the sudden lump in her throat as he continued to move closer, vibrating with rage. "I got through to him…He understands now."

"Bullshit! Don't be an idiot. You're smarter than this! I saw his face at the crime scene…when he had that gun trained on you. He wanted nothing more in the world than to pull the trigger. The monster wants you dead!"

"So, we won't give him a weapon until necessary and…"

"*No!* I will not give him an opportunity to hurt you again! Do you have a fucking death wish, or are you just that stupid?"

The words cut her impossibly deep, but she refused to give in.

The entire room fell silent as Lilith and Chance stared each other down.

Finally, Lilith unclenched her jaw and gave him an answer. "No on both counts. That's why we have to win his loyalty, or he has to die in the line of duty so his father won't come after me. I am offering a logical solution! *You* are the one who can't control your emotions!"

She took a step forward until she was mere inches from him and defiantly met his eyes.

"At least I'm telling you my plan instead of manipulating my best friend and keeping secrets from the person I love."

The second his expression fell, wounded by the sharp words, she turned on her heel so he wouldn't see the tears in her eyes. She had gone too far, but so had he.

She stormed off toward the spiral staircase, speaking over her shoulder. "I'm going to call Agent Gorman and his partner to fill them in. Hopefully, they're still in the area and agree to join us. Tim, call the airfield. Have them gas up Dad's jet and have it on standby. We're flying to Alabama as soon as we can. If anyone doesn't like the plan, they're free to leave."

Lilith didn't wait for answers or objections. She simply marched up the stairs, walked into the bedroom, and slammed the door. Then she collapsed against it, tears spilling down her cheeks.

When Chance had agreed to let her question Boston, she thought he was finally on her side, willing to back up her decisions. But now…

"How did we end up here?" she asked the vacant bedroom. Lilith wiped at her face and slid down to the floor. Her life had felt disjointed and messy before, but the resurgence of the virus, the Grecian cult, and Boston's interference had thrown the only stable things she had left into chaos. She had no idea how to move forward, other than focusing on the task at hand.

They needed to stop Dr. Thomas and Dr. Wolfe, prevent a pandemic, rescue Cohen, handle the human FBI agents, and escape any retribution from the Durand and Boston's father. Everything else had to wait.

Chapter 36 - *Cohen*

Andrew sagged against the restraints when Jerry finally took a step back. *A temporary reprieve*, the inner demon reminded him.

The minion had broken all four fingers on his right hand, and Dr. Thomas still hadn't asked a single question. So far, Cohen had managed to bite back the screams, only providing strained grunts, but the woman's excitement piqued with even the slightest indication of pain. *Fucking sadist.*

"You know, I really should thank you." The woman's cheery tone didn't fit the situation.

For the third time, Andrew tried to latch on to her energy and draw it to him. He didn't care if it exposed his nature—he had no intention of letting any of them live long enough to pose a threat. Unfortunately, the woman sat just out of his range, close enough to taunt him but nothing else. He'd tried to draw on Jerry when the man reached for another finger to snap, but the man didn't broadcast enough for him to use. If he had any emotions, Andrew had yet to discover them.

"Why…is that?" He forced the words through gritted teeth, still struggling with the pain coursing up and down his arm.

"You saved us a great deal of trouble by showing up at the hotel."

"How so?" His eyes narrowed at the woman when she tilted her head as if he'd asked a stupid question.

"You saved us the trouble of tracking you down. After all, we couldn't take you at the gala, with all those cameras and witnesses."

"Then why invite us?" His glare narrowed, and another wave of agony emanated from the fractured bones.

Rachel's face split with a beaming smile. "Kelley wanted to meet you all, especially Ms. Adams. The man *does* have a flair for the dramatic."

"Did you take her too?" He swallowed the sudden lump of fear in his throat, uncertain if he wanted to know the answer.

"No. Why would we?" The woman appeared genuinely confused.

They targeted me specifically?

"Why me? If we were getting too close, Lilith is the obvious choice since she's heading the investigation."

Are you seriously arguing with this psycho about why Lilith is a better choice for torture? He ignored the intrusive voice.

"Because you have something we want, Andrew Farren, or rather, you can get us what we want."

The use of his real name hit him like a lightning strike. *This is about the Durand. Fuck.* "I'm not following," he lied with a tired sigh, hoping she hadn't seen the recognition in his eyes.

"You will." After flashing a dark smile, her gaze drifted to Jerry, and her head dipped.

Andrew's pulse quickened. The giant man stalked behind him, and Cohen's head whipped around, tracking the emotionally-stunted minion.

"Wait! Why hurt me before you've even asked a fucking question?" Panic laced his voice, and the man's sweaty palm touched Cohen's right elbow.

"Because, my dear detective," a voice boomed from the stairwell, capturing his attention, "*basanos* is the only way we can assure your complete cooperation." Dr. Wolfe strolled into the room with an air of complete confidence. "Typically, I like to drag this out a bit, but we are short on time, thanks to your nosey little friends. Once I'm convinced that you will do what is required, the torment will stop."

"*Basanos?*" The foreign word sparked a distant memory that hovered just out of reach.

The man pushed the black hair from his face and smiled, pacing closer. "The Greek tradition of truth-seeking through torture. It is the only way to reveal one's true self."

The lump of fear dropped to Cohen's stomach, souring its contents. He locked his narrowed eyes on the archeologist with a menacing glare. "I will keep that in mind when the roles are reversed."

A hearty laugh echoed off the walls. "Quite feisty of you, Detective, but I think you'll find you're quite outmatched. You're human, after all."

Confusion contorted Andrew's face, and he leaned back against the wheel, studying the odd man. *They think I'm human, but they know my real name*…His mind flashed through all the possible scenarios and finally landed on one. *The website for PMIC. This is somehow about the company. It has to be. And if he's not human, what is he?*

"Pegasus Medical. That's what this is about, isn't it?"

"How very astute of you." Kelley didn't display an ounce of surprise. The man had been waiting for Cohen to come to that conclusion. He peered over Andrew's shoulder and nodded, taking a seat beside Rachel.

Before Cohen could process the movement's meaning, a hand struck the back of his elbow with crushing force, sending bone shooting through his skin. He couldn't hold back the scream this time. It echoed through the room and summoned the memories of similar sounds eight months ago, under Luminita's knife.

"Thank you, Jerry. You know what to do next."

Dread tightened around Andrew's lungs, and sheer agony wracked his body. He couldn't think clearly past the unrelenting torment burning through his arm. Blood gushed over his skin. *Shit. They ruptured an artery.*

As soon as the overweight man gripped his forearm, Cohen sensed the glow of pride, latched on, and tore it away. The pain eased, and the bleeding stopped.

The overweight man stumbled and backed away.

The screech of metal chairs on concrete filled his ears, and when Andrew peered up beneath his brow at Rachel and Kelley, they were standing, their faces frozen in soundless gasps. The sudden fear they exuded was more powerful than their excitement had been, extending farther, hovering closer.

A malevolent grin spread across Cohen's lips, and he grasped the edge of their energy, ripping it away viciously. They both lost their balance and sank into the chairs, draining of color, while Cohen slowly flexed his fractured fingers. The bones popped back into place, knitting together, healing with each movement.

"Hmm." The contented growl made their terrified faces pale even more. "Guess I'm not…human."

Kelley's head snapped toward Jerry, and he gestured to Cohen. The heavyset man approached with caution, opting to move behind the wheel and out of sight, but Cohen tracked the fear rolling off him in waves. Jerry stopped behind his left side, and once again, Andrew tapped into his minimal emotions. They weren't as strong as Kelley and Rachel's, but every little bit helped.

Unfortunately, it didn't stop the devastating blow to his left elbow. The skin split wide open, and blood gushed from the wound. *Fuck. He ripped open another fucking artery.*

Concentrate or you're going to bleed out! the inner demon screeched in his head.

Not helping, he retorted with an angry growl.

"That's enough! Jerry, come here," Rachel screamed.

Cohen drew just enough from Jerry, who backed away to join his masters, to slow the bleeding. *Not enough to heal, but at least I won't die in seconds.*

"Why don't you just get to the part where you tell me what you want?" Andrew snarled.

Kelley gathered his strength and stood, straightening the line of his tuxedo. "Very well." The man recovered quite well…all things considered. "You are going to take us to Pegasus Medical's headquarters and grant us access to the research labs."

Andrew's eyebrows rose, nearly touching his hairline. "I'm sorry? I don't think I heard you correctly."

The man's face hardened, and he took a step closer. *A bold strategy.*

"You are going to give the collective access to the building."

It was Andrew's turn to laugh. "You are fucking joking. You won't live long enough to regret that decision. You have no idea what you're dealing with!"

Dr. Wolfe's head tilted, and he continued to approach. "No. I don't think *you* know what *you're* dealing with. Your little magic trick was impressive, but our virus will reduce you to nothing over a few short months. You'll suffer, and you'll die, like all the rest of them, you soulless monster."

The truth in the man's words distracted Cohen, and fear clutched his heart. *They are behind the virus…*

Before the thought fully formed, a fist cracked against his cheek, splitting the skin. Spots invaded his vision. While Cohen struggled to stay conscious, the man gripped his chin in a painfully tight hold.

"You *will* take us there!"

Cohen cracked a delirious smile, still unable to focus. "No. Nothing you can do to me will change my mind. The people that own that building would do far worse than you can imagine."

Another vicious hit made his vision go black for a few seconds, and the noise in his head grew louder.

"I won't…help you."

"Art!" Rachel hollered from the far side of the room, and the sound rattled painfully through Andrew's aching head.

Kelley turned back in her direction her. Cohen tried to draw Wolfe's energy toward him, but he couldn't concentrate past the spinning room.

"I have a better idea." The tone in her voice chilled him to the bone.

Footsteps retreated, taking the man's energy with them. When the dizziness finally faded, Andrew glanced up. All three of them stood out of reach, but his vision halted on Rachel's menacing smile.

"He's right. Nothing we can do to *him* will change his mind."

Kelley started to protest, but she laid a hand on his shoulder, and her smile broadened. Then her brown eyes moved to Cohen with shrewd viciousness.

"You will do as we ask. You will follow every direction we give you."

"Or what?" The simple question sounded haunted, even to him. *You know where this is going. Your one fucking weakness.* He tried to ignore the inner demon but knew it was right.

"Or we'll infect Lilith. We have eyes and ears everywhere. You know we can get to her." Rachel took a step forward, and Andrew's heart thrashed against his ribs like a wild animal.

"No. I don't believe you." The lie didn't sound convincing to him either.

"Thanks to Renee…"

Her vision swung to the woman with the silver bob still standing by the stairs. He'd forgotten about her.

"We know where she lives, and I'm not talking about her apartment." Rachel's gaze drifted back to him. "I mean the seemingly abandoned warehouse outside of Manhattan. The one she shares with Chance Deveraux."

Fuck.

"One wrong move and we will give the word. She'll suffer. I helped revive the virus, and I know exactly what it does. Lilith is an *Empusa*. It's specifically designed to tear them apart from the inside, bit by bit. There's a possibility she might survive…but she'll wish she hadn't."

Andrew swallowed hard around the lump wedged in his throat. *Here's your fucking moment. Do you really care about her more than your own skin? The Durand will do more than end your life if you betray them. Are you willing to suffer to spare her that fate?*

"Do you hear me, monster?" Rachel spat the words and stepped closer, inches from him.

He could draw on her essence again, steal that feeling of victory, but if he did...

The woman's hand clutched his jaw, jerking his head up until he met her eyes. "I saw you at the gala, watching her." The woman's lips curved into another malicious smile. "Poor sad demon. Are you willing to spare her a tortuous fate, even if she doesn't want you? You know that, don't you? She *doesn't* want you."

Rachel echoed the words of his intrusive voice, and hearing them out loud fractured something deep inside his soul, causing more pain than the shattered elbow. He tried to look away, but the woman yanked his jaw again, forcing his attention.

"So, what will it be, demon? Will you help us and save Lilith from paying the price for your refusal?"

Desperation clawed at his insides, settling into the bone-chilling sensation of defeat.

You know the answer. The only answer. You aren't a fucking hero because you'd burn the world to save her. For once, he agreed with the intrusive demon on his shoulder.

Rachel's smile spread impossibly wide as he dipped his head in surrender.

Chapter 37

When the bedroom door slammed closed, everyone downstairs froze. Chance stood in the middle of the room, staring up at the bedroom and replaying everything in his head. *Calling the FBI, taking Boston as part of the team, raiding the Durand stronghold...It's all crazy. Isn't it?*

Nicci cleared her throat, breaking the uncomfortable silence. "Well, that was...dramatic." She glanced over at Tim, who was still staring at Chance with a worried expression. "Sounds like we have work to do, buddy."

"Wait." Chance turned toward them, exhaling slowly. "Do you really think this is a good idea?"

Nicci tilted her head, and her mouth stretched into a half-smile. "As insane as it sounds, it's logical. A lot of things need to go right, but the woman is smart. The FBI presence will most likely force the Durand's cooperation. If they help us stop biological terrorists, it will paint them in a good light, so perhaps they won't come after us later. The one thing I'm sure of is, she's right about the virus. Even if it's already out there, we don't want to see how Ashcroft's blood will mutate it. Ultimately, I don't think we have a choice."

"And Boston?"

"It's risky but the best plan I've heard. If he dies in the raid, especially with other FBI agents as witnesses, everyone wins. As for him having a weapon...you were there when she got the truth from him. Do you think he's on our side?"

Everything in his gut screamed no, but if he was being honest... "I think he wants to hurt the people that killed Cassie more than he wants to hurt Lilith...at least for the moment. I still don't trust him."

"Nor should you. The man's judgement is fundamentally flawed. He's a rapist and a woman-beater. We all need to keep a close eye on him. In the meantime, Tim and I have to get things rolling, and you need to fix whatever the hell that was."

His gaze fell to the floor, but he nodded.

"Come on, Tim. Grab the first aid kit so you can patch up your handiwork." The two of them collected their things and rode the elevator down, while Chance still stared at the hardwood floors.

Everything feels so...off. I don't know how to get back to who I am. I just want to protect her, keep her safe...Where the hell did things go wrong?

"Mr. Deveraux, are you all right?" Brittney's tentative voice broke the silence, reminding him he wasn't alone.

"Yeah..." After raking his hands through his hair, he strolled toward the counter and picked up the nearly empty bottle of Jameson.

"Is everything okay between you and Lilith?"

His eyes fell to the counter as he poured a shot and knocked it back.

"I'll take that as a no."

After pouring a second shot, he downed it and slammed his glass on the island. "I thought you weren't supposed to talk about your clients."

The woman shrugged her narrow shoulders. "I'm concerned."

"Things are crazy, but we'll be fine." He met her eyes with a less than friendly glare and poured himself a third shot.

Meanwhile, Dr. Price took a small sip of hers, leaned back on her stool, and continued to study him.

"No offense, but I've had my fill of shrinks trying to diagnose me." He purposefully avoided her gaze this time. The last thing he wanted to do was invite more personal questions.

"I apologize. I didn't mean to make you uncomfortable...and I'm not trying to diagnose anyone. You were kind to me earlier, about Renee, and I wanted to return the favor."

"That's really not necessary." Chance raked his hand through his hair again, his frustration and anxiety building.

"Mr. Deveraux?"

He stopped and finally met the woman's eyes again. She pushed her glasses back in place and frowned in concern.

"May I explain one thing? After that, I'll leave you alone. I promise."

He heaved a heavy sigh but nodded. If saying her piece meant she'd leave him alone, then fine. He could endure a few moments of supposed insight.

"I've observed the two of you together several times now. You have a strong connection, but there's something you need to understand."

She waited until his eyes met hers again before continuing.

"The nightmare with the siren coupled with the actual attack in the medical center…that should have ended your relationship. The traumatic memories—real or not—coupled with instinctual fear and the drive of self-preservation…It doesn't matter how much she trusted you before, those events should have eradicated her ability to be vulnerable around you."

Chance sank onto the barstool across from her as she voiced his deepest fear.

"She sat in my office three days a week for eight months and never said a word until last week. She does not easily trust, and I suspect the events last year only made things harder."

"Yeah…"

"However, in your case, she chose logic and forced her fear of you into a hole so deep, it may never see the light of day again. That woman has the strongest will I have ever seen. Every day, she chooses you, trusts you, bases her world around you, and makes herself vulnerable to you, despite every instinctual reason not to. That is something to respect and fear, Mr. Deveraux."

"I…" Words completely failed him, and he struggled to wrap his head around the concept.

"May I offer some advice?" Brittney reached out, placed her hand on his arm, and waited until she had his attention again. "Return that trust. Be on her side. Trust that she is trying to find a way out of this mess. She needs to know that you choose her over vengeance, anger, and the need to control the situation."

As much as he hated to admit it, the woman was absolutely right. Lilith was the way back to who he was. He needed to let everything else go and simply trust her.

For a few moments, he stared at his hands, and then he met her gaze once more. "I don't have much reason to trust others either, but I choose her every day and always will, Dr. Price."

A smile stretched the woman's thin lips, and she patted his arm. "That's what she needs to hear."

"Thank you." Chance looked up at the loft bedroom. "If you'll excuse me…"

"Of course."

He pushed away from the island and made his way up the spiral staircase with purposeful strides.

"Special Agent Gorman? This is Lilith Adams. I realize it's a little late, but I have news."

"Quite all right, Ms. Adams. News, huh? From our...friend? That was faster than expected..." Apprehension peppered the man's voice. "Is he...?" The words trailed off as if he were uncertain he wanted to ask the question.

"Boston is alive. He's a little worse for wear but breathing."

A sigh of relief rushed over the speaker. "So, he broke down and told you something...about Cassie?"

"Yes, but the situation is more complex than expected." She paused to take a breath. Once she rang this bell, it couldn't be un-rung. Unfortunately, she didn't see any other way. The FBI had given them Boston on good faith, and they expected updates. Besides, with the Durand involved, they needed someone neutral with the authority to make them comply.

"Ms. Adams? Are you still there?"

"Yeah, sorry. The people who tortured Agent Cappalletty are in possession of a virus. We've seen a few cases in a limited section of the populace, but..." Lilith collected her thoughts for a second, striving to find a balance between truth and believability. "The perps believe something from Phipps Bend will help the virus spread."

"I haven't seen anything from the CDC."

"There have only been a few isolated cases, one of which killed the victim. It hasn't been reported yet. We're hoping to stop it before things get to that point."

Of course, if the blood supply down south is contaminated, we're past that point. If my original assumption is correct, vampires in the southeast are already infected...

Before she could spin out further, Agent Gorman spoke again.

"The CDC really should—"

"They are a government agency full of red tape. We are trying to prevent a pandemic. I believe the current strain can be contained, but if they get their hands on something that mutates the virus or increases the rate of transmission, the results could be catastrophic."

"How can I help?"

The tightness in Lilith's chest eased a bit. Overcoming the CDC argument was the first major challenge, but not the last.

"Are you and your partner still in New York?"

"Yes..." The tentative answer made her nervous again.

"Can you come to Manhattan? Boston gave us a lead. During their illegal investigation of Phipps Bend, Boston and his partner discovered that most of the bodies and biological evidence were rerouted to a private company—Pegasus Medical International Corporation."

"Never heard of it."

"Most people haven't. It's a highly secured facility with a lot of secrets. My best hacker had a hell of a time just finding the address. Anyway, the terrorist group kidnapped the CEO, someone you and your partner know—Detective Andrew Cohen."

"What? That makes no sense."

"I assure you, it does. His grandfather passed away several months ago and left him the company, so to speak. Andrew is their public face. He knows where the facility is located and has access, which is why they took him."

"Okay..." The man was struggling to digest her story, but at least he was trying. "So, this medical company is in New York City?"

"No. Huntsville, Alabama."

"What exactly are you asking from me here, Ms. Adams?" Frustration rang loud and clear in the clipped question.

"The building is highly secured. They won't let my team waltz in on a hunch. We need authority and back-up to enter PMIC, find Cohen, and stop the terrorist group. We have a private jet and were hoping you and your partner would accompany us."

As soon as the last sentence left her lips, she held her breath. *What if he refuses? How can we get to Cohen and prevent Wolfe's group from unleashing a deadly variant? We could try to fight our way in, but the Durand will probably shoot us on sight.*

"What's the Greek angle?"

She slowly exhaled and assembled her thoughts. At least the man was considering her request.

"The twins that lead the group, Thomas and Wolfe, were raised with Old World Greek beliefs. They think they are reincarnations of Artemis and Apollo. One of them, Dr. Wolfe, is an archeologist specializing in Ancient Greece, which is why they...prepared Agent Cappalletty the way they did."

"So, the virus is the other case you mentioned, the one you didn't think was connected?"

"Yeah. We didn't have much information at that point. Dr. Thomas is a paleovirologist we consulted on the case. Unfortunately, we discovered too late that she is a key player in this terrorist plot."

An awkward silence settled in, which made her chest tighten all over again. Lilith was about to say something, when Agent Gorman finally spoke up.

"We won't participate in anything illegal."

"If the guards won't let us in, we will have to force our way, but with you, we will have the law on our side. You have reasonable suspicion that a crime is being committed on their property. We only want to ensure Cohen's safety, retrieve illegally obtained evidence, and apprehend a terrorist group that kidnapped, tortured, and killed an FBI agent. By doing so, we also hope to prevent a pandemic."

"I'll have more questions."

"Of course. That's understandable. We will have a briefing before takeoff, and I'm more than happy to answer any other questions on the plane."

"Okay. Where are we meeting you?"

"I'll text you the address. It's a warehouse just outside of Manhattan. Thank you, Agent Gorman. If I'm right, we'll be saving thousands of lives."

"We still have to wrap things up in Millbrook, so we won't be there for a few hours. I'll text you when we get close."

"You're still at the crime scene?"

"No. Not exactly. I'll explain when we get there."

"Okay. See you soon."

Lilith ended the call and stared at the screen, praying she'd made the right decision. Chance was correct about one thing—she was making a lot of assumptions. Things could go south in a hundred ways, but what choice did they have?

As soon as she sent Gorman the address, a knock broke her train of thought, and she peered up at the heavy wooden door.

"Come in," she hollered, tossing her phone on the bed and mentally preparing for another discussion.

"*Cherie?*"

Lilith released a heavy sigh when Chance peeked into the room. She wasn't ready for this particular fight, so she tried to snuff it out early. "You're too late. I already called Special Agent Gorman—"

"I heard."

"Of course, you did. What do you want, then?"

Part of her wanted to run over, kiss him, and make-up, but his words still stung. He had made it perfectly clear he didn't trust her judgment. Hell, he wouldn't even let her fully explain the plan. He just shut her down, and she didn't have the energy to convince him.

He opened the door enough to slip inside and gently closed it behind him. "I only want to talk, Lily."

"Look, Chance. I'm tired, and we have a few hours before the FBI arrive. I need some sleep. I don't want to waste my time arguing."

"I don't want to either." He held us his palms and slowly crossed the room. "I came to apologize."

She peered up at the unexpected gesture with suspicion. "Why?"

"We are in a real bad situation here, and you proposed a dangerous but logical solution. I overreacted, and I'm sorry, *mon cherie*. I haven't been...myself lately."

Some of the tension eased from her shoulders, but she knew he wasn't finished. "Continue."

A half-smile tugged at one corner of his mouth. "You know me too well. I have a suggestion...a slight modification."

"I am *not* staying behind."

"Lily—"

"No! For two reasons. I could never send you, Tim, and Nicci into that devil's nest while I sit here in safety. And if I'm wrong about Cohen, I need to see it for myself."

Chance stepped closer, running his hands up her arms with tears misting his eyes. "I know, but—"

"You can't protect me," Lilith finished.

When he nodded, a tear fell on his black T-shirt.

"I'm not asking you to." She hooked a finger under his chin and lifted it until he met her eyes. "I don't want a bodyguard. I want someone who will fight alongside me—a partner, a soulmate. That is who you are to me, and I need you to see me that way."

"I just…can't lose you, Lily." The raw pain infusing his words made her throat tighten. "The very thought has me tangled up in knots. I'm spinning out of control here."

"Then do this *with* me…" Her voice broke before she finished, and he moved closer to cradle her face in his hands.

"I need you to know one thing, Lily. I would follow you into hell itself, *amour de ma vie*. No matter how angry I am or how much I dislike a plan, I will *never* abandon you! I will always choose you because I love you, Lilith."

"I love you too."

The words escaped in a rushed breath seconds before their lips collided in a heated kiss, and the moment his tongue caressed hers, a dizzying jolt of electricity raced down her spine.

A deep guttural growl vibrated over her skin when he grabbed her hips and pulled her body against his. The impassioned rush left her breathless, and she clung to him with a desperate need to erase the fights, the awkwardness, and both of their insecurities.

Her palms slid over his shoulders, up his neck, and sank into his tousled hair. Then she broke the kiss, pulling back enough to meet his eyes. "I can't do any of this without you."

Tears filled their eyes, and Chance leaned his forehead against hers while dragging in uneven breaths. "You'll never have to."

They both knew there were no guarantees with the dangerous mission. Death was a high probability, but neither of them wanted to focus on reality. They needed the illusion of control to face what lay ahead.

His lips brushed against hers, the sensitive skin barely touching as their breath mingled. The gentle caress only made the fire burn hotter, and she leaned into him, lightly capturing his bottom lip with her teeth.

A rumbling moan escaped his throat, and his hands surged down her hips. In one quick motion, he picked her up and wrapped her legs around his waist. As soon as she gripped his shoulders, he leaned forward, and they both crashed onto the bed.

Lilith giggled and grinned until his lips found her throat. Goosebumps and shivers raced over her skin in the wake of each tender kiss, and his hands caressed her hips before scrambling to unzip her jeans.

Alarm bells rang in her head when he gripped the waistband. Dr. Price, Tim, and Nicci were downstairs, waiting to finalize their plan. They needed to prepare before the FBI arrived. They didn't have time for this, no matter how much she wanted it, needed it.

Chance sensed her sudden panic and stopped, with her jeans halfway down her hips. His fingers sank into her hair, and he claimed her lips in a fiery kiss that stole her breath again and eradicated her objections.

When he pulled back, they both panted, hearts racing and their tenuous control nearing the breaking point. She gazed into his hazel eyes flecked with green and saw everything in their depths—over a decade of unrequited love, the joy of sharing his life with her, the overwhelming drive to keep her safe, the lack of control, the rage he harbored for those who hurt her, and most of all, the raw desire that continued to vibrate over his skin.

"*Cherie…*" The low rumble of his voice made the warmth in her belly spread until the sensation enveloped every part of her. "We don't know what will happen in Alabama."

For a second, his gaze fell under the weight of that sentence, but when he met her eyes again, his shone with fierce determination.

"We deserve this moment, to remember what we are fighting for…I don't care about the world, the virus, Cohen, Boston…only you, *mon amour*."

Lilith pulled him closer, kissing him deeply, with tears on her cheeks. All thoughts of anything else dissipated like smoke, banished by the frantic compulsion to touch his skin.

When her arms wrapped around him, she grabbed his T-shirt and tugged, breaking the kiss only long enough to pull the shirt over his head. Her palms surged over the hard contours of his back, memorizing every line and curve.

His hand tightened in her hair, and his body moved against hers, eliciting a breathy moan that rushed over his lips. The simple sound broke his fragile control.

After pushing off the bed, he stood and pulled her to her feet, making her crash into him. For a moment, he studied her face, and brushed a stray curl behind her ear. She drew in rapid breaths, drowning in lusty need, then his hands surged up her hips, gripped her shirt, and tugged it over her head.

Before the Led Zeppelin shirt reached the ground, his lips found hers again in a kiss that made her knees weak, and he tightened his hold, pressing her against his body. The jolt that raced through her core was exhilarating, carnal, and addictive. She wanted more…*needed* more.

A sudden inescapable desire to pour everything into the moment overcame her. After all, Chance was right. They might not survive the raid on PMIC. *What if all we have is tonight? What if this is the last time?*

The bubble of anticipation grew until it burst in a frenzy. They shed their remaining clothing, removing every barrier, before tumbling back on the bed.

A sensual sigh passed her lips, and his body moved against hers in response. The decadent friction rippled through her, making her muscles tense beneath him.

God, this man. I need every bit of him. She reveled in the velvety texture and heady scent of his skin, surrounding her, caressing her, possessing her.

When his fingers twined with hers, she opened her eyes to gaze into his. A ravenous hunger burned in their depths that she still struggled to believe but couldn't deny.

"I love you, *cherie.*" The husky tone, thick with desire, cut through every trace of inhibition, and she wrapped her legs around him, pulling him closer.

"And I love you." Lilith closed the distance between them and lightly captured his bottom lip between her teeth.

When she let go, a rush of carnal need washed over them, burning away the flirtatious teasing until only the urgency to complete each other remained. The world narrowed to their panting breaths, arched backs, mewling moans, and thrusting hips, creating a delirious rush of pleasure. Their skin glistened with sweat, and the energy built like a rising tidal wave...looming over them...threatening to drown them.

When the wave finally broke, it tore a ragged scream from her throat. Every inch of her body pulsated, and she clung to him, nails digging into his skin. The room spun in dizzying circles as if caught in the undertow, powerless against it.

His forehead pressed against hers, and they both panted for breath, their chests heaving, muscles trembling, hearts racing. When the rush began to recede, he moved his arm around her waist, keeping their bodies interlocked, and rolled onto his side.

When his lips brushed against hers, they curved into an elated smile that made her quiver all over again. This was the moment, the bubble of happiness she wanted to live in forever.

Reality hovered on the horizon, infringing on her sex-induced high, but she shoved it away and nestled into him, reveling in his warmth, racing pulse, rich scent, and velvety touch.

His lips lingered over her neck, and he whispered against the delicate skin. "I am sorry for ever doubting you...doubting us." His teeth grazed the surface, sending shivers down her spine.

A mewling moan escaped her throat before her eyes fluttered open, meeting his. The same intense vulnerability and sincerity from the night of the gala shone in his eyes, but this time, she didn't shy away. Instead, she studied their depths, memorizing every nuance, before tenderly kissing his lips.

"I'm sorry I ever gave you reason to doubt." Her fingers brushed through his tousled hair, and she smiled softly. "You are the only one that I want. Now and forever, I'm yours."

His arms tightened around her, and he searched her eyes. "Marry me," he whispered before kissing her again.

At first, the words didn't register, but as his tongue caressed hers, the meaning finally sank in, and she pulled back.

"What did you say?"

A mischievous grin brightened his face, and he nipped at her lip. "You heard me."

"Chance…" She pulled back again, a soft frown forming.

"You just said you're mine, now and forever. You already know I feel the same way…After Alabama, let's make it official. No matter how prone we are to long life spans, we never know how much time we have." He pushed back her curls with tears in his eyes. "You are the love of my life and always have been. I don't want to waste a single day without you."

The exhilaration surging through her body didn't stem from carnal lust this time but still made her quiver, and he sensed every second of it. A low growl of contentment filled the air, and he closed his eyes, savoring the moment.

"Yes. Of course, yes." As soon as the words left her mouth, his eyes flashed open, and a delirious grin formed, matching her own. Once again, his lips claimed hers in a sensual kiss that sent her pulse racing. Their bodies moved against each other again, sparking a new warmth in her belly that quickly traveled lower.

"Chance…" Although Lilith had intended to interject a dose of reality and focus on the tasks that lay ahead, her breathy tone only increased his arousal.

When his lips grazed her collarbone, she squeezed her eyes shut and tried to focus.

"Chance…as much as I'd love round two, we need to…"

His lips trailed down until a hot rush of breath teased her nipple, momentarily halting her thoughts.

"You were saying, *mon petite cherie?*" He gazed up at her with a devilish grin, his lips still hovering over her sensitive peak.

After swallowing the lump of emotions and wanton desire lodged in her throat, Lilith found her voice again. "I need us both to survive so we can ravage each other to our hearts' content. That means getting dressed—"

The man frowned before his mouth claimed her nipple, growling in disapproval of her plan.

A gasping moan proceeded her words as she tried to continue. "...and form a plan before..."

After grabbing her hips, he rolled again, pulling her on top of him. She planted both palms in the center of his chest and sat up, trying to resist the subtle motion of his hips.

"We...uh...need to..." The words trailed off when the tattoo below his navel caught her attention. Her fingers traced the lily and scroll bearing her name. He'd been that sure of her over a decade ago that he permanently marked himself with her nickname, wore her on his skin every day.

The sudden tightening grip on her hips made her eyes flutter closed.

After a deep breath, she tried to inject logic again. "No. We *need*—"

Chance sat up, pulling her against him. "We need this. You said the FBI won't be here for a few hours." Fingertips traced up her back before sinking into her auburn hair. "Let go. Savor the moment with me. Everything will still be there afterward."

Both his hands rushed to her hips and gripped them tight as he thrust inside her, destroying all her objections like an atom bomb. Her hands clutched his shoulders, holding tight, her nails threatening to break the surface.

All thoughts of the people downstairs, the FBI, the Durand, Thomas, Wolfe, and Cohen evaporated into the ether. Nothing else existed in that moment.

Chapter 38

Lilith woke to the dings of several text messages. When her eyes fluttered open, she stared into Chance's sleeping face. A smile tilted his lips, and he still had his arms and legs wrapped around her, holding her close.

For a second, she soaked in the moment, memorizing the safety and security she felt, absorbing it into her core to carry with her.

The dings of three more texts sounded, and reluctantly, she started to untangle herself from him.

"What is it, *mon fiancée?*"

The low growl of his drowsy voice made her smile, but not as much as the new title. Still, Lilith reached for her phone and scrolled through the messages, while he tugged her close and nestled into the curve of her neck.

"Gorman and Hersch will be here in an hour, and everyone else is gathering supplies and equipment. Also, Tim called in some favors and got a few extra guys to help."

"Hmm." The rumble vibrated over her skin, summoning a heated flush of crimson, and he pressed his hips against her.

"You are insatiable." She chuckled and squirmed, but he held her tight.

"Perhaps..." Chance nipped at the delicate skin of her neck, and she pushed him away, far enough to meet his eyes.

"You know we can't stay here like this, as much as we may want to. Everyone is waiting on us, counting on us..."

He released a slow breath and stared over her shoulder. "I know. I just...I'm not ready to..."

"I'm scared too, for lots of reasons. You're right. There is no guarantee either of us will survive, but I'll do whatever it takes, and I know you will too."

His eyes watered, and he pressed his forehead to hers.

"Plus," she continued, "I'm not thrilled about being anywhere near the building where Gregor—" Her voice broke before she finished the sentence. After wiping the tears from her eyes, she turned onto her back and stared at the cedar-lined ceiling. "What I'm trying to say is that we can't hide in this bubble forever."

"I know, *cherie*." He leaned over, kissed her tenderly, and then slid off the bed. "I don't suppose we have time to share a nice hot shower?"

"I wish we did." Lilith scooted off the bed and hunted for her clothes.

"In that case, I need a quick, very cold shower." Chance grabbed her bra off the chair by the bathroom door and tossed it to her.

"Hell." After throwing her clothes on the bed, she hurried over and pointed a finger with a stern warning. "A very quick one."

The roguish grin spread, and she immediately amended her statement. "Shower! A very quick shower!"

He leaned closer, his lips hovering just out of reach. She barely resisted the urge to close that distance.

"If you say so, *mon avenir*."

"I've never heard that one. What does it mean?"

Their lips almost touched as he whispered, "I'll tell you in the shower."

About ten minutes later, Lilith and Chance emerged from the bedroom fully clothed but still wrapped in the magical moment. Lilith peered over the railing, but the living room and kitchen were deserted.

"Everyone must be downstairs."

When she turned back around, his infectious grin brightened.

"You have got to wipe that grin off your face. We have serious work to do."

"I'll try, but…" He grabbed her hand and slid his fingers between hers. "You agreed to marry me, *mon cherie*." He tugged her closer with an elated smile.

"Which I can't do if we die or end up in jail." After a quick kiss, Lilith slipped from his grasp and started down the stairs.

"Congratulations," a soft voice echoed from outside the bathroom under the stairs, causing Lilith to miss a step and almost tumble.

After catching herself and slowing her racing pulse, she glanced over at Dr. Price, who stood at the bottom with a guarded smile.

"Seems like you two made up…and then some."

Judging by the woman's facial expressions and body language, she clearly considered the engagement a bad idea. However, Lilith wasn't in the mood to find out why.

"Yep. I'd love to tell you all about it, but we have work to do before the FBI arrive." The defensive sarcasm made her words clipped, and she walked past her.

"I'm not convinced that bringing human law enforcement into this mess is a reasonable plan."

"Well, luckily, I'm not seeking your approval. I didn't ask for your help or advice. You are here for your protection—nothing more." Lilith continued toward the elevator, Dr. Price matching her stride.

"Lilith. You risk exposing us all. Come on, you have to admit you aren't thinking clearly right now."

She rounded on the therapist with a harsh glare. "What the hell does that mean?"

The doctor crossed her arms over her chest and raised an eyebrow. "Seriously? You are making major life decisions during an emotionally charged crisis."

"That is none of your business!"

"It *is* my business. You are my patient."

"Your job is to decide whether I'm fit for duty, which has nothing to do with my personal life."

"Of course, it does!"

"Doc," Chance interrupted from the foot of the stairs. "You are the one who helped me sort through shit and see the light."

The woman's face turned crimson, and she whirled to face him. "I told you to make things right, not propose."

"Wow. This is beyond inappropriate." Lilith shook her head, anger bubbling up to the surface once again.

"Lilith, calm down. All I'm saying is…now isn't the time to make these decisions."

"You are wrong. I see clearer than ever. I know what's important." As Lilith spoke, her gaze drifted to Chance, who stood at the foot of the stairs.

Dr. Price glanced back at him again and then returned her focus to Lilith. "It only seems that way because you're facing a life-and-death situation with thousands if not millions of lives riding on the outcome. You feel forced to pack an entire relationship into this one moment…"

As the doctor spoke, Lilith and Chance locked eyes, both searching for a sign Dr. Price might be right.

"No," Lilith declared in a firm voice before meeting the doc's stare. "No. I don't need some dramatic situation to force me into a commitment. I love him. That's the only reason that matters."

When Lilith looked over at him again, a brilliant smile lit his face, and he strolled toward her.

"Not that you care, but she's not forcing me either." Chance winked at the shrink, but she shook her head like a disappointed parent. "Now, if you'll excuse us, we have work to do."

Chance grasped Lilith's hand and led her into the freight elevator before adding a final thought.

"Oh, and Doc? Perhaps you can make yourself *useful* and whip up some food we can take with us. You're welcome to use anything you find." He closed the gate before Dr. Price responded and jabbed the down button.

"Sorry about that." Lilith nestled into him to hide her embarrassment.

"You have no reason to apologize, *mon petite cherie*." He placed a kiss on top of her head as the elevator rumbled to a stop.

Once again, he lifted the gate for her, and she slid past him, stealing a quick kiss.

When she turned to face the lower floor, everyone stopped in mid-motion to stare at them. The awkward moment stretched out until Nicci jogged over with a smile.

"Did you get some…rest?" She jabbed Lilith's side with her elbow and chuckled. "Seriously, Chance. You need to invest in some sound proofing."

"Does everyone—" Lilith's entire body flushed as she peered around the room.

"Know that you guys *made up*? I'm just teasing. We moved down here to give you some privacy before Chance went upstairs…Well, except for Dr. Price. I think she's too scared." Nicci shrugged. "Doesn't matter. Come on."

After grabbing Lilith's hand, she pulled her toward the tables they'd set up.

"We pooled our resources. I borrowed some walkies and earpieces from the precinct. Tim scrounged up some tac vests, knives, and assault rifles. He also pickup up a couple of passenger vans from Solasta and called in a few army buddies."

Nicci pointed to three guys in back who were cleaning and assembling several guns.

"This is Keller"—a short but well-built man with close-clipped blond curls, red cheeks, and a goatee—"Xander"—a tall, lanky man with a deep tan and long brown hair pulled into a ponytail,—"and Gibson." The last man sported shoulder-length black hair and dark stubble.

"Thanks for the backup, fellas. We really appreciate the help."

All three men nodded in response before returning to their tasks.

"So, when do Gorman and Hersch arrive?" Nicci asked, wandering over to the tactical vests.

"Anytime now. I told them Cassie's case is connected to a virus we've been chasing. I didn't go into details. Gorman wanted to call in the CDC, but I explained the stakes. Hopefully, we can stop it tonight and avoid the panic."

"And what if you're wrong?" Nicci asked without any animosity or blame. "The virus is already out there."

"Then we won't have a choice. I doubt Wolfe's cult knows about the Durand, which means it spread from us to them. The likelihood of it infecting humans is too great to do nothing. If we fail tonight or don't find the original source, we call the CDC and deal with the consequences later."

Nicci took every word in with calm composure and nodded. "Good. Aaron will be pissed if that happens, but fuck him."

"Chance!" Tim hollered from across the room.

"I better see what he needs. Good job, Nicci." Chance kissed Lilith's cheek before hurrying over to his best friend.

"About time you came downstairs." Tim winked and nudged him in the ribs.

"Thanks." Chance rubbed his side and tried to frown but failed. *How can I after everything that happened upstairs?*

"Yeah, well..." Tim returned to plugging mics and earpieces into walkies. "Once the feds arrive, we're good to go. Jet is fueled and waiting... Gear is almost set up..."

"Good, and thanks for bringing in some extra muscle."

Tim put down the last walkie and faced Chance. "Three guys from my old unit. Dependable, loyal, but Keller and Xander are human. Just a heads-up."

"You think that's wise?"

Tim raised an eyebrow. "Lilith invited the FBI, and you're worried about two men that protected my back during a war?"

"Point made." Chance nodded thoughtfully, but his best friend wasn't fooled by the feigned seriousness.

"Okay. What is up with you? I'm talking shop, and you look like the cat who ate a canary. I mean, great sex is one thing, but this is something else." Tim folded his arms over his broad chest and leaned against the table.

Chance raked his fingers through his hair and struggled to retain his composure. Under any other circumstances, he'd be ecstatic to share the news with the man he trusted most.

"Now's not the time. I'll tell you when we get back."

"Bullshit. Talk now."

After glancing around the room, he stepped next to Tim and leaned against the table beside him. "Keep it quiet. I'm only telling you because you're my best friend, and I know you won't let this go."

Tim peered over at him and arched an eyebrow. "Just spit it out. We have shit to do."

"Okay, okay. I...uh...asked Lilith to marry me."

"You did what?" Tim's loud voice echoed through the entire lower level, grabbing everyone's attention, including Lilith's.

She peered over at Chance with a confused frown, and he mouthed, *Sorry*, while elbowing Tim playfully in the gut.

"Damn, man. I said keep it quiet."

"Sorry, bud. I just didn't expect that. I mean...things have been a little rocky lately."

"You were right. I needed to get my head on straight, and I did."

"I wasn't talking about *that* head." Tim chuckled, and Chance elbowed him again. "Sorry. Low-hanging fruit...so to speak. So, I'm assuming by your grin she said yes?"

His cheeks heated, and he nodded. "You know, a year ago I never thought dating her was possible, and now..."

"I know, man. I'm happy for ya, and I'll buy you a beer when we get back, but it's time to get to work." He nodded toward the approaching headlights. "Pretty sure the feds are here."

"Show time." Chance took a deep breath. *No turning back now.*

Lilith made her way to the bay door, and Chance jogged to catch up, then fell in step beside her.

"What was Tim hollering about?" she whispered as they reached the threshold.

"I'll tell you later." His hand squeezed hers before resting on his gun holster.

Special Agents Gorman and Hersch exited the car and peered around the dark industrial park until they spotted Lilith and Chance.

"Ms. Adams, Mr. Deveraux, good to see you again so soon. You two might have to come work for me. I could use your interrogation skills." Gorman flashed a wide smile full of almost white teeth.

"Thank you for coming. I realize it's a lot to ask."

"Can we see Agent Boston?" Hersch still sounded skeptical, as if she expected a trap. Of course, the fact she was there at all said a lot about how much she trusted her partner.

"Of course." Chance flashed a smile and turned back toward the warehouse. "Hey, Tim. Can you retrieve our guest?"

"You got it, boss." The man's heavy footsteps echoed as he made his way to the holding room.

A few minutes later, he escorted David out of the warehouse. The man wasn't restrained, but the grip Tim kept on his arm was just as effective. Of course, there wasn't much they could do about his swollen eye and bruised face.

"Damn, David." Gorman rubbed at his chin and looked the man over. "Looks like you've had a rough day."

Boston's one good eye hardened, and he glared at the Agent. "Yeah, I'm sure you wouldn't know anything about that, would ya?"

"Are you okay?" The matter-of-fact tone Hersch used made everything seem impersonal. In fact, a few subtle indicators of satisfaction lingered on her features. She clearly wasn't one of Boston's admirers.

"No permanent injuries." The man's bloodshot eye turned to Lilith. "Ms. Adams and I reached an agreement."

Of course. He wanted as much leverage as possible, so she'd be forced to keep her word.

"I told her what I know. Now she's taking me along so I can ensure justice for Cassie."

The tall agent stepped forward, his dark brow wrinkled in concern. "I don't think that's the best play. Even if you were emotionally stable, you can't see out of your right eye. You'd be a liability."

"I'm going!" David stiffened, and his hands clenched into fists. "She was *my* partner!"

"Agent Gorman," Lilith interrupted, stepping in front of David. She needed them to go along with the plan. If David didn't go with them, he'd never stop hunting her. "I made the man a promise, and I keep my word."

"I will keep a close eye on him." When Chance spoke up, Lilith whirled around with a shocked expression, but he continued anyway. "I warn you. The man pulled a gun on her. I'll keep him out of harm's way if I can, but make no mistake, *she* is my top priority."

Some part of her wanted to be mad. They should have discussed a plan before laying it out for the FBI, but what was the point of being angry? He wanted to protect her as much as possible. How could she fault him for that?

"Very well, Mr. Deveraux. Agent Boston is your responsibility."

David's one good eye widened, and he turned toward Chance, but didn't say a word.

"Since that's settled, come on in. We will brief everyone on the situation and load up."

"The jet is fueled and waiting at LaGuardia, so let's make this quick," Tim hollered, ushering Boston back inside.

As everyone gathered around Lilith, her nerves kicked in. *Am I doing the right things? Am I leading them into a suicide mission? What if we never get past the front door? What if we fail?*

Chance leaned in, kissed her cheek, and whispered, "You got this, *cherie.*"

When he pulled back, their eyes met, and a flash of memories from upstairs burned through her anxiety and left her cheeks flushed.

"So, what is your plan?" Gorman prompted her, and she shook off the brief daydream.

"Yes, right. Our destination is Pegasus Medical in Huntsville, Alabama. It is a secretive company that operates outside of standard corporate law. Merely tracking down the address took a tremendous effort, and they won't want to let us in. That's why I've asked the FBI for help. I'm hoping their official standing will open the front door. Special Agents Gorman, Hersch, and Boston are joining us.

"Our mission has four main components: stop the group of biological terrorists led by Dr. Rachel Thomas and her brother, Dr. Kelley Wolfe; contain the virus in their possession; retrieve illegally obtained evidence from Phipps Bend; and rescue their hostage, Detective Andrew Cohen." Lilith scanned all their faces, waiting for objections, but everyone remained calm and receptive.

"I'll pass out pictures of our main targets on the plane," Nicci added, then nodded for Lilith to continue.

"The virus is transmitted primarily by blood, and there is no cure, so be careful. Assume the terrorists are armed and dangerous. They have already kidnapped, tortured, and killed an FBI agent."

Boston stiffened when she mentioned Cassandra but remained silent.

"This group is merciless, and they want to see the world burn."

Gibson, the army guy with black hair, raised his hand before speaking. "What's the plan for entry, ma'am?"

"We will attempt diplomatic methods first. Myself, Deveraux, and Agent Gorman will approach the front and speak with security about the situation. Hopefully, they'll let our entire team enter."

"And if that doesn't work?" Boston's cold tone was difficult to ignore.

"Forced entry through the parking garage. There's a metal door with a simple card key lock, easy enough to bypass. It leads to a stairwell with a key-carded elevator and a door to the main floor. The building is twenty stories with no thirteenth floor. We don't know which one the labs are on, so it might get bloody."

"Any idea how much security is on-site?" Gibson spoke up again.

"No. These people have unlimited resources, so expect a lot. But remember, we aren't there for them. Hopefully, we can convince them that cooperation is their best move."

"We don't have much intel." Nicci hated admitting it and took it as a personal failure—that much was obvious. "The building's blueprints are nonexistent. All I could find was the address. All the plans filed with the city were either copies of other buildings or corrupted. These people have friends in high places."

"What are the team assignments?" Xander stared at Lilith expectantly, and her brain froze.

Thankfully, Chance had that covered. "All right. Listen up. Detective Nicci DeLuca is our tech. She will handle data retrieval. Xander and Keller, you will accompany her. Lilith Adams is our forensic expert and is vital to both evidence retrieval *and* containing the virus. Myself, Boston, and Gorman will accompany her. Tim, you'll take Gibson and Hersch as our advanced team, scout, and clear the way. Any issues?"

When no one objected, he continued.

"On the subject of our final objective, rescuing Detective Andrew Cohen…"

Lilith's pulse quickened when he broached the subject, and he glanced back at her for a second.

"He is also known as Andrew Farren, the public face of PMIC. All efforts should be made to keep him alive and apprehend him. The man may know more about the Phipps Bend evidence breach."

"All right. Listen up!" Tim's voice boomed through the space with authority. "Everyone wears a vest. If you don't have your own, grab one off the table. Load up on weapons, ammo, and anything else you need before getting in one of the Solasta panel vans. We roll out in twenty!"

Everyone jumped into motion—some hustling around the tables, and others loading duffels into the vans.

"Tim, can you help Boston suit up while I give Lilith a hand?"

Tim turned and frowned at Chance for a moment before cracking a wide grin. "Sure. It's under the table there." Then he clapped a hand on David's shoulder and guided him into the milling crowd.

"What's under the table?" Lilith tried to peek, but Chance slid his hands up her arms with a soft smile.

"Are you sure about this? Going into the lion's den?"

Although her nerves were rattled, she summoned a resolute nod. "I'm sure."

"Okay. I ordered you a vest a few days ago…when Boston came to town. Tim picked it up earlier. One size doesn't always fit most." He grabbed a plastic bag from under the table and pulled out a black vest.

On the front, it had the NYPD insignia on one side and MCU (Major Crimes Unit) on the other. When he turned it around, large white letters on the back read: "CSI."

"I mean…it's not a diamond ring, but hopefully, it'll keep you alive until I can afford one."

Lilith leaned up on tiptoe and placed a sweet kiss on his lips. "Thank you, for everything."

"You're welcome"—a roguish grin curled his lips and made her pulse quicken—"for everything." The added wink made her chuckle. "Come on. Pull this over your head, and I'll help you with the straps."

The thing felt odd and bulky. As a CSI, she never had a reason to wear one—another example of how violent and messed up her life had become.

As Chance tightened the final strap, Agent Gorman approached. "Could I have a quick word with both of you before we head out?"

"Of course." Lilith shifted, trying to get comfy in the stifling vest.

They followed the man as he stepped outside and rounded the corner. He peered around to ensure they were alone before speaking.

"My partner and I found the crime scene."

When Lilith and Chance exchanged a confused look, he clarified.

"The actual crime scene—where she was tortured, where she died…"

"Holy shit," Lilith blurted out in shock. "How did you find it?"

The agent shrugged his broad shoulders. "Hersch is a genius. I can't take the credit. Transporting an entire tree was a risky move, so she started searching nearby properties that fit the criteria you provided—a place where someone could grow a tree in a controlled environment."

Gorman dug a pack of cigarettes and a lighter out of his pocket and lit one. After a long drag, he continued.

"That's when she found the Bennett School for Girls in Millbrook."

"A school?" Chance sounded more than a little skeptical.

"It's a thirty-two-acre property, originally built at the turn of the twentieth century as a luxury hotel and lodge by New York publisher H. J. Davidson Jr., but it didn't do well. In 1907, May Bennett created a school where girls could complete high school and two years of higher education. Eventually, it just became a girl's college. Enrollment declined as co-ed schools grew, and they abandoned the place in 1978."

"That's…a very detailed history." Chance raised an eyebrow, and the man chuckled.

"I'm a history buff, remember? When Hersch found the place, I looked up the background."

"What did you find there?" Lilith interjected to keep them on track.

The man released a large puff of smoke first. "There was a ballroom with a huge glass ceiling. That's where they grew the trees."

"Trees? Plural? There's more?"

"Yeah, two more, and these ones still had fruit on them...lotus fruit—a rare commodity with hallucinogenic properties. We also found vials of ketamine and fentanyl. I'm guessing that's how they kept her alive. Techs also found two containers with blood residue in the ballroom."

Gorman swallowed hard before taking another drag.

"I was right about the breaking wheel...We found it in the basement. They had thirty chairs set up in the room. They watched...Maybe even participated." The man's jaw clenched tight, and smoke bellowed from his nostrils.

"Did you find anything else?" Lilith still hoped they'd find proof they had access to the database. The transcript from her therapy sessions were damning, but she wanted concrete proof. Plus, their computers might not be as heavily encrypted as Dr. Nichols's, and if they had notes on the virus, perhaps they would help Dr. Scott make a vaccine.

"Yeah, some high-tech labs. One seemed medical, and the other held a ton of Greek artifacts."

"Any computers in the medical lab?"

"One."

"After this mission in Huntsville, could my partner, Detective Nicci DeLuca, take a look at it? She is a gifted hacker, and there may be useful information on that computer about the virus."

Gorman nodded thoughtfully. "I think I can arrange that." After a sigh, he glanced at them both again. "There's something else. We found an armory—empty gun racks, tons of ammo boxes, even a wooden crate labeled: 'grenades.' That's why most of the things you told me on the phone didn't surprise me much."

Lilith's heart sank, and she peered over at Chance. *Thirty armed fanatics?* All this time, she'd been more worried about the Durand, not a pack of delusional professors and history buffs. Even if the Durand helped, things could still get very bloody.

"Can I ask you something, Ms. Adams?" Gorman took another drag while studying her face.

"Of course."

His tawny eyes narrowed for a moment before exhaling another puff of smoke. "This facility is so hush-hush that you struggled to find the address and couldn't get the blueprints...but you know about the key-carded door in the parking garage, the security measures on the elevators and interior doors, how many floors the building has, and that they don't have a thirteenth floor. You've been there."

"Yes," she stated firmly. There was no point in denying the fact. "Cohen's grandfather hired us to solve the Voynich Manuscript robbery at the Yale Library last year. We've only seen two floors. The nineteenth floor is mostly offices and conference rooms, and the sixteenth floor was just a bunch of hotel suites."

Despite her best efforts to keep the tragic memories at bay, they flickered through her mind anyway. The images made her stomach churn, but she maintained the illusion of being calm and focused.

The agent watched her, the skin around his eyes tightening slightly as he debated whether to push for the truth or not. Why they had been there and what happened didn't change her intel, so hopefully the simplified explanation would satisfy him for now.

"All right." He squeezed and twisted the cigarette's filter until the cherry fell on the ground. Then he stomped it out and slipped the butt into his pocket. "The troops are waiting. Let's get moving."

Chance nodded at the agent. "I'll tell Tim we're all set." After a brief glance at Lilith, he disappeared around the corner.

"I have to ask…" Gorman paused until he had her full attention. "Are you sure about taking Boston? I need to know your plan."

This was the question she had hoped to avoid but knew would come up eventually. No matter how many angles she explored, she came back to the same answer—the truth. The man wasn't a pushover, and if he sensed a lie, he might back out entirely.

"I'll be honest. Boston is a problem in a lot of ways, but primarily because of his father. Taking him is the only solution. If he survives, I'm hoping he'll let go of his grudge. If he doesn't survive…"

The fear won, making her words come to an abrupt halt, but he didn't need her to finish the sentence.

"He dies a hero in the line of duty. I hope it doesn't come to that. Boston is a black mark on the Bureau, and I don't see him changing his ways, but I can't condone murder."

"I would never ask you to."

"Don't make promises you can't keep. I'm smart enough to understand David is more than a mere personal annoyance from your past. The man is capable of causing you genuine harm, both physically and legally. If this mission of yours turns into a real fight, the temptation to eliminate a threat with a little friendly fire will be hard to overcome." The man leaned a little closer and lowered his voice. "I'm not onboard with that outcome."

"I understand, and I'm not either. However, if he turns on me like he did at the crime scene, I *will* defend myself."

The agent leaned back against the wall with an unexpectedly warm smile. "You're a bright kid. Boston is a damn black hole, and I'm glad you escaped his gravitational pull. I only wish I could say the same for poor Cassie. Such a damn shame."

"Thank you, and I'm sorry Agent Cappalletty got caught up in all of this."

"Hey, partner! Wanna give me a hand?" Nicci strolled out of the warehouse with a duffle slung across her back, one gripped in each hand, and Lilith's forensic kit tucked under her arm.

Lilith turned back to Gorman with a grateful expression. "We better get loaded up. Thank you for filling us in on what you found."

After the agent gave her a smile and a nod, Lilith jogged over and grabbed a bag from Nicci. "Is there a reason you grabbed my kit?"

Nicci shrugged. "I figured it might come in handy at some point. Better to have it and not need it."

Once they reached the relative privacy of the van's rear doors, Nicci leaned over and whispered, "Everything okay?" She thrust her chin in the direction of Special Agent Gorman.

"Yeah, I think so. He knows we've been to PMIC before, and he's nervous about Boston."

"Understandable. So, what did you tell him…about PMIC?"

"Just that they hired us to solve the Voynich heist."

"Okay…Phase one is complete. Everyone is alive, and no one's in handcuffs." Nicci slid the bags into the back before leaning against the door. "Here's hoping we can talk some demons into helping us defeat a Greek-obsessed terrorist cult. Sounds simple enough."

Chapter 39

As soon as the jet reached cruising altitude, Nicci passed out keyrings with laminated pictures of Cohen, Thomas, Wolfe, Renee, and anyone else she could ID from Wolfe's entourage at the gala. Once everyone had them clipped to their vests, Tim and Chance handled any lingering questions, while the others tried to sleep.

The four-and-a-half-hour hop down to the Huntsville International Airport had them scheduled to land just before noon, and according to Nicci, no one else had slept last night.

Still, a dismal sense of doom permeated the cabin, stimulating their sympathetic nervous systems, which favored anxiety and panic over sleep and relaxation. Lilith doubted a single person on the plane was capable of truly resting, herself included.

The more she contemplated the task ahead of them, the more difficult it became to remain optimistic, especially after what Gorman had told her about the cult's stronghold. At least thirty delusional, violent, and dedicated terrorists waited for them, armed with guns and grenades, and that was only if they made it past the emotion-feeding demons and their army of SWAT lackeys.

As Lilith obsessed over every possible scenario for the hundredth time, Nicci collapsed into the seat beside her.

"I can't sleep." The petite Italian rubbed her face and then peered over at Lilith. "Did you get some sleep?"

"A little...earlier."

Nicci displayed a wide grin, resting her chin on her palm and her elbow on the armrest. "So...how was your make-up session?"

"Um..." Lilith gazed around the cabin, but no one was paying attention. *Still...* "I don't think this is the time."

"Oh, come on. After what happened earlier, Alicia will probably dump me. I need to live vicariously through you."

Lilith chuckled, and her cheeks flushed. "Let's just say it was...eventful."

Nicci frowned at the odd word choice. "How so?" The woman's warm brown eyes continued to study her, which only made Lilith blush more.

"I'm not sure I should say anything."

"Woman, I am your best friend, and you know it. Come on. What do you mean by eventful?"

A sigh rushed past Lilith's lips, and she leaned closer. "Chance...He... asked me to marry him."

Nicci sat back with a stunned expression Lilith almost found offensive. "Seriously?"

She flashed a tight smile and nodded, the nerves kicking in. Dr. Price had no problem voicing her disapproval, and Nicci never had an issue speaking the truth, but before Lilith's anxiety shifted into overdrive, Nicci leaned in again with a greedy grin.

"I need details."

The abrupt shift left Lilith rubbing the back of her neck and squirming in the seat. "Uh, yeah...Well, it's not a story we'll be telling at dinner parties."

"Spicy! *Molto speziato!*"

"Shh." Lilith's entire body burned with embarrassment as several people peered in their direction.

"Okay, but I get details later, right?"

"Sure." Reality cut into the happy moment, draining all the warmth from her. "Assuming there *is* a later."

Nicci bumped her partner's shoulder and flashed a resilient smile. "We've survived some hairy situations. Have a little faith."

After flashing a smile neither of them believed, Lilith lied through her teeth. "You're right. I'm sure everything will be fine."

What's the sense in pointing out the obvious? So many things can go wrong. If the Durand say no, we might end up fighting two armies. Hell, if Chance is right and Cohen is playing us, this whole thing might be a trap.

The weight of every life on the plane sat heavy on her shoulders. She slumped into the seat, closed her eyes, and pretended to sleep.

The Lotus Tree

As soon as the plane landed, Nicci and Hersch left to pick up the rental van from AVIS, while everyone else unloaded the plane. Well, everyone except Gorman, who stepped away from the main group to chain-smoke half a pack.

No one spoke much. The oppressive awareness of their own mortality in the face of less-than-favorable odds didn't leave room for idle conversation. Lilith spotted Chance smiling at her a few times, but the affectionate gaze quickly melted into his business-like mask, as if he were frightened of dwelling on their happiness and missing something or jinxing them.

The ride downtown wasn't much different. The tense silence felt stifling. Everyone mentally prepared for the task before them and checked their gear one more time.

When they arrived at the PMIC building, Lilith, Chance, and Gorman stepped out into the afternoon sun. She shielded her eyes and gazed up at the uninspired monstrosity composed of concrete and dark glass. Except for its height, which dwarfed the surrounding buildings, the entire thing appeared bland and mundane, as if it housed an insurance conglomerate or something else uninteresting.

Lilith stood still, trying to regulate her racing pulse and imagine a host of boring suits inhabiting the place, but the building loomed over them, dark and ominous. Death resided in those malevolent halls. Perhaps not hers, but she knew in her gut they wouldn't escape unscathed.

Chance squeezed her hand and smiled down at her. "You ready?"

After one last gaze at the tower's sinister form, she exhaled slowly and nodded. *This was my idea. I can't back out now.*

Gorman dropped his half-smoked cigarette and ground it into the pavement with his shoe. "Let's get this done."

The three of them marched toward the darkened front doors, wearing bulletproof vests, pistols in their side holsters, tactical knives on their hips, and assault rifles slung across their backs. But Lilith felt naked, memories of her last experience whirling through her mind. *This is not enough. We are not enough.*

She tried to silence the disparaging mantra, but it kept repeating, and her hands started to shake. *Come on. Get it together.*

Chance reached for the door, but when it didn't budge, his brow wrinkled in confusion. It was one o'clock on a Monday. The place should have been open.

"Perhaps they take clients by appointment only?" Gorman suggested, surveying the entrance.

"There's no buzzer." Lilith's pulse raced, and she frantically looked for an explanation. *My plan is dying before it's even started.*

Chance cupped the sides of his face and peered inside. "There's another set of glass doors, and…" He adjusted his angle, crouching down to catch the light from the foyer. "Seems like metal behind them."

He quickly stood up with a deep frown.

"Shit."

"What?" Lilith searched his face for some glimmer of hope but found none.

"I think we're too late for plan A."

"Why do you say that?" Gorman took a step closer.

"I'm guessing the metal I saw are security doors. I think the place is in lockdown." He studied the building's façade, working the problem in his mind. "We can try the parking garage, but there may be heavier security than we expected. If PMIC security is in the middle of a fight, I don't think they'll take kindly to our presence."

Lilith closed her eyes. The worst-case scenarios flew through her head, making her anxiety almost unbearable. "Damn it. One time! One goddamn time, I'd like things to go our way! Fuck!"

"*Cherie*, stop." Chance moved in front of her and slid his hands up her arms. "You asked these people to help us." He nodded toward the van as Nicci peered out of the passenger side window. "You can't afford to lose your shit. Besides, we don't know anything for certain yet. Let's get in the van and circle back to the garage, okay?"

"You're right." Lilith took a deep breath and stretched her neck before meeting his gaze again. "Thank you."

A roguish grin curved his lips before he turned his attention to Gorman. "Looks like it's forced entry. Are you still okay with that?"

The agent took a second and glanced back at the front doors. "If you're right about the place being in lockdown, there's an active threat inside, and it's my duty to investigate." With that, the FBI agent strolled past them and climbed back into the van, with Chance and Lilith close behind.

"Tim, prep your team. I'm sure we'll have to deal with added security. Nicci, take us around to the garage."

"No one home?"

Chance shrugged and slid into the seat beside Lilith. "Guess we'll see."

"All right, kids. Looks like we're gonna see some action. Hersch, Gibson, get your gear." Tim swapped seats with Nicci and then double-checked his weapons and walkie.

Of course, when they arrived at their destination, a steel gate bared their progress, and Lilith struggled to contain her frustration. Thankfully, the entrance was in an alley that appeared to have very little traffic, and all the windows facing the area were blacked out. The Durand probably owned the surrounding properties to ensure their privacy. For once, their endless resources came in handy.

Gibson, Tim, and Hersch—the advanced team—hopped out of the van, cautiously approached the gate, their assault rifles at the ready, and did a preliminary sweep. Once they declared the area safe, Gibson got to work, while the other two stood guard.

Lilith expected him to bust out a lock cutter and attack the thing, but the man simply pulled out a foldable tablet and typed away. Apparently, Nicci wasn't their only hacker. After about ten minutes, the gate groaned into action and slowly rolled up.

With the way ahead clear, they moved forward in a three-man formation, their rifles aimed and ready with Gibson in the lead. When he swung left, Tim took point and directed Hersch to the right.

Everyone in the van remained silent, fixated on the garage entrance. They strained to hear any signs of trouble and the seconds seemed to stretch into minutes as they waited.

Lilith was so focused that when "All clear" crackled over the walkies, she nearly jumped out of her skin.

Chance nodded to Nicci, and she put the van in gear, slowly edging it into the cavernous garage. Cars filled every space on the ground level, which didn't lift Lilith's spirits. The Durand were here...lots of them. She had no idea how many inhabited the building, but there were at least seventy-five cars on the ground level alone.

When she spotted the blue metal security door, a flood of memories washed over her, and her pulse quickened again. She recalled equating the door to a mouth, ready to swallow them all whole, and that sensation still lingered. Nothing good waited for them inside. That was her only certainty.

However, as they drove closer, she realized the door wasn't closed, and apprehension tingled up her spine.

When the van came to a stop, she hopped out and peered at the mangled metal door barely hanging on its hinges. Chance stepped up beside her with the same confused frown.

It looked like someone had busted through the door with brute force, or perhaps set off a grenade. Lilith stepped closer and spotted a trail of blood across the concrete, leading away from the door. She followed the trajectory of splotches and drips to a hole in the fencing between two concrete columns.

"What the hell?" She plucked a piece of flesh from the sharp metal wire, and fear prickled over her skin.

Lilith leaned through the hole in the fence and peered down the alley both ways. No broken doors or windows, only a few drops of blood that led nowhere, a rusting dumpster, and a half-disassembled motorcycle.

"Lily. We need to get in formation. This is a hostile scene." To his credit, Chance kept his voice low, steady, and calm—the exact opposite of how she felt. Whatever escaped was long gone.

"Of course." Lilith shook off the chilling sensation, grabbed her assault rifle, and joined the others.

"Let me double-check everything."

When Chance strolled up to her, she saw all the barely restrained emotions on his face. He swallowed hard, checking her vest and then clicking the safety off on her rifle. His eyes finally met hers, and she saw how desperately he wanted her to stay in the van, but he never voiced that desire.

"Tim's team will take point, but we will all move together. Boston will be in front of me, and I want you behind me, with Gorman at your back. Once Gorman is in place, he'll tap your shoulder to confirm. Then you tap mine. You do not break formation without asking. Understood?" His hazel eyes misted as she nodded firmly. "I need to hear it, Lily."

"Yes. I understand."

His gaze fell to the pavement for a moment, as if he was hoping she'd change her mind, but then he stole a brief kiss and turned around before she could respond—or perhaps to stop himself from saying anything else.

As he stepped forward, Lilith noticed Boston staring at her with an odd expression she struggled to interpret, but it wasn't entirely friendly. Before she could decipher it any further, Chance shoved David toward the door, and she hurried into position behind him.

Between the backup flood lights and the flashing emergency lights, the splatters of blood and bits of concrete littering the ground became glaringly obvious. She turned to study the inside door frame—no blast damage. Whatever had wrecked the door wasn't a grenade.

A trail of bullet holes at roughly chest height ran along the concrete leading up the stairs, which were smeared with blood and high-velocity drops.

"The elevator's locked down. I've got another door here," Tim hollered from the front.

"The lab won't be on the first floor. Take the stairs."

Once Chance gave the order, Tim, Hersch, and Gibson moved up the stairs like one smooth unit, while the rest of them waited below. They turned the first corner, disappearing out of sight, but not for long.

"Stairs are a no-go." Tim jogged back down to join them. "Looks like a grenade blast or something. Took them out just before the second landing."

"This building is too large to have only one set of stairs. It would violate fire codes," Hersch interjected, rejoining the group. "If we cross the lobby, odds are, we'll find a matching set on the other side."

"All right. You heard the woman." Tim smiled over at the agent before taking point again. "First team goes right. Second team stays center. Third team goes left. Everyone get in position."

While Gibson stepped up with his tablet and a plastic card connected by wires, Gorman tapped Lilith's shoulder. She passed it on to Chance, as directed.

Once Gibson swiped the card, he typed a few things, and a green light blinked to life. He nodded at Tim, stowed his gear, and took his position next to Hersch.

Tim swept the door open with his foot, and the hinges groaned, announcing their presence.

Lilith heard a voice from inside. It sounded artificial and repetitive, but she couldn't make out the words. However, when she followed Chance into the dark lobby, the sound became clear, and it was far from comforting.

"*Security Breach, Level 4, Research Labs. Evacuate all floors. Security Breach, Level 3, Training Facility. Evacuate all floors. Security Breach, Level 2, International Arms and Security. Evacuate all floors. Security Breach, Main Level. Evacuate all floors.*"

The robotic announcement looped over and over as they stepped inside. Then the smell hit her. The overwhelming stench of blood, death, and evisceration saturated the air, so thick she could taste it on her tongue. The sour odor of perforated bowels always made her gag, and she wasn't the only one. The entire team, including the humans, stopped in the doorway, coughing on the contaminated air.

Once everyone adjusted and moved further inside, Lilith finally got a peek at their surroundings. Chance was right about the security doors. Sheets of thick metal covered the entrance, cloaking the entire room in darkness, except for the strobing emergency lights.

Each flash revealed a new horror. Men in full tactical gear were strewn across the floor, surrounded by pools of blood. Red splotches covered the walls and every visible surface.

Something horrific had happened here.

"Tim, can you do anything about the announcement?" Chance called over to him when they neared the security desk.

Lilith stopped beside a body and bent down to inspect it. The right arm had been ripped from the shoulder, and shreds of flesh and tendon still clung to the joint. Most of the throat was missing or so badly mutilated she couldn't detect tool marks, and the abdominal cavity was ripped open by four sharp lacerations, exposing loops of tattered intestines. The man's face was frozen in a horrified scream—pale and lifeless.

"Something is wrong." Lilith stood straight up, shaking and unable to tear her eyes away from the damage. *This looks like Isadora's handiwork, but she's dead…No human could do this…*

Chance turned around as the overhead announcement finally stopped. "What is it?"

"This man…wasn't shot." Her eyes roamed the lobby, and her chest tightened. Between the flashes, an eerie darkness drowned the bloody scene and left her chilled. "Is the area secure?"

She peered up at Chance, who merely frowned in return.

"I need to see the other bodies. You told me to ask before breaking formation."

After a quick survey of the area, he called out to the other team leads. "What's the verdict? Are we all clear?"

"Secure on our front, but I can't do anything about these fucking emergency lights. They have to be turned off at the original source. My guess is the lab," Tim hollered from the security desk.

"All clear here too," Nicci shouted from the far side of the vast room.

"Stay in sight and don't roam too far." Conflicting emotions still lingered in his features, but they only made her appreciate his vote of confidence more.

After a brief smile, Chance led Gorman and Boston to the front desk, while Tim's team spread out and guarded the right flank, mirroring Nicci's group.

Lilith moved quickly from one corpse to the next, briefly assessing their wounds—ripped-off limbs, deep lacerations, torn-apart ribcages missing hearts, necks so savaged a few barely clung to the spine. One was entirely decapitated.

With each mangled body, the knot of dread grew until true terror blossomed in her chest. None of them had bullet wounds. Not a single one. Someone or something had torn these men to shreds and escaped through the parking garage.

It was out there...free.

She sprinted to the security desk. The strobing lights continued to bombard the grotesque scene, flooding her vision with crimson. While rounding the counter, she slid on a pool of congealing blood and nearly lost her footing.

"The bodies..." She panted for breath, and Chance helped steady her. "Thomas and Wolfe's people didn't kill them. They weren't shot. They were torn apart like—" She stopped short when she remembered Gorman and Boston were present. Part of her kept forgetting they were working with humans. They were on the same side, but only because they didn't know the full truth. If the FBI agents knew they were vampires, they might side with their enemies.

"Like what?" David spoke up first, suspicion leaking into his expression.

Well, shit. Of course, he'd hop on any sign of me withholding information. When in doubt, half-truths typically worked.

"A previous case. What do the cameras show?" She stalked past Boston, ignoring the man's scowl, and stood beside Chance as he pulled up the footage.

All four of them leaned in, trying to decipher what was happening on the screen. The bright strobe lights made motion difficult to track, but all Lilith saw were muzzle flares, blood, and body parts. The gunfire and blood-curdling screams rattling through the speakers in a blast of static grated down her spine.

"What the hell is it?" The curiosity in Boston's voice bordered on hysteria, and his breaths became rapid.

"I don't know." Lilith peered closer when Chance rewound the footage.

"With the flashes, it's impossible to tell. Whatever it is…it's fast." Chance frowned at the screen and tried to zoom in, but the pixilation only made things more difficult to see. Too bad they didn't possess the impossible tech of enhancing video footage like they did on TV.

"What the hell have you dragged us into?" Boston grabbed her shoulder and spun her around to face him. "You said you've seen this before!"

"I've seen something similar, but it's impossible. The woman is dead."

"Woman?" David's face scrunched. He took a step back and stared out at the bloody scene in shock. "That doesn't make any sense? No woman could do…that."

"Agent Boston raises a valid point. What are we dealing with here? This doesn't seem like the work of terrorists."

Both Chance and Lilith turned toward Agent Gorman, trying to form a response while the others wandered closer.

Thankfully, Chance recovered faster and took the lead once again.

"You're right. This is an unexpected development, but our mission hasn't changed. Agent, we don't know who or what did this, but we understand if you and your partner want to walk. You are under no obligation to stay."

"Oh, but I am? What about me? I didn't sign up for this."

Everyone ignored Boston's outburst, even Gorman, who studied the carnage. Flashes illuminated oceans of blood spatter, over thirty mangled corpses, and even a severed head sitting on a low couch.

"In all my years with the Bureau, I've never seen anything like this."

"Chance is right. We could really use your help, but you aren't obligated." Lilith desperately hoped they wouldn't walk away. She needed their help more than ever with this new development, but forcing their cooperation wasn't fair.

The man's gaze drifted until his dark eyes rested on her. "If you knew who or what did this…would you tell us?"

Lilith flinched as his discerning eyes bored into her, daring her to lie. "I swear to you. I don't know how this happened."

"That's not what I asked."

"If it was a matter of life and death, which it is…yes." To her surprise, she meant it. She'd do whatever it took to get them all out of this alive.

An uncomfortable silence stretched out while Gorman stared her down, assessing her truthfulness, until Boston couldn't take any more.

"Are you fucking kidding me? She's playing us. She's been playing us all along!"

"David, calm down." Gorman huffed like a tired parent and rubbed the bridge of his nose.

"No!" Before anyone could react, an arm circled Lilith's neck and dragged her backward. "I'm not dying because of this lying bitch."

Lilith choked and gagged from the sudden pressure on her throat. Boston took advantage of the distraction. He snatched the pistol from her holster and jammed the barrel against her temple.

As soon as the pressure registered, she squeezed her eyes closed, and tremors ran through her entire body.

"Whoa! Drop your weapon!" Chance shouted.

Everyone raised their guns and spread out, but Boston was too smart to give anyone a clear shot. The man dragged Lilith along until his back was against the wall and shielded himself behind her.

"No! Listen to me right fucking now! Everyone, out front!" Boston demanded.

Nicci, Keller, and Xander made their way around to join the rest of the group but kept their weapons trained on him.

As much as Lilith wished things were like Hollywood, they couldn't merely take a shot. Any shock to the system could tense his muscles, including his trigger finger, and with the gun still pressed to her temple, the result would be less than ideal. A movie vampire might survive a shot to the head, but real life didn't work that way, or her father would still be alive.

The tension against her windpipe eased a touch, and David leaned in close to whisper. The wash of his hot, sticky breath made her stomach churn.

"I should have known better. I knew there was something wrong with you. What are you? Some kind of demon?"

The words made her blood boil, but before she responded, Chance grabbed his attention.

"Boston. What do you want?" He took a step closer, his hands in the air, and tried to keep his gaze locked on David.

"Fuck you. Stop walking, or I'll empty the entire clip in her skull!"

When Boston shoved the pistol hard enough to tilt her head, the image of Farren doing the same thing flooded her mind and brought tears to her eyes. She'd almost died that day…until Cohen offered himself in her place.

Jenny Allen

Of course, Isadora's pets had attacked before he could make good on that deal, leaving a room full of corpses—just like this one.

Chance froze in place, and his gaze drifted to her terrified face. He sensed every emotion swirling in her brain. She wanted to squash the desperate panic in her gut for his sake, but she couldn't. David had wanted this from the moment he laid eyes on her at the station. He wanted to destroy her. She had never gotten through to him, not really. Justice for Cassie was nothing more than a fleeting distraction from his true desire—Lilith's death.

While her mind spun out, Chance swallowed hard before speaking again. "Let her go, and you can walk out of here."

"Bullshit. The second I drop this gun, I'm dead."

"David—"

His arm tightened again, cutting off her words, while he moved around the group, keeping a wide berth.

"I don't want to hear anything from your lying fucking mouth."

"I promise you won't be harmed if you just let her go. Please!" The strained plea in Chance's voice tore at her heart.

The man scoffed, and a cruel grin stretched his lips. "You're begging for her life? Come on. The sex isn't *that* good, as I recall."

Chance went absolutely still, and his eyes bored into Boston with laser-like intensity. The man continued to circle them, unfazed, heading for the door.

"You're finally gonna pay for destroying my life." The barrel of the gun dug into her skin, and his finger tensed on the trigger, making her heart stutter in her chest.

All her hard work, self-defense techniques, cardio, and she had no choice but to stand there, helpless, as the monster from her past brought it all to an end.

Her teary eyes drifted up to Chance. His chest heaved with panicked breaths. This was the worst part. He had to watch her die, powerless to help her. He would carry the guilt with him for the rest of his life, blame himself.

"David! This has gone far enough!" Gorman snapped the words with firm authority, but the effort was wasted.

"Fuck off, John. I know you handed me over to these savages. You and your partner. I won't forget that little tidbit, and neither will my father. You can kiss that pension goodbye. In fact, I think they'll be sizing you both up for orange jumpsuits."

"David, think about Cassie. She wouldn't want any of this."

When Agent Hersch held up her hands and stepped forward, he focused on her, and the tension in his gun hand eased slightly.

"Shut up. This has nothing to do with her."

"But it does. It has everything to do with her! She's the reason you came along, right?"

"Shut up, Eileen!" The gun against Lilith's head shook as he screamed.

"No." The petite woman took another step forward. "Cassie was a good woman, better than you deserved, and you knew it. She's dead because of *you.*"

"Stop!"

"You betrayed her trust, dragged her into your mess, and now she's rotting in the morgue, all because you couldn't let go of your fucked-up past. You're a pathetic excuse for a man."

"I'm fucking warning you, Eileen. Shut up!"

"No. You're an abusive piece of shit. It should be *you* rotting on that slab!"

"Fuck you!" In a split second, Boston swung the gun around and shot Hersch in the chest.

Time ground to a halt.

Everyone except Chance and Tim rushed to the fallen agent, and shouts echoed through the room.

The pressure on Lilith's throat had eased when the man pulled the trigger, and she shoved her hand between her neck and his arm while he was distracted. The rage and adrenaline forced her cartilaginous fangs to click down from the roof of her mouth. She opened wide and sank them into the man's forearm.

He wanted a monster, and by God, she was going to give him one.

As his shrieks filled the air, she rammed her elbow into his gut and scrambled away as fast as possible. Lilith skidded to the ground, her heart pounding.

Chance slid to his knees in front of her and frantically looked her over. "Are you okay?"

With tears in his eyes, he wiped the blood from her face, and when she nodded, he pulled her tight against him. His heart raced, thumping like a caged rabbit on speed. She nestled into his arms and cried.

If Hersch hadn't distracted him...

"I thought I was really going to lose you this time."

Motion caught her attention. Nicci and Gorman were pulling Hersch to her feet. The bulletproof vest did its job—thank God Boston hadn't aimed for her head. Either way, the woman had taken a bullet for her. At the very least, Lilith owed Eileen Hersch a beer.

Boston screamed again, and she peered over her shoulder. Tim forced the man to his knees.

"The bitch bit me!" Blood streamed down his cuffed hands from the two small puncture wounds.

Hopefully, she hit an artery.

"I'm fucking bleeding!"

The sound of his voice slowed Chance's pulse and made his muscles stiffen around her. When she pulled back, he was staring at Boston with the same impassive mask he wore when he had shot Spencer. Dread gripped her heart again.

"Chance."

His hazel eyes darted back to her for a moment, and then he stood, leaving her alone on the floor.

"Hey. What are you doing?" Lilith hopped up and stepped into his path. "Talk to me."

"I'm sorry, *cherie*."

"Wait. What? Sorry about what?"

Without another glance, he walked past her, drew his handgun, and came to a stop behind Boston.

"Chance. What are you doing, man? I got this." Tim frowned up at him in confusion until he spotted the gun in his hand. "No."

When Agent Boston turned, trying to look behind him, Chance squeezed the trigger—two quick pops to the base of the skull that thundered through the room. Then he dropped his gun.

Everyone yelled. Gorman and Hersch surged forward, their weapons trained on him. Chance held up his hands and got on his knees, his gaze landing on Lilith's horrified face.

"Fuck. Is he dead?" Hersch hollered.

Gorman grabbed Chance's wrists and cuffed him.

Tim shook his head, wiping blood and bone fragments off his tactical vest. "Yeah. I'd say dead is an accurate statement. Shit."

"Wait. What are you doing?" Lilith ran up to Gorman, her heart threatening to beat right out of her chest. "Come on. Boston had me at gunpoint."

The man's dark features contorted into an expression of disbelief. "Mr. Deveraux shot a federal agent in cold blood *after* he'd been subdued."

"He shot Hersch."

"In the vest. I'm sorry, Ms. Adams, but I warned you. I won't condone murder."

When Gorman walked away, Lilith collapsed in front of Chance. Her heart plummeted. "Why did you do that?"

He tilted his head and sighed while tears misted his enigmatic eyes. "You know why, *cherie*. He was too dangerous, and I had to keep you safe. I had no choice."

A moment of déjà vu struck her—sitting in her therapist's office as Dr. Price asked if she felt remorse. A sad smile crossed her lips when she realized he had killed Boston for the same reasons she had killed Peisinoe.

"I'm sorry, *mon amour*. I wanted to keep my promise to you. I tried."

"No. You were right. Peace was never an option, and I'm sorry for insisting it was." Lilith caressed his stubbled cheek and pressed her forehead to his, fighting to breathe past the lump of tears in her throat. This couldn't be the end to their story.

"Let's all slow down." Nicci's authoritative voice made everyone stop in their tracks. "We still have a mission to complete."

"I think we're past that point, Detective."

"Really, Agent Gorman? You're giving up because someone killed an abusive rapist who held a CSI at gunpoint and shot a federal agent? That man's justice is worth more than Agent Cappalletty's or the thousands of people that might die if this virus mutates?"

"Look—"

"No. You look. We are already here, so let's finish this. Release Mr. Deveraux. He's not a threat to anyone else. If you still want to take him into custody afterward, he's all yours."

"She's right, John." Hersch laid a hand on her partner's shoulder. "You know I don't endorse cold-blooded murder, but even subdued, Agent Boston was a threat to all of us, and we have more important things to worry about."

"I took an oath, Eileen."

"We both did, and we've both broken it. Handing Dave over to civilians wasn't legal, but you did it for very good reasons. Hell, we agreed to come on this mission off the books, which is enough to get us suspended. And don't forget how you helped me before any of this. That wasn't legal either.

Let's just see this thing through, okay? After that, we can discuss this further."

With an irritated grunt, Gorman nodded and pulled a cigarette and lighter from his vest. "Uncuff him." Once he gave the order, the man wandered away from the group and lit his cigarette.

Somehow, Lilith suspected a smoker lighting up in the Durand's corpse-ridden lobby was the least of their concerns.

Chapter 40

"Thank you, Agent Hersch." Chance smiled over his shoulder as she unlocked his cuffs.

"Please, call me Eileen." The woman tucked away the handcuffs and walked around to face him. "I can't officially say what you did was right, but..." The agent's eyes drifted over to what remained of Boston's skull. "The bastard had it coming."

"No—I mean, thank you for this—but I was referring to what you did for Lilith."

She turned back to him with a hint of pink in her cheeks. "I couldn't stand there and watch him destroy more lives. I'm just glad he aimed for my vest." Her features melted into a faraway expression, and she rubbed at the left side of her chest.

"Anyway..." The woman shook off the daydream and smiled up at him. "Lilith seems like a strong, smart woman, so I'm not surprised Boston wanted to break her."

"Sounds like you knew him well."

"No, but I know the type." A host of dark memories floated just beneath the surface—personal experience.

"We should get moving. This place obviously doesn't have an alarm that notifies police, but it's only a matter of time."

Agent Hersch strolled away to join Tim and Gibson.

Lilith jogged up and threw her arms around him. He held her tight, burying his face in her neck, and just breathed. *She's alive*, he reminded himself.

"I am so sorry, Chance."

"Shh, *cherie*." He stroked her curls as she cried against his shoulder. "Nothing is set in stone. There's still a chance they won't arrest me."

Lilith pulled back and frowned up at him. "But what if they do?"

One side of his mouth lifted in a weak smile. He wasn't ready to broach that subject or consider the possibility. He pressed his lips against her forehead and whispered, "We'll cross that bridge when we get to it."

"We need to move out!" Tim hollered at them from across the room.

Chance stepped back and brushed back the strands from her face. "Come on, *mon fiancée*. We have work to do."

A sadness lingered in his smile, tearing at Lilith's heart. Before he walked away, she rushed up and captured his lips in a tender kiss that she never wanted to end.

A genuine smile lit his handsome face afterward, and that was enough to lift her spirits…for the moment.

After grabbing her rifle, Lilith took her position behind him, and they crossed the lobby to join the other teams. When Agent Gorman passed by them, his dark eyes held a mass of conflicting emotions, and he avoided eye contact. *Perhaps Chance was right. Maybe his arrest isn't set in stone.*

"All right! Same drill. I will lead Gibson and Hersch in first." When Tim turned toward Agent Hersch, the corners of his mouth lifted, and an almost imperceptible blush infused his cheeks. Then it was gone, and he reverted to business mode. "Chance's team will follow, and Nicci's team will cover the rear. Our objective is the fourth-floor labs. Let's move."

Gibson swung the door open for Hersch and Tim, who entered the stairwell, guns aimed. After a few seconds, Gorman took the door as Lilith followed Gibson and Chance inside.

The strobe lights were still flashing, but this time, they only revealed sterile white walls and concrete—no blood or rubble to be seen. The entire group took their time climbing the stairs, pausing at each landing to check the doors—all secured by keycard locks.

As they approached the fourth-floor door, Gibson moved forward once again, and Tim guarded the ascending stairs. Just like before, he pulled out his folding tablet and connected a card with a wire. After one swipe, the little green LED lit up, and Hersch grabbed the handle, cracking the door.

She waited until Gibson stowed his toys, aimed his rifle, and nodded. The woman gave a silent count…*one…two…three*. The door swung open wide. Tim and Gibson rushed inside, surveying every angle.

After a few minutes, Tim gave the signal, and the rest of the group passed through the door. The dark hallway was flooded with flickering light every few seconds, which was quickly giving Lilith a migraine. She pinched the bridge of her nose and followed Chance further down the hall.

Then her foot hit something solid, and she stumbled forward, right into Chance's back. "Shit. Sorry. I tripped on something."

She glanced down at another mutilated corpse, but this one wasn't in SWAT gear. Blood covered his white lab coat, his pale face, even his broken glasses. His head bent unnaturally to one side, and the tattered remnants of flesh revealed bits of fractured vertebrae. *What the hell did this?*

"*Cherie.*" She peered up at the guarded expression on his face. "There's more."

Lilith stepped to the side and looked down the hallway. Dozens of bodies dressed in civilian clothes littered the floor, and torrents of blood and tissue clung to the gray walls. She could write the lobby off as over-enthusiastic self-defense, but this…this was pure slaughter.

Gibson and Hersch checked each door, picking their way past the eviscerated and savaged bodies. The stench became overwhelming in the confined space, and Lilith covered her nose as they peered into another bland office.

When the group paused at a corner, Lilith gazed down at the corpse lying next to her feet. The pale face summoned a spark of recognition. She squatted down and turned the head toward her.

"They were here."

Everyone peered over at her, and she stood up.

"It's the overweight guy from the gala. The one that parted the way for us."

"Seems like you were right about the target. Still no idea what did all this?" Gorman's gruff voice held a little more suspicion than it used to.

"No, but I'm hoping the lab will give us answers."

"Looks like it's just up this hall," Tim called from the corner. "Double doors with a keycard with about ten bodies piled in front of it. Looks like they were killed while trying to escape."

Yeah, but killed by what? Does the Durand have another necromancer, like Isadora? Did they create something new? With access to Ashcroft's DNA, anything is possible. Fuck. What did these demonic assholes do? Better question…how do I explain it to Gorman, Hersch, and the other humans when we find out?

The group turned the corner and covered her as Lilith stopped at each body. She found two scientists and handed one of their badges to Tim before moving on to three heavily armed civilians she didn't recognize, most likely part of Wolfe's group.

Then she spotted a shock of silvery-blond hair and shoved two middle-aged men off Renee. The woman's milky eyes stared lifelessly, blood pooling in the corners of her eyelids. Like the others, most of her throat was gone, but the damage extended up to her face. The stark angle of her mandible lay exposed and glistening in the flashing light.

Lilith averted her eyes, mixed emotions churning her stomach. Sure. The woman had violated her privacy and participated in kidnapping, torture, and murder, but the brutal manner of her death was still disturbing.

She tried to reign in her panic but glimpsed someone else familiar and rushed over to the man lying beside Tim. "Chance!"

As she removed the severed arm from the dead man's chest, Chance walked up behind her. "Holy shit. That's the reporter from the gala."

"Yeah."

The man had traded his boring navy suit for a sweatshirt and jeans, but she'd recognize his face anywhere.

"What's happening?" Nicci pushed her way past Chance, past Lilith digging through the man's pockets, and stopped in her tracks. "Oh my god...that's—"

"The reporter, yeah." Lilith pulled a leather wallet out of his back pocket and flipped it open. "Michael Higgins. He's an English professor at Penn State."

Nicci's sudden snort of laughter caught them all off guard. When she noticed everyone staring at her like she'd grown a second head, she shrugged. "It's smart...that's all."

"How so?" Chance quirked one eyebrow and glared down at the petite detective.

"Lilith's an intelligent woman, hot on their trail. It makes sense that they rattled her cage to throw her off balance before she met Dr. Wolfe. Of course, I think Aaron upset *you* more than their fake reporter."

"Yeah, well..." Lilith looked around at the other bodies and sighed. "I don't see Thomas or Wolfe in this pile. We need to keep moving. If they managed to escape, we're wasting time."

"All right. Back in position. I'll see if this works."

Everyone scrambled back into place and readied their weapons. Tim slid the badge Lilith had given him through the keycard lock. The LED blinked green, followed by the metal *thunk* of a heavy-duty lock disengaging.

After another silent count, Gibson and Chance pulled the doors open, while Tim and Eileen took point. A deep and ominous darkness saturated the room between flashes, and a buzzing alarm sounded from inside.

"Lily. Hold the door."

She picked her way past the strewn bodies and gripped the handle, taking over for Chance.

"Stay here until we clear the room, okay?" Once she nodded, Chance turned to Nicci. "Same for you. Gibson is great at hacking security systems, but not computers."

"Got it." The petite Italian nodded, took over for Tim, and patted him on the shoulder. "Be careful, big guy."

"Xander and Keller, stand watch at the corner. Gorman, you can either stay here until we clear the room or come with us. Your call."

The man's dark brow furrowed deeply, and he considered the options. "I think I'll accompany you, Mr. Deveraux. Can't let my partner have all the fun." Nothing in his deep voice matched the jovial nature of his words. He didn't want to go in there—plain and simple—but he wouldn't abandon his partner either.

Chance glanced over at Lilith one more time, but her gaze was fixed to the flashes of glass and metal inside. A mixture of fear and curiosity swirled inside her, and she knew Chance sensed all of it.

However, when he moved forward, she touched his arm, drawing his attention. "You be careful too. Can't have the love of my life dying on me, right?"

A smile crossed his lips at the familiar phrase. The words were strikingly similar to the ones he had told her before she descended into the bowels of the Phipps Bend basement last year.

After stealing a quick kiss containing everything he didn't have time to say, Chance followed Tim and the others into the dark room, leaving Lilith and Nicci alone in the hallway.

"Hey partner, are you okay?"

Lilith gazed down the bloody hallway. The light continued to flicker, illuminating a host of horrors drenched in red. "When is this shit gonna end? Ashcroft, the Durand, a psycho cult, and now this?"

"I'm sure that's not the only thing on your mind."

"What do we do if Gorman insists on arresting Chance? I can't let him go to jail."

"We'll figure it out, but you're right. He can't go to jail." She peeked into the room before whispering, "He may be a half-blood, but the database showed something else in his blood…something not human. It's too risky."

Lilith paled, realizing what Nicci meant. It wasn't a matter of whether Chance went to jail. It was a matter of whether Gorman *insisted* on being a problem.

She liked the history buff, and she hadn't invited him along just to kill him later. There had to be a mutually beneficial way to resolve things, even if it meant breaking her own rules.

Suddenly, the strobing lights stopped, plunging the hall into unsettling darkness. Nightmarish images of animated corpses shuffling through the black flooded her brain, making her pulse race furiously. Fear tingled over her skin, and she broke out in a nervous sweat. *No. Keep it together. This isn't a dream. This is real, and bodies don't more on their own…not usually.*

Her panic reached a fevered pitch before fluorescent bulbs flooded the hallway with blinding light. After a few seconds, Lilith's eyes adjusted, and the bile rose in her throat.

The grotesque hall was even worse under the harsh and unforgiving lights. The pale faces were contorted in fear. Blood soaked the carpet and formed deep pools in some places. Loops of shining pink intestines covered the floor, like a sea of skinless snakes. Blood and hunks of flesh clung to the walls, a few bits oozing slowly to the floor.

"*Merda Santa*," Nicci whispered, the color draining from her heart-shaped face.

Although Lilith didn't speak Italian, she got the gist.

"*The main lab is clear.*" The words crackled over the walkie, making Chance's voice almost unrecognizable. "*There are a few more doors to check, but we have a…survivor who needs medical attention.*"

A confusing mixture of hope and fear ricocheted down her spine. *What if it's Cohen? What if he's dying? Shit. What if it's not and he's already dead?* Lilith spoke into the mic, "Nicci and I are coming in."

They moved into the lab. The macabre display continued but with one noticeable difference—the corpses wearing lab coats and scrubs were riddled with bullet wounds. Thomas and Wolfe's cult had drawn blood before unleashing whatever terror destroyed them.

In the center of the room stood a computer station connected to a sizeable mainframe, which indicated a significant amount of data. It also meant they couldn't simply grab the hard drive and run.

"Well...looks like I have a date with this beauty." Nicci grinned, cracked her knuckles, and got to work, while Lilith continued to survey the room with a blossoming sense of déjà vu.

The octagonal room's outer circumference featured glass holding cells of various sizes, workstations, and several doors to other rooms. She'd never been here before, but the lab closely resembled the one from her nightmare...the one where she'd seen Gloria, the girls, and Nicci dead. *How is that possible?*

"Chance, where's the—"

"Over here." He stepped back with his gun still aimed, revealing a slumped figure on the floor. "Gorman and Hersch are searching the cold storage unit." He thrust his chin toward a heavy door beside the entrance. "I figured they'd recognize evidence from their case." He lowered his voice before continuing. "And it keeps them busy while we sort this out."

Lilith moved closer, peering at the man on the floor. Although she couldn't clearly see his face, she recognized the jet-black hair. The harsh dye job looked even worse against the current deathly pallor leaching the olive undertone from his skin.

Four deep lacerations cut across Dr. Kelley Wolfe's chest. The wounds made a wet sucking sound with every rattled inhale and gurgled bubbles with each exhale—at least one punctured lung, if not both.

Lilith wracked her brain for a moment, trying to think of a solution. She wasn't accustomed to performing first aid. Typically, the victims were well beyond saving when she arrived on the scene. "I need...a first aid kit and...plastic."

"I think I saw a kit, but what kind of plastic do you need?" Tim hollered from across the room.

"The thinner and more pliable the better...like cling wrap, or even a Ziplock bag." *Of course, none of that will save his life. I just need him alive long enough to answer questions.*

Tim and Gibson tore through the lab, pulling out drawers and ripping open cabinets to the sound of Nicci's furious typing. Meanwhile, Lilith grabbed gloves and knelt in front of Wolfe.

The sticky blood pooling around him soaked through her jeans, still warm from his body heat, and the unexpected ache in the roof of her mouth made her stomach churn. She'd never experienced a reaction from her cartilaginous fangs like this.

Sure, they had clicked into place a few times when she felt threatened or was dangerously low on hemoglobin, but they never caused...desire before, not even with the cab driver last year. That had been an animalistic need, self-preservation. This was...bloodlust, for lack of a better term.

It had to be all the blood, an ocean of crimson in one building.

"I got some baggies here, ma'am." Gibson's voice held a sharp Southern twang that still took her by surprise.

"Here. Take her this too." Tim shoved a first aid kit in Gibson's direction when he ran past.

"Thanks." Lily ripped open the kit, but apparently, they experienced a lot of injuries and never thought to restock the thing. "Shit. Keep looking for any kind of ointment—like Neosporin, Vaseline, Aquaphor, anything."

Wolfe gargled and coughed, sending flecks of blood flying as he tried to speak.

"Hold on. Save your strength and let me help." Then she glanced up at Chance, who still had his weapon aimed. "Can you help me lie him flat?"

Reluctantly, Chance clicked on the safety, let the rifle swing behind him, and grabbed the man's narrow shoulders. Lilith moved to Kelley's feet and slowly eased him down. Once he was supine on the blood-soaked tile, Chance resumed his guarded stance, weapon in hand.

Kelley jerked and released a gurgled scream when she pressed plastic against the sucking chest wounds. Unfortunately, between the thickness of the freezer bag and the congealing blood, she couldn't get a good seal.

"Chance, put the gun away and help me. This man is in no shape to attack anyone."

Before Chance responded, Kelley's hand clamped around her wrist, capturing her attention. "Not the..." The gurgled voice croaked from his throat along with flecks of blood. "Plan."

Lilith quirked an eyebrow and pressed the plastic tight against the deepest wound. "I figured being slashed open wasn't part of the plan. Where's Cohen? What happened here?"

The man's brown eyes with their shock of blue widened, and he struggled to drag in another breath. "Rachel...she...wouldn't..."

"Wouldn't what?"

The man's breaths became slower and more ragged.

"I found some A&D ointment. Will that work?" Tim hurried over.

Lilith sat back on her heels, staring at Kelley's lifeless face. "It's too late. Damn it!" She surged to her feet, pulled off the bloody gloves, and tossed them in the sink.

After a moment, she glanced back at Chance.

"What about you? Any sign of Cohen?"

The man's jaw clenched, and he shook his head. "We haven't cleared the other rooms yet."

"Well, there aren't any more threats in this room, so perhaps you should." She didn't mean for the words to come out clipped and irritable, but the frustration and fear were getting to her. "Shit. I'm sorry. I just—"

"I know." He walked over and tucked a few strands behind her ear. "We'll figure this out. We always do, *cherie*."

Dread strummed along her nerves, and she peered around the blood-soaked room. "I'm not sure I want to figure this one out."

"Say the word, and we can leave right now."

A large part of her was tempted to take his offer, but she knew better. They needed to uncover what happened and what had escaped. And whether or not Chance liked it, they needed to find Cohen. If he was alive, she needed the truth from him.

He didn't need her to voice the answer. The man knew her…better than anyone. "Check on Nicci. Tim and I will check the other rooms, while Gibson stands guard."

"Thank you."

Chance pressed his lips against her cheek in a quick kiss before joining Tim on the other side of the room.

After one last glance at Dr. Wolfe's body, she strolled over to the computer desk in the center of the room.

"Hey, partner. I've almost got the surveillance footage from the lab. Just a few more minutes."

"What's the open file there?"

"Specimen Omega. I copied it to my flash drive but haven't looked through it yet."

"Lily, first door leads to an operating room. It's clear. Moving on to the second."

She nodded in Tim's direction, but her eyes remained fixed on the open file in the tab bar. *Omega. What did they create?*

"Okay. Here we go. This is timed two hours ago, about ten minutes before the first alarm triggered."

Lilith gazed at the screen. Staff in scrubs, lab coats, masks, and face shields milled around various stations and wandered in and out of adjoining rooms. Nothing stood out or appeared abnormal...

Until Cohen, looking a little worse for wear, entered the room with Kelley and Rachel close behind him. Andrew's left eye was swollen shut, a gash in his eyebrow left blood trailing down his face, and a sling supported his left arm.

All the workers froze in place, except for an older man with sunken cheeks and a permanent scowl.

"Vhat are you doingk here? You may be ze company's poster boy, but dis area is off limits! Only my hand-selected team vorks here. Get out!" The man spoke with a Russian accent that was prominent but understandable, more so than Luminita's had been when Lilith first met her.

Andrew held up his hands and took a step forward. "Ivanov, this isn't what you think. I need you to remain calm."

The scientist, Ivanov, scoffed and continued forward. "I'll be calm vhen you and your riffraff are gone. Out!"

While the rigid man pointed at the door behind them, Rachel raised a pistol and fired several shots.

For a moment, the picture seemed frozen, and then everything descended into chaos. Other members of the cult entered the room and opened fire on the staff, who screamed and scrambled for cover.

"Get on the floor! Now!" Chance's sudden shout drew Lilith's attention from the surveillance footage. "I don't care! Get down!"

Lilith raced across the lab, following the voices to the second adjoining room, and pushed through the door.

Chance loomed over Cohen, the rifle barrel to his temple. Andrew held his shaking hands in the air while he pleaded.

"I swear to God, I didn't know!"

"Get on the fucking ground, or I *will* pull the trigger!"

Andrew swallowed hard and started to comply until his bloodshot eyes landed on Lilith. "I am so fucking sorry. I didn't know! I swear to you, Lilith! I didn't know! You have to believe me!"

Although the man appeared traumatized, he'd definitely healed since the video—no sling, no gash, no swollen black eye. Of course, the horrors in the other room had provided a veritable feast of fear and anguish, so she shouldn't be surprised.

Luminita's handiwork of faint pink scars on his face still remained. Once again, she wondered why those didn't heal the same way the rest of his injuries did. *Was it tied to the emotional intent? Did the ritualistic torture her father subjected Ashcroft to actually make a difference? After all, Ashcroft hadn't managed to heal those scars either.*

"Lilith! Please! I never lied to you! I swear it! I didn't know!"

Cohen's pleading cries pulled her from her wandering thoughts again, but before she responded, the stock of Chance's rifle collided with Cohen's head, providing just enough force to knock him to the ground. "None of us care about your apologies. Hands behind your back!"

Andrew's sky-blue eyes remained locked on her, and the desperate sadness in their depths made her uneasy. She knew he was adept at manipulation, but since the ordeal with Luminita, his emotions seemed erratic, raw, and most importantly, real. They weren't buried and concealed under layers of nonchalant arrogance like they once were. She could *not* bring herself to believe Cohen double-crossed them.

"Can you bring him to the main lab? Nicci has the surveillance footage pulled up, and I think we all need to see it."

The firmly pressed lips, clenched jaw, and furrowed brow all indicated anger, but Chance didn't argue. After a few tense seconds, his expression softened, and he cuffed Cohen's wrists before helping the man to his feet. "You heard the woman."

When Cohen didn't move, Chance shoved him forward with a little too much force. Andrew stumbled but quickly recovered and followed Lilith into the next room.

The demon's face paled when he gazed around at all the carnage. Apparently, he had ducked out of the room before most of it and hadn't set foot inside since.

"Chair. Now!"

Cohen complied with hesitation and sat on the edge of a blood-splattered chair. "I didn't know what they had. I swear to you! I had no idea Ivanov was working with Luminita."

As soon as the woman's name left his lips, a chill ran down Lilith's spine, and she whirled around. "What are you talking about?"

Frantic panic took over when his eyes drifted to the floor, and he struggled to breathe through it. Speaking her name had surely summoned a host of horrific memories he could never forget. The fine network of scars on his body were a permanent reminder.

"Andrew." Lilith knelt in front of him and waited until he met her gaze. "How do you know these scientists were working with Luminita?"

"The book…" His words trailed off, and his eyes drifted to the counter next to Nicci. "Shit! It's gone." The panic set back in, and his respirations quickened. "We need to go! We need to get out of here now!"

"Lil, he's telling the truth…About the book, at least. Come look." Nicci pointed at the screen.

Lilith gripped Cohen's knee until his wild eyes met hers again. "Andrew, calm down." As his breathing normalized, a wave of dizziness made the room tilt, and she pulled her hand back.

"Fuck. I'm sorry. I didn't mean to draw from you," Andrew added quickly.

Lilith swallowed hard and ignored the apology. "We're all leaving soon, I promise. But we need answers. I need to know what we're dealing with."

She stood up and started toward Nicci, but Chance stepped into her path. "Are you sure about taking him with us? This could still be a set-up. The man's harmless act in front of his grandfather was convincing too." He wanted her to say no, that much was clear, but none of the anger and doubt leaked into his words.

"Yes." Lilith stared into his eyes, begging him to trust her. "I believe him, and if I'm wrong, we'll need answers. Either way, he comes with us."

Once again, his expression softened, and he nodded. "Solid plan." He fell in beside her as she approached the computer desk.

"Sorry. What is it, Nicci?"

The screen was paused during the cult's fire fight, but nothing unusual jumped out at her.

"There." Nicci pointed to the desk at the bottom of the frame, the same one they stood at.

When Lilith spotted her uncle's journal—the Voynich Manuscript—sitting on the metal counter, her stomach lurched.

A barrage of memories flashed through her brain in quick succession—Miriah's tortured corpse lying on her desk…Her father revealing his violent past in a hotel room…Duncan shackled to the concrete floor, gnawing on his own limbs…The Durand executing her father in front of her…A thief with his jaw ripped off and ribcage torn open…Farren with his gun to her head…The screams as Isadora's zombies tore people apart…Peisinoe's shrieks slicing through her mind, like red-hot razor wire…The sickening sound when Luminita's scalpel nicked the bone while carving Cohen's flesh—all atrocities that occurred because of that infernal book and the dark secrets it contained.

What else would happen because of those cryptic pages? What new horrors awaited them because of its vengeful tale steeped in centuries of blood at the cost of countless lives?

Chapter 41

"Can you see who took the book?" Chance glanced at Lilith, probably sensing her mounting panic and despair.

"Let's find out." Nicci pressed play while Lilith, Chance, and Tim hovered over her shoulder and Gibson guarded the doors.

When the fire fight ended, Dr. Wolfe shoved Cohen against the desk, while his sister roamed the room.

"What do you want from us?" Cohen's voice held a cold, crisp edge that was difficult to ignore.

"We told you. The *Empusa* from Phipps Bend."

"The vampire? Ashcroft? He's dead. I thought you did your research."

"We only need his blood…his DNA."

"Those items would be kept in cold storage…*if* we had them, which we do *not*."

"I think you're the one who's misinformed." Kelley scoffed.

Rachel lingered by a reinforced-glass-and-concrete cell in the far wall. The light didn't quite reach that area, making her difficult to see, but whatever occupied that holding cell had captured her interest.

"Kelley. Over here."

"Watch him! We still need him to get out of here."

After he barked the order, Renee wandered on-screen with an assault rifle, guarding Cohen while Dr. Wolfe strolled over to his sister.

Then he stopped short and recoiled. "Holy shit! What the hell—"

Rachel interrupted him, but Lilith couldn't hear their conversation. "Can you turn it up?"

"Already at max volume on this thing. Their equipment sucks. I might be able to extract the audio once I get the files back home and amplify it. Depends on the camera's mics, though."

Lilith studied the twins. They continued to talk, and judging by their arm movements, gestures, and Wolfe's rigid posture, it was a heated debate, one he was losing.

Lilith glanced away from the screen to stare at the open glass door with an arterial arc of blood spatter covering it.

"*No!*" Kelley's robust shout from the TV drew her eyes back to the screen. The man stormed over to the computer. "That was not the plan, Rachel! We are supposed to grab the samples we need and go. We don't know what that…thing will do! Get what we came for so we can leave before someone sounds the alarm."

When Wolfe paced around the desk, he noticed Cohen staring in horror at the ancient book and picked the thing up, casually flipping through the pages. The Voynich Manuscript held nothing but pain and revenge, but he'd never know that. The book was impossible to read without the cipher, which didn't seem to be there.

Meanwhile, his twin bent over a case and pulled out something—*a syringe, perhaps?* The woman turned and glanced at her brother, then appeared to swap the item for something else.

Lilith squinted at the screen, trying to make out what she was doing, but between the low light in that section and the poor camera quality, the visibility was awful. *For a species with virtually unlimited resources, they sure skimped on the security budget. Of course, maybe that's on purpose. Perhaps they didn't want a highly detailed record of what they were doing here.*

"You're wrong, Art. The gods gave us a divine tool of vengeance, and I won't squander the opportunity to serve their purpose!"

Kelley put Duncan's book back on the counter with a confused frown and turned to Rachel, who was doing something to the cell.

"Rachel, no!" the man screamed, rushing forward, but not fast enough.

The door sprang open, and a dark figure stepped past the threshold, stopping in front of the virologist. For a few tense seconds, the two faced each other, then Dr. Thomas moved…

The shadow lunged, and arterial blood splashed against the glass before Rachel could scream. Only a gurgled cry emerged from her throat. The thing tore her right arm from the socket and threw it across the room.

Then the screaming truly started.

Cohen slammed a button, which plunged the entire lab into darkness, and a robotic voice issued a familiar announcement.

"*Security Breach, Level 4, Research Labs. Evacuate all floors.*"

The flashing emergency lights revealed blurs of motion, sprays of blood, glistening intestines, arms torn from the sockets as the guns they held fired, and rib cages rupturing open, a red mist filling the room. When the movement stopped, the book was gone.

"Goddamn. What the hell is that thing?" Gorman's voice made them all jump.

"Special Agent Gorman? What are you doing here?" Cohen's voice turned from panicked to icy wrath, and he glared over at Lilith.

"Backing up Miss Adams and saving your ass." The man clapped a hand on Andrew's back while wearing a somber frown. "Glad to see you in one piece…What happened to—" The agent's dark brows pulled together as he gestured at the thin scars on Cohen's face.

"The story is too long to tell at the moment. Is Hersch—"

"Right here, Andy." The cool tone didn't match Eileen's use of his nickname. Whatever happened between them, she wasn't entirely happy to see Detective Cohen.

"Now" —Gorman glared over at Lilith—"are you going to tell us what the hell that thing is?"

"As soon as I figure that out." Lilith sighed and hoped her partner could give them answers. "Nicci, are there any other camera angles? Perhaps one facing that holding cell, or one that will show us who snatched the book?" Lilith diverted attention back to their true concerns, which didn't involve Andrew's personal life.

"Let me dig for a minute."

"What about you two? Did you find anything in cold storage?"

"Just this." Hersch pointed to a box sitting on the floor. "Looks like most of the biologicals. They could have samples elsewhere. There's no telling."

"Okay. Thanks," Lilith replied absently, her gaze drifting back to the mysterious holding cell.

While Nicci typed furiously, the others watching her, Lilith wandered over to the shadowy spot. Dr. Thomas's lifeless eyes stared out from under her thick bangs, and Lilith thought back to the first time they'd met.

The woman's deep dimples and cheery disposition had thrown Lilith for a loop. She didn't seem like anything more than an overeager scientist— harmless but enthusiastic. Rachel had even fooled Cohen and his emotion-sensing talents. *Not even the Durand are infallible.*

Lilith stepped over the woman's corpse and searched the area. A plaque by the door read: "Specimen Omega"—the same as the open file Nicci had copied. *So, the thing has a name.*

As she stepped into the small six-by-six space, she noticed claw marks all over the cement walls. She traced the rivets with her fingertips, starting at head height in a downward swipe. *Talons...at least a few inches in length, four together...but the figure stood upright...like a human...*

A sudden dread blossomed in her chest, squeezing her lungs and twisting her stomach. *No.* Her brain tried to deny the conclusion.

"Got it!" Nicci hollered. "It was buried in heavier encryption. They definitely didn't want anyone else seeing this...Oh shit!"

Lilith swallowed the lump of fear wedged in her throat and turned back toward the computer. Chance's horrified face only made things worse.

"No...," he whispered before his eyes snapped up to Lilith.

"It's a person? What did this is...human?" Gorman took a step back, his eyes widening. "What's wrong with his face? Are those scars? They look like..." His head swiveled to Cohen with an expression of complete shock.

Lilith closed her eyes, sending a single tear down her cheek. Gorman's reaction narrowed the answer to two possibilities—either Luminita had succeeded in turning a Durand, or...

Her eyes flashed open when Chance softly gripped her shoulders. "Is it him?" As soon as the question left her mouth, she prayed he'd say no.

Chance swallowed hard, a lifetime's worth of apologies in his eyes. When he finally nodded, the answer hit her like a deathblow, and she collapsed against his chest.

The notion was ridiculous. It defied logic, but she felt the truth in her bones.

Gorman gazed around at their glum, defeated faces. His dark brow furrowed, and he rested a hand on his gun. "Are you people gonna answer me? How the hell can a man do all this, and how the hell do you know him?"

Lilith gazed up at Chance and locked eyes with him. "We only have two choices here. Aaron is still a threat, and we don't have enough proof to go to the Elders. We're on our own...perhaps worse. If Aaron convinces the Elders that we're the enemy...we'll be hunted by more than the Durand. We need to find this monster and stop him...permanently."

For a moment, he studied her face, an internal debate waging war in his head. The man was trained to eliminate threats, including humans who knew too much.

"You realize we'd be breaking our own laws. If the Elders find out, Aaron won't have to convince them."

"What choice do we have? We can't do this alone."

Gorman drew his gun but couldn't decide who to aim at, so he backed up to the wall. "Eileen. Get over here."

"John, calm down. You're right. Something very odd is happening here, but let's not escalate things. These people haven't threatened us."

Chance leaned close to whisper in Lilith's ear, while Eileen attempted to talk down her partner. "We only have one choice."

Lilith jerked back to stare at him with a disapproving frown, but he smiled softly.

"Not that one—the *right* one. Remember, I'm always on your side."

The frown melted into a grin, and she gave his cheek a quick kiss. "Thank you for trusting me."

"Of course, *mon cherie*."

"You better start talking, Miss Adams, or I'll call this in right now!"

After taking a deep breath, she turned to face Agent Gorman. "If that's what you want."

"Of course, it is—"

Lilith held up a hand, and he stopped short.

"Both you and Agent Hersch are smart people, and I trust you, but I also need to impress the gravity of this situation. This information is dangerous, possibly more so than the monster that did all this. If you call this in, you'll be condemning every person who enters this building."

"Lilith! What are you doing?" Cohen surged to his feet, and his face turned red. "You cannot do this! Don't be fucking stupid. You'll condemn us all!"

She met Andrew's eyes for a moment and shook her head. "You saw the footage. You know what's out there. We're already condemned."

Before he replied, she turned her attention to the federal agents.

"This info can get you killed. Cohen isn't exaggerating. You can walk away right now, and I will never contact you again. But…if I tell you the truth, we will need your help."

Gorman's shoulders relaxed, and the gun fell to his side, but he didn't put it away. "And what if I don't want to help?"

"You will. I know what kind of man you are and what you're willing to sacrifice when thousands of lives hang in the balance, but I won't force your hand. This needs to be your choice. Lots of powerful people will want you dead if they find out what you know."

"I'm in." Special Agent Eileen Hersch stepped forward with her chin held high, and her eyes briefly darted to Tim.

"What are you doing?" Her partner frowned while he rubbed anxiously at his neck.

"Come on, John. You knew this wasn't a normal case from the moment we set foot on Cassandra's scene. We came here, off the books, to help these people. As I see it, they need our help now more than ever. Whatever slaughtered these people is on the loose."

"We do, and to be clear, Cohen is correct. By revealing secrets, I'll be putting *all* our lives in danger—Cohen, Chance, Nicci, and myself—not just yours. Unfortunately, I'm backed into a corner with no other options."

"And you'll tell us everything? No holding back. No secrets."

"I promise."

"*We* promise," Chance corrected. Then he glared over at Cohen with all his pent-up hostility. "Right?"

The demon stared at each person in turn as if they'd all lost their minds.

"You already told us you don't have any other allies. That's why you came to *us* for help. Right? There's no other possible reason. Do you think your…family will understand all this? They will kill you."

Andrew clenched his jaw and stared daggers at Chance, but ultimately, he inhaled deeply and sighed. "The Cajun giant has a point." Cohen sank into his chair, seething with anger, but he couldn't deny the logic. "I'm already dead. Why not take the fuckers down with me?"

His eyes narrowed in on Chance again in a less-than-friendly expression.

"Since we're allies, can you uncuff me?"

After a defiant staring contest that grated Lilith's nerves, Chance nodded to Tim, who crossed the room. When he leaned down to remove the cuffs, Tim whispered something in his ear, and Andrew stiffened. Then Tim walked away and resumed his position.

"So, who did this? Who is that man on the screen?" Gorman shoved his gun back in his holster but still wore a suspicious frown.

"Ashcroft Orrick is not a man."

"Who?"

"This is a lengthy conversation. One we shouldn't have here for multiple reasons." Cohen stressed each syllable to ensure they understood.

"It's only a matter of time until the Durand discover their security measures didn't work and send reinforcements. We *need* to go!"

"The Durand?"

"I promise we'll tell you everything once we get out of here, but each second that we stay puts us all in more danger than you realize." Lilith silently prayed the FBI agent would trust them long enough to escape and regroup.

Gorman's lips mashed together in a thin line. He shook his head and paced the floor. When he reached his partner, he stared at her but kept moving. "And you're onboard with this?"

The woman replied without any hesitation. "Yes, John. What we've seen here…I can't explain it. Can you? I want to hear what they have to say. I need to know."

Gorman studied each one of them in turn until his tawny eyes rested on Chance. "And you…you killed a federal agent."

"No. I killed a corrupt bully who liked to rape and beat women. One that shot your partner, threatened to destroy your lives, and held a gun to my fiancée's head. I will *not* apologize. It may not align with your laws and ethics, but I did what was necessary for all of us."

The agent put his hands on his hips and sighed. "See…the problem is…I think you planned to kill him all along and were simply waiting for an excuse or permission. I don't believe you had any intention of letting him walk away."

"You're right. I did plan to kill him. Hell, I wanted to. I know his type, and they don't change. They're mad dogs, rabid with the desire for control. They sustain themselves by breaking others. I would have killed him the very first night, but I made a promise, and I kept it until Boston made that impossible."

"At least you're honest." Gorman shook his head, still trying to decide how he felt about the whole situation.

Meanwhile, Cohen strolled toward the door. "Well…sounds like I've missed a lot." An odd sadness lingered beneath his nonchalant statement, and he avoided looking in Lilith's direction. "If you two have things settled, can we leave now?"

"I'll call the airfield and get things set up." Tim reached for his phone, but Lilith interrupted.

"No. We can't use the jet, and we can't leave. We just need to find a safe place to hole-up nearby where no one will look for us."

"I know a place we can go, but we can't keep talking here. Agent, are you in or out?" Andrew gestured to the camera's red light with a tight frown.

When the man didn't answer, Cohen glared at Agent Gorman, who was shifting his weight from one foot to the other.

"The people who own this building guard their secrets with *extreme* prejudice. When they see this footage and discover our intention to reveal them…"

Cohen's steely gaze shot over to Lilith, and he exhaled sharply before turning back to Gorman.

"They will hunt us all. And when I say *hunt*, understand these people have virtually unlimited resources and unfathomable weapons. Our odds are *not* good, and they decrease every second we stay here."

Gorman's face clouded, but after a few tense seconds, he nodded. "Well…sounds like we better move."

"Finally." Cohen sighed in dramatic fashion. "The United Nations make faster decisions."

Everyone ignored the snide comment as Tim rallied the troops. "Okay. We should resume our team assignments in case we encounter hostiles on the way out." While Tim spoke to the entire group, his eyes lingered on Agent Hersch.

"Right. Tim, Gibson, and Hersch, clear the hall and resume the lead. Nicci, once you have everything, grab Keller and Xander and explain the situation—basics only—and follow Tim. Cohen, you're with Gorman, Lilith, and me."

"I got what I can." The petite detective snatched a flash drive from the computer, shoved it into a pocket in her tac vest, and zipped it shut.

"Wait. Do I get a gun?"

Although Cohen peered around the room at all of them, Chance was the one who spoke up first.

"If you need one. Until then, no." He stated the decision in a matter-of-fact tone without bothering to face the man.

"I had nothing to do with this, Deveraux. You saw the footage."

Finally, Chance turned to face Andrew with calm indifference. "Doesn't mean I trust you, *démone*." For a split-second, his eyes moved to Lilith, and Cohen picked up on the subtext.

"What? Do you honestly think I'd put a bullet in your back over—" He stopped short, becoming painfully aware of his surroundings and who occupied them. "Never mind. Let's go. We're wasting time." He rushed through the words and glared at the tile floor, while Tim, Hersch, and Gibson strolled past him.

When Nicci approached him, she veered off course and marched right up to Andrew. "You need to get your shit together!"

The man's lightly scarred brow furrowed, and he opened his mouth to speak, but Nicci barreled ahead.

"I know. Life has shit on you a lot, especially lately, but get control of yourself. Like I said before, you've acted like a moody hormonal teenager since you arrived, and it's not attractive or helpful."

An almost imperceptible blush graced his cheeks, and he stared down at the petite detective. "It's a little more complex than that."

"No. It's not. Bad things happened to you, horrible things I'd never wish on my worst enemy, but snap out of it! Your emotional baggage is wearing us all out. We can't work together if you don't *deal* with this."

Nicci continued into the hall, leaving Cohen in stunned silence. Then he noticed Gorman, Chance, and Lilith staring at him.

"I, uh...think I'll wait in the hall."

"I feel like I'm missing something here." Gorman watched Detective Cohen disappear through the door before turning his stare on Chance and Lilith.

While her cheeks flushed, Chance saved her from fumbling through an answer. "Chalk it up to conflicting personalities. The detective and I don't like each other much...for a multitude of reasons."

"Hmm. Now that you mention it, Eileen didn't seem thrilled to see him either. I always thought she was sweet on him. They did a lot of one-on-one brainstorming during the Phipps Bend case. I barely saw my partner while he was in town, but she never really mentioned him afterward."

"Yeah, well...He has that effect on people. We should move out. As much as I hate admitting Cohen's right, we're wasting time."

The agent nodded, grabbed the box of evidence from cold storage, and headed for the door. Chance turned to Lilith and caressed her cheek.

"You ready, *mon petite cherie?*"

"More than ready." Lilith gazed around the blood-soaked room, her stomach churning.

Ashcroft was out there somewhere, alive and absolutely vicious. He had torn through every person he saw, regardless of whether they were a threat.

His actions weren't cold, calculated, and methodical, as they'd been in Tennessee. This...This was primal, animalistic, unrestrained slaughter.

Hopefully, Nicci's flash drive held the secrets of how they'd brought him back and why he'd changed so drastically.

Suddenly, she recalled Dr. Thomas having crouched over a case, just before she opened the cell. It almost looked like she'd switched items…

Perhaps she gave him something. Maybe a sedative of some sort so she could take more than a sample. She doubted any normal tranquilizer would work on him, but what if it had the opposite effect? An extreme reaction…Or perhaps…*no.*

As soon as her mind landed on the most logical answer, Lilith shoved the thought away, refusing to acknowledge its existence. Ashcroft being alive was bad enough without him being infected with a virus, which caused encephalopathy and violent behavior. Hopefully, her gut instinct was wrong. If Dr. Thomas had been dumb enough to infect him, they'd failed their mission on every possible front.

"Guys, I picked up chatter on the walkie!" Tim burst back into the room, breathing heavy. "Reinforcements are arriving. We have to move now!"

Dread clutched Lilith's gut. They all whirled into action, sprinting through the door, hurdling over bodies, and racing for the stairwell. As they all clambered down the steps, the distant thud of boots echoed from above.

"Stop before you enter the lobby. Security protocol is a double-sided sweep—one team lands on the roof, and another enters through the parking garage." Cohen shouted the warning as they passed the third-floor landing.

"Tim. How bad were the stairs on the other side? Can we scale down and avoid the lobby?" A hopeful tone infused Chance's voice.

"A ten-foot drop, at most."

"Take the second-floor entrance. We'll cut across, avoid the lobby, and try to sneak out to the van, assuming they didn't disable it."

"Affirmative."

By the time Lilith reached the landing, Gibson already had the door open and was ushering everyone inside while watching the stairs. Once Gorman—the last one in line—passed by, Gibson sprinted back up to the front, and they ran down a long corridor lined with glass cubicles.

"Wait!" Cohen veered into a room with wall-to-wall screens, and Lilith screeched to a halt.

"Andrew, what are you doing?"

"Lily, come on!" Chance shouted, slowing to a jog. When she followed Cohen into the glass room, he stopped. "Damn it! Tim secure the door and hold." After barking the order, he rushed back for the two strays.

"This is the security hub. It has access to all the cameras," Andrew explained, pulling up footage of the lobby, stairwell, and parking garage.

Chance studied the footage, calculating their best route. Avoiding the lobby was a smart move. At least fifteen heavily armed men were scattered around the room, lying in wait.

Chance pressed the button on his mic. "Tim, we have two men guarding the stairs near the parking garage, one at the van, and two more at the garage entrance." Then he turned his attention to Cohen. "Can you show me the roof team? Where are they at?"

After clicking a few buttons, a shot of the Durand Council courtroom appeared on the screen, and a ton of horrific memories flashed through Lilith's mind. As the three-man SWAT team cleared the room, the memory of Farren shooting her father replayed so vividly, she thought she heard the shot.

"We still have time, but we need to move fast." Cohen clicked several buttons, racing through past footage. "I can delete the past hour, but not the cult. They need an explanation. Of course, it still implicates me, but you'll be left out of it for now."

A few more clicks, and every screen went dark. "I'm rebooting the system. It should take several minutes for it to come back up so they can't track us. Let's go!"

Andrew sprinted through the door and down the hall, with Lilith and Chance close behind. When they reached the stairwell, Tim, Hersch, and Gibson were already gone.

"They went ahead to ensure we can get down the stairs." Gorman paced back and forth.

"We don't have another option. We have to make it work." Chance swung the door open slowly and spotted Tim at the edge of the crumbled stairs.

Tim silently signaled to him, and Chance glanced back over his shoulder to relay the message. "Hersch and Gibson are in position, guarding the bottom. We are gonna move slow and quiet. Once everyone is past the gap, we'll guard the lobby door while Tim's team clears the way to the van. Understood?"

Once everyone nodded, Chance held the door. He waited for Xander, Keller, Nicci, Gorman, Cohen, and Lilith to sneak into the stairwell, before covering the second-floor hallway.

One by one, Tim helped each person down the ten-foot drop until it was Lilith's turn. Her heart raced impossibly fast, and her eyes widened when she stared down at the ten-foot drop.

"You got this, Lil. We're almost home free. Come on."

Lilith nodded a little too much and stepped to the edge.

"Just turn around, give me your hands, and I'll help ease you down, okay?"

Once again, she nodded emphatically and followed his instructions. When her boots touched the rubble below, her pulse eased a little, and she crept up behind Cohen, taking slow deep breaths.

The Durand peered over his shoulder at her. "You okay?"

She nodded but his eyes lingered on her face, studying her.

A few seconds later, Tim snuck past them, resuming his role in front, and Chance took position behind Lilith.

"Get your knife out and don't use your gun unless necessary."

When Chance whispered over her shoulder, she immediately complied. The last thing they wanted to do was announce their presence.

After a deep breath, Lilith peeked over the railing. Hersch and Tim went in different directions on the bottom floor, creeping up behind the two guards. Almost simultaneously, they sprang on their targets, covered their mouths, and slit their throats in one smooth motion. Then they gingerly lowered the victims to the ground and took positions on either side of the door leading into the garage.

After Tim gave a thumbs-up, they all moved to the first floor as quietly as possible and huddled near the lobby door. Tim signaled Gibson to take over his spot. The man hustled into place, and Tim crouched to peer into the garage, waiting. The guard must have been facing the door because Tim didn't move a muscle.

Everyone waited in tense silence. Anticipation and dread prickled over their skin with increasing intensity. They remained so focused, the elevator beep made them all jump.

"Tim," Chance hurriedly whispered into the walkie. "The elevator is coming down…at the fifth floor. We gotta move!"

Without hesitation, Tim rushed to the van in a crouched sprint and disappeared.

The elevator dinged again…Fourth floor.

Gorman and Chance flanked the elevator, guns at the ready. while everyone else crept closer to the door, their hearts racing.

Another ding…Third floor.

Lilith heard a small thud and leaned to peek into the garage. Tim lowered the guard to the ground, jogged around the van, climbed into the driver's seat, and gave a signal. Hersch and Gibson slid into the garage, guns trained on the entrance, and motioned for everyone to follow.

Another ding…Second floor.

Xander, Keller, Nicci, and Cohen clambered into the van. When Lilith raced across the concrete, she glanced back.

Chance followed close behind, with Gorman sprinting through the door as a loud ding echoed in the cavernous space.

First floor.

Lilith leapt inside, crawling past Cohen, when gunshots rang out with a deafening pop. Hersch ducked behind the van, and Gibson squeezed a few rounds at the half-open door. But Lilith's eyes landed on Gorman, who squirmed on the concrete, holding his left leg.

Chance rushed over. Gibson continued to provide cover fire while Chance tossed the agent over his shoulder. A muzzle peeked through the door, but a shot from Hersch made it pull back.

Gorman grunted and panted as Chance helped him into the back row. Once he was seated with his leg propped up, Chance's eyes darted to Lilith for a second, and then he hopped out of the van.

Her heart sank. *Shit.*

She leaned forward in her seat, peering through the windshield. Chance yelled for everyone to get in, and Tim turned the key. The engine roared to life.

Movement through the open door caught Lilith's eye. The men guarding the entrance were moving in, creeping past parked cars, trying to get closer.

Lilith slammed the button on her mic. "Two hostiles at three o'clock."

Hersch scrambled into the backseat to help her partner, and Gibson climbed inside. A shot hit the vehicle's side with a loud *thunk.*

Lilith grabbed her assault rifle, crouched on the floor by Cohen, and squeezed off a few rounds, making the assailant duck behind an SUV.

"Chance! Move it!" she shouted, squeezing off another shot. A loud bang sounded overhead, and she glanced up to see Cohen aiming her Beretta, the barrel smoking.

When Chance suddenly appeared in the doorway, he came to a halt. For a tense second, Cohen kept the gun aimed at Chance's surprised face, and her heart nearly stopped.

Another shot hit the van, shattering the glass, and Cohen lowered his gun. Chance immediately hopped inside, slammed the door closed, and crawled into the passenger seat.

"Drive!" As the words left Chance's mouth, Tim threw the van in gear. The tires screeched, and shots peppered the van's side. The thing lurched into motion, rocketing past the parked cars.

Chance clicked his seatbelt and glanced over his shoulder at Cohen. The skin around his eyes tightened.

If Cohen noticed the suspicious glare, he didn't acknowledge it. The man merely slid the pistol into Lilith's holster as she climbed back into her seat.

A shot hit the back door with another heavy thud, and Lilith peered through the rear window. Men were filing through the blue door with their weapons aimed.

"Hold on!"

When Tim hollered, Lilith whipped around.

The security gate was closing. She braced herself and silently prayed. The vehicle slammed into the lower edge of the metal link, which sent sparks flying.

Tim made a sharp right turn that slammed her into the window and stomped on the gas, weaving through light traffic and taking as many turns as he could. He pulled into a busy Wal-Mart shopping center and brought the van to a screeching halt.

"Gorman. Are you okay?" Tim twisted in his seat to peer at the back row.

"He's fine. A through-and-through." Hersch grabbed the first aid kit from the back and rummaged through the contents. "Just get us out of here!"

"First, I need everyone's phones. You can have them back, but I'm taking the SIM cards, and they stay turned off, understood?" Everyone passed their phones to Chance.

Tim turned and fixed Cohen with a steely stare. "Where are we going? You said you knew a place."

Chapter 42 - *Ashcroft*

Everything from the moment the woman had jabbed a needle into his neck until he reached the parking garage was a blur of blind rage, blood, and gore. So many bodies, but they weren't enough to quell his desire for revenge. He'd shred the throat of every Durand for what they had done to him—months of calculated torture and starvation, testing the limits of his regenerative power. One by one, they *all* would die screaming…after he finished his war with Gregor.

However, when Ashcroft tore through the fence and stepped into the alley drenched in late-morning sunlight, every inch of exposed skin burned as if coated in napalm. His ear-piercing screech ripped through the air, and he shot toward the closest cover—a rusting dumpster.

His body still smoldered with the lid slammed closed.

The stomach-churning stench of refuse, intensified by the summer sun, assaulted his nostrils, and the sweltering heat threatened to suffocate him, but the UV rays kept him trapped in the hellish metal box. He couldn't move until sunset.

For a while, Ashcroft lay across the garbage, prioritizing the need for cooler air over his need to escape the horrid odors. His mind fixated on the humans and Durand he'd slaughtered, the memory of every death rising from the blood haze, each one widening his wicked smile. The fear and pain of his victims sang through his veins like a drug. He craved more…wanted more…needed more.

Next time, I'll go slow. I'll savor each tendril of terror and slowly drink them dry…like Miriah. His slender body trembled at the thought. He'd made that one exquisite piece last almost two days. However, the true delight had stemmed from Duncan's despair and disgust while being forced to witness his daughter's torment until his mind broke, shattered into a thousand painful shards.

A sinister sigh of desire slithered past his thin lips. *Soon I will do the same with Lilith and Gregor. Soon, but never soon enough.*

Ashcroft's head whipped in the direction of the parking garage when he sensed others approaching—five humans, five vampires. Centuries of practice had gifted him with the ability to differentiate the subtle nuances between species. It also allowed him to recognize unique emotional signatures, and two of the vampires were more than familiar—Lilith and Chance.

A delirious grin curved his lips until he remembered the sun holding him prisoner in the malodorous sweatbox.

She is so close. I can taste her terror. It's even more delicious than in Phipps Bend. He panted with an almost irresistible craving.

Then his attention moved to the woman's betrothed, who vibrated with fear, not for himself, but for *her.*

A ragged gasp escaped his throat, and he drank in the whisps of energy he could gleam from them. *A taste, but not enough.*

The very thought of his knife on Lilith's porcelain skin, making it blush before the blood welled around the blade, sent shivers through his body. But forcing Gregor and her beloved to witness every devious act, violation, slow slice, for hours and hours…it would be the ultimate high.

A growl of frustration formed when his coveted prey wandered further into the building. *Too far away.*

Ashcroft glared at the ray of sunshine peeking between the dumpster's lid and side. A sneer contorted his angular face, pulling at the tight scar tissue he'd endured for six hundred years, the ones Gregor had gifted him.

Soon. Be patient.

Ashcroft had slowly dealt justice to Gregor's extended bloodline for centuries, but now the end goal loomed so near, his body curled in on itself with ravenous hunger.

The moment had slipped through his fingers in Tennessee. He'd had her restrained, and both Gregor and Chance had been present to witness his wrath. But he'd let the lecherous Durand detective sway him. The thought of an ally, a true disciple—unlike Spencer, who was too weak of mind and body—had been too enticing. He'd stayed his hand in exchange for Detective Cohen's cooperation, and the bastard had betrayed him.

Ashcroft's lip curled into a venomous snarl. The detective would pay too. *Perhaps I'll save him for last. I'll make him watch the others die first. Of course, the dark seduction of so much suffering might finally draw him to my side. With my help, nothing could hurt him again…or stop him.*

Some time later, Lilith's group returned to the parking garage, but something had changed. She'd traded a human for a Durand—Detective Cohen.

His nefarious heart fluttered with a deep-seeded desire. All the pieces—minus Gregor—were right there…mere feet away!

Ashcroft glared maliciously at the wicked sunlight keeping him from his prize. All he had to do was take her, and everyone else would follow, just like before. *Everything I need is so close!*

Talon-like nails screeched against the metal when gun shots rang through the alley. Frustration and rage burned through every cell while he screamed and thrashed against the dumpster's interior.

Ashcroft's prey retreated, racing away from him.

"No!" he screeched, powerless to stop them.

When Lilith's group receded into the background, a murderous resolution settled over him, granting a temporary calm.

Once darkness falls, the world will pay. Every last human, vampire, Durand will pay with their blood until I find them.

"May the mysterious gods take pity on their souls. I certainly won't."

Chapter 43

"Take I-565 East toward AL-79 South. It's about an hour drive," Cohen stated calmly.

The frown on Tim's face clearly showed his dislike for the cryptic answer, but he decided not to comment.

"You're sure the Durand doesn't know about this place?" Chance remained guarded and skeptical but hadn't openly objected to the plan.

"Yes. I paid for the land in cash under a pseudo name, and I pay the guy who owns the other cabins under the table for the upkeep."

"A cabin. You…" Nicci looked him up and down suspiciously, pointing out his expensive charcoal gray suit. The thing might have been rumpled and blood-stained, but it probably cost more than Lilith's rent on her apartment in New York City. "*You* own a cabin?"

Cohen stiffened in his seat, smoothing out the wrinkles in his slacks. "Yes. It's on a lake near the Cathedral State Park, in an area called Angler's Retreat."

"Angler? As in fishing?" Lilith frowned, trying to reconcile two very different pictures of Cohen.

After a sideways glance at her, he nodded stiffly, and Nicci burst out laughing.

"I'm sorry." The petite detective covered her mouth and tried to contain herself but still giggled several times.

Cohen's cheeks turned red. "Yes, yes. Very funny. Fishing is not a hobby of mine…Not in the traditional sense." The man loosened his tie and unbuttoned the top of his shirt before continuing. "It's the last place anyone would look for me, which is why I chose it. I needed a place to escape Farren when he was on one of his rampages."

"So, Luminita—"

"Has never been there." He interrupted Lilith's question and turned to face her. "Ironically, I never brought her there because I didn't want to put her in danger. If Farren found out we were close, he'd kill her, like everyone else in my life."

The memory of Farren holding a gun to her temple while Cohen pleaded for her life flashed through Lilith's mind again. His grandfather had stolen so much from him, and the only thing he didn't—Luminita—betrayed him in every possible way. She was out there somewhere, still trying to create an abomination through torture in the hopes of advancing their species. The same torture that left permanent reminders of her betrayal on Cohen's face.

"And that's enough of that. I don't need anyone's pity." He stiffened again and stared straight ahead, slipping back into his impassive mask.

"Can we discuss the matter at hand, then?" Gorman leaned forward, resting his arms against the seat in front of him.

Before Lilith opened her mouth, Chance answered his question. "Let's get to the cabin, make sure the place is secure, and settle in first. Everyone needs to be involved in the conversation, and it should be face-to-face."

Lilith peered over her shoulder. Gorman was considering Chance's suggestion. After glancing at his partner, the man nodded and settled back into his seat.

Meanwhile, Nicci dug out her laptop, unzipped her pocket to retrieve the flash drive, and plugged it into the computer. The sound of her furious typing filled the van. Everyone else sat in silence, anxiously waiting for the next revelation and desperately hoping it wasn't more bad news.

"Man...the explosion sure did a number on him." Lilith peered over the seat, trying to catch a glimpse of Nicci's screen. "Burnt to a crisp but mostly intact. How do you come back from something like that?"

"I shot the bastard at point-blank range and took half his head off. Somehow, he still functioned enough to heal himself." Chance shivered, the scene most likely playing behind his eyes.

"He did what?" Gorman exclaimed from the back seat.

"The monster can regenerate at an alarming fast rate. We'll explain everything else later. I promise. What's in the file, Nicci?" Lilith turned in her seat to get a better look at the screen.

"Looks like there's a narration to time-lapse footage. Should we wait and watch this all together?"

"I, for one, don't mind skipping the burnt body recovery," Tim hollered without taking his eyes off the road.

"Just go ahead and play it. The audio should be enough," Chance chimed in from the front passenger's seat.

"Specimen Omega vas recovered from a hostile site in Knoxville, Tennessee."

Lilith immediately recognized the subtle Russian accent—Ivanov, the scientist in the surveillance footage.

"Our partner supplied the body and other evidence to assist our research, vhich is beingk conducted in secret. Vhen it arrived, I thought he'd betrayed us. Regeneration seemed impossible. De tissue vas burnt vell into de skeletal muscle layer, and even areas of bone vere degraded."

Then the pictures began to change. Lilith watched in horror as the skeletal remains began to form subtle bulk beneath the blackened skin.

"As you can see from de time-lapse, regular infusions of Durand and vampire blood initiated a healingk process deep vithin the body's core, but de progress vas slow, occurring over several veeks…"

"I'm sorry. Did he just say vampire?" Gorman balked and shook his head.

"Yes, but can we hold the questions for now?" Nicci sighed and pressed play again.

"Luminita suggested ve feed de subject vith more than blood and provided details on de specimen's previous eatingk habits. Vhen ve brought in humans to prepare in de manner described, ve lost a few lab technicians and supporters, but de results vere all dat mattered."

"Oh my god." The color drained from Lilith's face, and she covered her mouth. "They tortured people…like Miriah." Lilith blinked back tears and faced away from the scream, thankful there were only pictures of the atrocities and not sounds.

"The healing process vent much quicker after dat. Muscles formed, tendons and ligaments reattached, but de outer layer remained unchanged for quite some time. I grew impatient and took de specimen into surgery. Vhen I cut into de burnt husk, I found young healthy tissue below, so I debrided all de dead tissue."

Unable to resist, Lilith glanced back at the screen. On the operating table lay a body devoid of hair, with skin so thin the arteries and veins were visible. It looked like a clone still growing in the pod of some sci-fi movie, but the scars were still there.

She spotted the faint names of Gregor's family on its chest and the light lines upon its barely formed face. *Why? There is no reason they should still exist. The burn damage went deeper than the scars. Are they part of his DNA somehow? What makes them different from any other damage he incurred? The head doesn't show any scarring from Chance's bullet.*

"At four months, de subject is fully intact and physically healed, but has not voken up. De team vorries dat brain function may not return. Luminita reassures us dat dis is temporary."

There he was…on-screen, lying on a hospital bed…the monster from her nightmares, breathing and alive. He almost appeared peaceful, sleeping without hatred and vengeance contorting his face.

"Four veeks after my last entry, the subject has voken. Tests show he is neurologically intact vith full reflexes. He follows basic commands, and each day, he seems more oriented. Luminita vill arrive tomorrow to interrogate de subject and determine if he is of use."

"All right. They brought him back to life. We're all up to speed. Can we turn the thing off now?" Cohen shifted in his seat, clearly uncomfortable and not in any hurry to hear Luminita's voice.

Nicci glanced over at her partner, who nodded softly.

"Uh yeah. Sorry. I can watch the rest in private and give you all a report later." Nicci closed the laptop, slipped it into the bag, and stowed it under her seat.

"Thank you." The words emerged lifeless and flat. Cohen continued to stare at the windshield, but saying those words at all was a rarity for him.

The thought of Ashcroft out there on the loose sat heavy on everyone's shoulders the rest of the drive. They might have survived the Durand stronghold, but what waited for them out there was more deadly, and they had an obligation to stop it.

T im pulled into a gravel drive winding around several tall pines until they faced a quaint Southern cabin, and Lilith smiled. The pristine yellow paint glowed from the evening sun, and the white front porch seemed welcoming and warm. It was the sort of place Lilith imagined curling up with a great book and sipping lemonade, not hiding out from demons.

"Okay. Gibson, Xander, and Keller, I want you scouting the surrounding area. Tim and I will clear the building. Hersch, you can help Gorman onto the porch so you'll have room and light to bandage him up properly. The rest of you, stay in the van until we give the okay."

As soon as Chance finished rattling off assignments, the doors opened, and people climbed out, leaving Lilith, Nicci, and Cohen in awkward silence.

"So…" Nicci glanced at Lilith, hoping for some sort of assistance, but she merely frowned in confusion. "Sounds like that Russian doctor had other supporters? Possibly on the Council?"

Andrew inhaled and exhaled slowly. "I wouldn't know anything about that, Detective DeLuca. I didn't know what was happening in that lab."

"Yeah, I know, but…perhaps the Russian doc had friends you were aware—"

He turned in his seat before she finished, and a chill filled his eyes. "I've been kidnapped, beaten, and forced to betray my people, only to find out they've been conducting unsanctioned experiments on a monster. I'll be number one on their hit list. Perhaps I can have a little time to process that before you needle me with questions like I'm a fucking suspect."

Nicci swallowed hard and sank back in her seat. It was the first time Lilith recalled seeing the woman intimidated, or perhaps that wasn't the correct word. Shock and embarrassment seemed like a more appropriate description.

"Lil, do you mind if I step out for a second?" Nicci avoided looking at Cohen, but he continued to stare at her with chilling animosity.

"Yeah, of course."

"Sorry, Andrew," Nicci mumbled, scrambling out of the van and closing the door behind her.

"That was a little harsh, don't you think?" Lilith fearlessly met his gaze, her arms folded over her chest.

The man relaxed into the seat beside her, and his eyes drifted to the floor. "I don't want to answer questions right now."

"She was only trying to do her job."

"Her job is a thousand miles away."

"Come on, you know what I mean."

After another sideways glance, he sighed. "Fine. I'll apologize."

"Thank you."

"And what about you?" His gaze lifted to stare through the windshield. "Are you really engaged, or just lying to law enforcement again?"

The unexpected question sent her mind reeling. "Hell of a subject change."

When he peered over at her, his eye color had changed to a warm hazel, but his face remained the same impassive mask. "I'm curious."

"Um…yeah, it's real this time."

As she stumbled through the answer, his eyes narrowed as if sensing something, and then he chuckled.

Lilith frowned at the odd reaction and leaned back against the window, putting more distance between them. "What's so funny?"

"I honestly thought he wouldn't tell you. He did tell you, though, didn't he?"

"Tell me what?" As the words left her mouth, she knew they were pointless, and when Cohen merely raised an eyebrow, she sighed. "Fine. Yes. He told me about your—" She couldn't make herself finish the sentence.

His gaze wandered to the windshield again, and his lips pressed into a thin line. "I keep underestimating him. He loves you in a way I haven't seen in a very long time."

"Did you just compliment Chance twice in one breath?" When in doubt, she always turned to sarcastic humor.

An amused smile tilted his lips, and he gazed out at the cabin. "I suppose I did. How unlike me."

"Why didn't you—"

"Say something?" He finished the question and met her eyes again, but this time, sadness lingered in his face. "Because I know how you feel about him, and because I trust you."

When she still appeared lost, he continued.

"You know my history with Farren. I haven't allowed myself to care about many people…only one person actually, and we know how that turned out."

He turned in his seat to fully face her, a myriad of emotions flickering across the surface.

"I trust you, Lilith Adams. You have always been straight with me, even when it was inconvenient or uncomfortable. That means something to me, something I would never risk losing. I'm not asking anything from you beyond returning the favor, and perhaps, your friendship."

"I do trust you, Andrew. When Nicci told me where Aaron transferred the bodies—"

"Aaron? Your uncle Aaron?"

"Yeah. Enemies on all sides. I think he was conducting illegal research at Goditha too. A database with DNA sequences of virtually every vampire and then some. The doctor he worked with was Dr. Thomas's mentor. He funneled the information to her, which is how they found out about Ashcroft."

"So, your uncle is working with Luminita?"

"It appears that way, but we don't have any hard proof to take to the Elders. Until we find something solid, we have to stay off their radar."

Cohen leaned back against the seat and shook his head. "We both seem to attract a lot of trouble. Not a good combination."

A sudden knock on the window made them both jump. Lilith peered around him. Nicci waved emphatically as Cohen opened the van door.

"Hey, the cabin is clear. We can go in." After a quick glance at them, Nicci turned on her heel, her long ponytail swishing with the movement, and marched away.

"I suppose that's our cue." Cohen straightened his suit jacket, despite it being speckled with blood, stepped out of the van, and turned back to Lilith. "I appreciate you talking to me honestly about everything. You didn't have to. I will help in any way I can."

"Thanks, Andrew, but I needed to. There is too much at stake, and you deserve the truth." A warm smile curved her lips, and she slid out of the van, still marveling over the oddly frank discussion they'd shared.

Perhaps he was tired of the mask, weary from putting on performances, and wanted a change. A lifetime of Council politics, false facades, and traitorous subterfuge had all resulted in Farren's sick control and Luminita's betrayal after years of manipulating him. It was enough to make anyone want a change.

She stopped in front of him, peering up at his hazel eyes, and held out her hand. "It's nice to finally meet *you*, Andrew Cohen."

A slight blush colored his cheeks. He flashed a tight smile and shook her hand. "Let's get inside before your fiancée tears out my spine. It would somewhat hamper our investigation."

Lilith chuckled and fell in step beside him. They made their way across the gravel and onto the front porch. Chance opened the door as she reached for the handle, peering at Cohen before his gaze landed on Lilith.

"The others just returned. Everything's good." Once again, he focused on Cohen. "You have a nice place here."

"Thanks, Gigantor." Cohen patted him on the shoulder and strolled into the cabin.

"Still friendly as ever, I see." Chance sighed and shook his head.

"Actually"—Lilith nestled into him, and he wrapped an arm around her shoulders—"he paid you two compliments a few minutes ago, but don't tell. It's a secret."

"You two can have the master bedroom if you can separate long enough to catch everyone up to speed," Cohen hollered from inside, but it lacked his usual bitter tone.

"See? Compared to when we first met him, he's downright cuddly."

Chance chuckled, kissed the top of her head, and led her inside. "Let's get this over with. We all need some sleep."

"What about Tim's guys, Xander and Keller? Are they in?"

Chance nodded as they strolled down the hall to the spacious living room. "Yeah. Tim vouched for them. We're breaking a lot of rules, but they understand the risks. We should also call Dr. Price at some point and tell her to go home before she finds the expensive liquor."

A small chuckle escaped, and Lilith nodded. "I'll take care of it."

"Gotta have something to celebrate with when we get home." Chance's touch lingered on her left ring finger with a blushing grin. But when they entered the living room, he released a sigh and released her hand.

Lilith came to a stop and gazed around at all the expectant faces—Nicci, Tim, Hersch, Keller, Xander, Gibson, Cohen, and Gorman. This was a huge gamble, and she hoped it paid off. If the Elders found out what happened, revealing secrets to humans and a Durand, they'd be ostracized from the vampire community, cut off from their resources.

Her hand slid into the pocket where she had stashed the blood caplets—*only four of them, two days at best. One problem at a time.*

"Okay." Lilith took a deep breath, glanced back at Chance, who nodded, and then faced the room. "I need to tell you all a story about a girl named Mary."

To be continued…

About the Author

Jenny Allen, the author of The Lilith Adams Series, also published several poems and short stories in University journals while spending time as a reporter and photographer for the Chattanooga State College newspaper. Ms. Allen studied forensic science, compiled extensive research in world myths, and applied them into a thrilling supernatural series. Her background as a published photographer and award-winning artist helps her visualize scenes when writing, contributing to her unique style of vivid imagery.

Born on a Royal Airbase in Lakenheath, England, she left the U.K. at age nine to travel the United States and Germany. In her Sophomore year, she began writing poetry after the suicide of a close friend in San Antonio, Texas. She later graduated to short stories and narratives until, in 2002, she wrote her first novel, Lilith in London, which was never published but still exists as 432 handwritten pages. Over twelve years, it underwent a metamorphosis, eventually becoming her first published novel, Blood Lily.

Currently, Ms. Allen lives in York, Pennsylvania with her husband, Eric Deardorff, and their two sons, Kaidan and River. When not working as a full-time RN, she is writing the fourth book in the series, Ghost Orchid. She plans to continue her book series while pursuing her medical career.

"More than anything, I wanted to challenge the concept of reality and the supernatural while truly digging into the emotional grit of tragedy. I often began writing with a clear goal in mind, but the characters swayed me in different directions. I've fallen in love with the ways they've developed and grown over the first three books, and I look forward to discovering the surprises they have in store for me in the future."

Milton Keynes UK
Ingram Content Group UK Ltd.
UKHW040713201123
432908UK00001B/332